# BLOOD

Joseph Glass is a pseudonym for a *New York Times* best-selling author. He lives with his wife and daughter in Scottsdale, Arizona.

*Blood* is the sequel to his first Susan Shader novel, *Eyes* (also available in Pan Books).

*By the same author*

EYES

JOSEPH GLASS

# BLOOD

PAN BOOKS

First published in the United Kingdom 2000 by Macmillan

This edition published 2001 by Pan Books
an imprint of Macmillan Publishers Ltd
25 Eccleston Place, London SW1W 9NF
Basingstoke and Oxford
Associated companies throughout the world
www.macmillan.com

ISBN 0 330 35380 2

3 5 7 9 8 6 4 2

A CIP catalogue record for this book is available from
the British Library.

Phototypeset by Intype London Ltd
Printed and bound in Great Britain by
Mackays of Chatham plc, Chatham, Kent

Visit our website at: www.panmacmillan.co.uk

TO SUSAN

# ACKNOWLEDGMENTS

I would like to thank David Rosenthal for his interest in my work. Sincere thanks also to Zoe Wolff for expert editorial advice, and to Beverley Cousins of Macmillan Books for unfailing professionalism and patience.

My heartfelt appreciation goes to Ernst H. Huneck, MD, for indispensable technical advice.

*In the very act of observation, the scientific investigator alters the material he observes.*

*Quantum Theory*, Jones, Burns, Hamann et al.

*First do no harm.*

Hippocratic oath

# PROLOGUE

The killer stood shivering in the cold late-morning air. November in Wisconsin could be bitter, he mused. He wasn't dressed for it. Overalls, a wool shirt and a cap. He needed a heavy coat with lots of down. But it wouldn't create the right impression.

The parking lot was full of yellow school buses. Field trips. Grade-school kids with their teachers, coming to see how Mother Nature could create wonders.

He ducked into his van to warm up. The thermos still had some coffee, and he poured it into the lid. He could see his breath. A nasty day for a hunt.

More buses coming in . . .

The girl was angry at her parents.

The hills and pastures moved slowly by outside the window of the school bus. She kept her eyes on them, ignoring the noisy conversation of the children around her on the bus. She wanted to be alone with her own thoughts.

But it was more than that. She wanted to run away. She hated the idea of going home tonight. She wished this bus was a Greyhound which would take her to some faraway place like California, instead of a school bus which would return her to school late this afternoon, where her mother would be waiting to pick her up.

Her mother and father had been talking about getting a

— 1 —

divorce since last spring. They had first brought it up the week after her birthday. She was playing with a stuffed animal, one of her gifts, when her mother called her into the living room.

'There's something important that your father and I need to discuss with you.'

Daddy came into the room a moment later and they both sat on the couch looking at Harley. They looked embarrassed, sheepish. All the authority had gone out of their faces.

'We don't think it would be a good idea for us to live together any more, honey.' It was Mother who did the talking. 'We've been getting more and more unhappy, more and more troubled.'

'I didn't notice that.' It was Harley herself who said this. It wasn't quite true, but she felt she had to do something to stop them.

'Well, I'm afraid it's true, nevertheless,' her mother said. 'The situation is getting worse, and we feel that this is bad for you and Chase as well as for us.'

Chase was her brother. He was five years old. Mother said he was too little to be told about this.

'Harley, you're getting to be a big girl now, and we didn't want to proceed any further without talking with you about this. The thing is, honey, when a man and a woman are no longer happy with each other, it makes it very hard for them to be a good Daddy and Mommy to their children. Sometimes the only thing you can do, for the good of the whole family, is to separate. Then you can go on loving the children in a better and healthier way.'

'Does this mean Dad won't live with us any more?' Harley asked. The sound of her own voice amazed her. It was cool and evaluative, like the voices of adults she had heard on TV. She felt cut off from herself by this thing they were doing.

Mother nodded. 'Dad will live in his own place. You'll be able to visit him there, of course. You and Chase. You'll spend some weekends with him, and some vacations. And you'll be able to call him up any time you want to.'

Dad was looking away. She could not tell whether he was guilty or sad. He looked both.

'But it will be better all around. We both feel sure of that,' Mother said.

'Then why are you asking me?' Harley asked, in another voice that was not quite her own. A voice made new by the fear inside her.

'We're asking you because we love you.'

'But you're *not* asking. You're *telling*.' Harley's anger made her astute. 'You don't really care what I think. You're just doing what you want.'

'Honey . . .' It was Dad who said this. He was looking at Harley, but he didn't quite meet her eye. 'We're telling you about this because we love you. We need you to know—'

'You don't love me!' the girl cried. 'If you did you would stay together.'

He leaned forward, but she shrank away from him on the couch. Mother was leaning toward her too, as though to stop her. She felt surrounded. She jumped up from the couch and stood confronting them.

'I don't care what you do.'

'Honey, please. Try to understand.'

'I understand. I don't care what you do.'

And she ran up to her room and locked the door.

That was six months ago. They had tried to engage her in further discussion of the divorce, but she wouldn't listen to them. She told her mother to do what she wanted and to stop talking about it. Sometimes there were tears in Mom's eyes when these exchanges took place. Once there were tears in Dad's eyes as well. But Harley refused to be moved by them.

She was eight years old and she knew enough about the truth to know when she was being lied to. They didn't care about her, and they didn't care about Chase. They only cared about themselves.

The killer's coffee was gone. He sat watching the buses unloading. He glanced at his watch. It was getting near lunchtime. Some of the kids were carrying lunch bags.

He was hungry himself. And soon he would need to use the bathroom. But another need was rising to a fever pitch inside him as he watched the small legs and heard the girls' voices calling to each other.

He had to stay. A little while longer. The important thing was to be patient.

There were other children of divorce at school, of course. But the little circle of Harley's friends – Linda Begg, Karen Zwick, Elise Gillespie – all came from families with two parents. True, Karen had a stepfather, but at least she had two parents.

Harley turned around long enough to see the other kids behind her. Elise and Linda were sitting together, with Karen and Julie in the seat behind them. Harley had not intentionally refused to sit with them – one of the five had to be separated, after all – but her isolation repeated a pattern that had started after she heard about the divorce, and gotten worse since. She felt cut off from her friends. She had not told them the truth. Part of her hoped that it would never come to pass. Perhaps it was just a thing that Mother and Father talked about. Perhaps they would never have the courage to actually do it.

On the other hand, if they went through with it, Harley would just run away anyway. She would never have to explain it to her friends, because she wouldn't be here any more. She would be gone, probably to California.

She had gone on in this uneasy way, feeling things get worse even as she hoped for the best. But yesterday had brought the final straw. One of the mean girls from the other homeroom, Deborah Hartmann, had been exchanging insults with Harley's group in the hall outside the gym. Linda told Deborah she was white trash. Deborah pointed at Harley and said, 'Harley's no better than I am. Her parents are getting a divorce.'

Karen had turned to Harley and asked if it was true.

'Of course it's not true,' Harley had said, turning white.

'It is so,' Deborah called out. 'My mother heard it from her next-door neighbor. They're getting a divorce next year. And Harley's mother has a boyfriend.'

'Is that true?' Karen asked. 'Does your mother really have a boyfriend? Is that why they're getting a divorce?'

Harley turned on her heel and walked away.

Her shame had increased as the day wore on. Later, at home, she asked her mother whether it was true that the divorce would come after the New Year.

'It's true that we're thinking about it for this winter,' Mother admitted. 'Who told you that?'

'Is it true that you have a boyfriend?'

Mother blushed. 'Where did you hear that?'

'Everyone knows about it.'

'Honey, that's not something for you to worry about. We'll talk about it another time perhaps.'

'Will your boyfriend be living here with us?'

'Darling, no! Who told you that?'

So it was true.

Harley had gone upstairs and spent the evening in her room. This morning, when she got up for the field trip, she refused to kiss her mother goodbye. She could hardly wait to get out of the house. She took the lunch bag from her mother, and the warm coat for the trip, but refused to talk or answer questions. Mother was looking at her sadly through the living-room window as she got on the bus.

Half an hour ago, when they were on the highway, Karen Zwick had come to Harley's side and asked, 'Is it true about your parents? I heard from Sandy and some other kids that it is true.'

Harley had looked away without answering. Now her friends were in their seats behind her, perhaps looking at her. She kept her eyes on the hills outside the window. She wished the subject would never be brought up again. She wished she was in California right now. She wished she was dead.

The Cave of the Mounds was a popular place. There were lots of other buses there, some of them yellow school buses and some of them large tour buses with dark-tinted windows. Mrs Willard gave a long speech about staying close together and being extra careful inside the cave. Harley only half listened. She had been here before with her first-grade class. She found the cave boring. It wasn't nearly as interesting as the pictures suggested. Just some dark rooms, musty-smelling, with a few display cases.

She saw the man during the confusion of getting off the bus. He looked like a bus driver. He had some sort of uniform on, overalls and a cap and a name tag. He was handsome. He beckoned to her. When she hesitated, he put his finger to his lips and made a silent shushing face, as though it was a secret between them.

She looked back at Mrs Willard, who was talking to one of the other girls. Karen and Linda and Elise and Julie were gathered around the teacher, pulling on their warm coats. Harley hesitated to join them. She did not want to go into that cave and be asked more questions about her parents. She had had enough questions.

She looked longingly at the tour buses with their dark windows. She thought of California and of running away. Turning back to the stranger, she saw that he wore a secret smile, inviting her to him.

The cold made her shiver. In California there were warm beaches and new friends, and no more questions. Maybe the stranger would take her to California.

She skipped quickly toward him, seeing her friends disappear behind her. He was laughing. It would be a good joke on all of them. She saw it in his eyes.

# PART ONE

# CHAPTER 1

GRAND JURY INDICTS SAEGER KILLER

*A Wisconsin grand jury has handed down an indictment
in the murder of Harley Ann Saeger, the Wisconsin
third-grader whose disappearance last month sparked a
nationwide search until her body was found in a
muddy farm field on 24 November.*

*Calvin Wesley Train, a career criminal who has been
convicted of violent crimes in half a dozen states and
spent much of his life behind bars, is accused of the
abduction of the Saeger girl while she was on a school
field trip to the Cave of the Mounds. After repeatedly
raping and sodomizing the girl over a one-week period,
Train allegedly strangled her and dumped the body in a
field a half-mile from Interstate 40 in Oklahoma.*

*Train was arrested in El Paso, Texas, by FBI agents
acting on a tip in early December. Fiber evidence
linking the victim's body with Train's van was presented
to the grand jury, along with blood evidence linking
his semen and saliva to the girl's body. Witnesses to
Train's presence in the parking lot of the Cave of the
Mounds visitors' center the day of the abduction
testified, along with witnesses who placed Train near
the scene of the dumping of the body a week later.*

*Train was represented by a member of the Public*

*Defender's office in Madison, but a spokesman has confirmed that Alexander Penn, the controversial criminal defense attorney known for his work in high-profile cases, has volunteered his services to Train.*

Calvin Wesley Train had spent nearly half his life behind bars.

The son of a mentally ill barmaid who was seventeen at the time she bore him, Train had no idea who his father was. He spent eight years with his mother in Tulsa until she committed suicide. Then he was passed from aunt to uncle to grandmother to landlady until he ran away at age ten. His first felony was an armed robbery in Oklahoma City at age twelve.

He spent most of his adolescence in various correctional facilities and was released at eighteen, an adult in the eyes of the law. Arrests for armed robbery in Oregon and Washington led to suspended sentences. By nineteen Train had been arrested for a variety of sex crimes, including exhibitionism, window peeping and rape. His third conviction for robbery netted him seven years at Folsom Prison. After his release he held jobs as a service station manager and security guard until another conviction for rape put him behind bars again.

By age twenty-seven Train had done time in five prisons and been convicted of the standard array of crimes attributable to the career criminal with sexual inclinations. He had done a stretch at the Colorado State Hospital for the criminally insane, and been pronounced cured by the resident psychiatrist, Dr Thamdantung.

At twenty-seven Train changed his pattern. After escaping from the state penitentiary in Kansas he stayed out of prison for six years. His movements and behavior during that time were a mystery. He was not arrested once. Then, at thirty-three, he was convicted of aggravated assault and rape after taking a young girl hostage in an Amarillo movie theater and sequestering her in a motel room. He spent six years in prison.

With time off for good behavior, Train was paroled after six years. Four months later he abducted and murdered Harley Saeger.

Train was being held in maximum security at Wisconsin's Waupun Penitentiary. His trial for the murder of Harley Saeger was scheduled for 1 May in Madison. The defense, now headed by renowned criminal defense attorney Alexander Penn, had petitioned for a change of venue and been turned down. Train would be tried by a jury taken from Wisconsin residents who lived near the spot where the child was abducted.

On 16 January Train was to be interviewed by Dr Susan Shader, a Chicago psychiatrist and psychoanalyst who had been retained as an expert by the prosecution to render an opinion as to Train's sanity at the time of the crime. Dr Shader, an experienced forensic specialist whose publications about the criminal mind were well known in the medical and legal community, was to interview Train for a total of as many as twenty hours.

In a news conference Alexander Penn had announced that his client had no memory of anything that happened after his abduction of the Saeger girl. 'He remembers speaking to her in the parking lot at the Cave of the Mounds, and he remembers waking up in a motel room in Oklahoma a week later,' Penn said. 'That is all he knows about Harley Saeger.' From this announcement it was clear to legal observers that Penn was planning a temporary-insanity plea. The prosecution would have to fight Penn on the legalities of the insanity defense, and through expert psychiatric testimony.

Penn was making the smart move. The insanity defense, with amnesia, neutralized the physical evidence. The trial would be reduced to a battle between psychiatrists and a contest between the lead attorneys for the jury's sympathy. Penn would spin an oratorical web around his client, painting him as a victim, a martyr, and the defense could combat this only by oratorical means. This was to Penn's advantage, for his skill at manipulating juries was legendary.

Susan Shader woke up early that morning as usual in her Lincoln Park apartment. She showered and washed her hair before checking in with her answering service. She glanced out of the window at the lake, which was steely grey under a grim sky. She dressed carefully, looking in the full-length mirror to see the effect of the skirt and jacket she had chosen.

The face in the mirror looked tired. *Wake up*, she told herself. She went back into the bathroom to add a touch of color to her cheeks. The Chicago winter was draining her face of life.

Another look in the full-length mirror revealed a self she could live with. Not as young as she might have liked, or as innocent. But the years had given character to a face that still had a girlish quality when the right mood struck her.

Taking her briefcase with her, she locked the apartment and went down to the car. The drive to Madison took two and a half hours. In the car she thought about what lay ahead.

Calvin Wesley Train was a career criminal. If the cops and lawyers who had come into contact with him were to be believed, he was intelligent. It would be Susan's job to learn as much of the truth from him as she could. She doubted this would be easy.

As the flat farm fields of Illinois gave way to the prettier hilly country of southern Wisconsin, Susan thought about the victim, Harley Ann Saeger. Susan's son, Michael, was one year younger than the Saeger girl. Though Susan had seen and heard almost everything in her years as a psychiatrist, she always felt shocked by crimes of violence committed against children. She told herself she shouldn't be – after all, violent crime was in its essence a regression, so the choice of children as victims made some psychological sense – but she was anyway. Crime was an adult business, an expression of rage and rebellion suited to adults. It didn't seem fair to victimize children, who were the only truly innocent human beings.

The interview took place in Train's cell. Train was shackled to his chair in standard maximum-security gear, his arms chained to his chest, his feet chained to the chair. He could not get up, so he extended a hand painfully as the guard ushered Susan into the cell.

'How do you do, Doctor?' Train said. His voice was deep and rather mellifluous. It bore a Great Plains accent tempered by his many travels.

'How do you do?' Susan gave him a polite smile as he shook her hand. His handshake was warm and dry. She found his touch oddly reassuring. It was an eloquent handshake, neither too distant nor too firm.

*You are my sunshine*. The words rose from underneath Susan's consciousness and skipped off it like a stone skipping off the surface of a lake. She did not notice them.

'I'm sorry I can't offer you better accommodation,' Train said. 'You can have the bed. I'm kind of locked into this chair.'

The guard remained in the cell, watching in silence as Susan sat on the hard little bed. She felt Train looking at her legs. She had opted not to hide her femininity in choosing her outfit. It was important to see how Train related to women in a social sense. She had even ducked into the ladies' room at the prison to make sure her hair was in place.

She took in Train's physical presence. It was quite different from the mug shot that had appeared in the newspapers. Train was a handsome man. He was above average in height, just over six feet, but he seemed smaller somehow. He still wore the thick moustache he had worn when he was captured in El Paso. His skin was the color of coffee. His hair, receding, increased the expanse of a brow which gave him an intelligent, thoughtful look.

He was well built, with a deep chest and broad, square shoulders. He had expressive hands with very long fingers. Despite his tattoos he seemed sensitive, even refined. His nose was aquiline, his lips thin. He had high cheekbones, which lent a hint of Native American genealogy to his face.

The eyes were dark, the irises shading ambiguously into the pupils, which were contracted in the harsh light of the overhead bulb.

Train regarded her curiously.

'At least you don't look scared,' he said.

'Have many of your visitors seemed scared?' she asked, smiling.

'Sure. They act like they're being locked in a cage with a rattlesnake. People don't understand perpetrators.'

Susan weighed his use of the professional term. She knew he was intelligent. His IQ had tested at 150 at Folsom Prison.

'What don't they understand?' she asked.

'We're not dangerous to someone like you, in a place like this,' Train explained. 'We're only dangerous under certain circumstances. And we're human, too. That's what they don't see.'

Susan nodded. 'I'm afraid convicted criminals are victims of prejudice, just like other minorities,' she said. 'It's difficult for others to put themselves in their place.'

'The nature of the beast,' Train agreed. 'If people were a little more tolerant, men like me would not exist.'

'What do you mean?'

'It takes years of prison to make a headstrong young kid into a real criminal,' he said. 'The early offenses are really pretty innocent. Prison changes that. When you've been in long enough, you stop caring. You lose the ability . . .'

There was a silence. Susan was watching him attentively.

'What ability?' she asked.

'The ability to believe that you can make a difference in what happens.'

'Don't you feel you're making a difference in the world when you commit a crime?' Susan asked.

He shook his head slowly. 'Not at all,' he said. 'That's not how I look at it.'

'How do you look at it?'

He thought for a moment, studying her.

'You know,' he said, 'they should let you pull the switch on me when the time comes.'

'Why do you say that?' Susan asked, surprised by the change of subject.

'I don't know. You look like a nice woman.' Train was studying her, his hands clasped in his lap. 'I'd like to get it from a nice person when the time comes. Add a touch of humanity, if you know what I mean.'

There was a silence. Susan pondered the subtlety of his overture. In one brief formula he had sketched a scenario of intimacy with her, expressed contrition, respect for her and the desire to die. It was a remarkable display of intersubjective manipulation. Of seduction, even.

'Do you want to die?' she asked.

'Doesn't make a lot of difference what I want,' he said. 'Not at this stage. I'm only talking about the way I'd like to go. I know these boys are all gonna be looking at me and pointing the finger when I get the juice. It's a lonely thing to look forward to. I just wish it could be gentle. At least in a way.'

Susan nodded, letting the line play out.

'From what I hear, you haven't been the recipient of much gentleness in your time,' she said.

'Not a lot, no.' He gave a brief laugh. 'But you'd be surprised, Doctor. I have my happy memories to go along with the bad. There were days when I had hopes for myself. I wanted to be somebody. Even to do good.'

'Perhaps it's not too late,' Susan offered.

'There I have to disagree with you,' he said.

He shifted in his seat, apparently uncomfortable in the tight shackles.

'Is that hurting you?' Susan asked.

'Hell, no.' He smiled. 'It reminds me of where I am, that's all. You have to learn to stay within yourself, in a place like this. I don't mind any more.'

Susan watched him, a mild look in her eyes.

'Now, don't tell me,' he said, observing her. 'You're thinking about some of the stuff that's happened to you in your own life. Some of the not-so-gentle stuff.'

She smiled. 'I wasn't, exactly. But you're right, Mr Train. When I look at you, I can't help thinking of the things I went through myself.'

'You're wondering how the hard knocks turn one person into a criminal and another into a productive member of society.' He raised an eyebrow.

'I suppose so,' she said. 'It's never possible to predict how a person is going to turn out. We make our own lives out of the raw material we're given.'

'That's one way to look at it,' Train said.

'What is the other way?' she asked.

'Some of us work with raw material that's already rotten,' he said. 'We try for a while. But you can't build a cathedral out of quicksand.'

'I'm not sure I understand you,' Susan said.

'I hear you have a little boy,' Train said.

Susan tensed slightly at his words. 'Yes, I do,' she replied. 'How old is he?'

'Seven.'

'That's a nice age, seven. I remember it like yesterday. You know, when I was seven I had already lost my virginity.'

'How?'

'My mother had a lot of boyfriends.' Train was looking steadily at Susan. 'A couple of those guys had an open mind about sex, and who they did it with.'

There was a silence as Susan pondered his words.

'Mom was no slouch herself,' he said. 'She used to tie me to the kitchen table and play games with me. I was plenty sore afterwards, if you know what I mean.'

'Sexual games?' Susan asked.

Train was silent. He looked at Susan. His eyes moved over her body. Strangely, she did not feel violated. The despair in his look was its most salient feature.

Then he looked at the guard, who was sitting impassively by the cell door.

'Ewing, can I have a cigarette?' he asked.

'Sure, Cal.' The guard produced a pack of Camel Filters, lit one with a butane lighter and placed it between Train's lips.

'I'm sorry,' Train said, gesturing to Susan. 'You want a cigarette, Doctor?'

'No, thanks.' She shook her head. 'It's been a long time. I wouldn't want to get started again.'

'I don't have to smoke,' Train said. 'If it bothers you.'

'Not at all. Feel free.' She smelled the acrid smoke. There was a time when that aroma was a constant companion to her. Like many other things, she had left it behind her. It did not bother her to look back on it.

Train took a long puff, and blew the smoke out through his nostrils and the corner of his mouth.

'What were we talking about?' he asked.

'I believe we were talking about quicksand,' Susan said.

He laughed. 'Yeah, quicksand. By the time I was old enough to know what was happening, things were already out of control. That's what it's like. At each moment there's an element of choice, but you've already fucked up so badly that your freedom of choice has been whittled down, so to speak.'

'What had you done wrong?' Susan said. She did not want to repeat his language, but she wanted to hear his answer.

'Been born,' he said.

He puffed at the cigarette.

'Was that your fault?' Susan asked.

Train smiled. 'It was somebody's fault,' he said.

She let his point sink in. She was impressed by Calvin Wesley Train. He was intelligent, that was obvious. Many career criminals intellectualized their careers, but he spoke with a rare lucidity and eloquence.

She decided to move forward quickly. Train was creating the mood, molding it with his personality. It was time for her to push back.

'Tell me about the Saeger girl,' she said.

He darkened. He inhaled smoke.

The silence stretched.

'What were you doing up there?' Susan asked.

'Nothing. Hanging out. I'd been in the neighborhood.'

'The neighborhood of the Cave of the Mounds? There's not a lot up there.'

He nodded. 'Yeah.'

Another silence. Train tapped at the loose ash of his cigarette with a long finger.

'Were you visiting?' Susan asked. 'Or on business?'

He gave her a little smirk. 'Business, you could call it. I boosted a few cars, a couple of houses. The pickings were slim. People up there aren't well off.' He breathed in and out. 'It was time to move on, but I thought I would check the parking lot at the Cave of the Mounds. Tourists aren't too bright about what they leave in their cars. I figured I might help myself to some cash, or something I could fence off, like a camera.'

Susan nodded. 'Then what?'

'I saw the kids getting off the bus,' he said. 'This one little girl was a little bit separated from the rest. She looked at me. She looked lonely, kind of. It all happened real quick. I just beckoned to her. *Come here a minute*. Like that. It was just an impulse. She came over. We started talking. She asked me if I'd been to California. I told her yes. I sort of moved her over toward my van, away from the school bus. She didn't resist. She seemed eager to skip out on her field trip.'

'Then what happened?' Susan asked.

'I don't know. That's all I remember.' Train gave her a sidelong look.

'And the next thing you remember after that?' she asked.

'Waking up in Oklahoma,' he said. 'I was in a fleabag motel. Seven o'clock in the morning, the TV playing. A truck starting up outside the window.'

'Were you frightened?' Susan asked.

'Of what?'

'Of waking up with no memory of how you got where you were?'

'Somewhat.' He thought for a moment. 'At first I thought I might have had a few too many beers or something. But then, from watching TV, I began to realize a lot of time had passed. Yes, I was worried.'

'Had this sort of thing ever happened to you before?'

He smiled. 'Not as an adult. But I remember it happening to me as a boy. I would tune out for days at a time.' He smiled at Susan. 'Remember what I told you about the kitchen table?

Sometimes I didn't hang around to feel everything that was going to happen.'

Susan nodded. Train's story had been rehearsed. The insanity defense would be anchored in Train's past, and particularly in the sexual abuse he suffered as a child.

'Tell me, if you can, the last thing you thought you remembered, as you woke up in the motel room.'

'You mean the last thing I could remember from before that moment?'

'Yes.'

Train pondered, his brow furrowed.

'I'm not really sure about that. Wisconsin, I guess. I looked at that TV screen and wondered whether I was still in Wisconsin. Where I was. That sort of thing.'

'What happened next?' Susan's face expressed polite interest, not challenge.

'Well, nothing much. I got up, walked around, looked at my face in the bathroom mirror. Tried to clear the cobwebs.'

'Did you begin to recognize the motel room?'

'Not at all. I did see my stuff on the floor, though. My duffel bag, my shoes. I knew I hadn't been dumped here. I had come on my own power.'

He frowned, his eyes half closing.

'Then I saw the news on TV. The Saeger girl was all over the headlines. There was a picture of her face. When I saw that, I remembered the parking lot at the Cave of the Mounds. I began to think I was in trouble.'

'What kind of trouble?' Susan asked.

He took a deep breath, looking at her. 'I kind of thought I might have killed her.'

There was a silence. Train seemed stricken. His cigarette had gone out. He slumped on the bed, his eyes downcast.

'What made you think you might have killed her?' Susan asked.

'My memory of meeting her in the parking lot.'

Susan sat looking at him for a moment.

'Let's go back to that memory, if you don't mind,' she said. 'You said you spoke to her about California. As you did so you led her away from the buses.'

'I sort of backed away. She followed me.'

'Tell me again what you were thinking at that moment, just before the memory loss intervened.'

Train thought for a moment.

'Just that she seemed lonely. Troubled. I was lonely myself. I wanted to be close to her.'

'Did you reflect on the fact that you could not be close to her without breaking the law?'

'What do you mean?'

'Without abducting her. Without hurting her.'

Train shook his head. 'There's one thing you've got to understand, Doctor. I never wanted to hurt that little girl.'

Susan nodded.

'What else do you remember from the moment in the parking lot?'

'Nothing. Just that feeling of being alone, being cut off. I saw it in her eyes too, when she looked at me. That loneliness. I wanted to be close to that in her.'

'But you knew you were doing something dangerous. For instance, if one of the teachers from the field trip had seen you with Harley at that moment . . .'

'Yes. I see what you mean.'

'Did you have a feeling based on that knowledge?'

'Maybe. A feeling of risk. Furtive. Yeah. Maybe.'

He looked steadily at Susan.

'All right. Now, Mr Train, you had abducted girls and women in the past, is that true?'

Train nodded, his eyes clouding.

'You had raped women?'

'Uh-huh.'

'And little girls?'

Silence. Then, 'Yes, that's true.'

He glanced at Susan's body, then looked away. Comparing her with his victims? Possibly, she thought. It was a man's look. Sexual, evaluative. Many men found Susan attractive. She expected her skin to crawl under the gaze of a killer like Calvin Wesley Train. For some reason it did not.

'So you had to suspect that if the Saeger girl came with you at that moment, she was likely to be hurt.'

He sighed. 'I didn't want that little girl to be hurt. I didn't want to hurt her.'

'But you knew you might have to. You knew it might happen.'

Abruptly Train's eyes filled with tears. They remained expressionless as the tears flowed down his cheeks.

'I didn't want to,' he said.

'I don't think you're being entirely honest with me,' Susan said. 'I don't think there was that much doubt in your mind about what was going to happen.'

He wiped at the tears with the heel of his hand. He looked curiously childlike at that moment.

'Shows how much you know,' he said.

'Mr Train,' Susan said, 'I want to understand what happened. I want to hear it in your own words. But it won't help either of us if you leave anything out.'

'I'm not leaving anything out.' He took a deep breath. 'You don't understand. You can't understand. I had no desire to hurt her. I just wanted – not to be so lonely, for a little while. I wanted contact with a human being. She seemed human to me. That's all there was to it.'

'Then why, when you woke up in Oklahoma, did you suspect that you might have killed her?'

He sighed. 'As you say, I don't have the best record. I thought it was possible.'

'And how did that make you feel?'

'I don't know. Empty. Hopeless. I don't know.'

'Hopeless?'

Train looked at her. 'There's this feeling you get. I don't mean *you* – I mean me. A feeling that everything is out of control. That things follow their course on their own. That you can't control them. That feeling is pretty hopeless. I felt that.'

Susan nodded. 'Now, after your awakening in the motel you took steps to avoid arrest, didn't you?'

He nodded. He knew his movements had been tracked and documented. He had hidden in out-of-the-way places, shaved off his moustache and asked friends for help.

'Did you consider turning yourself in?' she asked.

Train shook his head, a rather arrogant look on his face.

'Why not?' Susan asked.

'I wasn't feeling too good, but I wasn't feeling like moving to Death Row either,' he said.

'And how did you feel when you were finally arrested?'

'Relieved. I just wanted it to end.'

'Wanted what to end?'

'Everything. All of it.' He looked at Susan. 'I still want it to end.'

'Are you afraid of being executed?' Susan asked.

'Not at all.' He shook his head. 'This has gone on long enough. I want it over. And I am truly sorry that little girl got hurt. You may not understand that, but it's true. I'm sorrier than you are.'

'Do you believe you killed her?' Susan asked.

He nodded. More tears had welled in his eyes, but did not flow down his cheeks. 'I have to believe it. My common sense tells me it had to be me. I can't run from it.'

'And how does that make you feel?' Susan asked.

'Did you ever read *The Stranger*?' he asked.

'Camus?' She raised an eyebrow in surprise.

Train gave her a twisted smile. 'What's the matter? Didn't you think we could read?'

'It's been a long time for me,' she replied. 'I read it in college, I believe.'

'When they give the guy the death penalty,' Train said, 'he reflects that it was all coming a long time ago. That it started long before the crime he committed. It was coming all his life. He had never had a chance.' He exhaled. 'That's how I felt. It was too late a long time ago. That little girl's luck ran out when they first pulled my pants down as a little boy. I just want it to end.'

There was a silence. He looked at Susan.

'If it was you dropping the juice . . .' He smiled through his tears. 'That's something I missed out on – what your little boy has. If I knew that a woman like you was going to help me out of this world, I wouldn't mind at all.'

Again his eyes were on her in their probing, appraising way. He was seductive, there was no doubt about that. Susan looked at her watch. Their time was up for today.

'Thank you for seeing me,' she said. 'We have a lot to talk about. I appreciate your honesty.'

'It's about all I've got left,' Train said, holding his hand out as far as the harness would allow.

She had to bend down to shake his hand. She felt his breath on her cheek. She noticed the tattoo on his right hand. She turned his wrist to see it better.

'What's your tattoo?' she asked. The design began on the back of his hand and extended up his forearm.

'Just an error of my youth,' he said. The tattoo on the back of his hand showed a woman's face. Extending from it, up his arm, was her body, which was the body of a snake. It looked like a boa constrictor.

'Are you right-handed?' she asked.

'Sure. Aren't you?'

'No.'

*You are my sunshine*. This time the words broke through to Susan's conscious mind. A smell of coffee seemed to come with them. A fugitive sense of something pleasant came over Susan, followed quickly by its opposite.

Susan held on to his hand, studying the tattoo. The colors were faded. She wondered whether the snake's blue body was intended to cover needle tracks. She also thought about a couple of other possibilities, neither one pleasant.

Train was passive, enjoying the contact with her.

*All's well that ends well*. These words seemed to be spoken by a voice, perhaps a long time ago. Again Susan felt the jagged confluence of something terrible and something restful.

She forced herself to endure the handshake for another moment. Then she stepped back. He let his hand fall to his waist.

'I'll see you next time,' she smiled.

'I'll look forward to it.'

The guard let her out of the cell as Calvin Wesley Train stared at her from his sitting position. His right hand was open, the fingers moving gently, like worms.

# CHAPTER 2

It was a long trial.

A parade of medical and forensic witnesses were brought to the stand by the prosecution to testify to the scientific probability that Calvin Wesley Train was the killer of Harley Ann Saeger. Traces of Train's blood, along with semen, saliva and hair, left no reasonable doubt on this score.

Alexander Penn attacked these witnesses aggressively. He argued in a scattershot manner that the medical evidence against Train was tainted, and that it might have been planted by police who knew of Train's long criminal record and wanted a scapegoat in the Saeger case. He also argued that the heavy publicity surrounding Train's arrest had prejudiced those witnesses, impairing their scientific judgment. Finally he played the race card, hinting that as a black man Train was a tailor-made scapegoat who could not get a fair trial.

Penn was one of the most flamboyant criminal defense attorneys in the nation. He had long white hair, originally a sandy blond but now bleached to give him the air of a venerable soothsayer. He wore expensively cut Italian suits which made him seem even taller than his six feet one. He had very large hands, which he used as eloquent props, pointing at the jury, sketching little patterns in the air, ostentatiously running his fingers through his hair. Most of all he had a deep, resonant voice which boomed through the high-ceilinged old courtroom, sometimes smooth and cajoling, sometimes bitterly sarcastic.

Thanks to Penn's high profile, the case was getting a lot of attention from the press. Sound trucks from networks and cable stations were camped in a parking lot a half-block from the courthouse. Penn gave a brief news conference every afternoon at the end of the court day, always making sure to include at least one quotable soundbite.

By the time Susan took the stand the Train trial had occupied banner headlines for two months. Susan was the first psychiatrist to testify for the prosecution and, according to informed observers, the most important.

Jay Braden, the prosecutor, was an aggressive man in his early forties, with thick graying hair and sharp eyes. He spent twenty minutes leading Susan through the long list of her degrees, qualifications, honors and writings on violent criminals. Susan, wearing a summer suit with a light blue blouse, had little to answer except 'Yes' during the litany.

When the credentials were finished Braden wasted no more time. 'Dr Shader, how many hours did you spend interviewing the defendant?'

'About twenty hours.'

'You talked at length about the murder of Harley Ann Saeger?'

'Yes, we did.'

'Doctor, is it your expert opinion that the defendant, at the time of the abduction of Harley Saeger, knew the nature and consequences of his act?'

'Yes. That is my opinion.'

'Was the defendant irresistibly impelled to perform that act, in such a manner that he could not at that time exercise his free will and judgment in deciding not to perform the act?'

'No. He was not irresistibly impelled.'

'Was he under the influence of a mental illness or other similar disturbance which attenuated or excluded his ability to exercise free will and judgment in contemplating the act?'

'No, he was not.'

'He could have abstained from the act?'

'Yes, he could.'

Braden stood with his back to Susan, looking at the jury.

'Doctor, what is your opinion as to the defendant's claim that he remembers nothing from the time he first met Harley Ann Saeger until he awoke in a motel room in Oklahoma?'

'I believe his claim is not truthful.'

'On what do you base your opinion?'

'There are two types of significant memory loss which we see in psychiatry,' Susan said. 'The first is called the fugue state. It can last a few hours or, sometimes, much longer. It often includes the manifestation of a second personality, usually a more gregarious and extroverted one than the patient's normal personality. The second is amnesia, which usually follows upon a traumatic event. In amnesia the subject normally appears confused and cloudy.'

'And did the defendant's behavior during the week following the abduction fit either of these paradigms?' Braden asked.

'No, sir. The defendant was engaged in criminal behavior – the torture and murder of the victim – and in evasive behavior designed to elude the police and subsequently to dispose of the victim's body. None of this behavior is characteristic of a person in a figure state or a state of amnesia.'

'Did the defendant then, or does he now, feel remorse over his act?'

'No.'

The gauntlet was down. The rest of Braden's direct examination consisted of a detailed and ultimately horrifying description of the acts of torture and sexual perversion carried out on the helpless little girl by Train, and of repeated opinions by Susan to the effect that at all times Train was legally responsible for his actions and felt no remorse.

Two hours after he had begun the direct, Jay Braden was ready to conclude.

'Now, in your opinion, Doctor, why did the defendant commit these acts?'

'For the sake of sexual pleasure,' Susan said. 'And to cause suffering.'

'What brings you to this conclusion, Doctor?'

'The acts themselves. The lengthy sequestration of the victim. The defendant's behavior in my interviews with him.'

'The defendant understood the nature and consequences of his actions, was not irresistibly impelled to commit them, and did so for the sake of sexual pleasure and to cause suffering to the victim?'

'Correct.'

'Thank you, Doctor.' Braden sat down.

The judge motioned to Alexander Penn, who approached the stand with his eyebrows raised in surprise.

'Doctor, you've been talking about some pretty frightening things,' he said.

'Murder is a frightening subject,' Susan replied. She looked very small in her chair on the stand. Penn towered over her like a prophet.

'According to your notes on this case, the defendant suffers from a very serious mental disorder, does he not?'

'He suffers from what is termed a narcissistic personality disorder,' Susan said.

'And would it be correct to say that the abuse the defendant suffered at the hands of his mother and her various lovers played a critical role in creating that character disorder?'

'I would speculate that that abuse played a role, yes,' Susan said.

'The abuse was sexual and physical as well as emotional, was it not?'

'Yes.'

'It included forcible sodomy?'

'Yes.'

'Sequestration?'

'Yes.'

'Torture?'

'Yes.'

'Burning of the skin?'

'Yes.'

'So you do not consider the defendant a normal individual, in psychiatric terms?'

'No, sir.'

'You consider the defendant a severely disturbed individual, do you not?'

'Yes, I do.'

'Now, Doctor, you have stated that in your opinion the defendant does not suffer from the kind of mental disease that would compromise his ability to understand the nature and consequences of his act.'

'Correct.'

'If the defendant *did* suffer from such a disease,' Penn asked, 'would he be considered legally responsible for his acts in this case?'

Some of the legal observers present nodded to each other at these words. Penn was laying the groundwork for an attack on Susan's diagnosis. All he had to do was convince the jury that there was doubt about which mental disease Train suffered from and there would be doubt about the question of responsibility.

Susan's answer took him by surprise.

'If he did suffer from such a disease, he never would have committed those acts.'

'Objection!' Penn shouted.

'Counsel approach,' said the judge.

There was a lengthy sidebar. Both attorneys whispered earnestly. The judge listened with an impassive face. Susan waited, her eyes meeting those of the jurors. They looked interested, but also skeptical. Of her? Hard to tell. The only thing that made jurors more skeptical than a psychiatrist was a lawyer.

'The response will stand,' the judge announced.

Penn knew he was in trouble now. Susan had given the jury rope to hang his client with. Not only was Train not suffering from an incapacitating mental illness, but his acts themselves were strong evidence of his sanity.

Penn came forward and leaned over Susan like an angry father.

'Are you trying to tell this jury, Doctor, that the insane, monstrous acts committed on the victim in this case are proof of the defendant's *sanity*?' The last word was shouted.

'The defendant kept the victim alive as long as he could,' Susan said. 'He did so with the intention of enjoying her sexually for as long as possible. The torture he inflicted upon her was calculated so as not to cause her to die before he wanted her to die. A severely disabled mental patient could not have carried out such an organized series of acts.'

Looking daggers at Susan, Penn changed the subject.

'Now, Doctor, you have testified that in your opinion the defendant feels no remorse for his acts. Is that correct?'

'That is correct.'

'Doctor, I read to you from the transcript of your sessions with the defendant at Waupun Penitentiary.

"TRAIN: I am truly sorry that little girl got hurt. I'm sorrier than you are.

"TRAIN: There's one thing you've got to understand, Doctor. I never wanted to hurt that little girl.

"TRAIN: I just want it to end. Anyone who could do what happened to that child deserves to die.

'Now, Doctor, that sounds an awful lot like remorse to me. Why doesn't it sound like remorse to you?'

'The defendant is very adept at feigning remorse,' Susan replied. 'However, he betrays by various signs in his voice and manner that his emotions are not genuine.'

'Can you explain that, Doctor?'

'When a perpetrator feels remorse, the remorse shows in ways he can't control. Nervousness, tics, inappropriate tears or laughter and so forth. Nothing spontaneous like this happens with Mr Train. Everything is rehearsed. He is giving a performance of remorse.'

'Is this your opinion as an expert, Doctor?'

'Essentially, yes. But what I am describing is quite often visible to ordinary people, when they see someone lying or putting on an act.'

'Would it be visible to this jury?' Penn asked sarcastically.

'If you put your client on the stand I'm sure you'll find that out, Mr Penn.'

'Objection!' Penn thundered.

'Overruled,' said the judge. 'You asked the question, Counsel.'

Penn was visibly shaken by the course his cross-examination had taken so far. Susan's testimony was devastating to his client. The only way to undo the damage was to destroy her credibility.

'Now, Doctor, you are psychic, are you not?'

Jay Braden objected to the question. 'Irrelevant to her testimony as a psychiatric expert, Your Honor.'

The judge thought for a moment. 'I'll rule on that, Counsel. I'd like to hear her answer first.'

'Yes, I am,' Susan said.

'You believe in the reality of psychic phenomena, also known as parapsychological phenomena.'

'Yes, I do.'

'And you have written articles to that effect in scientific journals, have you not?'

'Yes, I have.'

'And you have given lectures and talks to scientific and parapsychological assemblies on that topic, have you not?'

'Yes, I have.'

'Doctor, does your belief in the supernatural affect your—'

'Objection to the word supernatural.' Jay Braden was on his feet.

There was a silence.

'Objection sustained.'

'Semantics, Your Honor,' said Penn. 'Would the word paranormal be more acceptable?'

'All right.'

'Doctor, does your belief in the *paranormal* affect your judgment of mental phenomena or psychological phenomena?'

Susan knew this was coming and had her answer ready.

'It does not affect my judgment as a psychiatrist in a context such as the one we are concerned with,' she said. 'I do consider it a theoretical issue worth pursuing in a scientific vein.'

'Can you explain?' asked Penn.

'I think the reality of psychic phenomena is something that needs to be examined scientifically. I also think the scientific criteria regarding certainty need to be examined where psychic phenomena are concerned. Moreover, I also think those criteria of certainty have already been challenged by modern scientific thought, especially in physics and mathematics.'

'Thank you, Doctor. Now, in your own publications and lectures on parapsychology you have stated that extra-sensory perception is not a thing that can be turned on and off at one's whim. Is that correct?'

'Yes. That is correct.'

'One cannot repeat a psychic experience on demand. The psychic impressions come and go when they please. Is that right?'

'Yes.'

'Would it not be possible to say, conversely, that one cannot prevent psychic impressions from coming when they wish?'

'Yes, I think that is correct.'

'Doctor,' Penn asked slowly, 'did your psychic powers play a role in your interviews with the defendant?'

'No. Only my observation as a person and as a psychiatrist.'

'How can you be so certain? Couldn't your conviction of the defendant's state of mind have been influenced by psychic impressions?'

'No, it couldn't.'

'Are you sure, Doctor?'

'Psychic feelings are like any other feeling or intuition that operates in the mind. They are often important, but they cannot be used to produce scientific conviction. The role of an expert witness is to testify based on his professional skill, not his feelings.'

'Doctor, did you ever have physical contact with the defendant?'

'We shook hands.'

'Did you at any time extend that handshake contact of your own volition?'

'I don't know what you mean.'

'Did you hold the defendant's hand longer than the handshake, and ask him a question about his hand?'

'Yes. I asked him about a tattoo that covered the back of his hand and his forearm.'

'And what was your purpose in asking this?'

'Curiosity.'

'Doctor, did you at any time receive impressions of a parapsychological nature from your contact with the defendant?'

'No, I did not.'

Penn looked at the jury.

'Doctor, you seem extraordinarily certain of your opinion as to the defendant's unstated motives in the commission of these acts.'

'I have a reasonable scientific certainty,' Susan said.

'Are you sure that your psychic gift had nothing to do with your testimony in this case?'

'Yes, I am sure.'

Penn took a deep breath, held out his hands as though in surrender and exhaled.

'I have nothing further, Your Honor.'

As Susan left the stand and walked quickly toward the exit she noticed that Alexander Penn shifted his position so as to block her view of Calvin Wesley Train. She caught a brief glimpse of Train's eyes, which were focused on her in a look of the purest hatred.

# CHAPTER 3

The case ended twelve weeks after Susan's testimony.

In a bold move designed to appeal to the jury's sympathy, Alexander Penn put Calvin Wesley Train on the stand in his own defense. Train repeated for the jury many of the statements he had made to Susan in their interviews. He detailed the sexual and physical abuse he had suffered as a child and as an inmate in penal institutions. He described the amnesia that had followed his meeting with the Saeger girl, and his horror when he realized, a week later, that it might have been he who killed her. He told the jury of his newfound interest in counseling other violent criminals.

'I thought I wanted to die, just to stop the violence I had caused,' he said. 'I think I could do more good by staying alive. I have an understanding of the kind of life that produces violent criminals. I think I could help them as a prison counselor to understand their own anger and hopelessness. That might prevent them from repeating their violent behavior when they get out of prison. If I could do some good with the years remaining to me, I would feel less bad about the things I have done in the past.'

The closing statements were long. Jay Braden went over the massive physical evidence against Calvin Wesley Train in painful detail, evoking with each piece of evidence the atrocious sufferings of the victim. He appealed to the jury members' love for their children as well as their sense of justice in asking for a conviction.

Alexander Penn stuck to his planned defense to the end. He claimed that the evidence against Train was tainted, and that some of it was planted in an attempt to frame the suspect. He claimed that the state's expert witnesses were prejudiced, that they were part of an unconscious conspiracy intended to punish the defendant in order to assuage public outrage over the crime. He intimated that the defendant's race played a role in this conspiracy.

Not scrupling to avoid self-contradiction, Penn claimed that Train's childhood of severe abuse and his long years of institutionalization had made him into a monster, a creature who had lost all sense of his own free will and of right and wrong. He attacked the criminal justice system for creating this monster and for freeing Train at the same time. He challenged the psychiatrists' diagnosis of Train as a sociopath. He attacked the legal definition of responsibility itself, saying it was outdated, prejudicial and completely inadequate for a scientific assessment of a mentally ill person's degree of understanding and self-control.

He singled out Susan Shader for ridicule, citing her belief in psychic phenomena as proof that she could not be relied on as an expert in forensic psychiatry. 'This was a real crime that took place in the real world. Yet the state bases its case on the intuitions of spiritualists.'

He concluded with an impassioned description of Calvin Wesley Train's tortured life. He cited the defendant's intelligence and his potential for rehabilitation.

'The state wants you to assuage the community's horror at this terrible, tragic crime by putting my client to death,' he said. 'An eye for an eye. A death for a death. No more, no less. What we have here is not a prosecution, not a fair trial, but a conspiracy to convict. You cannot allow such a travesty to take place. You must send them a message, ladies and gentlemen. Our courts should be a place of justice, not of revenge.'

Susan was at home, in jogging shorts and a T-shirt, working on an article for a psychiatric journal, when David Gold of the Chicago Homicide Division called to tell her the verdict was in.

'Can I come over and watch with you?' he asked.

'Sure. Come on over.'

The jury had been out since this morning. The deliberations had taken twelve hours.

Susan put away her work and glanced around her before going to her bedroom to change clothes. The apartment was like a theater in which the living room was the stage, brightly lit and prepared for all to see, and the rest of the rooms were the dark and cluttered wings. The living room was large, with armchairs, a glass-topped coffee table and a rather expensive couch. During the day it had a magnificent view of the Loop and the lakeshore. A cheerful carpet covered the floor.

The other rooms were a different story. There were piles of medical journals on the floors, boxes of 'stuff' Susan had brought with her when she first moved to Chicago and never bothered to unpack. A battered desk bought at a garage sale contained Susan's personal and financial papers. The curtains, bedspreads and rugs were no-frills. Susan sometimes reflected that the cardboard boxes represented her two-edged attitude toward her past. She could not make up her mind either to put it in order or to throw it away.

Only the bedroom Michael slept in when he visited showed personal touches which sketched a unified picture of Susan's life. Here were the family photos that reflected Susan's personal history. Herself as a child with her brother, Quentin, her parents' wedding portrait, studio portraits of herself with

Michael, and Michael's favorite picture of Susan and her father sitting on a picnic table in a Pennsylvania state park, taken when Susan was ten.

In the small bookcase were books Michael liked, along with coloring books, toy soldiers and stuffed animals. There were also recent pictures of Michael with Nick, Susan's ex-husband, and his new wife, Elaine. Prominently displayed was a blown-up snapshot of Michael and David Gold wearing matching T-shirts which bore the legend AREA SIX VIOLENT CRIMES. Michael idolized Gold, and never let a vacation go by without paying a visit to Gold's office in the Loop.

The apartment was emptier now that Susan's roommate Carolyn, a news producer at WGN, had left to move in with her boyfriend. However, Carolyn's cat, a ten-year-old former stray named Margie, remained here because Carolyn's boyfriend was allergic to cats. As Susan passed through the bedroom the cat opened one eye to acknowledge her passing, then went back to sleep.

Susan gave herself a quick look in the bathroom mirror.

*I look like hell*, she thought. Fatigue had combined with a long and busy day to leave her hair awry and her make-up smudged.

'Oh, well,' she said aloud as she wiped off her eye make-up entirely. 'He can stand it if I can.' She unpinned her hair, made a half-hearted effort to brush it, then tied it back in a ponytail and left the bathroom.

David Gold was Susan's closest friend on the Chicago PD and the man who had convinced her, eight years ago, to become a psychic consultant to the police. Gold had seen her at her worst in their years together. Police work seldom leaves a woman time or energy to look her best. Still she felt the need to look at least halfway attractive for him.

Gold arrived just in time to hear the reading of the verdict. The jury found Calvin Wesley Train Guilty with Special

Circumstances. In a prepared statement the jury foreman expressed the panel's desire that Calvin Wesley Train be executed to ensure that he never be at large again in the event of changes in the death penalty laws.

After being dismissed the jury gave a news conference. All twelve panelists said they had found the deliberations comparatively easy because of the massive evidence against the defendant. They also said that Calvin Wesley Train's own testimony had worked against him.

'We agreed with Dr Shader's view that the defendant was putting on a performance of remorse,' said the foreman. 'He seemed rehearsed to us and not sincere.'

The jury had been convinced by Susan's explanation that a truly incapacitating mental illness would not have allowed the defendant to deal with his victim in so organized and sadistic a manner. 'Dr Shader's testimony was a great blow to the defense,' said one juror. 'She stood up to Mr Penn and stuck to her guns.'

David Gold accepted the beer Susan held out to him.

'Well, you did your job,' he said.

'It wasn't pleasant. Did you see the way Train looked at me?' Susan sat down on the couch and crossed her legs.

'Yeah. I don't think he likes you.'

Susan shook her head. 'I hope he stays behind bars. I wouldn't feel safe if he got out.'

'He won't get out.' Gold shook his head. 'As long as there is a Death Row, Cal Train will be on it. I never saw a meaner guy.'

'Mean, yes. But subtle, too,' Susan said. 'It makes him scarier. In my conversations with him I found something almost spiritual about him. As though he were wedded to evil in some transcendent way.'

'Like being with the Devil himself?' Gold asked.

'I don't believe in the Devil.' Susan laughed. 'At least I

didn't up to now. But, yes, that's what it was like. He has a kind of spiritual thrust or power. He's very frightening.'

'Well,' Gold said, 'you're pretty frightening yourself.'

'Is that a compliment?' she asked, smiling.

He let his eyes rest on her. In her jeans and T-shirt, she did not look a day older than she had the first time he met her. Her hair was shorter now, and her eyes bore the look of hard experience in the professional world. But she had another quality, hard to name, that never failed to charm him and raise his spirits. A kind of innocence, perhaps, that only grew deeper as she matured. It stood out more sharply when she dressed informally.

At that moment the cat appeared in the doorway and gave Gold a long look. Gold turned to acknowledge her, but she was already padding away toward the bedrooms.

'Checking you out,' Susan said. Margie was a naturally aloof animal who had taken over a year to get used to Susan. But the cat's territoriality would not allow her to permit strangers in the house without at least one withering stare.

Gold stayed long enough to chat with Susan about his daughters and his wife, Carol, a violist with the Chicago Symphony. Gold asked Susan how Michael was doing, and she brought him up to date. Her custody arrangement with Nick was amicable, but she missed Michael terribly when he was not here and kept in close touch by telephone and e-mail.

Gold was reasonably sure that he and Carol would have no more children, so that made Michael officially the son he had never had. Gold looked forward to Michael's regular trips from California and took him to ballgames when he was in town.

At ten-thirty Gold looked at his watch and stood up. 'Long day,' he said. 'At least we got the news today.'

'I'm glad, too.' Susan gave him a tired smile.

'Get some rest,' he said. 'Talk to you tomorrow, maybe.'

'Good night, David.'

After Gold left Susan went through the apartment, turning off lights and peeling off clothes in her passage. She rarely stayed up this late.

She took a hot shower, called her answering service and checked her answering machine. There were several messages of congratulations from friends and colleagues who had heard about the Train verdict.

One of the messages was from Nick, Susan's ex-husband in California.

'Your verdict was on every station,' Nick said. 'Good work, Susan. Call me when you get the chance. Michael wants to speak to you, too.'

She would call tomorrow, she decided, when Michael got home from school. Right now she felt too exhausted to talk to anyone.

She threw her terrycloth robe on the chair in the bedroom and got into bed. She was glad the trial was over. The verdict had pleased her, but the Harley Ann Saeger case had left a chill in her nerves that might last a long time. In the course of the trial she had come to know the girl's parents, who had suspended their plans for divorce after her abduction, but now intended to go through with it.

Both parents had been devastated by the testimony they heard in court. Their daughter's sufferings had been unspeakable. The mother, June, was haunted by guilt about the planned divorce and its effect on Harley's last few months of life. She could not escape her morbid suspicion that in some way Harley's pain and alienation, due to her parents' problems, had had something to do with her vulnerability to Train's seduction at the Cave of the Mounds. Susan had tried, without much success, to reassure her. She suspected both parents might need some therapy in the future, despite the relief they felt at the verdict.

Susan lay in bed, her unpinned hair splayed over the pillow. She listened to the silence of the apartment. She thought of opening the book she was reading, but changed her mind and turned out the light.

Her eyes closed almost immediately. Images from the trial jittered before her mind, accompanied by the voices that had rung in her ears for so many weeks. It was impossible to turn it all off. She tried to call forth her son's face, as she often did at bedtime, just to contemplate it and to think about her love for him.

But something got in the way. She saw the photograph of Harley Ann Saeger that had been shown so many times in the media over the past year. She saw the face of Calvin Wesley Train, handsome, dark, intelligent. And the face of Alexander Penn, indignant and angry as he attacked her.

For one long moment she allowed herself the emotion she had banished all these months. The fear the doomed little girl must have felt came to her. Her breath came short, her hands grew cold. Her nipples tightened. Tears welled in her eyes.

*Where are we going?*

*Please. No.*

*Please . . .*

With a deep breath Susan got control of herself and forced the terror down. It belonged with the feelings she could not allow herself to feel.

Her effort seemed to work. After a few minutes her mind began to wander. Dream images bumped softly against each other like clouds meeting in a windy sky.

But the truth opened Susan's eyes before sleep could close them for the night. She lay staring at the ceiling, remembering.

She had lied to Alexander Penn and to the jury.

Her second sight had played a role in her conclusions about Calvin Wesley Train.

The day she shook Train's hand and touched the tattoo on his arm, she saw what had been in Train's mind when he watched the children outside the school bus and noticed Harley Ann Saeger wandering away from the group.

It was her vagina. He was looking at her legs and thinking about what her vagina would taste like.

That was the only thought in his mind as he beckoned to the girl.

# PART TWO

# CHAPTER 4

*Career criminal Calvin Wesley Train was found guilty
of First Degree Murder with Special Circumstances
today by a jury in Madison, Wisconsin, after a hard-
fought trial which took nearly seven months.*

*Train, who abducted and killed third-grader Harley
Ann Saeger last year, was defended aggressively by
high-profile attorney Alexander Penn. An eloquent
witness in his own defense, Train insisted he had no
memory of harming the girl . . .*

Loud music was playing, so it was somewhat difficult to hear
the reporter's voice. The bar was full of regulars who worked
in the Loop and were here for a beer or a cocktail before
heading for home.

Most of the dinner tables were unoccupied, but a few
patrons were having dinner at the bar. The place served a
variety of sandwiches and hamburgers.

Miranda Becker was drinking a margarita and waiting for
her Cobb salad. It had been a long day and she was too tired
to face going home alone and cooking a solitary supper. She
had been here before, with friends, and knew the food.

But there was another reason, one she did not like to
admit to herself. Doug might come in here on his way home.

He wouldn't be alone, but that was one reason she wanted
to see him. To see who he was with.

She caught a glimpse of herself in the mirror over the bar. She looked pretty, she thought. The slight pallor, the dark eyes, the long hair. She had lost weight, and was wearing a snug sweater and tight slacks she could not have fit into six months ago.

She looked like what she was: a woman who had cut her links to the person she was only a short time ago. A clean slate. A person trying to start over.

Unfortunately, the despair under her careful make-up and new clothes was as visible as the slight wrinkles around her eyes. She was not as young as she used to be. The clock was ticking. She had invested four years in Doug and got nothing out of them. Now she was four years older. Her market value was slipping with every birthday.

She sipped her drink and shook her head slightly. It was hard being a woman. She hated this jungle in which all unmarried women had to compete. There was no honor in it, no value. Only the frantic struggle to get chosen before others. The battle to grab off the available man before another attractive, smart, eligible woman got him first.

The face in the mirror was still young. But the battle she was fighting made her feel old before her time.

She remembered Jane Fonda in *Klute*, the prostitute dragging herself into a music bar to look for men, doing a half-hearted ersatz of swaying to the music with a bright smile, then abruptly faltering, sagging, her face expressing the disgust and loneliness she felt inside. Then pulling herself together, exhaustedly . . .

That was what Miranda saw in her own face as she looked in this mirror. A bright, eligible young woman trying to look attractive, trying to hide her emptiness and despair. This was not real. This was not living.

'Hello. Haven't we met?'

The voice belonged to a face that had appeared at her side in the mirror. He didn't look familiar.

'I don't think so,' she said, her voice intentionally off-putting.

'I guess I must have seen you here before. I'm in here pretty often.'

The bartender was approaching. The jukebox was playing the Phish tune she liked, 'Bouncing Around the Room'. The stranger ordered himself a glass of wine without offering Miranda another margarita. She studied his face in the mirror. A tall man, rather good-looking. Not in the way Doug was good-looking, but not bad.

He sipped at his wine in silence before turning to her. 'I hate this season.'

Miranda gave him a low-voltage smile. 'Why?'

'It's the doldrums,' he said. 'The weather stinks. Summer won't be back for a long time. There's nothing to look forward to but Thanksgiving with the relatives, and then the holidays. I'd feel better if it was March.'

'Then what would there be to look forward to?' Miranda asked, hearing her own depression in her voice.

'Summer, anyway.' He twisted the glass of wine, watching the pattern of the condensation.

'What happens in the summer?' Miranda asked, knowing she was encouraging him.

'I'm a sailor,' he said. 'I have a sailboat here in the marina.' He looked at her. 'Do you sail?'

'I have.' She nodded. 'But not in a long time.'

'I love to get my feet off dry land,' he said. 'It's an escape. I know it's dumb, but when I get away from the shore I feel free. I feel cleansed.'

She knew what he meant. But she had never felt that way, not at all. Boats stank of bait and fish. The slapping of the water against the hull grated on her nerves and she was prone to seasickness. She never felt liberated at all on a boat.

'Well, you can escape for a while,' she said. 'But you always have to come back to dry land.'

'I'm afraid that's true,' he said, smiling at her in the mirror. 'And dry land isn't all it's cracked up to be.'

To her surprise, she was getting over her embarrassment. He seemed a decent sort. Friendly, self-deprecating. She wondered whether he sensed her mood and was playing to it, or whether he himself felt sad and empty, as she did.

'Tell me,' he said. 'What do you do for escape?'

She thought for a moment.

'Think,' she said. 'Read. Music, sometimes.'

'I envy you.' He smiled. 'Thinking has never done it for me. All I do is brood.'

She nodded. But she had spoken honestly. Thinking was indeed her greatest escape. She could sit in a chair and let her mind roam aimlessly over a landscape made up of memory, reflection, imagination, mixing elements of them all, drifting through them without being held by any particular one. She had learned how to do this as a little girl, when her parents were fighting or when something at school got her down. The mind was a powerful escape if one knew how to use it right.

'It's a two-edged sword,' she said diplomatically. She could see he was the type who forgot his troubles through recreation. It would be difficult for him to understand her. She felt a bitter twinge of irony as she realized she was sizing him up for a relationship. She looked at his image in the mirror. Together they made a handsome couple.

'What kind of music do you like?' he asked.

This was the turning point, she told herself. One more personal word about herself and he would ask her to join him. It was up to her.

She glanced at the clock. Six-forty-five. Doug might still show up. If he did, he would not be alone. She hated the idea of letting him see her eating a solitary supper at the bar. Wouldn't it be better if she were with someone?

Besides, why not start over? What difference did it make if she had wasted four years of her life on one man?

*Ancient history*, she thought sadly.

She looked once more at the face in the mirror. Inwardly she sighed. 'Mozart,' she said.


Two hours later Miranda awoke with a crashing headache that forced her to keep her eyes closed.

The peculiar smell in her nostrils seemed to be the source of the terrible pain. Chloroform? She didn't know.

She was lying on her back, her hands and feet tied to the corners of the bed. Was it a bed? Or just a mattress? It felt strange against her skin.

She drifted in and out of consciousness. What was going on? What had happened? She remembered the stranger in the bar, a drive in his car, a drink. Then nothing.

She fought the headache, clenching her eyes shut and moaning softly. She suspected it was morning. Was she in his bed or hers? Had she done what she was afraid she had done?

He came into the room, interrupting her reflections. He was wearing a surgical mask and a scrub suit. He seemed busy, preoccupied. Miranda thought she was dreaming.

He knelt by her side, tied a tourniquet around her arm and stuck a needle into her. He was muttering to himself, but her terror combined with the effects of the drug to keep her from understanding.

Now she realized the ceiling was mirrored. She could see herself lying naked, tied to the mattress. This could not be a dream, she thought.

'Hold still,' he said.

A plastic bag was attached to the needle in her arm. She saw it filling with her own blood.

'What are you doing?' she cried.

Only the formless mutter answered her. She could feel her blood going out of her. She opened her mouth to scream, but passed out before she could utter a sound.

When she came to, she felt pain in her hands and feet. She instinctively tried to pull her hands to her face, but they were tied down. She knew now that this was not a dream.

'Help!' she screamed. 'Help me!'

He came back into the room. The look in his eyes had changed. They were sparkling with expectation. His hands were held up. He was wearing surgical gloves. In his right hand was a scalpel.

As he came closer she saw that he was naked from the waist down. A long penis swayed between his legs, erect and moist.

'Don't,' she said in a trembling voice. 'Don't.'

He crouched beside her.

'Just relax,' he said.

He placed the blade at a point just below her ribcage.

'The important thing is to relax . . .'

The blade cut into her, then downward. Pain exploded inside her. The scalpel fell to the floor with a clink. Now he was holding a long knife, poised in both his hands. The rhythmic mutter had started again behind his mask.

He raised the knife high with both hands and plunged it into her. The shock knocked the wind out of her, silencing the scream on her lips.

In the mirror blood formed a halo around her body.

Instinct told her that death was at the terminus of this moment, and the realization brought resignation in its train. She floated outside herself, toward the ceiling in which she was mirrored. She saw the spreading sea of blood, and recalled his description of leaving dry land for something liquid and free. She saw the half-naked man working over her naked body.

*Ancient history*, she thought. She was past caring.

But now, as she floated past him, she made out the words behind his mask.

'Blessed art thou among women . . .'

He was praying.

# CHAPTER 5

Susan was still under the emotional cloud of the Harley Saeger verdict. She wanted to get back to normal as quickly as possible. She had patients to think about, and writing, and plans for a visit to California to see Michael and to have a conference with his second-grade teacher.

It turned out she would not be able to catch her breath. David Gold was in her waiting room when her last patient of the day left. He looked overlarge and out of place in the leather armchair, a copy of *People* in his hands. He had crossed his long legs, and his shoulder holster bulged behind the lapel of his rather threadbare suit jacket.

'You again,' she smiled, her arms crossed.

'Got a minute?' he asked, throwing the magazine on the coffee table.

'Come on in.'

He entered her inner office, which was cluttered with books and computer supplies. A Macintosh of recent vintage was on the little table, attached to an external Zip drive. Susan was in the habit of writing down notes on her patient sessions on the computer during her lunch hour and at the end of the day.

'What's up?' she asked.

'We found the damnedest thing this morning,' he said. 'Out by the lake, near Grant Park. A woman's body. Stabbed to death. Really butchered.'

'Is that so unusual?' Susan asked.

'She was wrapped in a body bag,' Gold said, settling his long frame into the extra chair in Susan's inner office.

'A body bag.' Susan pondered the odd notion. 'That's certainly peculiar.'

'I've seen them in every place and container,' Gold said. 'Cut up in little pieces, in cars, in boats, even one in a coffin once.'

'In a coffin?'

'Right in the front parlor at Smithfield's Funeral Home, in Carbondale,' Gold nodded. 'The funeral director came down one morning and found a corpse laid out that didn't belong. We never solved that one either.' He shook his head. 'But a body bag – that's a new one.'

Susan said nothing. She sensed he was leading up to something.

'Pretty tragic,' he said. 'A young woman. Worked here in the Loop as editor of a business trade journal. Not married. Very intelligent, from what I can gather. She must have been good-looking, too – before.'

'Do you have any ideas?' Susan asked.

'Not a one,' he said. 'I went over to her office this morning. She had a small staff. They can't believe it. We called her family. The mother's dead, but the father lives in a retirement place down south. He's flying up.' Gold shook his head. 'A hell of a lot of stab wounds,' he said. 'She didn't have much blood left in her.'

He looked at Susan.

'ME has the body,' he said. 'I was there this afternoon. The techs dusted her apartment today, just in case. She lived pretty near you. Lincoln Park.'

'What was her name?'

'Becker. Miranda Becker.'

There was a silence.

'What have you got going?' Gold asked.

Susan smiled. 'Same old stuff.'

'Want to stop over there with me?' he asked. 'It's on your way home, almost.'

Susan looked at her computer. 'I have to write down a couple of things. Let me meet you there.'

Gold wrote the address on one of Susan's Post-it pads.

'We can have a drink after,' he said.

'All right.'

The apartment was in one of the older buildings in Lincoln Park, with a good view of the lake but very little floor space. It had a look that was at once feminine and businesslike. The curtains were bright, the fabrics on couches and chairs colorful. There were a couple of attractive throw rugs on a beige carpet. The bookshelves and cabinets were walnut, as was the computer desk, which dominated the small living-dining room.

On the walls were prints of paintings by old masters. Vermeer's *View of Delft* was on one wall, and Brueghel's beautiful *Hunters in the Snow*, a painting Susan knew, was over the couch. There were also a couple of Rembrandt por-traits and a religious picture that Susan guessed was by Botticelli.

There were heavy art books on the shelves, along with business and computer journals and paperback novels. While Gold talked to his office on the phone, Susan wandered past the books, letting her fingertips brush the spines. Many of the English and American classics were represented, along with modern novels that seemed well thumbed. Sue Miller, Toni Morrison, Ann Tyler. *The Good Mother* was a hardcover. *The Great Gatsby* was the old Scribner paperback, badly worn along the spine.

Miranda Becker was a reader. Looking into the small

bedroom, Susan saw a pile of library books beside the bed, all bearing bookmarks. Like Susan herself, Miranda must have liked to read several books at the same time, opening the one that appealed to her each night when she got into bed.

The TV was an old Sony portable. Significantly, there was no VCR. Miranda could not have watched much television. There was an exercise bike in front of the TV, a relatively new Tunturi similar to Susan's own.

On the bookshelves were pictures of Miranda, her parents and siblings.

'She has a brother and sister,' Gold called across the room. 'Both older, both married. The brother lives in Oregon, the sister in Tennessee. I've already talked to both of them.'

Only one of the photographs seemed recent, a Christmas family shot from a couple of years ago. The rest were older. Yearbook pictures of the brother and sister. A posed family portrait from a long time ago, when the siblings were all children. The faces were interesting, Susan thought. The brother and sister took after their father. They both had his sandy hair and square chin. Miranda, the youngest, resembled her mother, a handsome woman with dark hair and sad, intelligent eyes.

There were few things in the world Susan found more fascinating than family pictures and family albums. One could tell a lot about people from the way they posed when they were with members of their family. Particularly when the pictures could be compared to shots taken with friends.

Miranda Becker was very attached to her family, Susan guessed. There was a protective air about her older siblings in the photos. Miranda was at least five or six years younger than her brother and sister. A late child. The parents seemed loving but perhaps a little remote, as though they presided pridefully over their three children but did not know them terribly well.

A picture of the two sisters together was especially eloquent. The older sister was shorter than Miranda and heavier. She had the look of an aunt already, though she could not be much older than thirty. Her hand was on Miranda's shoulder, protective and, Susan thought, admiring.

'Do you know what the brother and sister do, David?' she asked Gold.

'The brother is some kind of businessman,' Gold said. 'The sister is a housewife, I think.'

That sounded right to Susan. The sister seemed homey and sheltering. Miranda, on the other hand, looked like the family's outsider, not only because she was physically distinct from her siblings but because there was something private behind her smile, especially as she grew older. Something she kept from the family.

'Look at this, Susan.'

Gold had opened the computer desk and was pointing to some manila folders.

'This isn't business,' he said. 'These look like manuscripts.' He had one open. 'Look. It's a short story.'

Susan looked at the folder. A manuscript of about twenty pages, printed in typewriter-style lettering, bore the title 'Ancient History'. She squinted to see the author's name. Camila Rhys, she read.

'Writing under a pseudonym?' Susan asked.

'With rejections, too,' Gold said, pointing to a handful of rejection letters from literary magazines. Susan caught a glimpse of one of the polite rejections: ' . . . writing is fine and fluid, but we felt the central characterizations lacked believable shape. The overall thrust of the story, we also feel, is too negative for our readers . . .'

'A closet writer?' Gold said, raising an eyebrow.

'Looks like it,' Susan said. 'I wonder if any of her work was published.'

'We'll find out,' Gold said.

Susan felt a brief pulse of awareness inside her. She sensed that these creative writings tucked into the dead girl's desk had been important to her.

'May I hold it?' she asked Gold.

He handed over the folder. Susan turned over the story's pages, one by one, letting her fingers brush the printed words. The first line struck her: 'I wouldn't go back there again. Not if you paid me.' The story seemed to be about a relationship. The last line repeated the haunting title: 'Ancient history.'

'David, could I read this?' she asked.

'Sure,' he said. 'Everything's been dusted already. I'll sign it out to you. Does it seem important?'

'I suspect it may be,' she replied.

She looked in the bathroom. Alfred Sung perfume, some Anne Klein toiletries. Nothing remarkable except the fact that the dead girl liked quality fragrances. Susan had the sense that Miranda was intelligent and cultured. Her disdain for television entertainment, her preference for reading and art books, rhymed with the expensive perfume and the elegant prints on the walls. A bright, upwardly mobile young woman who took herself seriously. Did her sophisticated tastes signify a loyalty to her parents or a rebellion against them? Susan could not tell.

'Do you know where she went to college?' she asked Gold.

'Smith, I think. Or maybe Sarah Lawrence. One of those chi-chi places back east. She went to private school, too. Rosemary Hall.'

'Were her parents wealthy?'

'I don't know,' Gold said.

An unmarried young woman who wrote fiction in her spare time. A lonely young woman, Susan guessed. With something to hide, perhaps.

The only remarkable thing about the bathroom was a rather large supply of sanitary napkins in the tiny closet. There were five large boxes of super-absorbent maxi-pads. Perhaps Miranda had been having trouble with her periods. Or perhaps she simply liked to be careful.

Gold was on the phone, talking in low tones. Susan opened the medicine cabinet. A bottle of Advil, some birth control pills. Melatonin. Bottles of Darvon, Percodan, the prescriptions dating from about six months ago. Also a bottle of Ambien, prescribed somewhat later. The girl needed some help sleeping.

Gold hung up the phone and came toward Susan.

'Something else,' David Gold said.

'What?'

'There's blood on her body that isn't her own.' Gold looked perplexed. 'Quite a lot of it. They're typing it now.'

'She must have fought back,' Susan said. 'Were there defensive wounds?'

'Not that I saw. But I didn't spend that much time with the body. We'll ask Wes later.'

'That, and the body bag . . .' she said.

'Yeah. Something isn't kosher here.'

Gold stood tapping his fingers against his pant leg. 'Anything else, Susan?'

Susan stood looking at the apartment. Gold glanced at his watch, but did not rush her. She had a strong feeling about Miranda Becker. A feeling of family, and of something else.

She went back into the bedroom. The bed was a double bed, attractively furnished with a fine comforter, pillow shams, a bed skirt. The young woman who slept here valued her sleep, and perhaps her comfort when in bed.

The bed was in a somewhat odd position, a bit too near the door. When Susan sat down on it she understood why. A person lying against the pillows could look out and see clouds or the moon, along with the tips of two large skyscrapers. The windows of one of the buildings reflected the lake. It was a tiny sliver of view, but it was eloquent and quite beautiful.

Susan let her fingers graze the pillow. Her eyes closed. She felt languid mornings spent floating in and out of somnolence, dreams alternating with waking thought, a long slow process of waking up.

*You have your whole life ahead of you.*

Susan's fingers were tingling. She felt something warm and something cold. A tremor went up her arm. The warm was family. A long time ago. Belonging, remaining. Happiness.

The cold was something internal and painful. Something hopeless.

Susan bent forward, holding her stomach. Gold, at the door, was watching her.

'She had an abortion,' she said.

'When?' Gold asked

'Recent. A few months ago, not more. That's why the sanitary napkins. And the pills. She had some bleeding for a few days. It . . .' Something took Susan's breath away. She stared unseeing at the wall above the window. 'She . . .'

*Ancient history.*

A bitterness, Susan thought. A deep, angry bitterness.

Gold was silent, waiting.

'She had a lot of suicidal thoughts in this bed,' Susan said. 'Some before the abortion, but mostly afterward. *I should never have been born*. Things like that. Also . . .'

Susan stood up and walked back to the living room. She picked up one of the family portraits which showed Miranda with her brother and sister. The family seemed so proud of her . . .

She struggled to clarify what was going through her mind. It was exhausting, for no message reaches a psychic unalloyed. The surface tension of the mind is so great that messages can penetrate it only at the price of a certain violence. Once a hole is punched, disparate signals from other sources rush in like detritus sucked into a vacuum. Some of these come from the past, others from the future. All have to compete for space with the psychic's own unconscious thoughts and feelings. And if there are resistances within the psychic to certain painful thoughts or themes, the psychic material may be distorted by these resistances, just as though it were a dream thought or an unconscious thought. Susan had written a paper on this phenomenon a couple of years ago.

'Sailing,' Susan said aloud.

Gold stood in silence, looking at her.

'Sailboats,' she said. 'Out on the lake. People . . . Sailing.' She shook her head as though trying to clear away cobwebs.

*You can escape for a while, but sooner or later . . .*

'The father doesn't know,' she said.

'Whose father? Her father?'

'The baby's father. Doesn't know she was pregnant. Doesn't . . .' Susan passed a hand over her brow. 'Doesn't know about the abortion. That's what she thought about at night. She couldn't sleep. That's why she got the sleeping pills. Her thoughts kept her awake. There was anger at the father. Grief over the dead child . . .'

With a last effort Susan grasped at the thread hidden among the others. 'There's something else,' she said. The quarry slipped away. 'I can't get it,' she said.

'Okay,' Gold said. 'We'll find the father. That's a good start.'

He waited another moment. Susan stood up, took a last look at the room and followed him into the living room. He helped her on with her coat. She caught a glimpse of herself in the mirror.

'She's looking at him in a mirror,' she said. 'She's suspicious. She's . . .'

A headache was creeping through Susan's temples. She shook her head.

'At who?' Gold asked.

'She's not exactly suspicious. A kind of bitter humor. Hopeless.'

Gold turned off the lights. They paused at the door.

'Who?' he asked. 'In the mirror. The boyfriend?'

She shook her head. 'The killer.'

# CHAPTER 6

'Sources close to the investigation have revealed a grisly detail,' the reporter said. 'The body of the victim was found in a rubber body bag. Police spokesmen refused to comment on the specific type of bag or its probable origin, but observers have suggested that the killer may work or have worked in a hospital, mortuary or other location where body bags are found. A possible connection to the armed services is also being explored.'

The downtown wind sprayed the reporter's face with frigid raindrops. She pushed a lock of hair from her moistened cheek.

'So far there is no evidence the victim had any enemies, or anyone who might have a reason to harm her,' she added. 'She led a quiet life as a writer/editor for a business journal here in the Loop. Her friends have expressed shock and disbelief at the crime. When it was suggested that she may have known her killer, co-workers said this was impossible.'

An image of a young man in a trench coat outside his place of work appeared on the screen. The video light glared off his glasses.

'I'm convinced she didn't know the killer,' he said. 'Nobody Miranda knew would be capable of a thing like this. This is some sort of crazy person, some sort of random killing.'

As the reporter's face reappeared the anchor man threw

in a question. 'Meredith, is the body bag the only unusual feature of the murder discovered so far?'

The reporter shook her head.

'Actually, Ted, the police are deeply concerned that the detail of the body bag was leaked,' she said. 'They have now clamped down on all details of the case and are refusing to confirm or deny anything about the victim or any suspects they might have. Incidentally, a grim nickname for the killer has already popped up based on the MO of the body bag. He's being called the "Undertaker". There is fear in some quarters that the murder of Miranda Becker was only the first in a series.'

'Let's hope this is the first and only crime by this perpetrator,' the anchor man said. 'Meredith Spiers, thanks for your report. In other news . . .'

The tape paused on the final image of the reporter. Beside her in an insert was a photograph of the victim. They bore a certain resemblance to each other. Both were young, both had dark hair and milky skin. They had intelligent eyes and the characteristic look of ambitious women. Crisp, straight, serious.

It was hard to say where the victim's photo had come from. It was too recent for a yearbook and too finished for a family snapshot. It looked like a studio head shot, dramatically lit and very attractive. Why would she need such a photo? She wanted to look good, even alluring. Why would an editor for a business journal want to look so good?

In any case, the glossy image increased her resemblance to the pretty journalist. They looked almost like sisters, framed together that way in the frozen image. Joined by youth, health, strength. Vibrant young women, one dead, one alive.

*Two.*

One of the mysteries of womanhood, the watcher reflected, was the exponential charge created by the sight of two women instead of one. Their combined attractiveness was infinitely more provoking than that of either one taken separately. There was something almost mystical about it. Like the tandem of Good and Evil, so much more powerful than Good alone.

He lingered over this thought for a moment. Then, still holding the remote in one hand, he pulled down his pants with the other. The penis rose proudly, its tip poised in front of the mouth of the reporter. He held it in his hand, feeling it pulse against his fingers.

He backed up the tape until the reporter was alone, then pushed the frame advance until the insert appeared with the victim's face in it. From one to two, he thought. The spiritual power of addition. Four breasts. Twenty fingers. Two tongues. Two women . . .

His breath was coming short. The shaft was straining in his hand. He let the remote drop on to the sheet. Without taking his eyes from the screen he picked up the glass from the table beside the bed. Warm to the touch. He brought it to his lips, taking in the coppery smell like a benison.

'God,' he thought, tasting the liquid.

The two faces rose before him, silent, mocking. He groaned.

'This is my blood,' he said, holding the glass out to them. Then, with a gasp, he anointed himself.

# CHAPTER 7

Susan spent the evening vainly fighting her headache and watching television. She took three Advil, but their effect was almost insignificant. The headache brought on by psychic activity was astonishingly resistant to medication. Only time and rest could cure it.

David Gold called after nine to tell her that the foreign blood found on Miranda Becker's body did not result from a defensive struggle. It was deliberately placed there by the killer.

'That's strange,' Susan said. 'Have you ever seen such a thing before?'

'Not really, no.' Gold sounded perplexed. 'I don't like it. It's too much like a signature. I think we may have a serial killer on our hands.'

'Have you found the boyfriend?' Susan asked.

'Not yet. I've been through her papers and her old correspondence. No diary. No letters from the guy, whoever he was. I'm thinking maybe she held a grudge and destroyed all traces of him.'

'I wouldn't be surprised,' Susan said. 'I picked up a lot of anger today. And bitterness.'

'Well, I'll get back to you tomorrow,' Gold said. 'We'll run him down one way or another.'

In the end, despairing of her throbbing head, Susan went

to bed. Troubling, confused dreams bore her deep into sleep. The next morning she woke up feeling slightly ill.

Her first session of the day was with Wendy Breckinridge, a girl from a venerable Chicago family who suffered from a variety of problems more or less directly related to her sexuality.

Wendy was early as usual. She got up from her chair when Susan opened the door, throwing the copy of *North Shore* down on the coffee table. As always, her clothes were striking. She wore a very short skirt with high-heeled shoes, and a knit shirt that had an athletic look to it. But her hair, normally a lush mane of light brown curls, was pinned back severely and she was wearing glasses. There was a crucifix around her neck.

The lower part of her body made no bones about its 'come hither' attractions. But her face and hair told a different story. Especially given her eyes, which had a tense, frightened look.

'I didn't know you wore glasses,' Susan said.

'I don't, usually. I wear contacts. But today I thought I'd wear the glasses, just for the heck of it.'

She sat down without crossing her legs. She had attractive legs, slim and shapely. Her body was delicate. She could not weigh much over 110 pounds. But her moods could overwhelm the basic physical facts of her body. She had a chameleon-like way of changing her colors radically. When she first came to Susan, now nearly two years ago, the changes had sometimes startled Susan. Now she had learned to expect just about anything when Wendy appeared.

'How are you doing?' Susan asked.

'Oh, great.' This was a standard response from Wendy. It was not a denial, but an overture. She looked miserable.

'What's been happening?' Susan asked.

'Not much. Ian came over last night.'

Ian was a frequent date and erstwhile lover, a young attorney Wendy had met at a party a couple of years ago. He had asked her to marry him after their first few months together, but she had refused. For good reasons, Susan thought. Wendy was a deeply troubled girl. At twenty-seven she was a long way from being ready to become a wife.

'Was it a good evening?' Susan asked.

The girl laughed. 'A joke,' she said. 'He told me he's engaged. I don't know why he had to come all those miles to tell me. He could have called me on the phone.'

'Who is he engaged to?'

'Some girl he knew in law school,' Wendy said. 'He used to talk about her. She was married, but she's divorced now. She used to be a public defender, but now that she's divorced she's working for a big firm in the Loop.'

Susan was silent, returning Wendy's angry stare with a neutral look of curious interest.

'I know what you're thinking,' Wendy said.

'You do?' Susan smiled.

'You're thinking I asked for this.'

'Why would I think that?'

'You know. Because of who I am.'

One of Wendy's strengths was her awareness of the severity of her problems. She was the black sheep of her socially conscious family. In school she had had discipline problems and received grades far below her ability. She had attended three colleges, finally getting her BA from a small women's college in southern Illinois after a total of six years. She now worked in the Loop as an assistant in an investment firm, a job procured by her father.

She was a reliable worker, but obviously unhappy in her lowly job. She had been engaged twice, both times to eligible young men from her parents' social set. She had broken off both engagements. She was considered desirable but wild. She had stopped taking the experimental drugs she had flirted with in high school and college, but she was well on the way to re-enacting her mother's hypochondria. She was adept at wringing prescriptions for tranquilizers, antidepressants, diet pills and other medications from a variety of internists. She often looked physically ill when she came for her sessions with Susan. Over the years she had suffered on and off from anorexia nervosa and later bulimia, and was always on one fad diet or another.

'Who you are in what way?' Susan asked.

'All ways.'

'Sexually?' Susan asked.

'Sure. Why not?' Wendy's voice was bitter.

'Who are you, sexually?' Susan asked.

There was a silence. Wendy looked away.

'A loser,' she said at last.

Sexually Wendy was anesthetic with the 'eligible' men she dated. However, she could experience satisfying orgasms, provided that the man she slept with was beneath her socially or in some other way off limits. The psychology was obvious. Wendy could only experience sexual pleasure with a man she knew her family would disapprove of. She had embarrassed her parents during her college years by bringing home a collection of seedy boyfriends.

But there was obedience underneath her rebellion. Since such men were off limits to her, they were not a threat to her underlying dependence on her family. She had never come close to a commitment to a man her family would not approve of.

She had many dates. It was easy for her to attract men with her willowy body and the sparkling smile she could affect despite her underlying depression. The men who dated her hungered after her body, but many of them dropped her even before having sex, because her instability was so palpable. They thought her a scatterbrained nutcase, more trouble than she was worth.

'Does losing really have anything to do with sexuality?' Susan asked.

'Yes. No. I don't know.' The question had upset Wendy.

'That's a good answer, for this office.' Susan smiled. 'Ambivalence about important questions can be a valuable clue. If you don't know the answer, that means there is something you can learn about yourself.'

Wendy looked away. A cloud outside the window darkened the day. Her face clouded with it. Unhappiness spoke eloquently from her tired eyes. Sex was a painful subject with her. As painful as family.

Her isolation was without a doubt the worst obstacle facing her. Her parents and their friends had little patience for her difficulty in finding herself. At home she was pigeonholed as the 'problem' daughter. At work her sex and her alluring looks brought only bigoted responses from her bosses. This constant insult to her ego fed her sense of guilt, which so far had managed to outdistance Susan's attempts to bring it under Wendy's control.

Her strong points were her innate intellect and her stubbornness. She refused to give up on understanding why she was so unhappy. She was bright enough to see that her life was being wasted on complexes and acting-out of one sort or another. She had been to several other psychiatrists and psychologists before becoming Susan's patient. 'Shopping around,' she said cynically.

Therapy was a convenient way to embarrass her parents while spending their money. But Wendy honestly wanted to help herself before it was too late. She worked hard as a patient, and was often courageous and insightful. Though her problems were of long standing and threatened to outrun her efforts at adjustment, she was not a quitter. Susan felt that with hard work and a few lucky events in her life, she could grow into a valuable and happy person.

'Something else is upsetting you today,' Susan said. 'What is it?'

Wendy chewed her lip nervously. She raised a severely bitten fingernail to her lips and gnawed at it.

'I promised myself I wasn't going to tell you this,' she said.

'Tell me what?'

The girl sighed. 'You're going to think I'm crazy.'

Susan smiled. 'I doubt that. Tell me, and I'll tell you what I do think.'

'Did you read about the girl who got murdered?' Wendy asked.

'What girl?'

'The girl on the North Side, the one who was stabbed all those times. Miranda Becker.'

'Yes, I did.'

'Pretty gruesome, huh?'

'Yes,' Susan said. 'It was a terrible thing.'

'I knew her.'

Susan tried not to show her surprise. She simply nodded.

'We were in private school together,' Wendy said.

'At Rosemary Hall?' Susan asked.

'Yes. She was in my class. We weren't close, but I knew her to talk to.'

Susan was looking steadily at her patient.

'It can't be easy to hear this news about someone you knew,' she offered.

Wendy shrugged. 'Worse news for her parents than for me.'

Susan thought this choice of words significant.

'Did you know her parents?' she asked.

'No. I think I remember seeing them at school, though,

when they came to visit. They were very handsome people. Her dad was distinguished-looking, silver hair, tanned face, all that. Her mother was very thin, a pretty woman.' She sighed. 'They looked loaded, but later I found out they weren't rich at all. That surprised me.'

'Did Miranda get along well with her parents?' Susan asked.

Wendy shrugged. 'In those days we all said we hated our parents. It was our way of bonding. For some of us it was more true than for others. Miranda, I never really knew. As I say, she and I weren't close.'

'Did she have a different circle of friends?' Susan asked.

'Not really. She hung out with a group that I knew pretty well. But she was a good student. She was always studying. She didn't join in our late-night gabfests very much. She was on a scholarship.'

She paused, looking thoughtful. Susan waited patiently for her to continue.

'I do remember, though, seeing her saying goodbye to them one day. It was in the fall, when we had all just arrived at school. I don't think it was freshman year. Maybe sophomore year. I knew Miranda by that time. I happened to catch sight of her hugging her parents goodbye. Her mother was crying. Then, after they had gone, I saw Miranda coming up the stairs of the dorm. She was crying, too. She looked really sad. She was wiping away the tears . . .'

There was a silence. Wendy's face bore a look of yearning which left little doubt as to the effect of the memory on her.

'That's an interesting thing for you to remember,' Susan said. 'How did it make you feel?'

'And there was another thing,' Wendy said, ignoring the question. 'She broke up with her boyfriend. A guy from some fancy prep school, I can't remember which one. He came from a rich family, the Pullmans I think. Yes – Bob Pullman.

I remember. I used to see him pick Miranda up. He was a nice-looking boy. Filthy rich. His family was really snooty. Like my parents. I don't think they approved of Miranda. She wasn't rich enough.

'Anyway, they went together for a long time. Two years at least. Then one day she came in and a couple of us were sitting in her room. She said she'd broken up with Bob. She didn't show any emotion about it – just mentioned it casually, as though she was talking about grades or midterms or something.'

'Was that an unusual thing?' Susan asked.

'Yeah. All the girls were always crying buckets every time they broke up with some guy. But Miranda just said it, just like that. And this was a long-standing thing. Everybody kind of figured Bob was a great catch for Miranda, a prize. With his family, and all his money and all that. Most girls would cry all night after losing a guy like that. But Miranda didn't. Not one tear.'

'Was it Bob who dumped Miranda?' Susan asked. 'Or was it a mutual decision?'

'Didn't I say it was Miranda who dumped him?'

'No.'

'Well, it was. She told us that much when we asked, but she wouldn't say any more. Just said the relationship wasn't going anywhere. Something like that.'

'How did that make you feel?' Susan asked.

Wendy was looking at the painting on the wall beside her chair. It was an early Miró, a picture of a clown.

'It made me feel strange,' she said. 'I knew Miranda had feelings, like everybody else. I was sure she felt something for Bob. It amazed me that she could be so cool about it. Not that she was indifferent; I don't mean that. She was just very firm, very calm.'

'As though she was holding a lot in?' Susan asked.

'You could say that. Yes. Holding it in.'

Wendy's eyes rested on the picture. This happened often in her office visits. The painting was remarkable for the concealed emotion it revealed. Its surface meaning was clear – the clown was sad underneath his mask of gaiety – but the more one looked at it, the more levels of feeling it implied. At times the clown seemed exhausted by his effort to appear happy. At other times he seemed secretly pleased to be safe behind his mask. The image seemed a good metaphor for mental life with all its subtleties and contradictions.

'Was Miranda normally a private person?' Susan asked, remembering the dead girl's apartment and her collection of short stories.

'Sort of. I guess, yes.'

'How did you feel about her?'

'Well, as I say, I didn't know her very well. But I respected her. I thought she was a reasonably good person. Which was saying a lot, at that school.'

'Do you have any other significant memories of her?' Susan asked.

'I guess not. Not that I can think of.'

'Why do you think those two have stayed in your mind?'

'I don't know.' Wendy's tone was evasive.

There was a silence.

'Well,' Susan said, 'one of them is a scene in which Miranda surprised you by showing emotion toward her parents. The other is a scene in which she surprised you by showing so little emotion about breaking up with her boyfriend.'

Wendy nodded, interested but noncommittal. 'Uh-huh . . .'

'How do you imagine her life with her parents?' Susan asked.

'I don't know,' Wendy said. 'I just have this vision of her, going home for her next visit and telling them she broke up with Bob.'

'How do you suppose they took the news?' Susan asked.

'I don't know.' Wendy darted Susan a sharp look. 'Why do you ask?'

'Don't you have a guess?' Susan asked.

Wendy sighed. 'I think they were glad. I think they wanted what was best for her. If she was unhappy with Bob, they wouldn't want her to go on being unhappy. They would...' She looked away again. 'They would trust her judgment.'

All at once her eyes misted. 'Think how they must feel now,' she said.

The mother, Susan knew, felt nothing because she was dead. But Susan could not tell Wendy this, or anything else she knew about the Becker girl.

Wendy's pretty features had contorted in anguish. 'God...' She was chewing her lip nervously.

'What are you feeling?' Susan asked.

'Sadness. I don't know. Sadness.'

'What kind of sadness?'

Wendy thought for a moment. Her sharp intellect was visible in her eyes, as was her ambivalence.

'Jealousy,' she said at length.

'Why?' Susan asked. 'Because Miranda was so close to her parents?'

Wendy nodded. 'Yes. I guess.'

'That was a feeling you never had, wasn't it? Parents who approved of your own choice and judgment?' Susan spoke gently.

Tears had welled in Wendy's eyes.

'Yes.'

They talked for a while about Wendy's parents. Her mother was more her overt adversary than her father, a remote figure for whom the family did not mean very much in the first place. However, the father did manifest some incestuous feelings toward Wendy, in his protectiveness of her and his suspicion of her boyfriends.

Not very surprisingly, the battle between Wendy and her mother was for attention from the father. The mother had had a series of illnesses over the years, most of which sounded to Susan like attempts to extort sympathy from her husband, who had had quite a few affairs. Wendy was following in her mother's footsteps on this score, falling ill when it suited her and gained her an advantage within the family.

Wendy's mother seemed to understand this, and often accused Wendy of malingering when she showed signs of illness. At other times, though, the mother showed affection for Wendy as the fifth wheel, the prodigal daughter she herself had never dared to be. But these displays were rare. For the most part she treated Wendy as a failure and an embarrassment. 'Why can't you be more like your sister?' was her refrain. Barbara, Wendy's older sister, was a former debutante who now lived quietly on the North Shore with her husband and two children. A well-behaved overachiever, Barbara was adept at meeting other people's expectations, and had never given her parents a moment's worry.

The relationship between Wendy and her father, a retired investment banker, seemed to Susan a lost cause. Wendy's prodigal behavior was too painful a reminder of his own sexual peccadilloes. As his youngest child Wendy represented his failure to produce a son. Susan also suspected that Wendy had not been wanted, at least not when she was conceived.

Susan looked at the clock on her desk.

'I think we're out of time,' she said. 'You've done some good work today.'

'Really?' Wendy looked surprised. 'I thought we were just talking.'

'You opened some doors behind which there was a great deal of emotion,' Susan said. 'I think there is more work for us to do on some of these issues.'

Wendy took her leave brusquely, without a goodbye. She often left the office in a great hurry, like a schoolgirl leaving a hated classroom at the end of the day. Almost from the beginning of the therapy Wendy had tried to cast Susan in the same colors as her parents, teachers and family doctor. Her transference of her resentment toward authority figures onto Susan was obvious. Gaining the girl's confidence was a slow process.

Susan sat looking out the window for a moment. In many ways, some more subtle than others, Wendy reminded her of herself, though not at the same age. By age twenty-seven Susan had finished medical school. No, it was herself as a teenager that she saw in Wendy. A girl hell-bent on rebellion, but eaten up inside by reproaches directed only at herself.

Susan was pondering her own memories of those painful years when the phone rang.

It was David Gold.

'Susan, I've got Miranda Becker's father in my office. He just got here from Florida. Can you find some time to talk to him today?'

Susan glanced at the datebook on her computer screen. 'How about lunchtime?' she asked.

'Twelve-thirty?'

'Yes.'

'I'll tell him. Thanks, Susan.'

Susan hung up the phone. Despite herself she felt an intense curiosity to meet the father. She was fascinated by Miranda Becker, a private young woman whose quiet life had ended so violently. There had to be a reason why. Susan planned to find it.

# CHAPTER 8

Miranda's father, Clark Becker, had checked in at his hotel and taken a nap by the time Susan arrived at Gold's office for their meeting. He stood up and shook Susan's hand in a courtly manner. Susan recognized him from the pictures in Miranda's apartment. He was a handsome man with a startling shock of white hair and clear blue eyes. Though he was smiling, his features were distorted by grief. He seemed almost unsteady on his feet.

'I'm still trying to take it in,' he told Susan when Gold had left the room. 'Miranda was my favorite. Eleanor's and mine, I mean. Eleanor died eight years ago, when Miranda was in college. Miranda took it hard. We all did.'

'Were they close?' Susan asked.

'Very close. Miranda was much closer to her mother than to me. That's normal, I suppose. But we had three children and Miranda was the youngest. It seemed to me that she was Eleanor's favorite child, the one she had been waiting for, if you know what I mean.'

'I think I do,' Susan said.

'The whole family seemed to jell after Miranda was born,' he said, a wistful look in his eyes. 'As though she was the missing piece of the puzzle.'

Susan nodded. 'I saw the family photographs in her apartment. I sensed a lot of love in those pictures.'

Grief constricted his face suddenly, and was pushed back.

Susan imagined the same kind of rigid control as a character-istic of his daughter.

'She was the youngest,' he said, 'but Patty and Richard actually looked up to her, in a way. She was a very serious person. And a talented one.'

After a hesitation Susan said, 'The police found some creative writing among her private papers. Did you know she was a writer?'

He looked surprised. 'She won some writing contests back in grade school, but I thought she had left all that behind.' He seemed disappointed to hear of a significant part of Mir-anda's life that she had not shared with him. 'Of course, she was very private,' he said.

'Did your wife's death have an effect on the closeness between you and Miranda?' Susan asked.

A minimal glint of anxiety shone in the blue irises.

'She was closer to her mother,' he said. 'When Eleanor died, the relationship between Miranda and myself became a little more – official, perhaps you could call it. We spoke on the phone. We sent letters. We saw each other at family gath-erings. We were friendly, but not close.'

'You didn't come up here to see her?'

'Almost never. She flew down to Florida on holidays.'

'I suppose, then, that Miranda didn't confide in you a great deal about her love life,' Susan said.

He shook his head. 'Not at all. She never spoke of a particular young man. Never mentioned a serious relation-ship. That doesn't mean she didn't have one, of course. It made me feel a bit guilty, because if Eleanor was alive I think Miranda would have confided in her about such things. As I say, Eleanor's death was a blow.'

'Did Miranda confide in her sister or brother?'

'You'd have to ask them. I would strongly doubt she talked to Richard about anything personal. Patty, it's possible.

Patty has always been a sort of big sister to Miranda. Protective, if you know what I mean.'

'As a father, did you have the feeling that Miranda was happy in love relationships?' Susan asked.

A sad, reluctant look came over Mr Becker's face.

'As I say, I can't really speculate. But I would have to say no. Miranda was a very attractive girl, intelligent, witty, well spoken. But it was my suspicion that she wasn't lucky in love. I never asked, of course. Perhaps she had important relationships that didn't work out.'

Susan had the clear feeling that the death of Eleanor Becker had damaged the family, and particularly the relationship between Mr Becker and Miranda. Many fathers depend on their wives to keep the lines of communication open with their grown daughters. When such a wife dies, the father and daughter are left without a clue as to how to communicate.

'Do you think Miranda was a happy person?' Susan asked.

Mr Becker's eyes welled with tears.

'I'm terribly sorry to mention painful things at a difficult time like this,' she said. 'Forgive me.'

'No, it's all right,' he said, pulling himself together. 'Your question is quite apropos. I did not feel that Miranda was a very happy person, at least not in recent years. She was happy enough as a teenager, and as a college student – but after graduation, in her twenties, she seemed troubled to me. At sea, perhaps. Looking for something from life that she wasn't getting.' He looked at Susan. 'I think her capacity for happiness was great,' he explained. 'I just think she was going through some bad years, if you know what I mean.'

'I understand,' Susan said. 'It's a common problem, especially for young women in their twenties and thirties. They feel pressures. Often a career and friendships don't make up for the lack of a stable love relationship.'

'Yes. Yes.' Again there was that hint of evasion in the blue eyes.

'Can you think of anything in your knowledge of Miranda that might help the police find her killer?' Susan asked.

The old man sighed. 'I wish I could. I wish I had been closer to her these past years. You see, of our three children Miranda was the most like Eleanor. That may have complicated things when Eleanor died. To be honest, I may not have handled Miranda well at the time. She reminded me so much of Eleanor. Even her feelings were like Eleanor's feelings. I might not have been quite as forthcoming as I should have. I was simply too broken up.'

Susan stood up and held out a hand.

'Mr Becker, you've been very helpful. I'm terribly sorry about what has happened.'

'Thank you.' The old man spoke with dignity.

'If you think of anything that might help us, I hope you'll get in touch.' Susan gave him her card after writing her home number on the back.

'I certainly will,' he said. 'And thank you for your concern.'

Looking very lost and miserable, Clark Becker left the office.

David Gold returned a moment later.

'So,' he said. 'Nothing, right?'

Susan nodded. 'If I didn't sense so much affection in his grief, I would say he barely knew his daughter.'

'That doesn't leave us with much,' Gold said. 'I had a long conversation with her older sister this morning. She doesn't know anything about Miranda's love life. Either that or she wasn't saying. As for friends and co-workers, I'm drawing a blank so far. Maybe you can do better.'

'Do you want me to try?'

'If you can spare the time.' Gold sighed, running a hand through his thick hair. 'Somewhere out there is a guy who impregnated her. From what I see of this girl, she didn't sleep around. The relationship meant something.'

'In most young women, that would create fall-out which would help us,' Susan said. 'Every girl has at least one confidante whom she tells about her major problems with men. My gut feeling is that Miranda was the exception. She kept it inside.'

The short story written by Miranda flashed before Susan's mind. She was eager to read it. She suspected it might contain secrets that Miranda had not confided to friends or family.

'I'm gonna go back to her Rolodex,' Gold said. 'So far most of the numbers are business contacts. But one or two seem to be college friends. I'll keep at it and let you know.'

'All right.'

'Did you get any feelings from the father?' Gold asked.

'A lot of guilt,' Susan said. 'I think it had to do with incestuous feelings toward Miranda, probably when she was much younger. I suspect he became somewhat distant toward her as a way of compensating for those feelings. When his wife died he was left in the lurch and didn't know how to communicate with Miranda.' She thought for a moment. 'I also suspect Miranda was aware of it, in some unexpressed way. There might have been a bit of outright conflict between her and her father. Something Mr Becker didn't want to admit to.' She shrugged. 'I couldn't push him on it, though,' she said. 'That would be too cruel. He's hard enough on himself already. Besides, I don't think it would help us.'

'What are you going to do now?' Gold asked.

'I have to look at the body this afternoon,' Susan said. 'I thought I would stop over at Miranda's office on the way.'

'Maybe you'll have better luck than I did,' Gold said, walking her to the door.

Susan did not have better luck. Miranda's employees – she was the editor-in-chief and office manager for the trade journal – liked and respected her but knew next to nothing about her private life.

According to Kim Davis, her assistant, Miranda worked long hours, sometimes staying late at the office to finish work she could have delegated to others.

'She was a hard worker,' Kim said. 'She set a good example. We worked hard to please her. But the office wasn't grim. She kept everything on a light note. Nothing was that serious.'

Kim thought for a moment. She was a pretty girl in her twenties, a bit overweight, with fresh blond hair.

'There was a girl here last year that Miranda had to fire,' she said. 'She just wasn't dependable. I know Miranda didn't like having to let her go, but she did it. Her standards were high. She was well paid, too. The company knew a good editor when they saw one.'

'Did you spend time with her socially?' Susan asked.

'Some, yes. We would stop for dinner after a long day, at some place informal. Once in a while we went to a movie. Miranda loved movies. She was a great Harrison Ford fan. She thought he was gorgeous. Did you ever see *Working Girl*, with Harrison Ford and Melanie Griffith? She liked that.' Kim thought for a moment. 'But mostly her tastes ran to the serious. She liked the movie *sex, lies and videotape*. She also liked *Pulp Fiction*. Things that were a little too arty for me.'

'Were there romantic movies she admired?'

'I don't remember . . . Wait, I do. She liked *Casablanca*. She thought Ingrid Bergman's choice between Bogart and Paul Henreid was good. Oh, yes – *The Heiress*, with Olivia de Havilland. I've never seen it, but she told me she liked it. Also *The Good Mother*, with Diane Keaton.'

Susan was surprised. These were very grim stories. Stories of love that led to loss, even to tragedy.

'Did she ever tell you anything about her love life?'

Kim shook her head. 'She was very private about it. I knew she dated men, because she was often busy on the weekends. I told her about my boyfriends, and she was a good listener. But she never reciprocated.' She hesitated before adding, 'I think there was someone serious. I couldn't swear to it, though. It was just a feeling. I'm pretty sure it didn't work out – whoever he was.'

'She never mentioned anyone specific?' Susan asked.

'No. As I say, she wouldn't talk about that kind of thing.'

'Did you feel shut out?'

'No, I wouldn't say that.' Kim thought for a moment. 'It's strange . . . I could spend a whole evening with Miranda, bend her ear about my problems with my boyfriend, and really feel a closeness with her. Then I would realize, after she was gone, that she hadn't said a single thing about her own private feelings. She sort of knew how to avoid that, without seeming standoffish. I've never met another person quite like her in that way.'

Susan recalled what Wendy Breckinridge had told her about the young Miranda Becker, how cool she had been after breaking up with her long-term boyfriend. Susan sensed something complicated about Miranda's love life. But she could not tell what it was. Kim Davis was her closest friend at work, and seemed to know next to nothing about it.

She recalled her extensive training as a therapist. Every therapist has to learn how to control the lines of communication with patients, so that the therapist can learn private things about them without revealing anything private about himself. Miranda was one of those rare people who behave in a similar manner toward their closest friends.

Yet Miranda had been pregnant and had had an abortion. Something important had happened to her and she had kept it entirely to herself.

Or had she?

It occurred to Susan that perhaps Miranda had been in therapy. She resolved to ask Gold to look into this.

Late in the afternoon Susan drove to 2121 West Harrison, where Wesley Ganzer, the Medical Examiner, greeted her warmly and took her to the autopsy room, where Miranda Becker's body lay on an examining table.

It was a grim sight. It was easy to see that Miranda had been an attractive young woman. The knife wounds were like grotesque embellishments to her flesh.

'We're talking about a five- or six-inch blade for the fatal stabs,' Wes said. 'Probably your basic hunting knife. However, some of the smaller wounds were most probably made with a standard scalpel.'

'Which one was fatal?' Susan asked, bending over the body.

'The deep cut to the abdomen,' Wes said. 'It caught the abdominal aorta. She was probably dead within a minute or two afterward. I think it was intended as the *coup de grâce*.' He looked at Susan. 'There's semen in it. Did I mention that?'

'No, you didn't,' Susan said, looking at the cruel wound with distaste.

'There are traces of semen on other parts of the body,' Wes said, 'but the bulk of it went right into the wound. He may have masturbated on her as she was dying. There is also the possibility that he actually inserted his penis into the wound. I can't determine that for certain, because he could have put his hands into the wound.' He grimaced. 'Or his mouth.' He shook his head. 'Anyway, that was how it ended,' he said.

Susan was looking at the wounds, mentally counting them up.

It had been a difficult job for the crime scene technicians, because the body bag in which the corpse was found eliminated all the usual crime scene evidence. In this case the bleeding pattern was important, and there was no rug or floor to tell the investigators what had happened. The ME had had to extrapolate from the body itself to theorize about the order of the wounds.

'I've done quite a few multiple-stab autopsies,' he told Susan. 'This one seems different somehow.'

'In what way?' Susan asked.

'Usually your rage stabbings will be more or less random, with defensive wounds on the hands and arms and sides, and the *coup de grâce* coming at the neck or trunk within a couple of minutes. I don't see that here. There's too much bleeding from the peripheral wounds. If you put that together with the ligature on the wrists and ankles . . .'

'What are you suggesting?' Susan asked. 'Torture?'

'Yeah.' He pointed to the wounds. 'He tied her up and spent some time with her before he started cutting.'

'Where did you find the foreign blood?' Susan asked.

'Well, the body bag and the transport of the body made it somewhat hard to determine that,' he said, 'but we found foreign blood in the wounds to the hands and feet. That had to be deliberate. And the abdominal wound.'

'How much foreign blood?' Susan asked.

'Can't tell. Her own blood loss was so massive, there's no way to really measure. He might have been dripping it out of a vial, or a blood bag. No way to know.'

*Civil blood . . .*

Susan looked at the feet and hands. The wounds looked strange.

'Are these scalpel cuts?' she asked.

'Yes and no. They're puncture wounds. But they could have been done with a scalpel, in a stabbing motion.'

*Civil hands . . .*

Susan was receiving signals from the body. She didn't want to draw attention to them or to slow down the ME. She touched the corpse's flesh, feeling her own skin crawl, and trying to learn what she could.

'The feet, the hands,' she said, have you ever seen that before?'

'Not really.' Wes frowned. 'Usually you get all kinds of defensive wounds to the hands and arms. The feet, nine times out of ten, are the one part of the body that is unscathed. The stabbing pretty much stops at the lower thighs.'

'When do you think the wounds to the feet came?' she asked.

'My guess is that they came early. The hands, too. There was steady blood flow from those four wounds throughout the rest of the attack. They're completely soaked.' He frowned. 'I found saliva in those areas. Elsewhere, too, but I would have to guess he was licking or sucking her at the hands and feet.' He shook his head. 'A real nutcase, for sure.'

She looked again at the initial wound. 'I suppose you couldn't establish a drip pattern.'

'We tried, based on the drying pattern,' he said.

'Was she on her back?' Susan asked.

'Definitely. She was lying down. Some sort of non-abrasive surface.'

Susan looked at the wound below the ribcage once again. The ME was watching her.

'Are you thinking what I'm thinking?' he asked.

Susan nodded. 'Crucifixion.'

The killer had deliberately patterned some of the wounds after a crucifixion. However, he had not gone so far as to tie Miranda Becker in an upright position.

Susan looked again at the overall pattern of the wounds.

'There's no doubt he's highly organized,' she said, 'at least in the opening stages of the execution. At the end he becomes frenzied, but at the beginning it's a ritual.'

Wes Ganzer was shaking his head. 'She won't be the only one,' he said.

Susan pointed to the small transecting wound at the base of the large abdominal cut.

'Was that done after or before?' she asked.

'Interesting you should ask,' Wes said. 'At first I thought he had done it as part of the initial incision, before he started stabbing. But the blood flow suggests to me that it might have been done at the very end, when she was already dead. Either as an afterthought or . . .'

'What does the shape of the wound suggest to you?' Susan asked.

'Well, a cross,' he said.

'An upside-down cross.'

'Right.'

Susan seemed thoughtful.

'What are you thinking, Doc?' Wes asked.

'Devil worship,' she said. 'The upside-down cross is a traditional symbol for Satanists.'

There was a silence as they both looked at the ravaged body.

'She had an abortion, by the way,' Wes said. 'Did I mention that?'

'How recent would you say it was?' Susan asked, not volunteering the fact that her second sight had alerted her to the abortion when she was in the victim's apartment.

'Less than a year, maybe less than six months.'

'I see.'

She looked at the wounds.

'The blood type of the semen and saliva you found,' she asked, 'does it match the foreign blood?'

'Some of it does, yes,' Wes said.

'What do you mean?' Susan asked. 'Not all of it?'

'We're going to have to wait for the DNA,' he said. 'But from a gross assay it looks to me like there is foreign blood from at least two sources of different types.' He shrugged. 'Maybe more. It's too soon to tell.' He gestured to the wounds. 'This was literally a blood bath.'

Susan thanked him and took her leave. Her sorrow and revulsion at what had been done to an innocent young woman were matched by a strong sense of intellectual dissatisfaction. The murder of Miranda Becker had been a ritual killing, highly organized and deliberate. But something on that examining table had not given up its secrets as completely as the young victim had given up her life.

*Civil blood . . .*

*Civil hands . . .*

Unnerved as she expected she would be after this examination, Susan went back to her office to think.

# CHAPTER 9

It was seven o'clock when Susan got home. She added some refrigerated water to the large plastic cup the cat liked to drink from and filled her bowl with food. Margie followed a special diet for older cats prescribed by Dr France, the vet.

For herself Susan had no appetite at all. The session at the Medical Examiner's office had seen to that. She ate a bowl of ramen and fixed a small salad from a head of romaine that would be brown by tomorrow if she didn't eat it tonight.

She took a long bath to clear her mind of the images left by the afternoon's visit to the ME's office. Then she lay down on her bed to read Miranda Becker's short story, 'Ancient History'.

The story was very disturbing. The protagonist was a young woman named Mary who had been dumped by the man she loved, and who subsequently found out she was pregnant. Her thoughts about her unborn child took her back to the time of her own conception and birth, when she was clearly not wanted by her mother, who however carried her to term as a means of capturing the man who had impregnated her.

As she struggled to deal with the foetus in her womb, which was obviously not wanted by its father, Mary came face to face with the symbolic issue of any human being's worthiness to live. She soon realized that she could not answer this question for another person, but knew the answer all too well for herself. The answer was no.

Mary's suicidal impulse must have pre-dated her discovery that she was pregnant, but it seemed as though she only discovered it now. She felt tainted in her essence by something which was not quite sin, not quite a personal failure. It was something more cosmic, more diffuse, which only gained in intensity by virtue of its mysteriousness.

'Why did I ever believe in the future?' Mary asked herself. 'The past is the only place I can end.'

The heroine's problem became to decide whether her unborn baby deserved to live when she, the mother, so clearly deserved to end her life. In the course of the story she wrestled with this painful issue. The irony was that she lacked the power and wisdom necessary to solve the problems that faced her as a person – the problem of love, above all – but she had the power of life and death, over her unborn baby and herself.

'I was of two minds,' she said, intentionally referring to her unborn child as well as herself.

The story became more painful to read with each additional page, because Susan feared that the whole thing would turn out to be a suicide note. Mary's suicidal impulse was overpowering. The question was whether it would extend to the child in her womb.

Late in the story the heroine had an encounter with a small child, a girl. The two had a casual conversation reminiscent of the disturbing J. D. Salinger story 'A Perfect Day for Bananafish', in which the hero puts a bullet in his head after a conversation with a child. Mary conversed easily with the little girl, who reminded her of herself at the same age. All the while she pondered her power to decide whether the foetus in her womb would ever become a child like this one. The temptation to cancel, to annihilate, was extreme.

As Susan read on the tension became almost unbearable.

On the last page the heroine went to the top of the building in which she worked, during the busy lunch hour. She stood on the roof looking at the city far below, the city where she had spent her entire life. 'Was this happening now,' she wondered, 'or was it happening a long time ago? The past was like a gas, spreading over everything in silence. A time when new things had not yet existed. What could be more tranquil than that? An emptiness silent as the grave, before anything had happened.'

The final image showed the heroine leaning forward on the balls of her feet, looking down at the city she had never before seen from this height, and repeating the bitter words that described her own unhappy life. *Ancient history.* Whether she jumped or not was for the reader to wonder.

Susan was impressed by the budding literary talent shown by Miranda Becker. Despite some minor rough spots in pacing, the story would have been publishable had it not been for the extreme negativity of the theme. The significance of Mary's pregnancy was not the question of whether her child deserved to live, but whether she herself deserved to live.

Disturbing though this connection seemed, it was full of psychological truth. Many women, faced with an unwanted pregnancy, make their decisions about abortion based on their own guilt feelings and their anger toward their parents. More than one of Susan's patients had terminated a pregnancy in order to punish herself, her parents or her husband – without ever realizing it consciously. The power of life and death over an unborn foetus created enormous ambivalence and pain. This was one reason – not the only one – why abortion often left after-effects which were not seen right away, and which could turn out to be incurable.

Hence the beautiful and frightening significance of the story's final line, in which the heroine repeats, to herself alone, 'Ancient history.' The theme of the story was the impossibility of deciding a current issue without being influenced, even dominated by the past.

Miranda Becker's identification with her heroine was obviously extreme. It was hard not to conclude that Miranda had suffered the same dilemma of being dumped by a man she loved and then finding out she was pregnant with his child.

As to the question of being unwanted, this was apparently not the case with Miranda Becker, who was her parents' favorite child. On the other hand, Susan's interview with Miranda's father had suggested that there were secrets in the Becker family which she did not yet understand.

Susan had closed the story and was sitting on her bed, thinking of nothing, when words suddenly came to her which she had not thought of since this afternoon.

*Civil blood...*

*Civil hands...*

The words had a familiar ring somehow. She went to the bookshelf in the living room where she kept her small collection of reference books. Bartlett's *Familiar Quotations* was no help. On an impulse, Susan took out her large *Oxford Dictionary*, whose definitions often included quotations from literature. She looked up the word 'civil', and found a quotation from Shakespeare given as an example of the word's usage.

*Where civil blood makes civil hands unclean.*

The quotation was from *Romeo and Juliet*. It referred to the long-standing feud between the Capulet and Montague families which ended in the deaths of Romeo and Juliet.

*Civil blood...*

Susan had not read *Romeo and Juliet* in many years, perhaps not since high school. She had no memory of those particular lines. Yet they seemed obscurely connected both with the subject of the story and with the grotesque murder of its author, Miranda Becker.

Susan was convinced the words had been communicated to her by her second sight. But their source remained a mystery.

She was returning the dictionary to its shelf when David Gold called.

'Becker was not seeing a shrink,' he said. 'At least, not from what we can tell. No checks or credit card bills, no insurance claims, no record of appointments in her calendar.'

'She might have been seeing someone under an assumed name,' Susan offered. 'Perhaps paying cash. It happens.'

'Yeah, I'll ask around. But don't hold your breath.'

Susan wondered whether Miranda could have afforded therapy on her salary. She would not be the first troubled person for whom psychiatry was off limits for financial reasons.

'Anyway, I've got some good news,' Gold said. 'I found Becker's last boyfriend. His name is Doug Maegher. He works in an advertising agency in the Loop. I called his number from her Rolodex and he told me straight out that he had been seeing Becker as of last spring. I didn't mention the abortion. He seemed shaken up by her death.'

'Do you think he's the father of the foetus she aborted?'

'I'll need you for that,' Gold said. 'I've set up a meeting at ten tomorrow morning at his office. Can you meet me there?'

'Let me see what I can arrange,' Susan said, writing down the address. 'I'll call you back.'

After Gold hung up she sat looking at her note pad, which bore, above the address of Doug Maegher, the enigmatic words, *Where civil blood makes civil hands unclean.*

# CHAPTER 10

Doug Maegher was a rising executive at the well-known Sterns, Charpentier advertising agency. He was more than a casual boyfriend to Miranda Becker. They had dated off and on for four years, their up-and-down relationship going through many phases before it ended seven months ago. It was Miranda who finally broke off the relationship. Doug accepted this and went on with his life, thinking of Miranda only casually until he heard the shocking news of her death.

Such was the story Maegher told Susan in his office at Sterns, Charpentier at ten the next morning.

Doug Maegher was a handsome, well-spoken man whose smoothness suited his profession. Well over six feet tall, he was a former college athlete who worked out in his spare time. In answer to Susan's question he said he had never been married.

'Did you consider marrying Miranda?' Susan asked.

'Yes, I did. We talked about marriage many times. As a matter of fact it became a sort of running argument with us. We always decided against it, though the reasons would vary.'

'What kind of reasons?' Susan asked.

'We didn't have enough in common. We were too different. We had different priorities. Things like that.' Doug was sitting back in his executive chair, his hands clasped behind his neck. He was very handsome, Susan reflected. His face was that of a male model, with a strong jawline, tanned skin and dark eyes.

'We went around and around with it,' he concluded. 'A lot of otherwise pleasant evenings ended up in arguments because of it. I think we were both relieved when we finally called it off.'

Susan did not need second sight to know that this statement was untrue. Doug Maegher might have been relieved, but Miranda Becker was deeply wounded by her loss of him.

'How did the break-up come about?' Susan asked.

Evasion glinted briefly in Doug's dark eyes. Susan was reminded of the evasion she sensed in Miranda's father when he talked about Miranda.

'I met someone else,' Doug said. 'It wasn't an ideal relationship, but it sort of threw a new light on things, for me. I finally realized that I was not the right man for Miranda, and never would be. I told her about it. She broke up with me then and there.'

'And you say she was relieved?' Susan asked, just to test the look in his eyes.

He nodded emphatically. 'I think she was fed up with me. She was wasting herself on me, after all those years. It was time for her to move on, and she knew it. I think it was painful for her, just at that moment, but I do believe she was secretly relieved to have it over with.'

'What do you mean, wasting herself?' Susan asked.

He thought for a moment.

'Miranda was a very serious person,' he said. 'She took herself seriously, and she wanted a man who was equally serious about himself and about the relationship.' He shrugged. 'I just wasn't that man. It may be my own personality, or the phase of my life that I'm in right now, but I simply wasn't ready to be so deadly serious about everything.'

'When you say she was serious,' Susan probed, 'do you mean unhappy? Or simply intense?'

He leaned forward, furrowing his brow.

'That's an interesting question,' he said. 'I do think she was unhappy. I can't say why; I never really knew. She was quite capable of having fun, laughing, having a good time. She could be very animated at parties. But underneath, there was sadness. I guess you could say she took everything very much to heart.'

'And this was a problem between you?' Susan asked.

'Not specifically a subject of argument,' he said. 'A feeling, you might say. A feeling of conflict. As I say, she was so serious about herself, about her life. I wasn't the ideal man for her in that regard.'

'Did you know that she was a writer?' Susan asked.

'A writer?'

'A creative writer. She wrote stories.'

'No. I didn't know that.'

'To your knowledge, was Miranda in therapy?' Susan asked. 'Or had she ever been in therapy?'

'Not that she told me,' he replied. 'It wouldn't have surprised me, though.'

He looked at Susan. 'How about some coffee?' he asked. 'Or tea? My assistant can bring some right in.'

Susan noticed a carafe of mineral water on a tray on the lowboy.

'A glass of water would be nice,' she said.

Doug Maegher poured the water and brought it to her. She allowed her hand to touch his as she took the glass.

'What about you?' he asked. 'Are you married?'

'Divorced,' she said.

'Bad luck for someone,' he smiled. 'Is there anyone serious in your life?' He did not hide his attraction to her.

'Yes, as a matter of fact,' Susan said. She felt offended by his interest. For herself and for Miranda.

He sat down behind his desk and gave her a steady stare that seemed calculated to impress her with his sex appeal.

'I don't want to pry, or to embarrass you,' Susan said, 'but I need to know enough about your sexual relationship with Miranda to clarify a couple of things.'

'Shoot.'

She sensed he was flattered to have the subject of his virility brought up. Also perhaps he thought the topic of sex brought him closer to Susan herself.

'If I were to tell you that Miranda was pregnant this past year, and terminated her pregnancy, would you think it possible that the child she aborted was yours?'

Her question clearly made him uncomfortable.

'Why do you ask?'

'I'm just inquiring as to the physical possibility,' Susan said.

'You mean, what kind of contraception did she and I use?'

'Yes.'

He thought for a moment. 'I suppose it might have been possible. I didn't use condoms. Miranda gave me to understand that she was taking the pill.'

'Did you ever see her supply of pills? In her medicine cabinet, perhaps?'

'No, I never did.'

'Does it seem possible to you that she might have intentionally stopped taking the pill in order to become pregnant?'

He frowned. 'That doesn't sound like Miranda. Of course, anything is possible . . .'

'Could she have simply missed a pill as an oversight?'

'I strongly doubt that. Miranda was a very controlled person.'

'Could there have been someone else,' Susan asked,

regarding him steadily, 'or was it your impression that Miranda was essentially exclusive?'

'Oh, exclusive. Definitely.' He nodded firmly.

'And you?'

He looked away. He seemed preoccupied with the cityscape outside the window.

'Well, there's no point in trying to deny it,' he said. 'I slept with other women. Now and then. There was no one really important, but I wasn't completely faithful to Miranda. As I say, she was so serious about everything. I just couldn't be as serious.'

'Did she know about any of these other women you saw?' Susan asked.

He thought for a long moment before replying.

'At the end, yes,' he said. 'She came over to my place one night when I had someone there with me. We had a scene later that night. She couldn't deal with it. She broke up with me then and there.' He furrowed his brow. 'Come to think of it, I never saw Miranda again after that night. Not to speak to, anyway.'

Susan gave him a long look.

'You weren't being candid, then, a few minutes ago when you gave me to understand that the break-up was a mutual decision.'

He let out a sigh. 'No, I suppose I wasn't. It's best that you know the whole truth.'

There was a silence.

'The other person you were with that night,' Susan asked, 'was she acquainted with Miranda?'

'No. They had never seen each other before that night.'

Susan thought this over. As she did so she noticed Doug Maegher looking at her.

'I've read about you,' he said. 'Seen you on television, as a matter of fact.'

Susan said nothing.

'What's it like to be psychic?' he asked with a smile.

'It can be very unpleasant, sometimes.'

'Why?'

Susan didn't answer. She was thinking how unpleasant it was to feel the selfishness of a man like this up close. One didn't have to be psychic to be turned off by him. Susan knew that Doug Maegher had hurt Miranda Becker as badly as anyone alive, except her killer.

'Can you think of anyone who might have wanted to hurt Miranda?' she asked.

He shook his head. 'I can't think of a soul. She had no enemies. Everyone liked her, respected her. Of course, it's possible there might be areas of her life that I don't know about. She was pretty private in some ways. I'm not an expert on her life.'

*Only on the part of it you wrecked.*

Susan studied his face. 'So you believe her death must have been a random killing?' she asked.

'I can't think of any other scenario.'

Susan stood up.

'Thank you for your time, Mr Maegher.'

'Doug,' he corrected her with a smile.

'Detective Gold or I may be in touch if there's something we need you to confirm,' Susan said. She felt his eyes on her as she picked up her briefcase.

'Don't hesitate to call,' he said, coming around the desk to take her to the door. 'I'm only sorry I haven't been more help.'

He dwarfed Susan as they stood together at the door.

'I didn't realize you're so small,' he said. His eyes took her in appreciatively.

'There's one thing that puzzles me,' Susan said.

'What is that?'

'You haven't expressed grief over Miranda's death, or loss,' she said.

The now-familiar look of evasion shone in his face. Throughout their interview he had rather the air of a man who was defending himself against an inquisition than that of a man overcome with grief at the death of a dear friend.

'I guess it hasn't completely sunk in yet,' he said.

Susan studied him with well-concealed distaste.

'Thank you again,' she said. 'Goodbye.'

She turned on her heel, seeming not to notice his out-stretched hand.


She met Gold for lunch at one of the downtown delicatessens he favored.

'So?' Gold asked, visibly hungry as he waited for his pastrami sandwich to arrive.

'He's a womanizer,' she said. 'Why Miranda got involved with him, I don't know. A breakdown in her better judgment, perhaps. He's very shallow, not much to write home about, but she wasted four years on him. I guess she wasn't the first woman who has fallen for the wrong man.'

'Too bad,' Gold said.

'He's the father of the aborted foetus, I'm sure,' Susan said. 'A blood test would prove it. It's academic now, of course.'

'He had no motive?' Gold asked.

'None at all. He's just a man who broke her heart.' It hurt Susan to think of all the profound emotion in 'Ancient History' being concerned with a shallow, narcissistic fellow like Doug Maegher.

'So where does this leave us?' Gold asked.

'I'm not sure.'

Susan was thinking.

Miranda Becker had been an unhappy person, but a

worthy one. She would have made a wonderful mother and wife. She simply used bad judgment in banking so heavily on Doug Maegher. Whether she got pregnant by him through accident or unconscious design, Miranda knew after the fact that the pregnancy was a mistake. She aborted the foetus in a spirit of depression and self-loathing. She could not bring herself to seek help for the pain and loneliness she was feeling. The result was an even deeper depression, which was in force when she died.

The only people privy to the agony Miranda had suffered were the magazine editors who rejected her short story for the very reason that they were disconcerted by the intensity of her sorrow.

Doug Maegher had nothing to do with her death. He was well out of it by then, and considered himself lucky to have washed his hands of her.

On the surface it seemed that Susan and the police were back to square one. It looked as though Miranda's death was a random and senseless event, unconnected to the life she had led.

Yet something told Susan this was not the case.

An aborted child, a woman crucified, drained of blood by a killer obsessed with blood.

The waitress arrived with a huge platter for Gold which included a hot pastrami sandwich, a mound of french fries and a generous portion of coleslaw. Gold dug in eagerly. Not for the first time, Susan reflected on the contrast between his tall, lean body and the enormous amounts of food he put away. He got virtually no exercise, yet he never gained weight. This was a constant chagrin to his wife, Carol, who was always fighting the scales and who claimed she could gain a pound by looking into a bakery window.

Gold looked up at Susan. 'What are you thinking?' he asked.

*Where civil blood makes civil hands unclean.*

'I don't know.' She shook her head.

The waiter was looking at Susan, apparently wondering if she didn't like something about her potato salad.

'Eat,' Gold said.

Susan smiled and did as she was told.

# CHAPTER 11

State's Attorney Abel Weathers did not like Susan. He did not believe in second sight, and he hated depending on it as an adjunct to his work. It was not he who had brought Susan in as a consultant eight years ago and he felt she had been pushed on him without his consent. 'Leave the police work to the police,' he liked to say.

Weathers also hated psychiatrists. In his mind they were nothing but hired guns used by defense attorneys to get guilty offenders off. He had personally conducted dozens of trials in which the overwhelming physical evidence collected by his cops was put up against a glib defense psychiatrist who claimed that the gang-banger or street punk who had committed the crime was not responsible. The fact that the prosecution also used psychiatrists did not comfort Weathers. He thought they were all witch doctors and he hated to see trials come down to conflicting opinions by shrinks.

Finally, Weathers was enough of a male chauvinist that he loathed having to share the spotlight with a woman.

For all these reasons Weathers accepted Susan's help grudgingly and never acknowledged her in his statements to the media. However, he agreed with Susan about the probable reason for Miranda Becker's brutal murder and its sinister significance for the future.

A meeting was held in Weathers's office at 26th and California to take stock of the situation. Present were two of

Weathers's prosecutors, three Homicide detectives, a representative from the Medical Examiner's office and Susan. Everyone seemed to agree on the worst news, i.e. that Miranda Becker was likely to be the first in a series of victims.

'The style of the execution is too bizarre,' said David Gold, who was sitting across the conference table from Weathers. 'There was some sexual frenzy at the end, but the girl was kept alive while the more shallow wounds were being applied. We're talking torture with a sexual aim, followed by execution.'

Susan said, 'I agree. If the killer had a motive to murder Miranda Becker, we might have seen a multiplicity of wounds, but they wouldn't have been so carefully applied. And she wouldn't have been kept alive as long as she was.' She looked at her notes. 'There is rage here, but the rage is completely displaced onto the larger sexual aim. The killing is a ritual. It has all the earmarks of a serial killer, and none of the characteristics of a rage killing with motive.'

'Tell me about the crucifix.' Weathers was looking at Susan.

'There seem to be two stages to the murder,' Susan said. 'First the killer enacts a symbolic crucifixion on the entire body, making cuts in the hands and feet. Then the stomach wound is applied.'

'While the victim is still alive,' one of the detectives threw in.

'That's right,' Susan said. 'The stomach wound is the *coup de grâce*. It looks as though he made the stab just below the thorax and ripped downward toward the pelvis. I suspect the two small incisions at the base of the wound, forming the upside-down crucifix, were made after she was dead. Wes seems to agree with me on this.'

'What about the semen in the wound?' Weathers asked.

'Probably applied as she was dying,' Susan said. 'Either

through masturbation or through penetration.' Her words brought a collective grimace. The cops and lawyers in the room had seen everything – Chicago was a big city – but the Undertaker's perversity shocked them.

'Take us through the religious symbolism,' Weathers said.

'I'm not an expert on it,' Susan said, 'but I do know that the upside-down crucifix is a classic symbol for Satanists and other religious iconoclasts. Like the Pentagram, or five-pointed star, which was an early symbol of purity or whole-ness. When the star was inverted, the two bottom points now pointed upward like the horns of the Devil.' She glanced at her notes. 'In the days of the black masses, the Devil worshipers would try to invert or pervert all the Christian sacraments. They would use a naked woman, often on all fours, as their altar. The Host would be replaced by some-thing black, like a turnip, and would be inserted into the woman's vagina, or sometimes her anus. The priest would make the sign of the cross backwards. Usually the mass ended in some sort of ritual copulation.'

Susan was the only woman in the room. Some of the men present seemed amazed by her cool presentation of such shocking material. In her white blouse and wool skirt, she looked like a college student giving a class presentation.

She looked at the others. 'This whole subject is shrouded in a lot of intentional obfuscation. But the main thing is that the Satanist has a deep inner belief in the very images he is trying to besmirch, and in the very laws he is trying to transgress. That's why the crime shows an obsessive concern with those images. Here the crucifixion. And, because of the adding of foreign blood to the wound, the concept of communion.' She frowned. 'I might mention that semen, in the black masses, was often mixed with the liquid sacraments. Also, the communion wine was replaced, according to legend, by the blood of a sacrificed child.'

'A Catholic killer?' Gold suggested.

'Can't tell,' Susan said. 'The Christian imagery is powerful with the general population.' She had seen many non-Catholic and even non-Christian patients whose hysterical symptoms or self-mutilations used Christ's stigmata as a model.

'The blood makes me nervous,' Weathers said. 'This bird brought blood with him to the scene. He had to have it in a bag or a vial or something. I understand there were probably two different types.'

'At least,' said the ME's representative, a serious-looking young man named Jarrett, who bore a startling resemblance to Ryne Sandberg. 'There could be more. DNA will take some time. We think he poured it in the wounds as part of the ritual. Probably before the victim died.'

Susan nodded. 'Blood means something to him. Enough to make it a key element of his MO. As a psychiatrist I would have to suspect that the significance of the blood goes beyond the religious symbolism. Blood can symbolize a lot of things. Cannibalism, virginity, menstruation – there's no end to it.'

'What about the body bag?' Weathers asked.

Gold shrugged. 'Could mean anything. It's a standard-issue bag, used by hospitals and police forces around the country. Manufactured in Indianapolis by a company that also makes a large line of synthetic products for medical and non-medical uses.'

'You think this bird worked in the medical field?' Weathers asked.

'It's hard not to think of hospital orderlies and other low-paid employees connected to hospitals or clinics,' Susan said. 'Most serial killers are under-employed low achievers. However, I wouldn't feel safe in concentrating on this to the exclusion of other possibilities. The killer could be anyone.'

There was an uncomfortable pause. Abel Weathers would

not be the one to ask Susan for clues based on her second sight. David Gold saw this and held up a hand.

'Susan, what did you pick up in her apartment?' he asked.

Susan thought for a moment. 'My most important feelings concerned her abortion. It was done in a spirit of extreme depression and anger. She had devoted years of her life to a man who didn't love her. She was hitting bottom, emotionally, at the time of her murder. But I saw no evidence that she knew her killer, or that he knew her.'

'Is that all?' one of the prosecutors asked.

Susan hesitated. 'There were other signals, but they're too ambiguous for me to mention.'

*Civil blood . . .*

*Civil hands . . .*

'I wish I had more,' she said. 'I'll keep trying.'

Weathers gave her a disgusted look.

'All right,' he said. 'Now, about the media. They're all over this and they won't let up. Nothing sells soap flakes like serial killers. Where they got the leak about the body bag, I don't know. But I'm gonna find out.' He pointed at Gold. 'Dave, I want you to work with me on special security for this investigation. No internal memos. No discussion of the case in common areas. No talking to the press. I want a tight lid on this.'

Susan could not disagree with this strategy. The media had evolved into a major enemy for those who wanted to prevent crime. In many serial murder cases the media became an equal partner in continuing the crime spree, egging the killer on by telling him what the police had found and what their theories were. The evidence indicated that most serial killers avidly followed the media stories about their crimes, and some used the media to communicate taunts or demands to the police.

And that was only the primary danger. The secondary and

perhaps worse effect of the media was its creation of copycats. The world was full of impressionable people whose mental health was unstable. They depended on the media for stimulation as well as information. A lot of them were more than capable of setting out to imitate mass murderers, serial killers or terrorists.

The present investigation had begun badly. The media reports about the body bag had already given birth to a nickname, the Undertaker. If the press got wind of the grisly and highly newsworthy MO of the killer, there would be no stopping them. Satanism was good press.

'Where does that leave us?' a detective asked.

Gold held up his pen, and Weathers acknowledged him.

'We're working with the bartender who saw the guy talking to her at Pulitzer's, the bar,' he said. 'He says he didn't know the guy. I want to show this bartender pictures of everybody in Becker's life. That includes friends, family, professional associates. We're going to check out all these people anyway, so we can kill two birds with one stone.' He glanced at the file folder before him. 'Then there are the people she knew without really knowing them. I want to check out people who knew her from a distance. We look at her daily routine, the people who went up in the elevator with her, the places where she shopped, the places she went in her spare time. Somewhere out there is a guy who crossed her path. So we retrace the path.' He saw the expressions on the others' faces, and held up both hands. 'I know it won't be easy. But no one is invisible, not even a murderer.'

Jarrett said, 'Then we have the blood. One of the foreign types is a probable match for the semen and saliva we found. We'll test it against that of all the known sex offenders and creepy-crawlers in the books.'

'Do you really think he would leave definite evidence of

his own identity all over the crime scene?' one of the detectives asked.

'Simpson did it,' said one of the prosecutors.

A grim laugh was heard from the detectives.

'That isn't as funny as it sounds,' Susan offered. 'The Simpson crime scene indicated a great desire to be caught and punished. We shouldn't be misled by the fact that in the end Simpson got off.'

Weathers shrugged. 'What are you saying?'

'It's common knowledge today that semen and saliva samples can give definitive blood types,' Susan said. 'If the killer knows this, he must think he is not losing anything by leaving his own blood at the scene. And if the desire to add his blood to that of the victim comes from some deeply rooted impulse, he would be inclined to give in to it.'

'On the other hand,' said Jarrett, 'he may know that there is no record of his blood anywhere. He may think the risk is minimal.'

'Okay,' said Weathers with a glance at his watch. 'Let's keep in mind that this may not be the guy's first murder. Or if it is, he may have committed assaults or rapes that have features of this MO. The feds can help us there. This crime is so stylized that I gotta believe the guy had some practice earlier on.'

'The military, too,' said one of Weathers's attorneys. 'We'll look for crimes near military installations around the world. Crimes committed by servicemen. The body bag could indicate military, so we'll work on that.'

It was Gold who summed up. 'If the guy left a trail along the way, we'll pick it up. We do have one thing working in our favor: he gave us a lot of clues. Becker isn't just a hooker in a dumpster on the West Side with stab wounds. She's a real encyclopedia.'

Heads nodded at his words. But the multiplicity of clues

on Miranda Becker's body was a two-edged sword. It was a powerful signature by the killer, but also a promise that she would not be his only victim.

'Is that it, then?' Weathers asked.

Eyes turned to Susan. Everyone in the room had plenty of experience in homicide investigation. They knew that the leads Gold had just outlined would probably not be enough. Not enough to stop the killer before he killed again, and possibly not enough to find him at all, unless some very good luck intervened.

That left Susan. Her second sight was the only instrument that might cut through all the tenuous possibilities to the actual identity and whereabouts of the killer. But so far Susan had told them nothing they did not already know.

They wanted and needed more. But Susan could not provide it. Not now, at any rate.

*Civil blood*, she mused. *Civil hands* ... With those enigmatic words at the back of her mind, Susan left the conference room.

# CHAPTER 12

Susan was a size 4 or 6, or in juniors a 5 or 7, depending on the manufacturer and sometimes the garment. Her T-shirts were usually Small. She liked sweatshirts and sweaters. Guess jeans fit her perfectly, Calvin Klein less so. She looked good in mid-calf skirts with boots. For work she bought conservative suits with relatively short skirts. She bought sportswear at discount houses as well as the department stores in the Loop, and found that Venture was represented in her closet almost as frequently as Carsons or Marshall Field.

Her ears were pierced, but she usually wore small gold studs. Loops only on special occasions. She wore no rings.

She hated pantyhose and regretted having to wear them in professional situations. They were hot and uncomfortable, and there was always a run in one leg. She hated high-heeled shoes even more. As a physician she considered them an orthopedic monstrosity. She wore flats at her office, but did put on high heels for police meetings, because without them she felt too short in the company of the tall cops and prosecutors.

She kept her hair pinned up at work, and sometimes at home. It was sandy, and would have turned blond in the summer had she gotten as much sun as she used to. She looked acceptable in a bikini, though childbirth had left enough of an effect on her shape to make her more comfortable in a one-piece suit. The Gottex suits that fit her best were difficult to find on sale, so her collection was small.

Her best features were, she thought, her legs and hands. Her worst was her shoulders, which were somewhat narrow and lacking in character. She envied women with square, athletic shoulders. She found her brown eyes bland, but had been told by friends and colleagues that they were hypnotic when she was concentrating on something.

She had a weakness for pizza, but had found over the years that her work had the advantage of taking her appetite away. She rode a Tunturi exercise bike in her living room, did sit-ups when she remembered and sometimes jogged in Lincoln Park during the daylight hours. She had given up her health club because she lacked the time to journey to and from it when she wanted to work out.

Tonight the dress she had worn was discarded on the armchair by the window, beyond which the lights of the city glowed ambiguously. Her bra and panties were on the floor. She lay naked in the arms of Ron Giordano.

Their lovemaking had left them pleasantly limp, and he was running a finger softly along her jawline, admiring the curve of her breast as her breathing slowed. Like her, he enjoyed silence, and could be comfortable with her for long minutes without saying a word.

She had met him a year ago, during the investigation of the murders of several coeds at the University of Illinois's Circle Campus, an investigation that had eventually led to the arrest of Arnold Haze.

Giordano was an Associate Professor of Anthropology at Illinois, and a former back-up quarterback and assistant coach for the Chicago Bears. He and Susan had started dating on the heels of the Haze investigation, and in the months since had settled into a close relationship.

They called each other at least once a day to exchange routine news and conversation. Once a week they met for dinner. And, to Susan's considerable relief, those dinners usually led to intimacy.

It was now seven years since Susan's divorce. In that time many men had shown an interest in her, but her occasional dates had led nowhere. Her marriage had been very satisfying before it collapsed, and she needed a kind of love that was apparently not easy to find among eligible men. This was one reason she felt such empathy for Miranda Becker, a lonely young woman ill-treated by the competitive sexual world.

Ron Giordano was the exception. Strong, gentle, aware of his own limitations and tolerant of hers, he delighted in her body and enjoyed her personality without trying to surround her or to judge her.

Ron was a veteran of divorce himself, and understood the damage it did to one's hopes as well as one's ego. He had the precious knack of giving a great deal of himself to Susan without demanding too much of her in return. The result was that Susan gave more than she had thought herself capable of giving.

'Don't move,' he murmured.

'Why not?'

'I love to feel you this way.'

She snuggled against him, her lips in the hollow of his neck. She loved the warm feel of his embrace, almost more than his lovemaking. Safety was a drug more powerful than erotic excitement. Even if it was the illusion of safety rather than safety itself, which was not really possible in this world.

'You're very small,' he observed with a smile.

'You always say that.' Susan was a small woman, five feet three in her stockinged feet, about 115 pounds when she ate enough, which was rarely. Work usually kept her under 110, which brought reproach from David Gold and Ron Giordano.

Ron, at six-two and 215, dwarfed her. He enjoyed her smallness, because he had seen her work and knew her capabilities. He thought of her as a person of weight and substance, and was always amazed and delighted to be reminded of how small she was, especially when her clothes came off in his bed. Her nudity made her seem waif-like and breakable.

He knew enough about her past to know that on some levels she was very vulnerable. He also knew her work exposed her to terrible things, more terrible by far than what he saw at the university. He was grateful for the opportunity to be her safe haven, in a sexual sense as well as an emotional one.

'How about a drink?' he asked.

She sighed. 'I'd better not. I have to be getting home.'

He kissed her hair and held her closer.

'Okay.'

There was a silence. The feel of her skin under his finger-tips told him she was more tense than usual tonight.

Over dinner she had told him about the difficulties of the Miranda Becker investigation and her role in it. She was frustrated and anxious. The more so because Miranda's eloquent, disturbing short story had made Susan feel the dead woman's life very strongly.

'There was a moral sense in her, almost too well developed,' she said. 'She was very rigid about herself, very unforgiving. She would have been an ideal candidate for therapy – she was intelligent, strong, introspective. But she never got any, as far as we can tell. She suffered in silence, alone.'

There was a time in Susan's life when she was out of

control and was as hard on herself as Miranda had been. The bad times went on for quite a while, in large part because Susan hid away from other people and punished herself with her own isolation. In those days her second sight had been like a curse. It gave her another reason to turn in upon herself.

Something about Miranda Becker's fate got under Susan's skin. Susan was haunted by the idea that the author of 'Ancient History', a woman so full of pain, could have had her life snuffed out by a killer when she still had so much to live for. It was as though Fate had cruelly gratified Miranda's suicidal impulses by making her the victim of a murderer. There was a perverse poetic justice in this.

And what had happened to turn the bright, self-respecting Miranda of Wendy Breckinridge's memory into the unhappy woman who suffered so much misery at the hands of Doug Maegher? Thirteen years of living, Susan guessed. One or two wrong turns that led to dilemmas Miranda might have solved had she lived on. But she did not live.

Susan sat up and squinted at the shadowy floor, in search of her panties. Ron's hand rested on her hip.

'Back to the real world,' she said.

'I hate the real world.' Ron Giordano smiled. 'It's over-rated and a complete disappointment.'

She looked down at him. 'Ah – but you're part of my real world.'

'Well. Since you put it that way.'

He glanced at his alarm clock. Ten-fifteen. Sometimes she stayed over, but usually she went back to her own place. The drive was only ten minutes or so. She liked to be home to get her messages. She didn't want to call patients or other doctors from here.

They had reached a point in their relationship at which a lot of couples would have moved in together, but something told him not to ask her. They had met at a painful time in her own life, and they were still getting to know each other emotionally. She was a complicated person with a past behind her. He felt ready for commitment, but wanted to give her plenty of time.

'What are you going to do tomorrow?' he asked.

'Rounds, supervisions. One new patient. A probable hospitalization, maybe two.' She sighed. 'The cold weather takes its toll. People come unglued.'

He nodded.

'How about you?' she asked.

'Same shit, same shovel.' He grinned. 'There's a curriculum meeting Friday. They're going to try to cut our core program. It will be a fight.'

'That's too bad.' Susan knew Ron took his teaching responsibilities very seriously. She had first met him while investigating the murder of one of his students. He felt an obligation toward them, and was offended by the professors he knew who had become cynical over time and no longer cared about their students. He was also offended by the university's administrators, who were always quick to sacrifice education to financial convenience.

'When am I going to see you?' he asked.

'I don't know. Soon.'

She bent to kiss his chest. She could hear the beating of his heart, the flow of blood through a powerful body that had once matched its skills against NFL defensive linemen and linebackers. He had back injuries that had forced his retirement. And, like all former athletes, he had knee problems, though he never complained about them.

She felt his fingers on her shoulder. Something urgent concealed itself in the softness of his touch. Her own flesh responded.

'Can you take pity on an old quarterback?' he asked.

# BLOOD

His hands slid down her ribcage to her thigh. She was tired, and she would be tired tomorrow. But being wanted was a balm more precious than sleep.

'It won't be pity,' she said, kissing his lips.

# CHAPTER 13

Wendy was hunting.

She wore a short leather skirt and low black boots. Her legs gleamed milky white in the glow of the evening. She took off her coat as she entered the tavern – a rather seedy place not far from the Water Tower – and flung it over the bar stool next to her own.

There was an audible intake of breath from the other patrons. Wendy's top was brief, hardly more than a halter. She wore a velvet band about her neck. Her hair was combed out, flowing over her shoulders. Her long, slim arms were as pearly white as her legs.

She looked too clean to be mistaken for a prostitute. But everything else about her appearance was so impudently alluring that few men could take their eyes off her.

That was her plan. She wanted to be noticed. But she wanted to be so outrageous in her pulchritude that most men would not dare to approach her. She was looking for someone confident, someone a bit wild.

She stood looking at herself in the mirror. A song she did not know was playing on the jukebox, the words completely drowned out by a thumping bass.

She did not have to wait long.

A tall man detached himself from the others and came toward her. His face appeared in the mirror next to her own before he spoke. The skin was olive, the brows dark. Latin, perhaps Italian, she guessed. Large shoulders, powerful pectorals under his dark shirt. A chain around his neck.

'Can I buy you a drink?' His voice was smooth. She heard the accent of the streets, mixed with something more subtle.

She didn't answer. She was looking at her reflection in the mirror. The face was expectant, alert. She had applied her make-up carefully. Her eyes stood out brightly.

'Come on,' he murmured. 'There's no harm in a drink.'

She gestured to the bartender, who came over with a wary look on his face.

'May I have a Glenlivet on the rocks, please?'

'Sure.' The bartender moved away without looking at the man.

'You have good taste,' the man said.

Wendy gave him a sidelong glance. 'Taste is a relative thing,' she said.

'That's true.'

She sighed. 'I wish I had a cigarette,' she said.

'What brand?' He was not intimidated. He was enjoying her performance.

There was a silence.

'When I was a teenager I used to smoke Virginia Slims,' she said. 'I thought they made me look sophisticated.'

He smiled. 'But now you're beyond all that.'

Wendy nodded. 'All our yesterdays . . .'

He went away for a moment. When he came back he placed an opened pack of Dunhills on the bar before her.

'Light?' he asked.

She looked at him without answering.

He tapped out a cigarette, placed it between his lips and lit it with a very old Zippo. She watched in the mirror as he held it out to her. When she didn't move, he placed it gently between her lips and let go. She felt the moisture of his saliva on her lips. She took hold of the cigarette and inhaled.

The smoke went straight to her head. It had been two years since she quit smoking. She watched the smoke curl between them. She smiled and picked up the glass of Scotch.

'Cheers,' he said, watching her drink.

'Thanks.'

He had not ordered anything for himself. He looked at her in the mirror as he sat down on the stool next to her.

'What's that?' she asked, noticing his tattoo.

'Nothing.' He clasped his hands on the bar.

She smelled him now. The faint aroma of sweat mingled with his cologne and with something else. She smelled cigarettes on his breath. He smelled very male, very attractive in a crude sort of way.

Her next swallow of Scotch left the glass half empty. It tasted astonishingly fresh and good.

He held out a hand.

'Tony,' he said.

'Tony what?' Wendy looked at the hand. It was powerful, with a broad palm and square fingertips.

'Garza.'

'That's an interesting name.'

'Thank you. What's yours?'

'Wendy.'

'Wendy what?'

'Just Wendy.'

He raised an eyebrow to acknowledge her refusal to identify herself.

'Like in *Peter Pan*.'

She gave him an appraising look. 'Yes. Like in *Peter Pan*.'

She had not taken his hand. He placed his hands on the bar again, watching her in the mirror.

'Aren't you drinking?' she asked.

'Not yet.'

She sipped again at the Scotch.

'Almost empty,' she said.

He smiled. He seemed amused by her.

'What are you waiting for?' she asked.

'Waiting for you to finish so we can leave.'

She shook the glass slightly, listening to the click of the ice.

'Where are we going?' she asked.

He shook his head. 'You don't want to spoil the surprise, do you?'

Wendy thought for a minute. She looked at his face in the mirror behind the bar. A ladies' man, a Lothario. Handsome, sexy, accustomed to getting his way with women. Perhaps violent when aroused. Perhaps, in some unforeseeable way, dangerous.

She finished the last of the Scotch and stood up. She picked up her coat without looking at the bartender.

'All right,' she said, holding out the coat.

Tony Garza helped her on with the coat, nodding at the bartender to indicate he would pay for her drink. She walked ahead of him out of the bar.

It was frigid outside, a cruel wind blowing off the lake. Her bare legs felt the chill instantly.

'My car is right here.' He pointed to a large American sedan, possibly a Lincoln.

The leather seat of the car was cold, but the heater warmed up quickly. He drove confidently through the downtown streets to a brick apartment building with storefronts on the ground floor.

He helped her to the door and upstairs, putting his arm around her to keep the wind off. When the door had closed behind them and she felt the heavy radiator heat, he held her by her shoulders and helped her off with the coat. Then he ran his hands down her bare arms to warm her.

'You should wear more in this weather,' he said. 'Does that feel better?'

She said nothing, but did not resist his touch.

He put his arms around her from behind. His hands slipped down across her tiny skirt to her legs, and rubbed gently at her thighs.

'A drink?' he asked.

But her hands were curling over her shoulders to caress his neck, his hair. He cupped his hands over her small breasts.

There was no more talk of drinks. He stripped her while they stood at the door. He sighed when the elegant lines of her naked body came free of her clothes. He picked her up and carried her to the bedroom, which was illuminated only by a dim lamp on the dresser. As she lay watching, he took off his own clothes. He had a hard, heavy body, obviously trained in the gym. Sexually he was well endowed. She congratulated herself on her luck.

He came to the bed and cradled her against himself. He was an accomplished lover, trying various caresses until he found the places that turned her on. She offered no resistance. When he produced a condom she pushed it away, saying, 'You don't need that.' But once he was inside her she tried to hold back, showing him hard eyes and a mocking smile.

He was not discouraged. He pushed into her with deep, slow strokes, his hands playing delicately over her hips and thighs. He kissed her, slipping a long, caressing tongue into her mouth. He touched her more intimately, and she began to melt. He pressed his advantage, coming deeper as he wrapped her legs around him. She cried out in protest when she knew he was making her come. He silenced her with another kiss, and finished her with a series of thrusts that seemed to come slower and slower. She lay limp and gasping when it was over.

They lay together for a while. She kept her eyes on the

ceiling, her scalded breaths finally ebbing to relaxation. Her hand rested on his hip. He took it and held it to his lips.

At length he turned to touch her nipple and asked, 'How about that drink?'

Before she could answer he was upon her again, this time harder and more demanding. He pushed her down into the sheet and took her with fast rhythmic strokes that seemed almost machine-like, shaking her, shaking the bed, until she came again with little cries like a child.

She lay stunned while he brought her the drink, a cheap bourbon whose taste she did not recognize. She drank gratefully.

'God,' she said, almost to herself.

'God, what?'

'I've never been so completely . . . fucked before.'

'You're all right,' he said. 'You just needed to have a real man for once. Those society boys of yours don't know how to treat a woman.'

'What do you mean, society boys?' Wendy asked.

'You're from the North Shore, aren't you?' He was looking at her curiously, not without affection.

'Does it show?'

'Written all over you.' He smiled. 'But that's okay. I'm broad-minded.'

He lay back with his hands clasped behind his head. She looked at his thick chest, his flat stomach. Between his legs was the thing that had given her so much pleasure. Nestled moistly in its thicket of curls, it looked oddly endearing.

She looked around her at the apartment. It was a tacky place, with cheap leather furniture and pictures of girls on the walls. He obviously saw himself as a playboy. The kitchen, on the other side of the living room, looked clean enough though.

'A bachelor pad,' she observed.

'You could call it that.'

'I take it I'm not your first date.' She underlined her irony.

'I don't think that surprises you,' he said.

'What do you do for a living? If you don't mind my asking.'

He grinned at her. 'I was a professor of philosophy at the University of Chicago,' he said. 'But my contract ran out while I was on sabbatical. So I'm between jobs at the moment.'

'That's what I thought.' Wendy was freezing up again, her eyes growing hard.

He did not react to the insult. Instead he placed a warm hand over her own.

'Ssshh,' he said. 'Just relax.'

She lay stiffly, accepting the pressure of his hand but resisting him inwardly.

'You're a real woman,' he said. 'You just have to get used to it a little. You're going to be fine.'

His affectionate manner left her off balance. She wanted to challenge him, to demean him. But he seemed to see through her. She realized that, sexually, she had not manipulated him at all. She had surrendered.

After a while she sighed. 'I've got to go.'

'No, you don't.'

Her eyes darted to his crotch. His sex had hardened at the sound of her voice. She really did want to go. She felt she had lost control of the situation. But her hand reached out to touch the large penis and her fingers curled around it.

She lay back, trembling. She felt his smile as he came to her again.

# CHAPTER 14

On Thursday morning Wendy Breckinridge came into Susan's office looking fearful and undernourished. She was wearing a black skirt and black sweater, and her hair hung lifeless around her pale face. She looked like a relic of the beatnik era.

After a few inconsequential minutes spent talking about her family, Wendy brought up what was really on her mind.

'This killer,' she said, 'this murderer. Do you suppose he knew Miranda before he killed her?'

'I don't know,' Susan said.

'I mean,' Wendy said, 'if he knew her, there must have been some reason why he would want to kill her.'

'It's possible, I suppose.'

'Well, I was thinking.' Wendy bit her nails nervously. 'I mean, if he knew her, knew a lot about her, maybe he knew the people she knew. Her circle of friends, so to speak.'

Susan gave Wendy a politely interrogatory look without saying anything.

'I know it sounds stupid,' the girl said, 'but how would it be if the killer knew enough about Miranda to know her friends. I mean, to know who I am, for instance.'

'That seems rather remote, doesn't it?' Susan asked. 'You hadn't seen her in many years.'

'Well, just suppose,' Wendy said. 'Just suppose he knew.'

'Yes?'

Wendy's eyes narrowed in an odd way.

'He might kill me, too.'

Susan suppressed the smile that wanted to come to her lips.

'Is that just a thought,' she asked, 'or is it something else?'

Wendy managed a small smile despite her obvious nervousness. In therapy she had learned to differentiate between ordinary reflections and what psychiatrists called 'supervalent' thoughts, thoughts whose excessive emotional charge betrayed their roots in unconscious emotional trends.

'I'm a little scared by it.'

'What is it that scares you?'

'The thought that he might know who I am. That he might have his eye on me. That he might . . .'

'That he might know what you had done wrong and be coming to punish you for it?'

Wendy looked away. Clearly she was in an anxiety state and not ready to deal analytically with her guilt.

'I know what you're saying,' she said. 'But I just – I can't help it. I'm scared.'

This was not the first time Wendy had seized upon a danger in the real world to let her guilt express itself. During her very first session with Susan, now two years ago, she had confessed that she was terrified of toxic chemicals and parasites. She used her fear as an excuse for a dramatic episode of anorexia nervosa that threatened her health quite severely. It took Susan several months to help Wendy explore the unconscious thoughts for which she was punishing herself.

The great fear of chemicals had passed, but other fears and inhibitions soon replaced it. Wendy's neurosis was powerful, having had over twenty years to develop and ramify inside her. Her clever mind found cruel ways to torment her with new obsessive ideas whose improbability in no way reduced their power to haunt her.

The fear of the killer was obviously tendentious, but it made Susan suspect that another revelation was on the horizon. She did not have to wait long to hear it.

'I went out again last night,' Wendy said, giving Susan a guilty look.

'Out where?' Susan asked.

'I picked up a guy. Downtown.'

'Did you sleep with him?'

Wendy nodded.

'Tell me about it,' Susan said.

'It was in a bar near the Water Tower,' Wendy said. 'I went in dressed to the teeth. He came right over and we talked. He took me to his place, an apartment building not too far away. He's this playboy type of guy, a ladykiller. The apartment was full of pictures of naked women. A huge bed, a bar stocked with lots of booze. That kind of thing.'

'Was the sex satisfying to you?' Susan asked.

'Actually, yes. He was a terrific lay, in a strange way. He was very slow, very accomplished. Quite a stallion.'

She gave Susan a composite look in which naughtiness mingled with extreme self-disgust and guilt.

'He took out a rubber, but I told him not to bother,' she said, rebellion in her voice.

'And what effect did that have?' Susan asked.

'He didn't seem to mind. He seemed pleased.'

This sort of revelation was not new to Susan. For a long time Wendy had been in the habit of cruising bars, restaurants and shopping places to pick up strange men. She knew how to dress her attractive body alluringly and to overcome her natural shyness in order to effect these meetings.

The sex she had with these strangers brought her the only orgasms she had had since her early adolescence. Her pleasure had to be bought, however, with danger. Nearly always she insisted on unprotected sex. She was intellectually aware of the contradiction between this self-injurious behavior and her morbid fears of infection, poisoning and the like. But her neurosis far outstripped her insight and she could not stop herself.

Wendy reported her exploits with an adolescent bravado that underlined her still-unresolved transference toward Susan as a mother figure and authority figure. Quite often a new sexual adventure would come along as a sort of defense against recent steps forward in their work together. Susan accepted this as a fact of life. She knew it was going to be a long battle to restore Wendy's sense of her self as a person with rights, a person of value worth protecting.

The subject of sex had a personal significance for Susan. As a teenager she herself had used promiscuity as a means of acting out her guilt and low self-esteem. Her problems had led to therapy, and it had made a great difference for her. It was hard to be a woman in that era. It was still hard. Girls and women often exploited society's tendency to use them as sexual objects. They threw themselves into this exploitation in order to hurt and demean themselves. It was an all too convenient trap to fall into.

'How did it make you feel?' she asked.

'It was intense.'

The present-day commonplace 'intense' was a favorite expression of Wendy's. It had a secret meaning for her. It meant deriving excitement, particularly sexual excitement, by putting herself at risk. The price in anxiety was always high but was conveniently displaced onto some other fear, usually something remote and even ridiculous.

'Fulfilling?' Susan asked.

'Yes. No. Yes.' Wendy's arrogant look disappeared, replaced by a worried expression.

Susan felt a brief throb of exhaustion. She had not slept very long last night. But her fatigue had more to do with the rigors of therapy than with her physical state. The problems her patients brought in were usually easy to locate and intellectualize, but the resources of their illness were enormous. The struggle to overcome them was like shoveling snow in the middle of a blizzard.

She had to laugh when colleagues in psychiatry bragged to her of curing patients in three sessions paid for by insurance companies. The technique of psychiatry had not advanced *that* much in ninety years. Therapy was still a lengthy business. Few patients could afford it. More and more Susan saw herself losing them to the fatal combination of illness and financial strain. They dropped out when they had a financial excuse, secretly relieved not to have to work through their problems. Months or years later they ended up in the hospital, crippled by the same problems.

Wendy was the exception, financially at least. Her family could afford therapy for as long as she needed it. Unfortunately, though, the family's affluence was part of her problem.

But she had, in the psychiatrist's phrase, a 'good neurosis'. A great capacity for mental health underlay her extravagant symptoms and her self-deceptions. Susan had hope that over time she could help Wendy overcome her visceral need to destroy herself.

As though on cue, Wendy now changed the subject.

'I keep thinking about Miranda, though,' she said.

'And what kind of thoughts are you having about her?' Susan asked.

'How he found her. How he chose her.'

'Assuming the killer is a man.'

'Yes.'

Susan felt caught in the middle. She knew a great deal more about Miranda Becker than Wendy did. She knew about her love life, her abortion, her frustrated ambitions as a writer, her struggles with loneliness. It was a dislocating feeling to hear Wendy's speculations about a virtually fictional Miranda, while Susan knew all about the real woman. A dead woman.

'How would you imagine he chose her?' Susan asked.

This was a frequent tool Susan used in therapy. When a patient brought up a subject that was obviously loaded, she would ask the patient to speak hypothetically about it, speculating as wildly as he or she wanted. The result was almost always a powerful clue as to what was going on in the patient's unconscious.

'He thought she looked lonely,' Wendy said.

'Was she lonely?' Susan knew the answer to this question.

'I don't know.'

There was a silence.

'Is that how the man chose you last night?' Susan asked. 'Did you look lonely?'

Wendy laughed. 'I looked ready, willing and able.' But her smile faded. 'Maybe . . . I don't know . . .' She sighed. 'This is ridiculous,' she said. 'I don't know why I keep talking about Miranda. She's ancient history.'

*Ancient history.* Susan was struck by the phrase, which had played so important a part in Miranda Becker's short story. She had to force herself to retain a neutral expression.

But it was Wendy who took her off the hot seat.

'I know what you're going to say,' she said.

'What?' Susan asked.

'That ancient history is the most powerful kind of history.'

Susan smiled. 'You've learned your lessons well.'

They spent the rest of the session sparring over the question of Miranda, who was assuming a portentous symbolic role in Wendy's imagination. Wendy knew from the press reports that Miranda had been seen with a strange man in the bar where she ate her last meal. This fact reminded Wendy of her own exploits with strange men in bars. She saw herself as a lesser, guiltier Miranda, a lonely young woman in a world full of hostile forces. It would take time to make her see that her own anger was at the core of her obsessive fears.

When the session ended Susan called her answering service and found an unusual message from Carolyn, her friend and former roommate.

*'Susan, I need a favor which could also be of help to you. A friend of mine wants to talk to you about a possible leak in the case you're working on. Her name is Meredith Spiers, and her number is 555-2958. Call any time, leave a message, and she'll get back to you. Thanks, honey.'*

Susan pondered the enigmatic message. She thought of calling Gold first to tell him about it. Then, remembering all the favors Carolyn had done her over the years at Channel 9, she made the call.

It was picked up on the second ring and a familiar-sounding voice came through the phone.

'Meredith Spiers.' It was the aggressive young reporter for Channel 9.

'This is Susan Shader.'

'Dr Shader, thanks for calling back. I hope I'm not inconveniencing you too much.'

'Not at all. What can I do for you?'

'It's what I can do for you. I should say, what we can do for each other. And for Detective Gold and the Undertaker investigation. I'd prefer not to say anything more about it over the phone. Could we meet sometime?'

Susan thought for a moment. 'My last patient is at four-thirty. Would you like to meet for a drink somewhere near my office?'

'30 North Michigan?' So Meredith Spiers knew where Susan's office was. 'Sure. How about Granger's?'

Granger's was a lounge just around the corner from

Susan's office. It was popular among professionals and office workers in the neighborhood. The front room was noisy, but the booths at the back were relatively quiet.

'Granger's would be fine.'

'Bring Detective Gold if you like. He'll want to hear what I have to say.'

'I'll see if he's available.'

'About five-thirty?'

'All right.'

# CHAPTER 15

Susan's last patient of the day was a manic-depressive reserve forward for the Chicago Bulls. She said goodbye to him at five-twenty, made some hurried notes on her computer and walked through a vicious lake wind to Granger's. When she arrived her hair was awry and her cheeks were red from the cold.

David Gold had called to say he would be a few minutes late. Susan looked around the bar and saw Meredith Spiers signaling to her from a booth. Pulling off her coat as she went, Susan joined her.

'How do you do?' she asked, extending a hand.

Meredith smiled. 'I recognize you from your pictures. I watched the Saeger case with great interest. I would have liked to cover it, but they assigned it to somebody senior to me. You look younger in person.'

'I was going to say the same thing about you.'

Meredith was a sleek, attractive young woman whose face had become familiar to Chicagoans and Channel 9's large cable audience thanks to her aggressive City Hall reporting. She wore her dark hair straight to her shoulders. Her naturally milky skin seemed to glow from inside and she had intense blue eyes. Her body was smaller than the impression one got from television. At five feet four or five, she probably weighed no more than 110 pounds. Her legs were shapely and hardened by workouts as well as the frantic routine of her work.

Susan guessed that Meredith was not yet thirty. She looked considerably younger in person than she did on television. There was something fresh and almost adolescent about her face. Her voice, too, had a youthful quality that was obscured by her on-screen persona.

She was obviously skilled at her work. Since she joined the Channel 9 team four years ago the ratings had improved significantly. She had won two coveted journalism awards for her investigative reports. With her attractive looks, she would probably be offered an anchor spot before long, either here or in some other major market.

'Thanks for seeing me,' she said.

'On the phone you said you had some information that could be of help to the police . . .'

'I received a very interesting e-mail yesterday,' Meredith said. 'Since it was anonymous, I didn't report it. But it seems to have come from someone close to the Undertaker investigation. I thought you would want to see it.'

Meredith showed Susan the print-out of an e-mail. Most of the page was cluttered with tracking information from the online service. The message was brief:

*Wounds in shape of crucifix.*
*Foreign blood found on body.*

There was no signature.

'I checked the address,' Meredith said. 'It's a phony. He used someone else's terminal. The screen name is phony too.' She gestured to the e-mail. 'It's true, isn't it?'

Susan looked at Meredith. 'Who do you think sent this?'

Meredith had taken out a pack of Winstons, and lit one now.

'I assume it's a leak from somewhere inside the cops, the State's Attorney's office or the Medical Examiner's. Who else could have sent it?'

Susan said, 'Detective Gold and State's Attorney Weathers would give a lot to know about this.'

'That's why I'm here,' Meredith said. 'I want to share it with them. But I want something in return.'

'What is that?'

'I'll tell that to Detective Gold myself.'

Susan ordered a glass of white wine and nursed it nervously as she waited for Gold to arrive. She tried to make conversation with the young reporter, but she felt preoccupied by the disturbing contents of the e-mail. This investigation could be hurt badly by leaks.

Gold swept in at five-forty-five, looking hungry.

'Do you two mind if I have something to eat?' he asked.

'Not at all,' Meredith said.

Susan was about to introduce them when Gold said he already knew Meredith. 'We've crossed paths now and then,' he said.

He asked the waitress for a Diet Coke and an order of onion rings. Then he looked at Meredith.

'What have you got going?'

'This.' Meredith showed him the e-mail. His face darkened as he read it. 'Did you show this to Susan?' he asked.

Meredith nodded.

'What about it?' he asked.

'I'll ask you the question Dr Shader didn't answer,' Meredith said. 'It's true, isn't it?'

Gold shook his head. 'No comment.'

There was a silence. He studied the reporter's pretty face.

'You're not going to use it, are you?' he asked.

'No. But I do think it's important. And, whether you

admit it or not, I think it's true. That's why I'm here. I want to make a deal with you.'

'What kind of deal?' he asked.

'I will promise not to air anything this guy tells me. Instead, I'll share it with you and you can decide what to do. In return, I want you to help me write a story that will scoop the other TV stations and the print media. I've got this ace in the hole and I want to get something for it.'

Gold was giving her his hardest cop stare. 'What makes you think it's true?'

'I'm willing to gamble on that,' Meredith said.

It occurred to Susan that Meredith was a good poker player. If the leak she had received was worthless, Gold would surely refuse her offer for a quid pro quo. If Gold accepted, that could only mean there was enough truth in the leak that he wanted to suppress it.

Gold looked at Susan. 'What do you think?'

'It's up to you,' Susan said.

'There's one more thing,' Meredith added. 'When the case is over, I want an exclusive interview with you and Dr Shader here about your work on it.'

Gold put on a sour look. 'I don't like publicity. And I don't like crime reporting.'

The journalist didn't seem offended. 'I don't blame you, I guess. Violent crime is great for ratings. Editors tend to approach it as sensationally as they can. But the exclusive I'm talking about will be different. It will be totally serious. No hype at all. Just an inside view of police work on a difficult case.' She sipped at her coffee. 'That's my deal,' she said.

Gold looked at her as his Diet Coke was brought. 'Why do you care so much?' he asked.

'It took some doing for me to get the Undertaker story,' Meredith said. 'I'm interested in you, in the work you do. I'm interested in Dr Shader's role. I'd like to write about you. That's all.'

Gold took a sip of his drink. 'You're not talking about a broadcast interview?' he asked.

Meredith shook her head. 'Print. I know neither of you wants to appear on TV.'

Gold thought for a moment. The reporter was driving a hard bargain, but she had strong cards. It was only natural for her to want to get a story out of whatever came up.

'Well, for openers you can count me out,' Gold said. 'I have a stake in staying out of the public eye. I can't help you there.'

They both looked at Susan. She did not relish being put on the spot. Gold looked uncomfortable. He knew how much Susan hated public exposure. She had made a virtual art form out of protecting her privacy despite the high-profile cases she had been involved in. Nevertheless, her name and face were far better known to the public than Gold's.

Susan picked up the e-mail and looked at it again.

*Wounds in shape of crucifix.*
*Foreign blood found on body.*

The e-mail had obviously been sent by someone involved in the Undertaker investigation. It was also explosively newsworthy. A headline about crucifix-shaped stab wounds would sell a lot of newspapers. So would the grisly MO of pouring blood into the victim's wounds.

Gold was looking away now. Meredith lit another cigarette. Susan took a sip of her glass of wine. It tasted as sour as her thoughts.

'A print interview,' she said. 'Like a feature story? What would it involve?'

'Some interviews with me in the course of the

investigation,' Meredith said. 'We could have lunch. I could meet you in your office when you had time. That sort of thing.'

'Where would it appear?' Susan asked.

'That remains to be seen. Maybe the *Trib* or the *Sun-Times*. Maybe the *Tribune Magazine*. Or *Chicago*. If none of them want it, I'll go to the professional journals. It won't be fluff, I promise you. As a matter of fact, you can approve it yourself.'

Susan twisted her wine glass. 'I'd like to think it over,' she said.

'Suit yourself.' Meredith puffed at her cigarette.

Susan was looking at Gold. He was clearly torn between his protectiveness of Susan and his worry about the leak Meredith had received. Everyone working on the case suspected that Miranda Becker would not be the only victim. The investigation could be seriously compromised by major leaks about the killer's MO or the cops' theories about his identity.

Gold gestured to Meredith's cigarette. 'How long have you been smoking?'

'Eight years.'

'You shouldn't smoke.'

'Keeps the weight down.'

Gold shook his head. 'You female reporters are a great advertisement for anorexia. I hate to let my daughters watch you.'

His onion rings arrived. He held out the basket to Meredith. 'Come on. One won't kill you. I bet you don't eat enough.'

Meredith laughed. 'Detective, I already have one Jewish mother. I don't need another one.'

Gold gave her a reluctant smile and poured salt on the onion rings before popping one into his mouth.

Susan was looking at the cigarette in the reporter's hand. Susan herself had smoked for a number of years, starting as a teenager. Quitting the habit had been one of the most difficult things she had ever done.

'Anyway,' Gold said, 'I do appreciate your coming to us. Most reporters would have turned on the camera and grabbed whatever mileage they could get out of this.'

'There are unscrupulous reporters,' Meredith said, 'just like there are unscrupulous cops. DAs even, sometimes.' She gestured to the e-mail. 'This had to come from somebody.'

Susan already knew what her answer would be. She could see how worried Gold was. There was little to gain by playing hard to get.

'You're serious about me approving anything you write?' she asked.

'Absolutely.' Meredith nodded.

Susan sighed. 'All right. I'll do it.'

Gold was visibly relieved.

'Are you sure?' he asked Susan.

'A feature story won't hurt me if it's responsible,' she said. 'And I think Meredith can help us.'

'Okay,' Gold told the reporter. 'I'll help you with your story. But if there aren't any more e-mails, or if they're bullshit from now on, the deal's off.'

'Fair enough.' Meredith crushed out her cigarette and slid out of the booth.

'Thanks to both of you for seeing me,' she said. 'I'll be in touch. You can keep the hard copy.'

'Is your computer secure?' Gold asked.

'Pretty much,' she nodded. 'I'll take precautions, though.' She shook Susan's hand. 'Doctor, I appreciate it.' Taking her coat from the rack beside the booth, she moved toward the exit with firm strides, her dark hair bouncing on her shoulders.

'Christ,' Gold said to Susan. 'That was good stuff, what she had. I'm glad she offered to deal.'

'Do you have any idea who the leak is?' Susan asked.

'Not a clue.' He shook his head. 'But now that I know there is one I can move a few people around. Process of elimination. It might work.'

There was a silence as he ate his onion rings, dipping them one by one into the lounge's special catsup. At length he looked up at Susan.

'Do you think she's pretty?' he asked.

'Very pretty.' Susan nodded. 'A very attractive girl.'

Gold took a long drink of his Diet Coke. He was a near-teetotaler where alcohol was concerned, but the calories in restaurant foods and snacks didn't faze him. He had an enormous appetite.

'I wonder if she gets those ratings because of her reporting or because of her figure,' he mused.

Susan said nothing.

'Ten to one she'll smoke her dinner tonight,' he said. 'You know how those news producers are. They like 'em thin.' He shook his head, picking up the last onion ring. 'Media,' he said.

# CHAPTER 16

The Undertaker was waiting in the rain when the girl came out.

She wore a white raincoat. She looked troubled. Her boyfriend was with her. He put his arm around her and gave her a quick hug. He himself looked worried. They had not brought an umbrella; that made sense. They were too preoccupied by the purpose of their visit.

They hurried down the street. The Undertaker followed them. The car belonged to the girl. They both got into it and sat talking for a moment. The Undertaker found shelter in the foyer of a shop and stood watching them.

Though it was her car, the man sat behind the wheel. They were talking over the counseling session. The Undertaker saw her shake her head in disagreement with something the man had said. Decisions, decisions. This was always a difficult time. The counselor had told them to think it over again, not to rush into anything.

After a few moments the man started the car, turning on the lights. The Chicago sky was crouched low over the city, dropping rain like the sweat of some huge gray beast. Despite the cold the streets smelled as funky as a locker room. The filth in the air swirled into the lungs like thick smoke, straight to the alveoli. What a godawful place to live.

The Undertaker frowned. Bad perceptions, bad thoughts. Let's focus on the job at hand.

The girl was perfect. Clean, fresh, vulnerable. A strawberry blonde. Milky skin with freckles. Natural grace to her movements. Delicate hands. And most of all, the sweet, troubled smile. He had seen it on her face when she used the pay phone in the store, with her boyfriend. She was a nice person. Deeply distressed by what had happened and by what must now happen.

Her name was Mary.

*Blessed art thou among women . . .*

*Blessed is the fruit of thy womb . . .*

He shook his head to clear away the thoughts. The car was signaling now, pulling away from the curb. He followed. The traffic was thick here, so he had no trouble catching up while they were stopped at the light. The heater was slow to warm up. This frigid rain made his fingers and nose cold.

He followed them east, toward Lake Shore Drive. They got on at the ramp and headed north. He followed from a safe distance; knowing already where they were going. The cars' red lights gleamed in the wet pavement, like beacons in a shining sea of black. In a sense it was a beautiful day, a day for dark and serious thoughts.

They got off at Lawrence. He followed. It took them ten minutes to get to her block. The boyfriend parked her car at the curb. They didn't go into the building. Instead they went into the coffee shop down the street. The Undertaker knew why. The counselor had made them both nervous. The girl didn't want to invite the man upstairs. She wanted to be alone with her thoughts. She had suggested that they have coffee so she could take her leave of him and go up alone. The Undertaker had not foreseen this, but it made perfect sense and fit into his plans.

After thinking the matter over for a long moment, he got out of his own car and went into the coffee shop himself. He sat at the counter across from their booth. Understandably enough, they were talking in low tones. A radio was on and there were other customers, so he had to strain to hear their conversation.

'Are you sure you're all right?'

'I'm fine. Why do you keep asking?'

'You don't seem fine to me.'

The Undertaker asked for a regular coffee and pointed to the doughnuts under the glass lid on the counter. He kept his conversation with the waitress to a minimum.

'Look, if you need more time ... We don't have to go through with this now.'

'It isn't a question of time.'

'Sure it is. You know that. You're already six weeks ...'

A blast of music from the radio obscured the rest of the sentence.

The Undertaker chewed mechanically on the glazed doughnut, not tasting it. He waited for the ambient sound to die down. But more customers had come in and were sitting down in the next booth. He could hear only snatches now.

'Look, I'm not trying to ...'

'I know what you're trying to do.'

He could hear conflict in the play of their voices. The girl felt alone. The final decision was hers. Quite rightly, she felt abandoned. It had taken two people to get her into this fix and now she had to deal with it alone. The man always took a step back at this moment – 'It's your decision.' But a woman wants above all not to be alone. The men do not understand this.

But the Undertaker did. And this was precisely the moment in her life that he wanted, the moment when she felt alone and needed love the most. For a long time he had not understood this, but now he knew. She must be soft and she must be sad. That was the key.

He finished his doughnut and declined a second cup of

coffee. The waitress smiled at him as he paid his check. Damn, he thought. She found him attractive. That might make her remember. He forced himself to smile back, not wanting to seem surly and thus remain in her memory. Everything bland, everything usual.

The rain was falling harder when he got outside, so he jogged quickly to his vehicle and got it started again. He rubbed his hands together, then held them under his arms for warmth. God damn this city. The weather was either bad or worse. Never good.

He turned on the radio and listened to the news. The stories were routine. Middle East, Northern Ireland, fluctuations on Wall Street. Nothing about the Undertaker. He was out of the headlines.

He turned off the radio. Normally he didn't watch the news and glanced at the paper only to see what was on television. He was an inward person. Introspective. Concerned with his own feelings and thoughts, and not inclined to lose himself in external distractions. Though he often characterized himself in the opposite way for other people, playing the role of a shallow extrovert.

This current thing, for instance. He had thought it over for a long time, analyzing, before he ever did anything. There was no point in rushing into something so grave.

He had pondered the morality as well as the impulse, the need. There were two sides to every question. No one knew that better than himself. It had caused him sleepless nights. A human life was a precious and valuable thing. It was unique. Once extinguished, it would never come again. The loss of one human being diminished the race in imponderable ways. Jesus was right. *If you hurt one of my brothers, you hurt me.*

He fully intended to be punished for this. That was part of the plan. To do it with impunity would be cowardly, selfish. When the time came he would take care of it himself, or arrange for it to happen. But first the whole thing had to be gone through properly, with no step left out. *Chapter and verse*, he mused.

They came out a few minutes later. The boyfriend walked her to her building, gave her a long, tender hug at the door and took his leave. She disappeared into the foyer. The heavy door closed, neon reflections hurrying across the large pane of rain-streaked glass. The boyfriend lingered a moment, then jogged down the sidewalk to his own car, which he had left there before. It was a Nissan that had seen better days. It took him a couple of minutes to warm it up and defog the windshield before he eased into traffic, his lights on in the rain.

The Undertaker waited. Traffic crawled by, slowed by the driving rain and the always-dilatory traffic signals.

She would be alone up there for at least two hours. He knew her routine. She studied in the afternoons and saw her boyfriend only in the evenings. She was an honors student. After undergraduate college she intended to get a doctorate in urban planning. She had lots of plans, ambitions. That was why she couldn't think about marriage now, much less children.

The Undertaker sat in the car, feeling the rain pummel the roof and windshield. The multitudinous drops crashing heavy as blood. Trying to get at him, he thought. Prevented by the roof. Staining drops . . .

He removed a photo from his shirt pocket and looked at it. The photo showed a young woman who bore a certain resemblance to the girl upstairs. Not really physical. What the French called *morale*. A psychological or spiritual resemblance. Youth, freshness, ambition. The girl in the photo was prettier, with her sleek hair and fine features. But in the moral way they were really about the same. Clean. Immaculate.

He let his finger run softly over the picture. His eyes half-closed. A brief tremor ran through him.

*Hood my unmanned blood, bating in my cheeks,*
*With thy black mantle til strange love grow bold . . .*

He knew the meaning of love.

The blurt of a car horn somewhere down the block broke the spell. He put the picture of the Virgin away and took a deep breath. Then he drove along the street another two blocks until he reached the convenience store. The phone on the side of the building was free. He pulled up and got out of the car.

The receiver was frozen by the rain, and wet. With distaste he picked it up and dropped a quarter into the slot.

One ring. Two rings. He knew the answering machine wouldn't pick up. She didn't use it when she was home. He sometimes called her because he liked the sound of her recorded voice. *'Hi, we can't come to the phone now. Leave a message and we'll get back to you.'* A hedge against cranks and burglars, the lie about 'we'. He liked her voice. It was crisp, kind. And in two more seconds he would hear it, live.

'Hello?'

The Undertaker's breath caught in his throat. She was so beautiful.

'Hello?' Suspicion in her voice now. Young, innocent, wary.

'Is this Mary?'

'Yes, hello? Who is this?'

'Mary, don't do it.'

The Undertaker had to fight the tremor out of his voice. She was electric in her innocence.

A beat. She was silent. He knew he had penetrated her defenses. She was worried anyway.

'I – I beg your pardon?' she asked.

'Mary, don't do it. You'll never be able to forgive yourself afterward.'

'Don't do what?'

'Mary –' repeating her name, hearing the fire on his own lips – 'you'll never sleep through the night again. You'll hear her calling out your name. You'll die a thousand deaths.'

'Who is this?' Now the tremor was in her voice. 'What are you talking about? What do you want?'

'Just don't do it, Mary. Listen to me. There is still time. Don't do it.'

There was a silence.

'Mary?' The name repeated, one more time. His knees were weak. The receiver trembled in his hand.

*Click*. She hung up.

She had fought him off. But in that last silence he heard her pain, her struggle. This was torture to her, this decision. And now the waiting was taking its toll. That was why she was so tense at the café with her boyfriend. She saw how fateful her plans were.

The Undertaker hung up the phone, slowly. A drop of rain slid down the shiny metal receiver, like a last tear joining him to her, to Mary, in this penultimate phase of the drama.

She was up there now, away from the phone, trying not to think about the voice in her ear. But it wouldn't go away. The voice was inside her, its warning coiled about her heart. He knew this as he got back in his car. This was their first intimacy.

She would be thinking about that voice, worrying about it, listening to its echo, until he called her again. It would trouble her sleep tonight. He was inside her to stay.

*Hood my unmanned blood . . .*

*Til strange love grow bold . . .*

He got into his car and drove away.

# CHAPTER 17

It was one of Susan's 'cloudy' days.

These were days when the boundaries of her mind seemed abnormally weak. Signals from disparate sources bombarded her, making her feel dizzy and depressed. Concentration was difficult. She had long ago realized that in the life of a psychic there are such trouble areas. They roughly correspond to the regular attacks that bedevil migraine sufferers or, somewhat less precisely, to the periodic mood shifts of manic depressives.

There was little to be done about it but to endure until the episode passed off. The signals could be anything, could come from anywhere. Things that were being said, or had been said, or would be said in the future. Things someone was thinking, or had thought, or would one day think. Events that had taken place or would take place or might take place. And any or all of them might be distorted in ways that could not be predicted. Some of the distortions could be caused by her own mental organism as it processed the signals. Others could be caused by the imponderable complexities of the invisible ether in which minds and events swam.

On a normal day Susan's mental boundaries were strong, as were her defenses. Psychic material would come through to her in scattered pieces, some comprehensible, some not. But on one of her 'cloudy days,' as she liked to call them, the external material flooded her and mingled confusingly with her own thoughts and mood.

Today she kept thinking about California, she did not know why. Images of the dirty beaches, the rolling hills, the crowded freeways and the Sierras. Images of San Francisco, of Berkeley, of the hills above Oakland.

She had lived in those hills, in a comfortable little house with her husband, Nick. It was in California that she met and married Nick, and lived her few years with him, working in a mental health clinic while Nick worked as a civil liberties attorney. They had been happy years, until the bewildering concatenation of events which brought both the break-up of the marriage and Susan's pregnancy with Michael. When the dust settled Susan had a new life in Chicago and Nick was married to Elaine.

Susan's memories of California were two-edged, ambivalent. It was a place where her life had gone sour. But it was the place where Michael had been conceived.

As she wandered round her apartment, she realized there was a focus to the images. It was Berkeley. The beautiful campus, the large trees and stately class buildings, the chilly bracing weather.

And something else. The hills above the town. The view of the Bay. Alcatraz, the Golden Gate . . .

*Methuselah*. The Biblical name popped up inside her mind. Completely without context, it bewildered Susan. It was accompanied by a smell of thick, dirty smoke. Susan paused as she was putting on her dress, noting the odd impression, wondering what it meant.

She went into the kitchen. Immediately she heard the cat leap off the living-room couch and come running. Margie stood in the doorway, her eyes widened in a look of patrician summons, and emitted a loud meow. This was her way of asking for a treat.

'Queen Victoria,' Susan smiled, getting one of the tiny dry biscuits from the box and holding out her hand. The cat ate the treat greedily, licking at Susan's palm with a rough, dry tongue.

Carolyn sometimes made Margie stand up on her hind legs to receive a treat, but the animal exerted herself with an air of outraged dignity so eloquent that Susan did not have the heart to make her do the trick.

Margie had only five teeth left – Dr France had had to extract the rest, which were severely decayed from the cat's long tenure on the streets – but they were more than adequate for the food she ate. Susan petted her head, admiring her beautiful blond and brown fur.

The phone rang, making her stand up. It was Gold, calling from his office. His news was bad.

'We have another body,' he said. 'Looks like the same killer.'

'How do you know?' Susan asked.

'The body bag, for openers. They found it in a dumpster up on the northwest side, near O'Hare. And the wound pattern.'

'A young girl?' Susan asked.

'College student. Her family lives here,' Gold said. 'She was living in an apartment in Rogers Park.'

'I'm sorry, David.'

'Yeah, well. I'd like you to take a look at her, if you have time.'

'Of course.'

Gold picked Susan up at her office and drove her to West Harrison, where they met Wes Ganzer and looked at the body together. The girl's name was Mary Ellen Mahoney. She came from a large Irish family which had been based in Chicago for several generations.

The girl had milky skin turned grey by death. Freckles

dotted her cheeks, which must have been vibrant and pretty in life. Stab wounds cruelly disfigured her body. The mortician's job would be a difficult one.

'The pattern of the wounds is the same,' Susan said, pointing to the hands and feet and the gaping slash in the abdomen. 'It's our man.'

'Yeah.'

Gold looked offended by the girl's condition. Though death had transfigured the girl, the cruel wounds made her look somehow alive. A sort of mortified dignity, rising above its own slash marks. Martyrdom, perhaps. Susan wondered whether this was the effect the killer had in mind.

Wes was pointing to the small longitudinal cuts added to the lower end of the stomach wound. 'There's your upside-down crucifix,' he said.

Susan asked the question that had been on her mind since Gold's call.

'What about the blood?'

'They did some quick typing today,' Wes said. 'It's not definitive until we get the DNA back, but there is definitely blood that wasn't the victim's. At least two other types.'

'Two,' Susan repeated ruminatively.

'Also, it looks as though he is intentionally applying the foreign blood in specific places,' Gold said. 'It's hard to tell precisely, because her own blood washed everything along with it. But Wes thinks he poured blood on the chest wounds and possibly at the hands and feet.'

Susan was gazing at the body.

'Are you thinking what I'm thinking?' Gold asked.

'Could he have poured blood from Miranda Becker into this victim's wounds?'

Gold nodded. 'When they did the post-mortem on Becker, they didn't say anything about needle marks. If he got blood from Becker, he must have inserted a needle.'

'And if there are two types of blood applied in this case,' Susan said, 'who is the other donor?'

'As with Becker,' Wes said, 'possibly the killer.'

The word *donor* made Susan cringe. She wondered whether the killer intended this effect as well.

'I have to talk to her family,' Gold said. 'I spoke to the mother on the phone half an hour ago. They know it's bad, but they won't be prepared for this.'

'I could come along,' Susan offered.

'No.' Gold's voice was firm. 'It's not your job.'

There was a silence. Susan could hear the city traffic going by outside the windows. It was another routine Chicago day. Ugly weather, of course. A harsh wind heavy with moisture from the lake. Pedestrians hurrying to their destinations, coats pulled around their necks. A city hunkered on itself, taking the blows of a harsh world on its famous broad shoulders.

Susan now asked the other question that had been on her mind all morning. 'Was she pregnant?'

Gold looked at her. 'Yes.'

'How long?'

'Maybe seven weeks,' Wes said.

There was a silence. From somewhere in the welter of her 'cloudy day' thoughts Susan realized she should have known this was coming.

'Was she planning an abortion?' she asked. 'Had she been to a clinic?'

'Yes,' Gold said. 'The number of the clinic is right beside her phone.'

They stood facing each other over the torn body of the girl. Now there was a clear link between the victims, not created by the killer's MO but by the victims themselves, their lives.

'The family doesn't know about the baby,' Gold said. 'I'm pretty sure of that. But I'm going to see a guy this afternoon who probably does. Her boyfriend. A student at DePaul named Paul Spreitzer.'

Susan met Gold later that afternoon at Mary Ellen Mahoney's apartment in Rogers Park. The neighborhood had unpleasant associations for Susan. It was here, last year, that Gold had rescued her and Michael after Michael had been kidnapped by Arnold Haze. She and her son came within inches of losing their lives in this neighborhood.

The building was vintage North Side, four brick stories and an alley behind. The entrances were sealed off by police vehicles. A cold rain was falling. The cops were sitting in their cars, looking unhappy. Gold spoke to one of them before returning to Susan.

'The social worker is with the parents now,' he said. 'Nobody's been here except the techs. Nothing happened here as far as they can tell. We can have a look around.'

The building's foyer was typical, with steel mailboxes, a threadbare carpet, thick whitewash on all the surfaces and that familiar Chicago smell whose source Susan had never succeeded in tracing. It seemed somehow related to the lake, the sewage and the city's humid air.

The Mahoney girl's apartment was small and well kept. A crucifix was on the wall by her bed, and a small picture of Christ was in the hall, but on the whole it looked as though she wanted to play down her religious past. The place looked very much like a student's apartment, with posters of foreign countries, a copy of the Lange portrait of Mozart, a picture of Chicago's skyline from Lincoln Park.

'She's a good student,' Gold said. 'Was, I mean. Working on a degree in urban planning. 3.6 average. Belonged to a singing group at the university, also the church choir. Not a lot of girlfriends at school. She seemed closer to her old friends from Catholic high school and family friends.'

Susan took a brief tour of the apartment. There were homey touches here and there that bespoke the proximity of family. A homemade afghan hung over the back of the couch. The throw rugs in the living room and foyer looked like hand-me-downs from parents rather than purchases from Good Will.

The refrigerator contained a couple of Tupperware containers with food probably left over from a Sunday dinner with the family. In the freezer were packages of meat, neatly labeled with a marker. Apples and oranges in the vegetable bin. Yogurt. Skim milk.

There were books on the shelves, including university textbooks, a Bible and some prayer books. The bathroom medicine cabinet contained medication for morning sickness.

Susan went into the girl's bedroom. She sat on the cheerful yellow bedspread and ran her hand over both pillows. Gold stood in the doorway, watching.

'Some of the sexual activity took place on this bed,' Susan said. 'She's quite serious about the boy, but . . .' She touched her forehead with two fingers. 'The pregnancy is a bone of contention. Or rather – they both want to terminate it, but she believes it will end her relationship with him.' She looked at Gold. 'Believed, I should say.'

She closed her eyes for a moment, as though trying to concentrate.

'I've been getting something ever since I walked in here,' she told Gold. 'Something confusing. A sort of noise. A mutter, a murmur. Indistinct. I can't figure out what it is.' She shook her head. 'I'm picking up a great load of guilt. Some of it is moral – she was Catholic – but most of it is more complicated. It has to do with her family, and with ambivalence about pregnancy. I don't think she told the father about her real feelings. She hid it.' She turned her face upward, her head cocked, eyes closed. 'Yes. She fears that if the baby is aborted the man will drop her. She knows this is selfish, she thinks that is unfair to the child. This brings her back to a purely moral worry about abortion. She can't shake loose of the pressure . . .'

Susan was having trouble staying focused. Signals were converging and diverging in her mind. Miranda Becker's short story about a girl named Mary, and now a murder victim named Mary. The ambivalence of the victim, and that of the short story's heroine. If I abort the foetus, am I doing so in order to get back at the father? If I complete the pregnancy, am I doing so in order to bind the father to me?

Susan stayed a minute longer, feeling a confusion of memories, impulses, voices of family members. Then she gave up.

A framed needlepoint, probably done by a mother or aunt, was on the wall above the phone. The pop-up directory next to the phone had a Post-it note attached to a blank page with the name of a clinic for women.

Gold pointed it out to Susan. 'See? Here's the clinic.'

Susan touched the phone.

*Don't do it.*

Her hand froze around the receiver, stopped by the soundless words that had leapt into her mind.

*There is still time. Don't do it.*

She looked at Gold. 'Someone called her.'

He looked at her in silence.

She picked up the receiver, held it to her ear.

*Don't do it.*

'A crank call,' she said to Gold. 'Warning her not to go ahead with the abortion.'

Gold looked at her through narrowed eyes. 'Man or woman?'

'Man.'

Susan stood with the phone in her hand, a peculiar expression in her eyes.

'Don't do it,' she said. 'You'll never be able to forgive yourself afterward . . .' Her voice sounded altered.

Gold took a step toward her. 'Is it the killer?'

She looked at him. 'I think so.'

They stood in silence for a long moment, waiting.

*You have your whole life ahead of you.*

Susan closed her eyes. 'There's interference,' she said. 'I'm not sure what I'm hearing. Something about a virgin. Religious imagery. Mixed with some sort of deep guilt and violence.'

'The Virgin Mary . . .' Gold said. 'Her name was Mary.'

'Yes, that too . . .' Susan's hands went to her temples.

She looked at Gold. 'He knew who she was before he decided to kill her. He stalked her. He – saw them together, her and the father. Knew about the pregnancy.' She held her temples harder. 'Now I know what I've been hearing, David. It's praying. Repeating prayers, very fast. Indistinct. Fast. Saying prayers . . .'

'Who?' Gold asked. 'Was it Mahoney? She was Catholic . . .'

'No. No.' She shook her head. 'It's the killer. He says prayers. He recites prayers over the victim. A kind of ritual. He moves oddly, a jerky movement. The prayers are coming out of his mouth very fast, almost garbled . . .' She closed her eyes. 'The female genitals . . . Conception, pregnancy . . . Blood from the vagina . . . Ouch!'

The effort of second sight sent pain stabbing through her head. She gasped. She looked at Gold. 'That's all, David.'

Gold came forward and rubbed her shoulders sympathetically.

'It's the same guy,' he prompted. 'It's our man, right?'

She nodded.

There was a knock at the door. Gold went to answer it.

He said something to whoever it was, then came back to Susan.

'The boyfriend is here,' he said. 'Are you up to talking to him? Want to take a minute?'

Susan closed her eyes for a moment, clearing her mind.

'I'm fine,' she said.

Gold went to the door and brought in a young man of college age. The young man's face was pale.

'Dr Shader,' Gold said, 'this is Paul Spreitzer. He was Mary Ellen's boyfriend.'

'How do you do?' Susan asked, holding out a hand.

The young man was obviously frightened. His hand shook in Susan's. His eyes darted over the bedroom, avoiding the bed itself.

'I've explained Paul's situation to him,' Gold said in an official-sounding voice. 'He understands that he's not under arrest, but that we need to talk to him.'

The boy was looking at Gold. 'Is it really true?' he asked.

'I'm afraid so,' Gold said. 'It happened last night.'

The boy looked shaky, but he didn't cry. Gold asked him if he wanted to sit down. This was the classic moment at which so many perpetrators showed inordinate emotion, and so many innocent people looked guiltily unmoved. This was because the grief reaction was so intense that their conscious mind blocked it out. Only in the weeks and months to come would grief surface in unexpected and sometimes permanent ways.

'When was the last time you saw Mary Ellen?' Gold was asking.

'Yesterday, at lunch. We ate together in the Union. We always did on Thursdays,' the boy said. 'She had a class at one, and I had my lab at one-thirty to four-thirty.'

'Was everything normal yesterday?' Gold asked.

'Yes. I'd say—yes, completely normal. Just lunch as usual.'

Gold sat down opposite Paul Spreitzer. 'Did she have anything on her mind, particularly?'

A shadow passed across the young man's face. 'No, I wouldn't say so. Nothing particular.'

Gold glanced at Susan. Her look told him to get to the point.

'Was Mary Ellen considering an abortion?' he asked.

The boy literally jumped. His face turned a shade paler than before.

'How did you know about that?' he asked.

'Were you the father?' Gold asked, rather tenderly.

The boy thought for a moment, then nodded.

'What clinic was she considering?' Gold asked.

'It's called North Side Women's Clinic,' the boy said. 'It's over near the Outer Drive. I . . .' Tears had welled in his eyes. 'Are you sure she's dead?'

Gold touched his hand. 'How far along was she, Paul?'

'Six weeks.' The boy's voice was toneless. He looked like a guilty man, though his crime was only that he had impregnated a doomed girl.

'So there was still time to consider things,' Gold asked. 'Had she looked at any other clinics?'

'No. She got the name of this one from a counselor at the university,' the boy said. 'It's highly regarded. She knew she didn't have to look any further.'

'What about having the baby?' Gold asked. 'Had she considered that?'

'At first, yes.' A sob choked the boy suddenly, and he couldn't speak for several moments. 'But I—we—I wanted her to terminate the pregnancy. I wasn't ready for that kind of commitment. Mary Ellen was ambitious, she was going to have a career. But she was torn. I think she wished she could have the baby. She was a very maternal person. Also, her family had beliefs about this kind of thing. They're Catholic.' He took a deep breath. 'But she was going to have the operation.'

Gold glanced at Susan, then looked back at the boy.

'Did her family know about the pregnancy, or about the intended surgery?'

Paul shook his head. He looked miserable. 'She worried a lot about that. I think she would have wanted their support. But she said they wouldn't understand.'

'Had she told any of her friends about the pregnancy?' Gold asked. 'Girlfriends?'

'No. Only she and I knew.'

'Nobody else that you might not be familiar with?' Gold probed. 'A counselor. A school psychologist. How about a priest?'

The boy thought for a moment. 'Confession . . . I hadn't thought of that. Her parish priest, his name is Father Dorsey . . .'

'Paul, I need to know if Mary Ellen had had any contact with people who tried to advise her against abortion. On the way into the clinic, for instance. Any hecklers, any crank calls—that kind of thing.'

The boy looked up. 'What do you mean?'

'You know. Pro-life hecklers. People trying to warn her against the abortion.'

Paul shook his head. 'I don't think so. I was with her every time she went there. There was nobody outside. Nothing like that.'

Gold gave Susan a look.

'All right,' he said to the boy. 'How about you? Has anyone called you or approached you about the abortion? A stranger. Something weird, perhaps.'

'No.'

'Paul, did you ever see Mary Ellen with a strange man?' Gold asked. 'Or did you notice a stranger in her vicinity? On campus, or anywhere else, in the past few weeks? Anything unusual at all?'

'No.' The boy shook his head. 'It was just us. The two of us. Talking about the pregnancy. We would meet here, or in a restaurant or something. We would talk. Everything at school was normal. The only thing different was us.' He looked at Susan. 'Are you sure she's dead?'

She touched his hand. 'Yes, Paul, she's dead.'

He stared at her. 'Do you think I did it?' The helpless look in his eyes made the words sound odd. He seemed to be asking not whether they considered him a suspect, but whether he had in fact committed the crime. If Susan answered yes, he would believe that he was in fact the killer. He wanted to be blamed for his girl's death, wanted desperately to be punished in her stead.

Gold spoke before Susan could answer.

'Paul, we're still considering all the possibilities. I'd like to take you down to my office and get your statement. Is that all right?'

The boy nodded numbly. As they moved away he gave Susan a longing backward glance, as though he wished she could take him in her arms and soothe away his pain.

Gold paused at the door to take in Susan's look, which assured him that Paul Spreitzer had had nothing to do with Mary Ellen Mahoney's death. Nodding, he led the boy away.

# CHAPTER 18

Night had fallen.

The scene outside Mary Ellen Mahoney's apartment was chaotic. Chicago PD black-and-whites were parked all over the street in a pattern designed to keep the news stations' sound trucks at a distance. A cordon of uniformed officers stood guard outside the building. Within a few yards of them, gathered like moths at a flame, were the journalists.

The word had already leaked out that Mary Ellen Mahoney was probably the Undertaker's second victim. The local news outlets would be saving ten minutes for the story tonight, and the reporters had to fill those ten minutes. With fact or with hype – the producers didn't particularly care.

The video lights shone in the frozen fog like beacons at street level, each one a halo around the face of a news reporter, male or female.

There were gawkers as well. Braving the humid cold of early evening, they bore serious faces, drawn by violence and hypnotized by its trappings. Now that the dead girl was officially the second victim of a serial killer, their vigil was more holy, their awe more profound. In that building a young woman had been sacrificed on the altar of violence. The reporters, like acolytes, hovered in the dark to pay homage to the gravity of the deed.

Two cops walking together in the mist kept the curious at bay while the murmur of the reporters carried on the frozen air like prayers of the faithful. The cops gestured to each other, deep in conversation when they weren't pushing back the crowd. An unmarked car came up with its siren sounding and was let through the cordon.

The Undertaker stood among the gawkers, his trench coat pulled tight around him against the cold. He surveyed the scene, impressed by the atmosphere of solemnity. It was like the Crucifixion, really, this respect in the face of sacrifice. Christ died for our sins. Did not this innocent young woman die the same way?

What was she guilty of? Being young. Needing love. Conceiving a child in the heat of that love, as God intended the female body to conceive. Young and in love . . . Were any of the faithful gathered here unaware of that equation? Were any of those who tuned in to the news reports and bought the newspapers unaware? Not really. All were brought here by the same recognition, the same seriousness. A mood of communion reigned.

It was that way whenever someone innocent died by violence. People gathered, drawn by shock, yet underneath aware of the secret syllogism which brought violence to the human victim by a logic greater than common sense. I am innocent, therefore I am punished. I have done nothing, therefore I am chosen.

The Undertaker removed a small container from the pocket of his trench coat. It was a thermal coffee cup with a plastic straw sticking out of it. He brought it to his lips thoughtfully, listening to the murmured conversation of the gawkers around him.

'I can't see . . .'

'Look by the right side. See in front of the cop car?'

'I'm freezing.'

'It's Meredith Spiers. See Channel 9?'

'Oh, she's pretty . . .'

The Undertaker paused at the sound of these words. He stood on tiptoe and craned his neck to see over the heads in front of him. Where? Where?

There she was, on the right, just outside the police cordon. Standing with her microphone in her hand, saying something to her cameraman. Someone came over to talk to her, then moved away. Time passed slowly as she waited, looking at her notes, fixing her hair, holding up the umbrella.

Then the video light went on and she stood in the halo, the young face glowing white, the eyes sparkling. She was speaking earnestly to the camera. The Undertaker couldn't hear her words.

'Isn't she beautiful?' a voice said.

'Who? Where? I can't see.'

On tiptoe again, the Undertaker took in the reporter. She was close in age to the victims, he mused. That alone must help her ratings. This was her first big criminal case. He could almost feel her excitement, even from this distance.

He brought the straw to his lips and took a long drink of Mary Ellen Mahoney's blood. His knees felt weak. Another sip, the chasm in his stomach deepening. The woman in front of him turned her head slightly, threatened to glance at him, did not. Could she feel the power of his ascension? Could she feel the burn of his homage?

Prudently he put the flask away. He took a last long look at the assembled crowd. The Adoration of the Magi, he mused. No medieval master had set the scene with greater panache. Giorgione should only be here tonight to see the lights glowing outside that building, the curious watching in silence, the reporters in the halo of their lights while the police stood by, hovering, protecting.

*Pray for us sinners, now and at the hour of our death.*

The Undertaker turned on his heel and headed for home.

# CHAPTER 19

Two days after Mary Ellen Mahoney's death Meredith Spiers did a special report on the murder on Channel 9's nine o'clock news.

Meredith scooped the other local TV and print reporters with the revelation that both of the Undertaker's victims had a connection to abortion. She also presented an exclusive interview with Lawrence Phelan, the Chief of Police, in his City Hall office.

The Chief confirmed that one of the two victims had recently had an abortion and the other was contemplating an abortion.

'It's a tenuous link, Meredith,' he said, 'but it's enough for us to warn all women in Chicago and the vicinity who are pregnant or who have had an abortion or are contemplating abortion to take precautions.'

In answer to a question from Meredith he specified that precautions meant not accepting invitations from strangers, not venturing into areas of the city not ordinarily explored and most importantly not going anywhere alone until the Undertaker was caught.

Meredith also showed parts of an interview with Wesley Ganzer, the Chief Medical Examiner, who confirmed that the method of murder strongly suggested a serial killer. 'I can't go into the details,' he said, 'because we need the clues we have in order to confirm confessions. But I can say that the two murders have all the earmarks of serial killings.'

Meredith returned to Phelan for the final comment. 'We have a number of excellent leads,' he said. 'We're following them aggressively, and we hope for a quick resolution of the case. But we consider this perpetrator to be a clear and present danger to the public. We urge all the women in our city to be careful. Remember, it is impossible for you to be abducted if you are not alone. Do not go anywhere unaccompanied.'

No further clues were included in Meredith's report, which had been cleared by David Gold. True to his promise, Gold had helped Meredith Spiers write a story that had truth in it. The anti-abortion connection was, for the moment, the hottest lead the police had going for them.

At a meeting the next morning Gold told Abel Weathers about Susan's feelings in the Mahoney apartment.

'When Susan examined the Mahoney girl's apartment she got some signals from the phone,' he said. 'Someone had called Mahoney to try to convince her not to abort the baby. *Don't do it. You'll regret it.* Something like that. A male voice. Possibly the killer, according to Susan.'

Weathers had put on his skeptical look. He knew he needed Susan's input, but he did not like hearing it.

'We're looking at pro-life fanatics,' David Gold said. 'People who hate abortion enough to kill women who terminate their pregnancies.'

Weathers looked worried. Predictably, he was thinking of publicity first in considering the abortion angle.

'Christ,' he said. 'That could bring some bad press.'

Gold shrugged. 'We don't have much choice. A lot of these people are sincere, but some of them are off the wall. Look at the bombings of clinics and the murders of doctors. The borderline between militants and crazies can be thin.' He glanced at his notes. 'We've got one victim who had an abortion a few months before her murder. A second victim who was considering abortion. That progression is interesting in itself.'

'What do you mean?' Weathers asked.

'Suppose we've got a nutcase here who wants to terrorize women into not having abortions. First he sacrifices a woman who has had one, then he kills a girl who was only considering it. How would you feel if you were pregnant and thinking about terminating?'

'I see what you mean.'

Weathers's chief assistant observed, 'The two women weren't using the same clinic, were they, Dave?'

Gold shook his head. 'Becker had hers done up in Evanston. Mahoney was using a clinic on the Near North Side.' He shrugged. 'But these pro-life people get around. They picket one clinic one week, another the next. They're highly organized. They even have assignments. They divide the work up.'

The bartender from Pulitzer's had helped a CPD artist create a composite sketch of the man who picked up Miranda Becker the night of her murder. The bartender remembered him as a tall, thin man with hollow cheeks and dark hair. No one considered thus far in the investigation fit this description.

'Let's check the pro-life crowd with that sketch in hand,' Weathers said.

'We will, but let's not be too narrow about it,' Gold said. 'Let me have men check out the crazies, whatever they look like. If we get a match to the sketch, fine. But the guy who picked Becker up may be innocent.'

The door opened and Susan entered the room, looking harried.

'Sorry I'm late,' she said.

Weathers motioned her to a chair. 'We're talking about the anti-abortion angle. What do you think of it?'

Susan said, 'I don't know whether it's the key factor. But from the two bodies it seems obvious that the killer has an obsession with pregnancy, conception and so on. It's very significant that he neither wounds the victim's vagina nor has sexual contact with it. He deposits his semen in the abdominal wound that kills the victim. Consciously or unconsciously he may be avoiding the vagina because he thinks of it as containing a foetus.' She glanced at Gold. 'In Miss Mahoney's apartment I got a clear signal that the killer prays over his victims. Probably as he is killing them. I kept hearing a fast, indistinct litany coming out of his mouth. Similar to the prayers that obsessive compulsives repeat when they're carrying out their rituals. Almost incomprehensible because spoken so fast.'

'Could the guy be an obsessive compulsive?' Gold asked.

'I would strongly doubt that.' Susan shook her head. 'Obsessive compulsives are some of the most harmless people around. They're so paralyzed by anxiety that they almost never get anything done. Most killers are narcissistic personality disorders with paranoid features. However, this man may have some obsessive features mixed in with his paranoid delirium.'

'We come back to the religious angle,' said Weathers, foreseeing more bad press in the event he had to arrest a Catholic for the crimes.

'The pouring of blood into the wounds suggests communion,' Susan replied, 'but communion can have different meanings for different people. The wounds themselves may symbolize female sexual parts in the killer's mind, with the knife or scalpel symbolizing the male organ.' She paused. 'Christianity is quite hard on sexual intercourse, as you know,' she added. 'The flesh is considered sinful in itself, in the Bible. Hence the theme of immaculate conception.'

'Isn't that a little exaggerated?' Weathers's assistant asked.

'Not if you compare Christianity to primitive religions that glorify the phallus and use it in fertility rites,' Susan said. 'Indeed, some scholars have identified Christianity as the first major religion to turn completely against the flesh. Most other religions sanctify the sexual act.'

Gold introduced Rich Sheehan, an Area Six detective with good street contacts and long experience in sex crimes as well as homicide. 'Rich is focusing on the Devil-worshipers,' he said.

Sheehan, a middle-aged detective whose long undercover experience had left him with a permanently seedy air, flipped open the manila folder he had brought with him.

'It's hard,' he said. 'These people don't advertise. They keep their activities a secret. But we have snitches who know some of them. I'm checking them out.'

'Don't some of these Devil-worshipers remove babies from women's wombs to use in their rituals?' asked Weathers.

'That's the myth,' Sheehan replied. 'The black masses call for the blood of an unborn child, or the blood of an infant that has not yet been baptized. But I've never heard of it actually being done.'

'Blood,' Gold said. 'We've got foreign blood drizzled onto our two victims' wounds. Blood that possibly came from previous victims. It's hard not to make that connection.'

'I agree,' Sheehan said. 'We'll follow it and see what comes up.'

Weathers leaned forward. 'We can't let this part of the investigation get out. There's nothing the media loves more than Satanism, Devil worship, that kind of thing.'

Gold was thinking of Meredith Spiers. He believed her anonymous leak had come from someone in Weathers's office, or from a detective. If this was true, the next leak might well involve the occult connection. Gold only hoped it would stop with Meredith.

'We're also considering a possible interface with the abortion angle,' Sheehan added. 'My guys are cross-checking pro-life freaks with Satanists and witches. It might turn up something.'

He looked at his notes. 'If there is a progression here, the killer might be looking to remove the foetus from the womb of his next victim.'

'Oh, Christ,' said Weathers.

'It's always possible that pregnancy is the common denominator, not abortion,' Sheehan said.

'Why didn't he remove the foetus from Mahoney?' Gold asked.

'Maybe he didn't know how to go about looking for it,' Sheehan replied. 'She wasn't far along, after all. Maybe the guy doesn't know enough about the female anatomy to search her for the foetus.'

Susan nodded. 'You're probably right. A lay person wouldn't know how to search the uterus for a small foetus.'

'But if he's as crazy as we think he is, he may raise the stakes as he goes along,' Gold said. 'Remember Charles Manson? His girls came close to removing Sharon Tate's unborn baby.'

Susan nodded. It was not a stretch to imagine a serial killer inspiring himself from a sensational crime like the Tate – La Bianca murders, even after so long a passage of time. Like patients who imitated well-known motifs from books and movies in their symptoms, serial killers were derivative by nature.

'Let's cross that bridge when we come to it,' Weathers said. 'For the moment, at least, the key motif is blood.'

'That brings up the vampire issue,' Sheehan said. 'Our man could be a vampire.'

Gold nodded. 'Guys who get off on drinking blood. They're not that common, but they do exist.'

Sheehan nodded. 'I've talked to a lot of whores who have come in contact with them. Some of them get off on menstrual blood. Others want to make an incision in a woman's skin and suck her blood like a baby. Some of them even have professionally sharpened teeth. It's a well-known perversion. Once in a while one of them will assault a woman for her blood, but normally it's a paying proposition.'

Susan said, 'Don't forget the necrophiliacs. They want the blood of a dead person or animal.'

'That's right.' Gold leaned forward. 'We don't know whether our man's main interest was the blood of Becker and Mahoney before he killed them or after.'

'Remember too,' Susan said, 'that he has methods of collection and preservation. Otherwise he wouldn't be able to pour foreign blood into the victims' wounds.'

The cops sighed. They realized the clues in these two crimes were opening too many avenues of investigation. It was almost as though the perpetrator wanted to overload the police with legwork.

'Okay,' Weathers said. 'We go with what we have and hope for the best. I assume you all saw the Spiers report on Channel 9. We had to open up the abortion angle for public education. But nothing else comes out without my approval. If anybody says a word out of school, I'll fire his ass.'

He looked at Gold. 'Dave, I want you to take manpower from wherever you need it and get this done fast. If you're right about the pro-life angle, a quick arrest could make a big difference.'

Gold nodded. 'My guys are interviewing all the doctors and other personnel at the clinic Mahoney was planning to use. Asking who has picketed the clinic or harassed the clients.'

Sheehan had closed his folder. 'I know most of the whores around town,' he said. 'If there's a vampire around who might be our man, we should be able to bring him in.'

The meeting broke up. Gold walked Susan to the elevator.

'I'll let you know how it's going,' he said. 'Let me know if anything else comes to you.'

The look on Gold's face told Susan what he could not say aloud. The net that had been outlined in the meeting would probably not bring in the Undertaker. Not before he found another victim, that is.

# CHAPTER 20

Wendy was having sex with Tony.

She was on her stomach in his bed. He was crouched atop her, thrusting rhythmically, his knees hugging her thighs, his hands on her shoulders. The bed creaked under Wendy. The rhythm was regular, almost mechanical. Tony had reached a plateau of excitement that he could maintain as long as he wished. There was something impersonal about this hot intimacy that Wendy enjoyed. She felt as though she were outside herself, part of a gigantic, inhuman pumping like that of a monstrous turbine or power source.

Tony sensed what she was feeling and stuck with the same rhythm. She began to moan, losing herself in what he was doing to her. When he felt her start to come he slowed his pace, letting her savor the full length of him sliding in and out, in and out. Then he paused, buried to the hilt inside her, and let her little spasms anoint him. Only when he knew she was all open to him, belonging to him completely, did he let himself go. The flow of his seed brought a great gasp from her.

'Oh,' she moaned. 'Oh, my God . . .'

As always, he had found a way to surprise her, to touch her in a new way just when she thought she knew all his tricks.

It took a long time for her scalded breaths to ebb. He

held her close, his sex silent inside her now, still hard, reminding her of its power.

After a while they separated. She lit a cigarette and lay listening to the city sounds outside the windows. Her glass of wine sat on the bedside table, half full. Tony was silent, watching her. She glanced around the apartment, taking in the crude paintings of half-clad girls with large breasts, the oversized furniture, the cheap rug. She smiled. She had come to like this place. Its very tackiness signaled that it was a place for pleasure, for dropping inhibitions, for forgetting what was expected of one.

Tony's lip curled as he watched her. She sensed his scrutiny and looked at him.

'What's the matter?' she asked.

'Nothing.' He shrugged. 'I'm just happy to see you so pleased with yourself.'

'With myself?' she asked. 'What are you talking about?'

His look darkened. 'Well, you got off again, didn't you?'

She smiled. 'Yes.'

'It must be nice having a stud all your own,' he said. 'At your beck and call, so to speak.'

Wendy frowned, the smoke from her cigarette billowing before her.

'Are you going to start that again?' she asked irritably.

He shrugged. 'Just calling a spade a spade.'

She sighed. 'I wish you'd stop saying that. I'm sick of hearing it.' Her impatience was obvious.

Tony lit a Camel Filter, the chain around his tattooed wrist clinking slightly as he popped open the old Zippo lighter.

Then he turned on his side to look at her. His sex nestled between his legs, still slightly tumescent from their love-making. He was very large, and proud of it.

He studied her body. She was elegant in her physical

manner, aristocratic. Not even her dirty language or her provocative outfits could hide this. It was what had attracted him to her that first night at Crandall's. She had stood out like an angel among the lowlifes in the bar.

The thought reminded him of the distance between them, and he brought it up again.

'Look, babe,' he said, 'I enjoy being with you. You're great in the sack, in spite of the way you were brought up. But I don't like playing games. I know what you need me for.'

Wendy sighed again. He was being difficult.

'Why don't you turn the record over?' she asked. 'I might as well hear the other side while we're at it.'

Tony puffed at his cigarette. He wanted to get off this subject too, but he couldn't stop himself.

'One of these days,' he said, 'you're going to get married to one of those society faggots your family picks out for you. I know it, and you know it. I'm just wondering where I'll fit in when that happens.'

'Jesus, Tony.' Wendy stubbed out her cigarette. 'When are you going to grow up?'

'That's a funny question, coming from you,' Tony rejoined.

'What is that supposed to mean?'

'You're a little girl, babe. You've never grown up. You like to play naughty games, and that's why you're here. But when push comes to shove you're going to do what Mommy and Daddy want you to do. You've never had an independent thought in your life. Why don't you just admit it?'

Wendy reddened. 'Do we have to go through this every time?' she asked.

'I don't mind playing games in the sack,' Tony said. 'I just like a little honesty when we're talking about real life.'

Wendy was angry. Every time she came here, it seemed,

the glow Tony left in her senses was spoiled by his angry possessiveness. He reproached her for slumming with him. He accused her of being insincere in her physical affection for him. He thought she was using him as a stud, with no care for his own needs or feelings.

It was difficult for her to deny, because it was true. As a man Tony had no more reality for her than the cab driver who had brought her over here. He was a lay, and a great one. She knew he got off on her body and on her sexual recklessness. Why, then, did he want it to be something more?

'I'm as honest as you,' she said. 'More so, in fact. We're consenting adults, Tony. Neither of us has any strings on the other, or wants them. Shouldn't, anyway. You're the one who's being childish.'

She felt him tense.

'Maybe I don't like being used,' he said.

'We're using each other,' she argued. 'That's what it's all about, isn't it?'

His face had turned serious. 'I don't think so.'

'My God,' she laughed. 'Look at these pictures on your walls. Look at this bed. You're a stud, Tony. A swordsman. I know I'm not the first, and I won't be the last. When I'm gone you'll fill this bed with other girls. It won't take you a week. Do you see me moaning and groaning over that? You've got your own life. I respect that.'

'I don't think you do.'

'What?'

'Respect me. Or my life. You don't give a shit about anything but yourself. And you haven't got much of a clue about that, either.'

He reached to flip the ash from his Camel into the ashtray. The powerful muscles of his forearms rippled as he moved. He worked out regularly, lifting weights to keep his body plated with muscle. He was a hunk, all right, she mused. If only he could keep his thoughts away from issues that were over his head.

'You're the one who hasn't got a clue,' Wendy said.

'Why?' he asked. 'Because I want to be something more than a cock with a man attached to it?'

Wendy sighed in exasperation. 'Because you want to make more of this than it is,' she said.

'It's already more.'

Behind Tony's dark, handsome brow she saw an argument forming. She knew it already. It was his core logic against her, and he had obviously put some effort into conceiving it.

'You wouldn't get off with me the way you do unless it was more.'

She shook her head. 'Can't you give it a rest?'

He touched her thigh, his broad hand closing around it easily.

'So much pussy and so little brains,' he said.

'Shut up,' she said, stung in her vanity by his sexism.

'When you marry one of those society boys you'll never have a single night to match what you get from me. But you won't care, will you? Because you'll be doing what Daddy wants you to do.'

Irked by his reference to the father she hated, Wendy bristled.

'You men are all alike,' she said. 'You think the sun rises and sets on your own little emotions. A woman is nothing to you but a slave. You expect her to give up her soul along with her body. If she doesn't think what you think, do what you want her to do, you think your manhood has been insulted. Why don't you grow up?'

Now both terms of their ongoing argument were in place. Tony insisted she was the slave of her society's rules. Wendy insisted her life was her own, and that Tony's possessiveness was no different from the repressive rules of that very society.

He liked to taunt her with references to her father; she fought back by identifying *him* with her father.

But their arguments, circular and interminable though they might be, could not change the kernel of their conflict. Tony did care about Wendy, in a way he had never cared for any of the countless girls he had bedded in the past. And Wendy did not care about him, though he gave her sexual satisfaction on a level she had never known before.

It maddened him to be able to give her a kind of pleasure she could never get from the tepid males of her society, but to get nothing in return from her. True, he was charmed and seduced by the hot responses of her body. But those responses made him want more of her, made him want something he did not understand. And he knew she would never give it to him. She couldn't even if she wanted to, because she was a child of her own upper-crust world.

Indeed, he knew she got off so heatedly with him because he was so far beneath her. Every time he had sex with her he became more aware of this painful contradiction. He almost hated her sometimes when he looked at her and saw how satisfied she was by him. She took what he offered, but gave nothing in return. And was this not the essence of her social class, in fact? To take from the common man and to give nothing back? To exploit?

'You just don't understand, do you?' he asked.

'No, I guess I don't,' she said. 'You think you own me just because you give me orgasms. Nobody owns me, Tony. Nobody ever will.'

She turned on her stomach, looking away from him. He studied her slim legs, her delicate ass. She was a prize, all right.

His hand shook sightly as he brought the Camel to his lips.

'So I don't understand, huh?' he asked.

'No, you don't.'

Perversely he held the cigarette above her ribs and flipped the ash onto her back.

'Ouch!' she cried as the ember seared her briefly before dying. She turned on her side, her eyes flaring. 'What do you think you're doing?'

'Nothing.'

'Jesus,' she said, rubbing the slight burn with a finger. 'You act like a little boy.'

'That sounds funny coming from you.'

She was looking up at the ceiling, her knees raised. 'I don't know why I keep coming here.'

'You don't?' Tony asked in a dangerous tone.

'No, I don't. This is a waste of time.'

He crushed the Camel in the ashtray and grabbed her by her hair.

'Bitch, I'll show you why you keep coming here.'

Cruelly he jerked her head to his crotch and shoved her face against him.

'Stop,' she cried, her voice distorted by the pain.

'Do you understand, bitch?' he hissed.

He was pulling her hair hard. She squirmed sideways to try to escape him, her legs flailing on the bedspread. He kept her face buried in his crotch. His penis was hardening at the touch of her nose and lips.

'Do you understand?' he repeated.

She wouldn't give up easily, she was too stubborn for that. She jerked this way and that, cursing him. He was touched by the sight of her body as she struggled. She was childlike in her nudity, her helplessness.

'Tony . . .'

'Bitch, do you understand?'

'I understand.'

He held her hair a moment longer, savoring her humiliation. Then he felt a pitying impulse and let her go.

'Never mind,' he said.

She turned away and lay on her side, still gasping from the pain. He measured her resistance to him. In a few minutes she would put that sweet little body into her expensive clothes and recede into her North Shore existence, looking forward to the next reception, the next cocktail party, the next Junior League benefit. And she would not give him another thought until the hungry thing between her legs brought him to mind.

She was getting up now, bending to pick up her panties.

'I've got to go, anyway.'

She pulled the panties up her legs and found the tiny bra she had worn tonight. Her golden hair fell over her shoulders like that of a princess.

It occurred to Tony that it might be a good idea to kill her. It would bring him peace of mind to know that she wasn't going anywhere, tonight or ever. That her roving eye would never come to rest on another man.

She seemed to guess at his thoughts, for she turned, her small breasts facing him, her eyebrow raised.

'What are you thinking?' she asked.

*As if you cared*, he thought.

'Nothing, babe,' he said. 'Not a thing.'

Something in his tone must have given her pause. She dropped the bra and climbed back on the bed.

'Why can't you just be nice to me?' she asked.

Her face came back to his pelvis of its own accord, and he felt her kisses on his stomach. She liked danger – that was obvious.

'Okay, I'll be nice,' he said, turning to cover her with himself.

# CHAPTER 21

It was Murphy's Law that almost got David Gold killed. In fact for years afterward, whenever Gold entered a room full of detectives, at least one would call out, 'Dave, how's Murphy?'

Area Six had been alerted to a possible barricaded suspect, a crazed militiaman named Vincent Carl Bruno. He had beaten his wife into a coma late last week and been a fugitive ever since. According to a neighbor, he had now returned home and was preparing for a stand-off with the police.

Bruno was the quintessential neighborhood bully. A Marine Corps veteran who had been granted a general discharge after a series of assaults on other enlisted men revealed his mental problems, he missed his chance to participate in the Gulf War and came home to take up a career as a gun dealer.

Since then he had been arrested for a variety of lesser offenses like illegal possession of a concealed weapon, disturbing the peace, driving under the influence, spousal battery. The veteran of two involuntary commitments to state hospitals, he was suspected of membership in several underground militia groups, all of which were on the FBI's watch list.

He had been married three times. All three wives had gotten restraining orders against him in their time. The first two had divorced him years ago. His two children wouldn't recognize him if they saw him.

The beating of his wife last week was the final straw. It was time to pull him in. Gold, as the head detective on the case, had to make the collar.

Bruno lived in a nondescript two-story house on a street of identical houses on the Near North Side. A blue-collar neighborhood full of factory workers, city workers and a few cops, it was the kind of neighborhood where militia types with private arsenals love to live. Just the sight of the endless ranks of frame houses made David Gold nervous.

The approach to the house was made cautiously.

The HBT Unit (for Hostage/Barricaded/Terrorist) was alerted to the planned arrest and about twenty men were sent as a precaution. They came in unmarked cars and wore plain clothes designed to make them look like neighbors or routine neighborhood figures such as mailmen, meter men, garbage men.

Gold was accompanied by two other detectives – both experienced hostage negotiators – and six back-up patrolmen. They drove up in three unmarked cars. The control van remained around the corner.

Gold sat in his unmarked car with Joe Riccio and Jason Kubik, the lead detectives. His first move was to telephone the Bruno house from a cell phone in the car. There was no answer.

'What about the surrounding houses?' he asked.

'The one on the right we evacuated,' said Kubik. 'A housewife and her little boy. The husband is at work downtown. The one on the left is empty. A factory foreman and his wife, no kids. They're visiting relatives, according to his boss.'

'Across the street?' Gold asked.

'We evacuated the three facing houses,' Kubik said, looking at his clipboard. 'Two housewives, one unemployed postal worker. Took them downtown.'

Gold nodded. 'No reason not to get started, then.'

Gold was to go up to the front door alone, with the HBT guys covering him from several vantage points. He was aware of the danger. He was in the Kill Zone. HBT language called the area inside the ring of police the Inner Perimeter. The Outer Perimeter was the larger area of the entire crime scene. The Kill Zone was the range of the suspect's possible weapons.

Whenever a suspect 'went barricade', as the saying went, the first order of business was to secure the area, getting rid of kibitzing neighbors and passers-by. The object was to close down on the suspect as much as possible. Limit him to his house or apartment, then to one floor of the house and finally to one room. There was plenty of time, no reason to hurry. The name of the game was containment and patience. Nine out of ten barricaded suspects eventually gave up out of fatigue and boredom.

The negotiators were typically detectives. The containment officers were usually recruited from the Gang Crimes units. None of the HBT personnel were permanent HBT. All were imported.

'Okay,' Gold said. 'Snipers ready?'

Kubik was on the radio, checking in with the shooters across the street and behind the house. They responded one by one. Gold also checked with the cars ringing the neighborhood. In the event Bruno escaped on the run, he would be pulled in easily.

Gold got out of the car. He was wearing a standard bullet-proof vest under his coat. It was freezing out. He went up the walk. The house looked innocent and respectable. The casual observer would never guess the basement was full of heavy artillery.

Gold knocked loudly on the door, four knocks.

'Police, Mr Bruno. Open up.' He called out the words loudly. The house responded with silence.

'Mr Bruno, Chicago Police. We need to talk to you. Open up!'

Gold turned slightly to glance back at the HBT. It was that slight turn of his torso that saved his life.

Something hit him just below the shoulder. It felt like the fist of a large man, or perhaps a baseball bat swung very hard. He went down in a heap, hearing the echo of a shot on the wintry air. Shouts sounded, shots were fired. Glass shattered somewhere to his left. He heard his name being called, then more firing.

The abrupt knock to his shoulder had spread through his chest and he felt numb. His blood pounded in his ears, louder than he could ever remember. He felt something damp, looked at the slushy stoop, and realized his blood was pumping out of his body in great tepid whooshes, mingling with the dirty city slush like oil poured onto vinegar.

That was his last thought. He was unconscious when they got him out.

When Gold woke up the next afternoon, he was in a private room in the Intensive Care Unit at Michael Reese Hospital.

Susan Shader was sitting in the visitor's chair. Vases of flowers from cops and their families crowded the windowsill and table tops. Gold was in intense pain, but he managed a small smile. Susan knew what he was thinking. *I'm alive.* To a cop who had felt a suspect's bullet enter his chest, that must seem a miracle.

'What happened?' Gold asked.

Susan stood up and came to his side.

'Vincent Bruno shot you,' she said. 'He was hiding in the house next door.'

'Oh, Christ.'

Susan had heard the whole story several times over from Terrell, Kubik and others. The cops had done their work. But they hadn't been quite thorough enough. They hadn't gone to the additional trouble of investigating all the neighbors for priors, especially crimes with violent tendencies. It turned out the neighbor on the left was a lodge brother of Vincent Bruno, and a militia type himself.

Bruno had a police scanner at home and had heard the cops' radio conversations as they came to the scene. He had gone next door to his neighbor's house and was hiding in the upstairs bedroom with a dozen pistols and rifles. While David Gold was calling through the door of Bruno's house, Bruno was coolly drawing a bead on him from next door. He used a hunting rifle with a sniper's scope. Taking aim at the tiny interstice where Gold's vest met his shoulder and armpit, Bruno had scored a direct hit.

Mercifully, Bruno had not used one of the expanding rounds which he possessed in great quantity. An expanding bullet would have killed Gold instantly, liquefying his internal organs like pulp inside a melon. The hunting bullet passed right through, leaving him critically wounded but viable.

'It feels like somebody lit a bonfire on the inside of my chest,' Gold said.

'That's what happens,' Susan said. 'Don't worry, though. It's not for long.'

The bullet had nicked a major artery, collapsed a lung, shattered a rib, and exited from his right side, leaving a wide swath of injury behind it. They transfused him in the ambulance and took him to surgery, where he spent two and a half hours having the artery repaired and the lung stabilized. He would probably need additional surgery, but he was out of danger.

'What are these tubes?' he asked.

'The one in your nose is oxygen,' Susan said. 'The one in your arm is isotonic fluids. They'll be in for a while.'

Gold gave a disgusted look. 'How long am I gonna be like this?'

'Like this, not more than another couple of days. You'll be here for a while, though. They need to monitor your vital signs and make sure the surgery was successful. And they're concerned about infection.'

'Hospital food,' Gold groaned.

'You'll survive,' Susan said.

Only now did Gold think to ask one more thing. 'What about Bruno?'

Susan shook her head. 'Dead.'

The gun battle that followed Gold's wound was unavoidable, because Bruno started throwing grenades at the cops and spraying the neighborhood with semi-automatic fire. In the end they had to assault the house and take him out. He was killed instantly by carbine fire from the assault team. In all that time he had not said one word to the cops.

Gold pursed his lips. 'Damn it.' Then he looked at Susan. 'Was anybody else hurt?'

She shook her head. 'Just you.'

He thought for a moment. 'Where's Carol?' he asked.

'Down the hall, getting the girls a Coke.' Susan smiled. 'Don't worry, she's fine. The doctors knew last night that you were out of danger. Carol had her sister take the girls overnight. She spent most of the night here with me.'

'With you?' Gold raised an eyebrow.

'She needed moral support,' Susan said. 'Besides, I thought I should keep an eye on you.'

Gold nodded. He was in too much pain to express his gratitude. He was glad to have received all the pertinent news from Susan rather than from other cops or hospital personnel.

'She's not too upset?' he asked.

'She's upset, yes. But she understands the situation.'

'What situation?'

'That you had bad luck. That you'll be all right.'

Carol was not an overly emotional woman, but she had never completely gotten used to her husband's profession. His wound came as a confirmation of fears she had entertained privately for fifteen years. Susan had prescribed a mild tranquilizer for her and kept her company during the vigil while Gold was having his surgery.

'Not bad luck,' Gold said. 'More like a comedy of errors. Keystone Cops.'

'You're being too hard on yourself, David. Accidents happen.'

Gold sighed. 'Christ.'

There was a silence. Susan stood, looking down at Gold.

'You're going to be fine,' she said. 'You'll end up good as new.'

'Wiser, I hope.' Gold wore a disgusted look.

'Shall I go get Carol?' Susan asked.

'Wait.' Gold held onto her hand.

'Yes?'

'See if you can get me some painkillers before you let her in. I feel like shit. I don't want her to see me like this.'

She smiled. 'All right. I'll get the doctor.'

'Is Riccio around here?'

'In the lounge with Officer Kubik.'

'Tell him I want to see him.'

'All right.'

'And Susan?'

She looked at him inquiringly.

'Thanks, kid,' Gold said. 'Nice of you to stay close.'

Susan left the room. For the first time she realized she herself was in a mild state of shock over what had happened. To her David Gold had always represented the most civilized and professional side of police work. He had never used his gun on the job and was proud of it. Seeing him in a hospital bed with the drawn look of a surgical patient was a frightening dislocation for her. She reflected that a split second and a half-inch of space were the only things that had separated David Gold from the examining table in Wesley Ganzer's office where Miranda Becker and Mary Ellen Mahoney had lain.

# PART THREE

# CHAPTER 22

Susan was to leave the following Thursday for a long weekend in California. She was to give a lecture on 'Distortion in Mental Life' to a group of psychiatrists who was meeting in Berkeley. She had accepted the invitation over a year ago and devoted considerable effort to the paper, so she could not have backed out now even if she wanted to.

But she did not want to, because she was to spend two days with Michael while she was there. She had scheduled her conference with Michael's second-grade teacher for this trip, and was looking forward to it.

There was another reason, a more private one. She wanted to get to the bottom of her unnaturally powerful mental picture of the hills above Berkeley. She had tried to write it off as an abnormally intense memory picture derived from her years in California and her anticipation of this trip, but she had become convinced that there was a psychic intuition mixed up in it somewhere. An intuition deriving from the Undertaker case. She hoped that when she was on the scene something would clarify her feelings.

She was loath to leave Chicago after what had happened to David Gold. His condition had been upgraded to 'serious', but he remained in a high-tech hospital room at Michael Reese, where he was still getting transfusions and respiratory assistance. Gold was weak, guilty and frustrated. He could no longer take an active part in the investigation and had to have the detectives touch base with him on his hospital phone.

Susan knew that with Gold out of action her own role in the Undertaker investigation would change. Gold was her chief defender in the CPD and the main buffer between her and Abel Weathers. Over the years Gold had managed to blunt Weathers's antagonism toward Susan through a combination of guile and diplomacy. When Susan's psychic intuitions led nowhere, Gold reminded Weathers of the times they had been crucial to the solving of cases. When Weathers lamented the embarrassment of the police depending on the feelings of a psychic, Gold subtly reminded him that psychics were good press. Susan was highly regarded in the media. Her stature redounded to the advantage of the State's Attorney.

Nevertheless, in the present circumstances Weathers would not be inclined to give much weight to Susan's input.

Susan was on her way to see Gold during evening visiting hours when she got a call from Meredith Spiers.

'I've got another leak. Do you think Detective Gold is up to hearing about it?'

'He'll be furious if he doesn't hear about it. Let's meet in his room.'

Susan arrived first. Gold looked miserable.

'Do you have pain?' Susan asked.

He nodded. 'It hurts to breathe. And this burning . . . Now I know why the guys who get shot are always so pissed off.'

Susan placed her hand against his cheek. He still had a low-grade fever.

'It's the trauma,' Susan said. 'When the pneumothorax is penetrated there is shock to a lot of different organs. Not to mention the surgical invasion. And, of course, there's nothing like a broken rib for pain. It's going to hurt for a while. Don't forget, also, that post-operative depression is almost unavoidable. You can't expect to feel normal, mentally, for at least a week.'

She did not add what she secretly knew to be the case: additional surgery might be necessary due to the combined insult of the bullet and the first surgery. Gunshot wounds were not pretty, medically speaking. The sequelae could be complex and very painful for the patient. In Gold's case empyema of the damaged lung was also to be feared. If it happened the doctors would have to insert a drainage tube in the area, in order to get rid of the purulent exudate. Gold would not be feeling normal for a long time.

He looked at Susan. 'Listen. You know Joe Riccio, don't you?'

'I've met him.'

Riccio was one of Gold's most trusted detectives, a veteran with an unblemished record and several decorations for valor. A handsome man whose taciturn personality belied his ruddy red-headed looks, Riccio had always treated Susan with a somewhat impersonal cordiality. She suspected he did not like her very much but was too much of a gentleman to let it show.

'Riccio will work with you while I'm down,' Gold said. 'When you get back from California he'll stay close to you. Take you places and report back to me.'

'All right,' Susan said.

A knock sounded at the door and Meredith Spiers came in, bearing a small vase of flowers, which she put on the crowded window sill.

'Detective, how are you feeling?' Meredith asked.

'Better now than a minute ago,' Gold said. 'Have you got something?'

'Yes, I do. It came in this noon.'

She handed him a print-out of an e-mail.

Gold squinted a little as he held the paper out in front of

him. He was beginning to need reading glasses, but didn't like to admit it. 'This light,' he muttered.

Then he read the contents of the e-mail aloud.

'*Semen in stomach wound. The crucifix is upside-down.*'

He frowned. 'A man of few words,' he said. 'And right on the money.'

'It's true?' Meredith asked.

'Yup.' Gold looked unhappy.

'What does it tell you?'

'It tells me this geek is very close by,' Gold said. 'Either he's with Weathers's staff, or the FBI, or one of my guys, or with the ME. No one else could know all this.'

'Have you discussed this with the State's Attorney?' Meredith asked.

Gold gave her an evasive look. 'I'm on it,' he said. 'That's all you have to know.'

Meredith nodded. In the brief silence that followed, Susan wondered whether Gold was hiding what he knew from Weathers. Weathers's insatiable hunger for publicity was common knowledge. It was remotely possible that Weathers knew who the leak was, and was allowing it to go on.

'Thanks, Meredith,' Gold said. 'It's good to have you on our team.'

'You gave me a good story on Miss Mahoney,' Meredith said.

'I'll give you another good one as soon as I get on top of this,' Gold said.

'There's one thing I'm worried about, though,' the reporter said.

'What's that?' Gold asked.

'If I don't use the stuff I'm getting, the leak may dry up. Or he may go to another journalist.'

Gold nodded. 'I see your point.'

'Whoever it is,' Meredith said, 'we need to keep him on the hook.'

There was a silence.

'Let me think about it,' Gold said. 'Maybe we can fudge it somehow.'

'The foreign blood,' Meredith asked, is it the same type as the semen?'

'Correct.'

'That leaves no doubt at all that it's the same man,' Meredith observed.

'Right.'

'How about the second type?' Meredith asked.

'Off the record – ' Gold gave her a sharp look – 'Becker's.'

'My God.' Even a hard-boiled reporter like Meredith Spiers had to grimace at the grisly MO. 'He's crazy, then.'

'Has to be.'

Meredith chewed her lip nervously.

'Well, I can't put any of that on the air,' she said. 'It might encourage a copycat.'

'That's good thinking.' Gold was impressed. The young reporter had some ethics, as well as an understanding of the unwitting role the press often plays in encouraging violent criminals.

A gentle knock sounded at the open door and one of the hospital's faceless series of doctors came in to take Gold's blood pressure. A night resident, Susan assumed.

'Sorry to interrupt, Detective. This will only take a moment.'

They all fell silent. Susan gave the physician a polite smile and stood up to look out the window while he was putting on the cuff and inflating it.

The familiar sigh of the air escaping the cuff sounded exhausted and somehow depressing. Susan realized she was feeling some of Gold's depression.

'Thanks, Detective.' The doctor swept out of the room without a backward look.

'Sit tight for a couple of days,' Gold told Meredith. 'I'll call you. We'll figure something out.'

Meredith stood up. 'Thanks, Detective.'

'Call me Dave,' Gold said. 'We're getting to be family.'

'Feel better,' Meredith said.

Susan went out into the hall with Meredith.

'Hospitals make me nervous,' Meredith said. 'For one thing, you can't smoke.'

'I understand,' Susan said. There was a time when the inability to have a Newport would have made her distinctly uncomfortable. Nowadays even the waiting rooms in most hospitals were non-smoking areas.

Meredith said goodbye and moved quickly away down the corridor. Susan watched her go. Meredith's remark about her nervousness had caused a small but definite pulse of intuition in Susan. Something was concealed behind Meredith's words. There was another reason, unconnected to smoking, why hospitals made her nervous.

Susan went back in to Gold. His face had changed now that Meredith was gone. Susan could see he had something on his mind.

'You know,' he said, 'I had a funny feeling when the bullet first took me down. I haven't told Carol about it.'

Susan looked at him expectantly, waiting for him to continue.

'A sort of letting go,' he said. 'A sort of . . .'

He paused, clearly upset about what he was trying to articulate.

'Peacefulness?' she offered.

'Yeah, in a way.' He looked into her eyes. 'Like I was ready to let it all go. Like I had been waiting for this all along. Just at that moment it didn't feel too bad. But later, thinking about it – it feels scary.'

'That bullet came close to killing you,' Susan said. 'You're not the first person who has had a feeling like that.'

In her time as a medical student and intern Susan had spoken to many patients whose near-death experiences had left powerful impressions on their minds. It made sense to her that the proximity of death would create uncanny emotions.

'It wasn't just the bullet,' he said. 'It was as though it was *me* letting go. That scared me, when I thought about Carol and the girls.'

She could see he was still unnerved by what he had felt.

'Did I ever tell you about my Aunt Frances?' he asked.

'I don't think you've mentioned her to me.'

'She came from the old country right after the war,' Gold said. 'She was my favorite aunt. She was my father's sister. She was the only one in the family who ever spoke Yiddish to me. My mother and father hated the old ways, they didn't even keep a kosher house. Frances was a curiosity. She had been a writer, a poet. Her books had come out in Yiddish, but one of them had actually been translated into other languages like Polish, Russian . . . I've got it at home, I'll show it to you sometime.' He smiled. 'She was a character. She used to tell me stories that had me on the edge of my seat. Stories of the old country, fairy tales. Dybbuks and all that. She was a hell of a storyteller. I couldn't get enough of her.'

'She sounds nice,' Susan said.

'There was some sort of beef between her and my father, I never learned quite what it was. She told him he was a lousy Jew, a traitor to his faith. He couldn't stand her. He thought she was a neurotic pain in the ass. But I thought she was terrific.' He thought for a moment, his eyes softened by memory.

'After her second divorce she got cancer. I think it was

uterine or ovarian, something like that. Anyway, it spread, and she came to our house to die. She was sick for a long time. I used to go in and read to her, talk to her. This was when I was about sixteen, seventeen. Christ, she was miserable. Most of the time I was in there she had her teeth gritted, moaning, sighing. They had her pickled in morphine, though I didn't know that at the time.

'Somehow I felt closer to her as she got weaker. She would hold my hand and talk to me with this terrific intensity, as though she was trying to leave something precious with me, trying to make sure I didn't forget it. She made me promise to say a special prayer of mourning over her when she was gone. "Your mother and father, they don't keep the Jewish ways," she said. "I want you to do this for me." She showed me the prayer. Made me memorize it in Hebrew, even. Christ, was that hard.'

He shook his head.

'I was sixteen, I wanted to be out playing ball with my buddies. But I did what she asked. When she finally died, she had been delirious for weeks. The ambulance came to get her before I could recite the prayer. I had to do it in the funeral home. She had already been cremated. I snuck in when nobody was there and stood over the casket. I worried that I was too late. I can still remember the beginning of it. *God, full of compassion, who dwells on high, grant perfect rest to the soul of Frances Gold, who is recalled this day in blessed memory.*'

He smiled. 'That one little phrase, *perfect rest*, struck me. In Hebrew it was *menucha nechona*. *Menucha* comes from a root that means quieting, like in birds settling down in a tree. It can also mean freedom from your enemies. *Nechona* means infinite, but it comes from a root that means firm, solid, like a house planted on firm ground. I really wanted her to have that. Some rest. She had had a hard life. She was a special person.'

He looked at Susan. 'That idea came back to me when I woke up here in the hospital. *Perfect rest.*'

'Is that what you felt when the bullet hit you?'

'Something like it, yeah. A kind of door opening. Behind it a kind of quiet I had never felt.'

'And you feel upset over having wanted it,' Susan offered. 'You reproach yourself for having been willing, at that moment, to leave Carol and the girls?'

He nodded, a small grin on his lips. 'I forgot you're a shrink,' he said.

'Those are very normal feelings, David. Something deep in us lets go when we're near death. It's not a betrayal of those we love. It's a mechanism in our body. A good mechanism, I think.'

He thought for a long moment. 'I've been a cop for so long,' he said. 'The idea of rest . . . When you're a cop, you live on the opposite side of the world from a thing like that.'

'I understand.'

She was standing by the bed. He took her hand and held it in his own.

'I formed a theory for myself,' he said. 'My idea is that the victims of violent crime, the dead ones I mean, can never find perfect rest until we catch the guys who did it to them. And punish them.' He looked at Susan. 'Magical thinking, huh?'

'I don't know, David. I'm a doctor. I don't know what happens after death. Your guess is as good as mine.'

Part of her felt sorry for Gold. Not because his private theory was so terribly fanciful, but because that theory must leave him in a permanent state of dissatisfaction. Many killers were caught, but few were really punished in proportion to the tragedies they had brought about. A lot of them plea-bargained their way to freedom, and killed again. Others languished in prisons, but gave little thought to the pain they had caused. This was the reason many sincere people wanted the death penalty never to be outlawed.

'What do you think?' he asked, an odd intensity in his tone.

'What do I think about what?'

'I don't know. Rest . . .'

She sensed there was something he wasn't saying.

'There is rest in letting go,' she said. 'I know that as a psychiatrist, and as a woman. There is also rest in loving those we love. Love is a renunciation of one's self in favor of someone else. In that there is rest, too. A kind of inner peace.'

'I guess so. Yeah.'

She thought for a moment. 'I believe there is more to death than violence. More than plain emptiness, too. But I don't know what fills that emptiness. I guess no one does.'

There was a silence. Gold looked down at her hand. Embarrassed, he let it go. His face hardened as he came back to more immediate issues.

'Riccio will call you as soon as you get back from California,' he said.

'I'm sorry to leave you at a time like this,' Susan said.

'Forget it.' Gold waved her scruples off. 'Get out of here for a while. A break will do you good.'

He managed a small smile. 'Give Michael a hug from Uncle Dave.'

'He's worried about you. He knows what happened.'

'He is?' Gold seemed distressed to hear this.

'I told him you're fine, but you know how he is.'

'Yeah. Maybe I should give him a buzz myself,' Gold said.

'He'd like that.'

She got up to leave, but turned back to look at him.

'What was that Hebrew phrase again?'
'*Menucha nechona*. Perfect rest.'
'It's a pretty language. I'll see you next week.'
He winked. 'I'm not going anywhere.'
'Take care of yourself,' she said.

# CHAPTER 23

San Francisco was cold and foggy. Susan remembered the winters here very well. The chill was not as overtly cruel as that of Chicago, but on certain days it penetrated deeper, filling the body with an almost gothic melancholy. She wore a sweater and a leather jacket, but it was difficult to feel warm.

Susan's lecture to the APA group went well, better than she had expected. The audience was erudite but not prejudiced. Often psychiatrists could be as clannish and narrow as anyone else. But today the questions were friendly, probing and interesting.

The thrust of her lecture was that, based on the inevitable conflicts between warring parts of the human personality, distortion is not an exception but a rule in mental functioning.

'As Freud said more than once,' Susan said, 'an entire life can be based on a single distortion in the subject's unconscious beliefs. The most well-known example is the person who compensates for his or her feelings of inferiority by a lifetime of ambition and achievement. Another is the person who sublimates his or her unconscious exhibitionism into a career as an actor – or, for that matter, as any kind of creative artist. Quite often the distorted view of the world that underlies the person's behavior can make him or her a great success in life. A success, indeed, whose contributions change the world. When this happens we have to wonder whether the person's choices are really a distortion at all.' She smiled. 'It wasn't a psychoanalyst but a very psychological writer, Marcel Proust, who spoke of life as a perpetual mistake. Pardon my French pronunciation, but the precise phrase was *"Cette perpétuelle erreur qu'est précisément la vie."* I'm not an expert on Proust, but I think he was saying that the constant contradiction between our beliefs and the reality we face is what gives our life direction and fruitfulness. In Proust as in psychoanalysis, it isn't so much the simple truth that matters as the complex ways in which the mind struggles to deal with truth. With life, I should say. Distortion in this sense can be viewed as the most powerful tool for learning which the mind possesses. I might conclude by reminding you of the dictum that modern physics takes for granted. The act of observation changes the object being observed. There is no such thing as simple objective observation. If this is the case, all knowledge is of necessity a distortion. The teaching of psychoanalysis, like that of art and perhaps religion, is that this distortion is not a negative thing. It can be the key to all our greatest insights.'

Only near the end of the question-and-answer period was the embarrassing subject of Susan's second sight brought up.

'Dr Shader,' asked a psychiatrist in the audience, 'it's pretty well known that you are gifted with second sight. I'd like to hear your thoughts about distortion in extra-sensory perception.'

'That's a very interesting question.' Susan smiled. 'Freud kept an open mind about the existence of psychic phenomena, despite his natural skepticism. However, he insisted that if psychic phenomena exist they must follow the same rules that govern dreams and symptoms. In other words, they suffer the inevitable fate of distortion – through condensation, displacement, secondary revision etc. – as other mental data. My own experience of second sight has been that distortion plays an integral part.'

'Does this distortion compromise the insights you have as a psychic?' the same questioner asked.

'Sometimes, yes,' Susan said. 'The truth as revealed by second sight is never simple. Even if it isn't cloaked by temporal complexities and interference from various sources, it has to pass through the final filter of the psychic's own mental organism. The defenses and repressions operating in the psychic can have a dramatic effect on the material intuited. Sometimes we are blind to a psychic insight that is staring us in the face. Not because of the insight itself, but because we repress it before it can become conscious. This can create problems.'

This was a painful subject with her. More than once her intuitions as communicated to David Gold, the FBI or others had turned out to be false, because of distortions originating in her own personality. On several occasions the crucial truth had been on the tip of her tongue, but had come out distorted, much like a dream image or a parapraxis. The result was a useless clue, when the truth was so close at hand.

Susan's conference with Michael's second-grade teacher went well. Not for the first time, Susan heard that Michael was a model student.

'Michael is right where he should be, academically,' Mrs Kittle said. 'He is in every way a normal healthy boy. I'm most impressed by the way he interacts with his classmates. He is kind and empathetic. He is very generous and helpful. I couldn't ask for a better student.'

As a proud mother Susan was thrilled to hear such praise for her son. As delicately as she could, she asked whether the teacher saw signs of fall-out from the divorce and Nick's remarriage.

Mrs Kittle shook her head. 'Unless that very stress has contributed to his extra balance and strength as a person,' she said, 'I can't see any ill-effect. Obviously he gets a lot of love from you. I've spoken to his father and stepmother, and they're very loving parents.' The teacher did not inquire about the circumstances of the divorce, or why Susan did not have custody of Michael. 'I understand you have him for summers and vacations. He's looking forward to this summer, very much. He writes about you often and draws pictures of you.'

Susan smiled. 'I know. He sends some of them to me. They're on my refrigerator back in Chicago.'

Two sensitive subjects were on Susan's mind, and she forced herself to bring them up, though she had to be evasive about the details.

'Has he shown any signs of stress consequent to a trauma?' she asked. 'He was put in a very stressful situation a year ago, something life-threatening. I've worried about it ever since.'

Mrs Kittle shook her head. 'Not that I've seen,' she said. 'Although I suppose it's possible. Michael is a very tactful boy. My guess is that he is the type who would keep painful things inside and present a smiling, helpful surface to others.'

Susan heard a description of herself in these words. It was not the easiest fate in the world to be a person who 'keeps things inside' and remains helpful to others. Yet the description of Michael was accurate. He had never acted out his bad moods, not even when he was a toddler. No doubt he would grow up to be a strong, helpful, private person. That was one definition of maturity, after all.

The final question could not be asked in any but the most evasive form.

'He's very intuitive, as you say,' Susan said, choosing her words carefully. 'I wonder if he feels isolated from other children for the very reason that he is intuitive.' She laughed.

'Naturally, as a mother I want him to fit in like a round peg in a round hole, never to feel different. I know that's not possible. But I do want him to feel part of the world. Not to feel isolated.'

Mrs Kittle smiled. 'I think your worries are unnecessary. The other children love Michael, and he thrives on that love. I've seen him playing with the other kids and overheard his conversations with them. He is not isolated, Dr Shader. He is not lonely. That I can promise you.'

Susan was relieved. A year ago, when Michael narrowly escaped death at the hands of Arnold Haze, he emerged from the experience with a gift Susan had never wanted for him – the gift of second sight. In her own youth second sight had played a complicated and painful part. It had come to her on the heels of her parents' deaths, and always been associated with survivor guilt in her mind. At all costs she wanted things to be different for Michael.

'Thank you so much,' she said to Mrs Kittle. 'Do you have any questions for me?'

'Only a comment,' the teacher said. 'I can see that you worry about the effects of the stresses Michael has been exposed to. Believe me, you're not alone in this, and neither is he. Most of my students have, in one way or another, experienced serious threats to the security they need to feel. Usually, of course, the stress comes from family problems. Some of the parents are too wrapped up in themselves to care. Others, like you, tend to agonize over the children. Try to remember that stress is part of every child's life. Coping with it is an inevitable part of being human. If you're sensitive to Michael's feelings, and if you're doing your best to be helpful and supportive to him, you're doing your job.'

Susan was grateful for this speech, though a bit embarrassed that her maternal protectiveness had kept her from knowing it for herself. She thanked the teacher warmly and took her leave convinced that Mrs Kittle was a fine and caring professional.

Susan felt she was on a roll. Her lecture had gone extremely well, without the outbursts of prejudice and ridicule that so often greeted her public appearances. The conference with Mrs Kittle had been reassuring. She took Michael to lunch at a coffee shop on Telegraph Avenue in Berkeley that she had often patronized when she worked here. Michael ate his favorite lunch, a baked potato with all the trimmings, and Susan had a Cobb salad which was three times too big, but delicious.

A brave winter sun had come out, turning the sky blue and making surfaces gleam, and Susan asked Michael if he would like to accompany her up into the hills above Berkeley. Eager for the adventure, he agreed, and they drove up through Strawberry Canyon and parked on a narrow road not far from the Berkeley Science Museum.

They sat down together between some eucalyptus trees and gazed at the magnificent view of the Bay. Michael was wearing a pair of jeans Susan had never seen before. His legs were visibly longer than they had been the last time she saw him. His hair was beginning to curl like his father's, and his fair skin showed a scattering of the freckles which ran in Susan's family. His eyes, always sensitive, seemed deeper now.

The fog had receded within the last hour or so. The Bay Bridge was clearly visible, as was the San Francisco financial district beyond Treasure Island.

'Is that Alcatraz, Mom?' Michael asked, pointing to the famous island in front of the Bridge's twin towers.

'That's right, honey. And that big tower there is the TV antenna at Twin Peaks.' Susan saw the freeway that had collapsed in the 1989 earthquake, and the Richmond-San Rafael Bridge with its lazy W shape. Berkeley stretched immediately below the campus, with Shattuck Avenue running north-south and University Avenue running east-west toward the Bay.

She could see traces of the devastation caused by the 1992 fire which destroyed 1,400 homes in the Moraga and Berkeley hills, as well as the hills above Oakland where her own house had been. She and Nick had gotten their divorce and sold the little house before it burned down. They had congratulated themselves on their good luck, but Susan had found herself looking back on the burned house as a symbol of her failed marriage.

Michael was thrilled by the view. 'It's beautiful, isn't it?' he asked.

'Very beautiful, yes.'

'Have you been here before?' He looked up at her.

'Oh, yes. I used to come here when I worked in Berkeley,' Susan said. 'As a matter of fact, you've been here with me. I brought you up here for picnics a few times, when you were still a baby.'

'Was Daddy with us?'

'Hmm,' Susan tried to remember. 'At least once, yes. But the other times we were alone. Daddy was working.'

'Did we have a good time?' Michael asked.

Somehow she knew he meant the time they were here as a family.

'Yes, honey. We had a very good time.'

'Did Daddy have a good time?'

'Of course. Daddy always had a good time whenever he was with you. Just as he does today.'

She knew her son was testing her memory of the good times they had had before her divorce from Nick. It fell to Michael, a child of divorce, to wonder about the time before his memory, about the time before unhappiness came, and doubtless to wonder whether he could have done anything to prevent the bad thing that happened.

'Did you come here alone?' Michael asked.

'Sometimes, yes,' she replied. 'When I wanted to get away by myself for a while, just to think. Or just to look at this beautiful view.'

'What did you think about?'

'Well, I thought about all the people who live around here, and across the water,' Susan said. 'I thought about where we lived, which is just over those mountains. I thought about your father, and I thought about you.'

There was a silence. She could see the boy's features clouded by intense thought. She knew there were painful things for him to ponder in his young life. It was her job, and Nick's job, to try to ease his way as much as possible through that process. The legacy of divorce was the onus of having to explain one's decision to the child whose life was fractured by the rift. The process was not simple. More importantly, it was ongoing. As a child grew older, his aware-ness changed, and so did his priorities. At age eight he might need a completely different kind of reassurance from the one that had worked at six. At thirteen it might no longer be possible to justify the act to him. A divorced parent's work in self-justification was never done.

Then, too, the parent grew older herself. At age forty the self-justifications that worked at thirty might no longer be effective. One never knew when the old solutions would start to weaken, like quiet hills under which a fault line kept its silent vigil.

*You have your whole life ahead of you.*

The words darted suddenly into Susan's mind. She remembered hearing them back in Chicago, in the course of the investigation. But she could not remember precisely when.

Their charge was much more powerful here. She wondered why.

Who had said them? What was meant? What was the situation at the time? A bad situation, Susan felt sure of that.

*You have your whole life ahead of you.* The helpful message of the words seemed eclipsed by a great surge of anger and of hopelessness.

Susan's brow furrowed. Those same words had been said to her not very long after her parents' deaths by a well-meaning therapist who tried to warn her not to let the loss affect her too deeply. 'You have your whole life ahead of you,' he had said. 'Grief can go too far. You have to think about yourself.' At the time she had paid no attention to the words, because she sensed her own grieving for her parents had not really begun. The school of her own suffering would lead to self-mutilation, promiscuity, and depths of isolation before she would begin to forgive herself for being a survivor.

*The important thing is to relax.*

These words impinged from another source. They, too, had crossed her path in Chicago. But their emotional co-efficient was very different. Something about them was frightening. Something terrible was happening, or was about to happen.

*The important thing is to relax.*

Susan had turned pale. She closed her eyes, struggling to focus on the context of the words. She could not recall anyone ever having said them to her. Unless, perhaps, her obstetrician at the time of Michael's birth.

But now she was hearing them with someone else's ears. Someone frightened, someone in terrible pain.

'Mom? Are you all right?'

At first she didn't hear Michael. A visual image was hovering before her mind, but just out of focus, just out of reach. She held Michael's hand to tell him she hadn't forgotten him.

'Mom?'

She shook her head to clear her mind, and looked at Michael.

'Yes, sweetie?'

'What were you thinking about?'

'Nothing. I was just trying to remember something.'

'What was it?'

'Oh, something someone said once. Something I had forgotten.'

She took the small notebook from her purse and found a pen. She jotted down the thoughts that were coming to her. Michael was looking at her quietly.

'Mom, who's Meredith?' Michael asked.

'Oh.' Susan smiled. 'Just a lady I know.'

'Is she a nice lady?'

'Oh, yes, honey. Very nice. She's very young, though. So young that it feels funny to call her a lady. She looks almost like a girl.' She started, realizing Michael had read her mind. 'How did you know about Meredith?' she asked.

'I don't know, Mom.'

He was looking out at the Bay, apparently unconcerned by his own intuition. Susan struggled to accept the fact that this was going to happen. Her son was psychic.

'Mom,' he said.

'Yes, sweetie.'

'What's an abortion?'

She regretted having brought him along. She should have come alone. She was on this hill for business, not pleasure. The truths she was seeking were ugly, painful truths. She should not have exposed Michael to them.

'Oh, it's a kind of surgery. An operation,' she said.

'Did you ever have the operation?'

'No, honey. I didn't.'

She finished writing, put away the notebook and looked at Michael.

'How shall we spent the rest of our day?' she asked. 'Shall we go to a movie?'

'Yes.' He was excited by the idea. He loved movies more than anything else. They stood up to leave. Susan paused, looking down at the Bay. Then she took out her notebook and wrote down something else.

'Sorry, honey,' she said, putting away the notebook. 'Let's go.'

They went back to the car and drove down into Berkeley. Susan called Elaine to tell her the plan for the movies. Then she placed a long-distance call to David Gold's hospital room. It was five o'clock in Chicago. Gold was awake, waiting for phone calls from the detectives about the investigation.

'Gold here.'

'David? This is Susan.'

'How's California? How's my boy?'

'Fine. Listen, David, I can't talk long, but I need to tell you something. The man you're looking for – he's been in your room at the hospital.'

'What do you mean? As a patient?'

'No. Since you've been there. He must have dressed like a doctor. He was there, David.'

Gold was silent.

'And something else, David. He's been out here, in Berkeley or the Bay area. I could feel him up in the hills today.'

'Lived there?' Gold asked.

'I don't know. I sensed it back in Chicago. I probably should have told you, but it seemed too tenuous. I'm sure of it now. He's been here.'

'Okay. I'll keep it in mind. It might help somewhere down the line. Got anything else?'

Susan hesitated. 'A couple of things, but they're just thoughts. I don't feel sure enough to say anything yet.'

'Okay. I'll put some guys on the hospital. Maybe work with hospital security. See what we can do. How did your lecture go?'

'Fine. Better than expected.'

'Good. Keep up the good work. And have a good time with Michael.'

'I will.'

She hung up and joined Michael. *Mulan* was playing in a theater not far from Nick's house. They had just time to make the beginning.

Michael took her hand. They hurried toward the car. A phrase trailed behind Susan, eclipsed on the hillside an hour ago, but clinging to her now like an angry insect.

*Hood my unmanned blood, bating in my cheeks . . .*

Preoccupied by other thoughts, Susan did not notice it.

# CHAPTER 24

On Friday night Wendy Breckinridge attended a benefit concert at Mandel Hall. The concert was being given for the benefit of children with AIDS, and was organized by a well-known North Shore charity whose founder and chief executive was Wendy's aunt, her mother's sister.

Ardyne Chrysler was the only relative Wendy liked. Though fabulously wealthy and superficially indistinguishable from her North Shore counterparts, Ardyne was a down-to-earth woman who lived unpretentiously and worked hard for charitable causes. Her husband had died of leukemia when she was in her thirties and Ardyne had decided not to marry again. She had genuinely loved him and felt that her personal life ended with his death.

Her generosity and integrity impressed Wendy. When Wendy was a teenager Aunt Ardyne was the only adult she confided in. Now that she was grown up she had lunch with Ardyne once a month or so, and sought out her advice while of course not confiding the disturbing details of her sexual and mental life. Ardyne seemed to understand that life was difficult for Wendy, and as far as possible she acted as a buffer between Wendy and her rigid family.

At the reception after the concert Ardyne introduced Wendy to a man whose face seemed oddly familiar. His name was Scott Carpenter and he came from a remote branch of a very old Midwest family whose money, originally made from the railroad expansion of the last century, had all been lost in the Depression.

Scott was about thirty and quite handsome in a freckled, boyish way. When Wendy told him he seemed familiar, he laughed.

'You have a good memory, then,' he said. 'That last time I saw you you were six years old and your mother was calling you in for bed. We were chasing fireflies on the lawn of your house in Lake Forest. That was the day I met you, and the last time I saw you.'

A dim memory stirred in Wendy, but slipped away before she could catch it.

'You're the one with the good memory,' she told him. 'What made you remember something so remote?'

'To be honest, I had a terrible crush on you,' he said. 'I was nine years old and you were this adorable little blond fairy. You were wearing a party dress which you had covered with grass stains, and there was something about you I never forgot.'

'What was it?' Wendy asked, interested.

'Your wildness, I suppose, combined with your delicacy.' He was looking at her through hazel eyes which betrayed a sentimental streak in his personality. 'You know, you haven't changed that much.'

Wendy frowned, wondering how much he had been told about her wild life. 'What do you mean?' she asked.

'You still look rather delicate to me,' he said. 'But I suppose you don't get many grass stains any more.'

'What about you?' she asked. 'What happened to you all these years? Why haven't I seen you?'

'We moved away after that summer,' he said. 'My parents got divorced. I lived with my mother in Florida. She found work as a secretary, then started her own business as a travel agent. She later remarried, but my stepfather died.' He looked around him at the aristocratic guests. 'I haven't been back to a North Shore gathering in all these years. Not since the day I played in your back yard, as a matter of fact.'

Wendy found herself having a good time. Scott Carpenter was an exotic creature to her. He came from her own society, but had spent his whole life far removed from it, in a modest lifestyle which she found refreshing. He knew nothing of her troubled girlhood or her wild ways. He still remembered her as a spirited little girl, and indeed still had a crush on her.

It was refreshing to be treated with so much respect by a man who was completely free of the prejudices that marked all those close to Wendy. She found herself opening up to Scott, first on general topics that interested her, and then about her own feelings. He drank her in eagerly, not judging her, but finding something to admire in all she said. When he talked about himself and his own life – he was a lawyer now, and would be returning to his practice in North Carolina after this visit – he was self-deprecating. Yet his intelligence shone through in everything he said, and so did a sensitivity Wendy was not used to in young men.

The operative issue was gotten over in a brief tactful exchange. Both Scott and Wendy were unattached, both were free agents. Scott took her to a lounge in the Drake Hotel, where they danced a couple of dances, then took her home in his cab, accepting her invitation to see her Gold Coast apartment for a nightcap.

'I've never seen such a beautiful apartment,' he said. He stood looking out the window at the lake and the traffic on the Outer Drive as she brought him a glass of brandy.

'Do you really think so?' Wendy asked. 'I'm so used to it now, it just looks like home.'

'I live in a little condo complex with a view of a parking lot and some railroad tracks,' Scott said. 'If you came from there you'd get a thrill out of this.'

She looked at her possessions through his eyes and had to admit they were impressive. The Aubusson carpet, the original paintings, the leather furniture, the fine crystal. They were lovely things. But they had all been bought with her father's money, and that tarnished any luster they might have had for Wendy. The only thing she bought with her own money was groceries. Even her clothes were far too expensive for her salary. She used her mother's credit card to pay for them.

'Coming from here, I'd probably get a thrill out of your place,' Wendy said.

Scott was looking at her curiously. 'Why do you say that?'

'Your place may be modest, but I'll bet there are no strings attached.'

'Only to the bank that holds the mortgage.' Scott was smiling, but her words had intrigued him. 'Do you mean family strings?'

She nodded. 'When you come from a background like mine, you miss having things that are completely your own.'

'I see what you mean,' he said. 'I suppose that's why they say money never brings happiness.'

He sipped at the brandy she had brought him. Wendy pondered the cruel simplicity of his words, and their rightness.

'What does bring happiness?' she asked.

Scott looked a bit taken aback. 'You're putting me on the spot,' he said.

'I didn't mean to.' Wendy sat down in the chair opposite him. 'I just wondered how someone like you would answer that.'

'Someone like me?'

She looked around her. 'Someone who doesn't live this life.'

'I'll tell you what,' he said. 'It's a hard question, but I promise to answer it if you'll answer it first.'

Now it was Wendy who felt cornered. A bitter look came over her face.

'Being your own person,' she said. 'Making your own mistakes and being able to learn from them. Not having to measure . . .'

'Measure what?'

'Measure up to ideas other people have about who and what you should be.'

These words had been spoken with undisguised anger. Scott was watching her with interest.

'That sounds odd, coming from you,' he said. 'You're such an independent person. I can't imagine anyone succeeding in telling you what to do.'

Wendy smiled sadly. How little he knew her!

'Now it's your turn,' she said. 'What makes you happy?'

'Being here with you.'

'Come on. Be serious.'

'I am serious. To me happiness means being able to leave my own boring alleys and wake up in a faraway place like this, with someone as unexpected as you.'

'Why do you say unexpected?' she asked.

'I'm not sure. I remember feeling that way about you when we were little.' He looked at his brandy glass, then at her. 'I was so dull, and you were so bright and airy and full of spirit. You haven't changed, you know. You really haven't.'

'Really.' His characterization amazed her. She considered herself a warmed-over person, a stale person without an ounce of real initiative or spontaneity. She hadn't done or even thought a thing in years that wasn't overladen with tired, empty misery. She wondered why he couldn't see that.

'I don't feel unexpected,' she said. 'I feel . . .' She let her words trail off. She didn't want him to know how she really saw herself.

'Lost?' he asked.

She nodded evasively. Yes, she felt lost. But that was only a small part of her unhappiness.

'I suppose it's natural to feel lost sometimes,' he said. 'But you're bright, you're beautiful and you have your whole life ahead of you. I think that's something to consider too.'

Wendy was still trying to get used to this unfamiliar version of herself when Scott looked at his watch and told her he had to go. He took his leave of her with a hug and a kiss on her cheek. When he was gone, she sat on her couch staring at the candle she had lit upon their arrival and savoring the strange sensations he had kindled in her.

It had been years since she had felt respected by anyone, much less admired. Her relatives and friends saw her as a scatterbrained, self-destructive brat who was not worthy of being taken seriously. Often she saw herself this way. She foresaw a long, empty life for herself, a life of cocktail parties, shopping for clothes, vacations in Hawaii or Europe, children, infidelity and constantly decreasing hopes ahead of her. It had been so long since she respected herself.

But Scott saw her as a lovely, talented girl with a future that was hers to create. And, in a way, she realized there was truth in his view, at least on an abstract level. Indeed, if she wanted to think of herself as someone worthy, someone lovable, what was to stop her? She had read the existentialists in college, like everyone else. One's life was a clean slate until one filled it with one's own choices. Despair was a choice, happiness was a choice.

She felt restless all at once. She paced the apartment, not sure what to do next. She was too keyed up to sleep. She looked at the clock. Only eleven-thirty. The night was young.

The compulsion to find a man came on her powerfully.

Scott had stirred some painful emotions in her, and the easiest way to salve them seemed to be a quick lay. She went to the closet, found one of her sexier outfits and quickly put it on. She stood looking in the mirror as she applied make-up.

Something stopped her. The girl in the mirror looked different. The face she was painting on, familiar and predictable, was trying to eclipse another face, one she had not dared to see for a long time. Wendy could not decide which way she wanted to go.

Still dressed in the tight outfit, she went to the phone and dialed Tony Garza's number. The four familiar rings sounded, then the sexy male voice with the music in the background. *'Hi, this is Tony. I can't come to the phone right now. Leave a message and I'll get back.'*

Wendy waited for the beep and said, 'This is me. Wendy. Are you home?' In the silence that followed she wondered whether Tony was out, or lying in the large bed with another girl beside him.

Pricked by jealousy, she hung up the phone and grabbed her purse, determined to go out and find another man at the nearest bar. But something stopped her. She stood listening to the silence of the apartment. The face of Dr Shader flashed before her mind.

*You're the one who decides who you are.* It was the doctor's voice she heard, echoing from one of their earliest sessions together. Wendy used to brag about being the plaything of other people's ideas about her. But Dr Shader never allowed her to get away with it. 'Pressures from other people are real,' she said, 'but the final decision is always your own. Learning to make that decision for one's self constitutes maturity.'

On an impulse Wendy went back to the full-length mirror and unzipped the tight dress, which fell to the floor around her feet. Her slender legs came free, her body clothed only by bikini panties and a tiny bra. She studied herself. For years she had looked in the mirror in two ways, first cynically appreciating her ability to attract the opposite sex, and then feeling a pulse of shame at the body she hated. The two impulses had come to be expressed by little physical tics: a raised eyebrow for the cynical self-appreciation, the curled lip and a small exclamation of disgust as the deeper shame made itself felt.

Tonight she looked different, because she felt different. Under her adult body she saw the little girl Scott Carpenter had admired. Idly she wondered how Scott's touch would feel on this body.

'Well, I guess I'm not going out,' she said aloud.

She hung the dress in the closet and took out a nightgown. Carrying it, she went into the living room, where the candle was still lit. She sat down on the couch, staring at the flame. Then she began to feel the cold, and got up and closed the curtains.

The apartment seemed empty. The silence was oppressive. Then, somehow, the emptiness and the silence were restful.

Wendy glanced at the phone.

*I wonder if he'll call.*

With that thought, she closed her eyes and fell into a completely unexpected sleep.

# CHAPTER 25

The Undertaker sat on the couch in his living room, staring at the Virgin.

She was young, pretty. She was not without the mild charm of all the Virgins painted by the old masters; but she was modern. A Virgin for our times. Fresh, young, full of energy and spirit.

She wore a business jacket and a blouse. Her hair was dark, worn in a conservative cut. Yet she was sensual. He had seen a publicity head shot of her with the hair brushed out in languorous waves. That shot had disturbed him. He had studied it with painful concentration, pondering the transformation of her purity into something so mysterious and sexy. He had spent hours trying to reconcile the two images.

In the end he had been forced to accept her as something multiple, a contradictory being in her essence. He thought about the great duality of Good and Evil, God and Satan. He realized there was a harmony of which evil was a part. Nevertheless her face troubled him, kept him awake at night. She could not be faithful to her own innocence.

There was a time, long ago, when his mother troubled him the same way. She had gotten rid of his father, 'to be alone with you,' so she said. She had spent long, languorous days with the boy, reading to him, cooking for him. This was before he started school. He quickly forgot about his father. His mother expanded to become his entire world.

A lot of the time she was naked. She said she liked being free and unencumbered when she was in her own home. She made the boy be naked with her. He was so small that it seemed natural to him. They took baths together. They slept in the same bed. Gradually he forgot that there had ever been a time before this intimacy.

Then there were men. He was startled the first time he saw one. She had gone out after supper, putting the boy to sleep, and came home with a strange man. They were laughing, talking loud. They fell asleep together. The boy peeked into the room, to the bed where he usually slept with his mother. A man's hairy body was draped over hers. The hairy center of the man rested against her hip as they snored together.

The parade of strangers made the boy feel like an outsider in his own home. He shrank into himself, to make room for the visitors and also to find safety. He was certain that sometime soon the men would be gone, as his father had gone, and she would be for him alone once more.

One night he peeked into her bedroom and saw her lying under a straining, grunting man, a stranger. Her legs were upraised, wrapped around the man's waist. The bouncing testicles alarmed the boy.

Then he saw something that filled him with horror. The man's sex was pumping deep into her private place, and when it came out it was covered with blood. In, out, in, out – redder each time, as though the hard shaft was destroying her stroke by stroke. And she did nothing to stop him. Her moans even seemed to encourage him. The ruined flesh anointing the staff . . . The boy was altered by what he saw. His eyes would never be the same again.

He felt tainted. He came to suspect that others could see the taint. When he went to school the other children made fun of him. He shrank into himself, trying to become invisible. He found ways to avoid being noticed. He polished the unremarkable surface of himself until he was like a pebble on the seashore, no different from a million other pebbles. Not worth picking up. Anonymous.

Each day he came home from school afraid of what he would find there. His mother was different now. She cried a lot. She drank whiskey and her breath had a sweet, stinky aroma. There were fewer men. She took the boy into her bed once in a while, but he didn't like being with her any more. Something about her repulsed him.

His withdrawal into himself seemed to have had unexpected effects. Since he hid so far beneath his own surface, he could no longer exert complete control over that surface. Things happened without him knowing about them. The teacher punished him for things he could not remember doing. His papers and exams came back with strange comments and bewildered questions. He had written things that upset the teacher.

One day he was taken out of his classroom by the principal and a police woman. His mother had died, he was told. He was taken to a shelter, where he remained several months until a foster family took him in. Whenever he heard adults talking about him there were murmurs about his mother and 'how she died'. He could feel the taint spreading deeper.

In sixth grade he was sent to the principal for fondling a little girl from the lower school. By now he was living with a foster family. When they were told what had happened, they sent him back to the shelter.

It became harder to find a home he could live in. He had to shrink further and further inside himself. They sent him to social workers, who asked odd questions, most of them about his mother. Through trial and error he found answers that made them leave him alone.

He moved from family to family. He was sent to special

schools. His grades improved. He was learning how to play the game. The disturbing ripples in his surface had disappeared. People paid less and less attention to him.

There was an older girl at the first special school. She let him play with her all he liked. She was thirteen. She met him in the woods beyond the playground and let him touch her. She tried to get him to put himself inside her, but he wouldn't do it. She asked him to use his tongue. The idea revolted him. He used his fingers. She would arch her back against the earth and beg him not to stop. One day he was pulling down her panties when he saw a string sticking out of her. She told him to pull it out, it didn't matter. He saw the blood, and that was when he wanted to kiss her, to taste her. She said that was disgusting, and never played with him after that.

Later he learned to go to prostitutes and ask them for that specific pleasure. They agreed willingly. He never had intercourse with them. Still he had never put his sex inside a woman. He would use his hand on himself while his face was covered with the blood of a whore.

It occurred to him that the very life of women was their blood, that he should see more of it. He asked one of them if he could cut her. She refused, saying not at any price. He asked around, tried others. They refused, saying they didn't want scars. In the end, maddened by frustration, he beat one of them senseless and used his pocket knife to cut her wrist. He drank the blood with great gasping moans.

By now he had found God and learned where the blood of women fit into the sacraments, the larger scheme of things. He realized his own actions and yearnings were not taking place in a vacuum, but had a moral context, a reason for being. He read the Bible and the great theologians, Pascal, Thomas Aquinas. They talked about communion, about Christ's blood and how we must drink it. About penance, about grace. Now he understood what he was doing, and why.

He was perfectly focused now. His grades were so high that it was easy for him to complete an advanced education and become a respected member of the community. He had friends, colleagues. He worked hard and distinguished himself. Sometimes women took an interest in him. He took them to dinner, talked to them, enjoyed the fact that they accepted him.

They couldn't see through him, but now he could see through them.

One night he killed a prostitute in a faraway city and drank as much of her blood as he could get down. As he lay admiring her body, it occurred to him that he must crucify her. He applied the wounds with care, devoutly. When the wound in her stomach beckoned to him, he entered her and gave her his seed, saying the appropriate prayers.

Now he knew what real communion was. His life took on a new clarity. He felt almost complete. The only thing he lacked was certainty regarding the future. He knew where he had been; he needed to know where he was going.

Then he found the Virgin. In that moment all his doubts about himself disappeared. He saw the entirety of his life, from its beginning to its end. He followed her, he studied her, he adored her.

*What love can do, that dares love attempt.*

His way was clear. She was his future. He prepared for his communion with her, which would be his last act.

Tonight he sat on his couch, staring at the image of her. Her hand was raised to a point just below her chin. This posture had become as integral to her image as the saints' inclined heads or Christ's body contorted by the Cross. She used this posture to speak. She was a teller of truth.

As always he marveled at her youth and innocence. Her girlish vitality filled his heart with yearning and pity and admiration. She was perfect. He was tainted. She was holy, he unholy.

'Darling,' he murmured. He was wet between his legs again. Anointed by her.

Sighing, he got up and went to the bathroom to clean himself. It seemed contradictory somehow, for his contact with her didn't sully him. On the contrary she cleansed him, she made him pure. And this was to be the crux of his approach to her when the time came.

After wiping his hands he put on his coat. He locked the house, got into the car, used the remote on the garage door and drove out into the night.

It was a beautiful night, clear and cold. One or two stars were bright enough to penetrate the city's canopy of haze. Beacons of hope atop the mire.

He took Lake Shore Drive into the Loop. He parked in a ramp and walked through the frigid wind to the hotel. He went through the lobby, pausing by a courtesy phone to glance at himself in the mirror. He heard the music from here. He followed it to the lounge, where a hostess led him to a table. He ordered a drink and turned his attention to the stage.

The musicians were in shadow. The girl was spotlighted, the microphone in her hand. She was sitting on a tall stool in classic torch-singer pose. Her dress was a dark burgundy, almost black. It made her skin glow pearly white under the bright lights. She wore loop earrings and a tiny necklace. Her hair, naturally auburn, fell over her shoulder. She was beautiful.

The tune was familiar, he had heard her sing it before. She had a husky crooning voice, rather subtle in the modulations from high to low, and quite striking in the low register. She had a way of using her hands to strike poses. She was schooled.

What attracted him was the contrast between her sophistication and her youth. She was only twenty-six years old; he had checked. The songs spoke of love, of longing, sometimes of cynicism and hopelessness. She sold the lyrics with all the facial cues of a much older woman. But her face was unlined, untouched by perversity. She was an angel singing the songs of a siren. A Virgin.

*Don't come back*, she sang. *I won't be here . . .*

The song was sad. She had lost her man.

*If you get lonely, call me last year.*

The conversations that were going on around the room ebbed as the seriousness of her words made the patrons take notice. This was just a hotel lounge, full of businessmen and bored bar patrons. But she was good at her craft, so good that sometimes she made them pay attention.

He nursed his drink, feeling his emotions stirred by her. In a spiritual sense he was amazed that he was actually in the same room with her. She was so exalted, while he was so impure. It was like a transgression of a spatial law.

He had felt that way the other night when he went into the detective's hospital room and found him with the two women. At first he had taken furtive pleasure from the notion that he was inside the enemy camp, if only for a moment. He had come in the expectation that Gold would be alone, or perhaps with his wife. Finding him with the psychiatrist and Meredith was a shock, a thrill.

He had to make his exit quickly, saying as little as possible and avoiding eye contact with them. But as he took the wounded detective's blood pressure he sensed the power of the two women behind him. Their beauty, their brains – and also their twoness, the sacred exponent of their charm. Four female breasts, twenty female fingers, four crystalline eyes focusing on him in that brief interval. If only they had said something, he could have taken their voices home with him and enjoyed them at his leisure. But they had fallen silent, waiting for him to leave.

He felt the same sense of invasion tonight. The singer sent out her words like omens that opened her very heart to him. And once in a while, as her eyes moved over the audience, they rested on him.

When she finished he applauded with the others. She had a shy, girlish way of acknowledging the applause, in striking contrast to her singing face, which was in character for the torch lyrics.

Though she sang all the usual numbers, and even took requests, it seemed to him that her natural inclination was to the saddest songs. He had read an interview with her in the Sunday *Tribune*, and she had told the reporter that the art of torch singing was dying out. 'The old songs have a lyricism and intensity that most of today's songs lack,' she said. 'We don't seem as focused on the tragedy of unrequited love as the songwriters were fifty years ago. That gives the songs a special poignancy.' She was articulate about what she did. Intelligent. Ambitious. She had not made a record yet, she was only a lounge singer, but she took her craft seriously and was honest about it. That was one thing that attracted him.

The other was her face. The way the spotlight framed it. The innocence of the eyes under the painted brows, the lips articulating the soft words of love and sadness.

The white pale skin and the lovely lush hair.

The blood coursing under the skin, making it glow.

*Hood my unmann'd blood, bating in my cheeks,*
*With thy black mantle; till strange love, grown bold . . .*

# CHAPTER 26

Susan was at the San Francisco airport, waiting for her flight to Chicago, when she learned that Calvin Wesley Train had been granted a new trial in the Harley Ann Saeger murder case.

The item was announced by a San Francisco anchor man whom Susan didn't recognize. It was not big news in California, so it was brief.

'Criminal defense attorney Alexander Penn won a victory for his client Calvin Wesley Train today,' said the anchor man. 'An appellate court judge in Madison, Wisconsin, granted Train a new trial after Penn argued that some of the key physical evidence in the case was mishandled by Wisconsin police.'

Susan did not have time to learn more about the decision until she got home. She called David Gold, who was furious at the news.

'Apparently they mislabeled a sample of the dead girl's blood,' Gold said, 'and introduced it into evidence for comparison with stains found on Train's pants. Pure bullshit, but the judge bought it.'

'Does this mean we're going to have to go through it all again?' Susan asked.

Gold knew she was really asking whether she would have to testify against Train again. 'Afraid so,' he said. 'I doubt that you'll have to interview the bastard again, but you will have to go up against Penn in the courtroom.'

This was bad news. Alexander Penn had been clever in the first trial, but Susan had managed to take him by surprise in her testimony. This time Penn would be ready for her, and would arm himself with a phalanx of defense psychiatrists to debunk her diagnosis of Train's character disorder and her claim that he was legally responsible for his crime.

It would be ugly. And there was little doubt that Penn would attack Susan by virtue of her record as a psychic.

She wanted to feel optimistic about the probable outcome of the second trial, but in today's criminal justice system anything was possible. Recent trials had made clear that in the hands of clever attorneys the truth can be only one small item in a blizzard of innuendo and suggestion.

Oh, well, she thought. This was why David Gold and his cop friends hated lawyers and judges so much.

When Susan arrived at Michael Reese, she was surprised to find Meredith Spiers sitting beside the bed in Gold's hospital room.

'Fancy meeting you here,' Susan said.

'She's got another message from her mystery man,' he said.

'How are you doing, Doctor?' Meredith asked.

'Not so good,' Susan said. 'You heard the news about Alexander Penn, I presume.'

Meredith nodded. 'Yeah, here we go again.'

She handed Susan a hard copy of another e-mail.

'This one seems off the wall to me,' she said. 'But I don't see how we can ignore it.'

Gold's best efforts to identify the source of the leaks had so far failed. However, through the stories he had confected with Meredith he had managed to keep the public in ignorance of the more sensational aspects of the murders. And the leaks had not dried up. Whoever was behind them seemed satisfied with the way Meredith was reporting the stories.

Susan read the brief message on the page.

'*He is in the arts,*' it said. '*He comes from Baltimore.*'

Susan looked at Gold. 'Do you understand this?'

'Hell, no,' Gold said. 'It's gibberish. There's nothing like this in the case.'

'You don't suppose this could be a lead that Weathers is following on his own?' Meredith asked. 'Or perhaps a lead the FBI has turned up . . .'

Gold grimaced. 'What are you saying?'

The reporter was silent, embarrassed. The obvious conclusion was that Weathers or the FBI had kept David Gold in ignorance of an important part of the case. Most probably because of his wound.

'I can't believe they would cut me out,' Gold said. 'Unless . . .'

'Unless what?' Meredith asked.

'Never mind,' Gold said. 'There's always politics, you know that. I suppose anything is possible.' He was thinking hard.

Susan was running her finger slowly over the lines of text on the page.

'What do you think?' Gold asked her.

She seemed thoughtful.

'I can't feel much,' she said. 'But I sense there is truth in here somewhere. Possibly disguised.'

'I'm gonna talk to some guys tomorrow,' Gold said. 'I need to know if Weathers already knows about this. If he doesn't, he has to be told.'

He gave a disgusted sigh. 'First Train's new trial, now this,' he said. 'Welcome to the criminal justice system.'

Meredith Spiers was looking sympathetically at Gold. She had come to like him a lot. His helpless condition made him seem less forbidding, more human. She liked his fatherly protectiveness toward her. It had been a long time since anyone took that kind of interest in her. She also enjoyed having Jewishness in common with him.

But she realized she had not brought him good news. The killer was still at large, and the investigation itself seemed to be slipping out of Gold's grasp.

Meredith took her leave after another couple of minutes. Susan came to Gold's side.

'There's something else I've been wanting to tell you about,' she said, indicating by her look that she had waited for Meredith to leave before broaching the subject.

'Something that's going to piss me off?' Gold asked. 'I've had my fill of bad news for today.'

'Something that may help,' Susan said. 'It's very tenuous, though, so I've been hesitant to mention it.'

'What is it?'

'Do you remember the religious signals I got in Mary Ellen Mahoney's apartment?' she asked. 'Something about a virgin. I've been getting that more and more. I have the feeling that the killer has a woman in his mind. It could be someone from his past. He calls her a virgin, or thinks of her as a virgin.' She thought for a moment. 'Possibly with a capital V. Like the Virgin Mary.'

'Uh-huh.' Gold's eyes were on the ceiling.

'She is like a Platonic Idea,' Susan said. 'And the victims are like simulacra of that idea.' She was remembering her philosophy from college.

'Can you talk English?' Gold grunted.

'Sorry.' She laughed. 'I think he sees these other women as lesser versions of the woman in his mind.'

'Clones.'

'Yes, I suppose you could say that.'

'Someone real? Someone he knows?'

'Or someone he once knew, someone he remembers,' she said. 'Whoever it is, or was, she symbolized youth and innocence to him.'

She looked out his window at the black evening sky. It was bitter cold outside.

'Virgin Mary,' Gold said. 'You mean like immaculate conception?'

Susan nodded. 'The killer is obviously worried about the womb as the site of sexual reproduction,' she said. 'Hence his obsession with abortion, and the fact that he doesn't touch his victims' genitals. The image of the Virgin would be highly reassuring to him. She conceived Christ and gave birth without sexual intercourse.'

'Is that why he puts his semen into her abdominal wound?' Gold asked. 'To avoid the vagina?' He reddened a bit at the thought of discussing sexual things so openly with a woman.

'The abdomen is where small children think babies grow,' Susan said.

'It's also where Christ had his wound.'

Susan nodded. 'If there is a real woman in his mind, he must have or have had an enormous obsession with her. He wants to harm her, but also to worship her, to put her on a pedestal.' She thought for a moment. 'There is a kind of man who covets virgins,' she said. 'The ultimate sexual fulfillment for such men is to deflower a virgin. I've had patients who have that preference. It shows great ambivalence. A respect for innocence which also sullies that innocence.'

'But this guy picks out pregnant girls,' Gold added. 'Girls who have had abortions, or are thinking about them. The opposite of virgins.'

'And instead of sleeping with them he kills them,' Susan

said. 'Of course, murder is a kind of intercourse, at least in a psychological sense.'

There was a silence as they both thought this over.

'David,' Susan said at length, 'there's one more thing I've been hesitating to mention to you. I don't want to muddy the waters, but it keeps recurring.'

'What is it?' Gold asked.

'Something about the Shakespeare play *Romeo and Juliet*. I got some signals from it at Miranda Becker's apartment. At first I thought it might have been in Miranda's mind, or perhaps she'd been reading the play. But I've been picking up on it everywhere else as well, including California. Lines from the play, images from it. I can't ignore it any longer.'

'What makes you think it's important?'

'One thing above all. In the play Juliet is a virgin. She falls in love with Romeo and wants to have him deflower her, but the conflict between their two families and Romeo's banishment after he kills Tybalt prevent the consummation from taking place. In the end Juliet dies a virgin.'

'Hmm.' Gold's voice was noncommittal. Susan suspected the literary reference didn't interest him.

'I'm sorry,' she said. 'I don't want to make things more complicated than they already are . . .'

'Don't worry about it,' Gold replied. 'You know police work. Anything can be important.'

'Yes, I guess so.'

Again there was a pause. Gold was looking at the TV mounted on the wall. The face of Abel Weathers was on the screen. Weathers, wearing his patented steely-eyed frown, was responding to an interviewer's question. The sound was turned off, so Susan could not hear what Weathers was saying. But his angry eyes could not conceal his enjoyment of the attention he was getting. Beside her she saw Gold smiling slightly at the screen. He was thinking the same thing she was.

He looked up at Susan. 'Who do you think she is?' he asked.

'Who?'

'This virgin. The one in the Undertaker's mind.'

'I don't know who she might be, or even whether she's real,' Susan replied. 'It might even be . . .'

Gold's eyes looked vacant. She realized he was too tired to talk any more.

'Anyway,' she said, 'I'll keep working on it.' She touched his hand. 'Take care of yourself.'

'Right. Keep in touch.'

She saw him lapsing into anesthetic-drugged sleep as she closed the door.


The Undertaker was washing his hands.

He looked at his face in the small mirror. Excitement, expectation. He dried the hands carefully, feeling his fingers tremble.

He fixed his hair, straightened his tie. He wanted to look good for her.

He mouthed a few words to himself in the mirror, an old incantation. Then he left the bathroom.

He went down the stairs and entered the basement room with a professional smile on his lips.

'Feeling groggy?' he asked with a smile.

The singer was lying naked on the mattress in the middle of the floor. Under her was a plastic tarpaulin, extra large. Her wrists were tied to the corners, her feet bound together at the bottom.

'Just a couple of things I have to do,' he said. 'Don't worry.'

He took her pulse. 100, predictable. Her breathing was shallow. Her eyes followed every move he made.

He found the vein at her elbow. He tied the tourniquet around her arm and pulled it tight.

'I need some blood for the ransom,' he said. 'Once they know it's your type, they'll give me what I need, and you can go home. Blood is better than teeth or ears or whatever, because your body replaces it.'

She seemed to be trying to say something.

'Never mind,' he said. 'There's no need to talk. This will just take a moment.'

He inserted the needle and got into the vein. She was staring at the bag.

'You may feel a little weakness when you stand up,' he said, 'but I'm here to help you if you need me.'

She watched her blood fill the bag. He could feel her fighting her own panic. She was praying he had told her the truth.

'That's a good vein,' he said.

He bent to kiss her breast. A stifled cry in her throat.

'Stop that,' he said. 'You'll ruin your singing voice. Nobody's going to hurt you.'

The bag was full now. He removed the needle from her arm and undid the tourniquet. He took the bag away and labeled it.

When he came back he was naked from the waist down. He carried another blood bag with him, this one full.

She thrashed spasmodically on the mattress. Blood from the needle puncture was flowing down her arm in a ribbon of red. Her skin was very white.

'It's all right,' he said. 'I'm not going to hurt you. Just stay calm. Remember, the important thing is to relax.'

But he had stiffened between his legs at the sight of her blood. And she saw.

He straddled her, his genitals against her pelvis. The scalpel was in his hand.

'Now hold still,' he said.

She knew who he was now, and what was to happen. Her eyes opened wider. The knowledge made her beautiful. An epiphany, he thought.

He made the incision in her palm. Sweetly, shyly, the blood came forth to greet him. His sex was on fire.

'Good girl,' he said. 'Brave girl.'

The long knife was at his side. The hands and feet would be done in another minute, and it would be time to finish it. But the sight of her wounded hand was too much for him. He bent to kiss it.

'This is my blood,' he said through dripping lips.

# CHAPTER 27

The name of the Undertaker's third victim was Marcie Webb.

She was reported missing when she did not show up for her Thursday performance at the Palmer House. The Homicide squad was on the alert, worried about the Undertaker, and an all-points bulletin was immediately put out on the missing singer.

When her body was found in a dumpster at a rest stop on Interstate 94, the body bag alerted the police to the Undertaker's MO, and a top-secret crime scene was created, with all media kept at least a mile away and no comment from the police about the crime or the victim.

The scene was scoured by crime scene techs and forensic specialists for twelve hours, with no success. Unfortunately it had been raining heavily at the time the body was dumped, so tire impressions or shoe prints were out of the question. When the body was taken downtown to the Medical Examiner's office, the usual array of evidence was found inside the body bag, along with the corpse of a twenty-seven-year-old woman.

The pattern of wounds was identical to those of the first two victims. Wounds in the pattern of Christ's stigmata had been carefully applied, and foreign blood poured into the wounds to the hands and feet. Semen was found in the deep abdominal wound.

Blood analysis was the top priority. There were at least

three foreign blood types present, possibly more. The FBI labs had now completed the DNA analysis of Miranda Becker's blood, and it was matched to one of the three. A second, tentatively identified by standard typing procedures, belonged to Mary Ellen Mahoney. The third type, 0, which matched the semen and saliva present, was presumed to belong to the Undertaker himself.

The Chief Medical Examiner determined that Marcie Webb had had an abortion, between a year and two years prior to her death.

Susan spent a painful half-hour at the ME's office, studying the body of Marcie Webb. Everything was the same. Even in the more florid moments of his sexual delirium the killer had stuck to his pattern.

'It seems clear that he applies the first incisions while the victim is still alive,' Wes Ganzer said. 'He gets off on the flow of blood. And, of course, he has to take some of her blood while she is alive.' He pointed to a needle mark at the corpse's elbow. 'He has some knowledge of anatomy,' he said. 'He knows how to take blood. I can't help thinking military. The body bag, the stabbing MO – this guy could be a veteran, a medic.'

Wes Ganzer had three grown daughters, two of whom were married. He was visibly disturbed by the Undertaker's victims, all young women close in age to his daughters. Each time she looked at him Susan saw increasing exasperation in his eyes. He was wondering when the police would catch up with the killer and end the agony.

Joe Riccio accompanied Susan to the small furnished room downtown where Marcie Webb had lived.

The place was obviously only a *pied à terre* for use when the singer was in the city. Marcie Webb's primary residence was her parents' home in Baltimore. She had visited them only two weeks ago. She kept most of her wardrobe at their house, and all of her memorabilia of childhood, high school and college.

'She was a home town girl,' Riccio told Susan. 'Had a lot of friends in Baltimore. Her professional career was moving slowly. She was thinking of setting up a little apartment in Manhattan, because most of the work is there. But she liked Chicago, according to her mother, and enjoyed working here.'

A poster of the 1997 NBA Champion Chicago Bulls was on the wall beside the late singer's telephone. But Susan barely saw it. She was pondering what Riccio had said about Marcie Webb.

*Baltimore.*

David Gold was being released from the hospital today. Susan would not be able to see him until tonight. She wondered whether he had drawn the same conclusions as she had about Marcie Webb's home town.


The singer's agent had flown in from New York the night before, and met Susan and Riccio at the apartment. A surprisingly elegant, urbane gentleman who looked more like a bank president than a music agent, he introduced himself as Orson Myers.

'This is terrible,' he said. 'Marcie was on her way to a great career. I really can't believe it.'

According to Myers, Marcie had finally scored a recording contract with a small record label based in Chicago.

'She had a growing local following,' he said. 'People know talent when they see it, and Marcie was very precocious. She had a maturity far beyond her years. If she had lived I think she would have become a star, as big as Maureen McGovern or Diana Krall, maybe bigger. This is just a tragedy.'

'Were you in close touch with her?' Susan asked.

'Reasonably close, for an agent,' Myers said. 'We spoke on the phone at least twice a week. I would call to ask how her sets at the Palmer House were going. She was very upbeat this last month or two. Excited about her singing, excited about the recording contract. We were picking out tunes and looking for musicians.' He shook his head sadly.

'Did Marcie express any concern or fear about anyone bothering her, following her, anything like that?' Riccio asked. 'Unwanted phone calls? Anything along those lines?'

The agent shook his head. 'No, not at all. She was upbeat, as I said. I wasn't aware of anything out of the ordinary.'

The manager of the hotel lounge, a man named Bob Inkster, was not much more helpful.

'Marcie always showed up on time, always did her work carefully and well,' he said. 'She never gave me a moment's concern. That's a rare quality among musicians, in case you didn't know. They can be unstable, temperamental. Alcohol tends to be a problem. But Marcie was a complete professional.' He shook his head. 'I'm going to miss her. This is a terrible thing. A terrible thing.'

In answer to Susan's question about threats to the singer, the manager shook his head. 'The usual occasional heckler. Some of these businessmen get drunk and make a nuisance. That's all.'

Susan got the impression that both men, Myers and Inkster, had had something of a crush on Marcie. Their grief was personal as well as professional. Susan wished she had seen the singer perform, but she had never even heard of her until her murder. The publicity photo that had been blown up into a poster at the front door of the lounge showed a fresh-faced redhead with freckles who looked somewhat unnatural in a fancy strapless evening gown and dramatic make-up. Marcie had been a very pretty young woman. Her eyes were her most impressive feature. They had the sparkle of youth, along with something melancholy and deep beyond her years.

The agent gave Susan a copy of the tape that had brought the recording contract, and Susan listened to it at home. Indeed, Marcie Webb was a very talented young artist. Her singing technique was flawless, and there was considerable depth in the way she handled lyrics.

Susan listened to the tape from beginning to end. There were several standards that were all sung with great eloquence and assurance, like 'These Foolish Things' and 'Ghost of a Chance'. Marcie Webb had also dared to perform the legendary Billie Holiday classic 'Travelin' Light', in a startling arrangement of her own which succeeded in selling the song without slavishly imitating the great singer's style or mannerisms.

But the highlight of the tape was a song entitled 'Call Me Last Year'. Composed by Marcie Webb herself, it had sad, somewhat bitter lyrics, evocative of a failed love affair, and they suited the subtle melody very well.

Susan could not get the song out of her mind. She found herself humming it on her way to work, and she listened to the tape again when she got home. Gradually she realized that something more than the song's musical qualities was preying on her mind.

She called Bob Inkster to ask him about the song, and he told her it was often requested at the Palmer House. He showed her the *Tribune* magazine article about Marcie Webb, in which the song was mentioned prominently.

The tragic loss evoked by 'Call Me Last Year' was too authentic to have been merely imaginary, Susan felt. Marcie Webb must have had an unsuccessful love affair somewhere along the line. That affair had perhaps been the source of her pregnancy and her abortion.

When Susan arrived at David Gold's little house in Franklin Park she saw Meredith Spiers's Honda parked outside on the street. Meredith herself answered the door. Gold was sitting in his favorite easy chair in the living room, wearing a V-necked sweater that looked new. He looked surprisingly normal, as though his unfortunate accident had never occurred.

'Want something to drink?' he asked.

'No, thanks. How are you feeling?'

'Functional.'

'Where's Carol?'

'Out shopping. She didn't have enough food in the house. I spent all of last week making up a list for her. I'm gonna chow down. Have to get my strength back.'

He gestured to Meredith. 'Do you want to say it, or shall I?'

'From Baltimore,' Meredith said. 'In the arts.'

Susan nodded, taking off her coat.

'Now we know the meaning of Meredith's e-mail,' Gold said. 'The bastard was telling us who his next victim was going to be. Marcie Webb was in the arts, a singer. She was from Baltimore.'

'We only had to substitute *she* for *he*,' said Meredith.

'So much for the leak theory,' Gold said. 'No wonder I couldn't find him. There's no leak. Your e-mails have come from the killer.'

They sat thinking that over for a long moment.

'I suppose we shouldn't be surprised,' Gold said. 'Serial killers love to taunt the police. The bastard couldn't resist.'

Meredith looked unnerved. 'I'm new at this part of journalism,' she said. 'Why did he pick me?'

Gold studied her face.

'You're pretty,' he said. 'You're attractive. Ten to one he simply has a crush on you.'

Susan had turned to look at Meredith as well.

'You're very visible,' she said. 'Channel 9 has been showcasing you for a couple of years now. And you were the first to report on the death of Miranda Becker. Serial killers have a complex relationship with both the police and the press. They taunt the police, but they also have a deep need of approval from authority figures. Quite often they will appear at the scene of their own homicides to help out as witnesses. Like arsonists. The police have learned to take careful note of all those who are to be found near homicide scenes. Often the killer is among them.'

'This guy gets around,' Gold said. 'If Susan's intuition was right, he was in my room at the hospital. I had Terrell talk to the nurses and the administrator. Nobody saw anything unusual.'

He looked at Susan. 'What did you find in her apartment?'

'Almost nothing,' Susan said. 'It was as impersonal as a hotel room. She put nothing of herself into it. I gather she kept most of her personal things in Baltimore at her parents' house. She was quite close to them, and to a lot of Baltimore friends.'

'We'll check out the Baltimore friends,' Gold said. 'I think you should go over to the Palmer House and have a good look at the lounge where she did her singing. Also the dressing room. See what you can pick up.'

'All right,' Susan said.

'Meredith,' Gold turned to the reporter – 'obviously you can't report the e-mail. I'll call Weathers and see if we can come up with something appropriate to give out. But there might be a silver lining here. Ten to one you'll be hearing from this guy again. When you do, we want to be ready.'

'How can we be ready?' Meredith asked. 'He's got the initiative. He's holding all the cards. We can't read his mind.'

She glanced at Susan, as though wistfully hoping that Susan's second sight could somehow rescue their collective effort. Gold was looking at Susan too, a reflective look in his eyes.

'We'll see,' he said. 'Time will tell.'

'By the way,' Meredith said, 'Has anybody noticed that all three victims have first names starting with the initial M?'

Gold looked at her. 'No, I hadn't.'

Susan shook her head.

'Maybe I noticed because my own name begins with M,' Meredith said. 'I suppose it's nothing, but . . .'

'Maybe it's not nothing,' Gold said thoughtfully.

Susan could see the notion connected to something in his mind which he did not want to talk about yet.


From Gold's house Susan drove downtown to the Palmer House, where Joe Riccio was waiting for her. They went into the lounge where Marcie Webb had performed. The room was silent, roped off from the lobby. A small sign apologized to the hotel guests for the temporary closure without mentioning its cause.

Susan took a long, slow walk around the empty room. It had a rug, which was quite dirty when viewed with the lights turned up. The bandstand was small, just big enough for the trio that had accompanied the singer. Sophisticated sound and lighting equipment was in evidence.

'How many nights a week did Marcie perform?' Susan asked the manager.

'Every night but Sunday,' he said. 'She did two shows, one at nine and one at eleven-thirty.'

'Were you here for her shows?' Susan asked.

'Usually, yes.'

'Do you remember any regular patrons? Anyone who requested songs?'

The manager thought for a moment. 'She got a lot of requests,' he said. 'She had a large repertoire for such a young singer, and she enjoyed performing different things. Also, as time went by, she got more requests for her signature items. "Travelin' Light" was one of them. And, of course, "Call Me Last Year," which was becoming well known.'

'Do you remember any particular faces?' Susan asked.

'Not offhand,' he said.

Susan wandered the room, circulating slowly among the tables. She stopped at one near the door and motioned to Joe Riccio.

'I'm getting a feeling from this one,' she said.

Riccio came to her side. He was watching her without expression. Like all the detectives, he knew David Gold trusted her insights completely. If he himself was skeptical, he didn't show it. He simply waited for her to continue.

'He came here many times,' Susan said. 'He requested songs. He sent her flowers. He – he always ordered the same drink. He was obsessed with her.' She thought for a moment. 'That's all I'm getting.'

'We'll talk to the cocktail waitresses,' Riccio said. 'One of them might remember a face.'

Susan nodded. She stood as though listening for something. Then she gave up and went backstage to the singer's dressing room.

The room was small and dirty, like all dressing rooms in theaters and nightclubs. But the vanity had been kept relatively neat by the singer. There were jars of make-up, flasks of powder, combs and brushes and hair-care products.

'Have they dusted everything here?' Susan asked Riccio.

'Yup. Touch anything you want.'

In one of the desk drawers Susan found an expanding wallet that contained fan mail. Most of it was addressed to Marcie Webb, Singer, c/o The Palmer House'. Some of it had found its way to her agent and been forwarded to her. There were no more than two dozen letters. Apparently Marcie had kept the letters for sentimental reasons, since they were the first of her career.

Susan read them one by one. Most were handwritten, with rather poor spelling and grammar, but all were admiring of the singer's talent and dedication to her craft.

Susan studied the ink on all the letters, looking for a signal of some kind. But nothing came.

She touched the impersonal make-up bottles on the vanity. She sat down on the chair and looked in the mirror. She was receiving signals that suggested worry, nervousness. But that could be consistent with the singer's keyed-up state of mind in the moments before each performance.

She looked at herself in the mirror. Her eyes narrowed. Something else was trying to make itself felt. Mirrors were a powerful tool for a psychic, because people who looked at their own reflections were always feeling the intense emotions that go with narcissism. Marcie Webb had felt something more than mere performance sweat in front of this mirror. Something had worried her, something had preyed on her mind.

Susan thought of the seat out in the lounge where she had sensed an obsession with the singer on the part of a regular patron. Could Marcie Webb have felt a threat somewhere in the audience?

She looked at the mirror again, but saw only the reflection of her own tired face. Her second sight had run dry, at least for now.

Susan got up and found Joe Riccio outside the door.

'Let's go.'

'Any luck?'

'Nothing definite.'

Susan called Gold from one of the lobby phones to tell him what she had found.

'I got nothing from the fan letters,' she said. 'I did get a feeling from one of the tables in the lounge, though. Someone came here often to hear her sing. Someone whose interest wasn't just musical. But I couldn't pin it down.'

She didn't mention the diffuse sense of anxiety she had felt in the singer's vanity mirror.

'By the way,' Gold said. 'Meredith's crack about the initial M. I'm not inclined to throw that out.'

'Three victims with the same initial?' Susan said. 'It seems remote, but I suppose . . .'

'It wouldn't be the first time a serial killer has picked out girls by their names or initials,' Gold said.

'I guess so,' Susan said without particular enthusiasm.

'And there's one more, if you think about it,' Gold said. 'Especially if your own theory is right.'

'What?' Susan asked.

'The Virgin Mary. That's another M.'

With those words echoing in her mind, Susan said good night.

# CHAPTER 28

Scott Carpenter called Wendy to ask her out.

They went to see *L.A. Confidential*, which was being shown again at a theater in the Loop. They both enjoyed the movie, though Wendy was privately a bit unnerved by Kim Basinger's role as a call girl. Kim Basinger's blond looks were similar enough to Wendy's to remind her of all the nights she had spent with strange men. But the movie's complicated plot and fast-moving narration distracted her, and after it was over Scott took her to a little restaurant on Ontario Street where they had a late snack.

Their conversation began with the movie. Wendy remarked, somewhat challengingly, that the Basinger character, a call girl made up to look like Veronica Lake, was a good commentary on men's use of women.

'They want to dress us up like movie stars, or models,' she said. 'Creatures out of their own fantasy life. I once read an article written by a prostitute. She insisted that what she did for money was not different at all from what most women did as wives and mothers – acting out men's fantasy of what they should be.'

'I'm afraid there's some truth in that,' Scott said. 'It's a mercy that the housewives and girlfriends don't end up like the prostitutes.'

'What do you mean?' Wendy asked.

'Oh, the dope addiction, the beatings. All that,' Scott said.

'Some wives do get beaten,' Wendy said. 'Killed, even. By jealous husbands.'

'Yes, I see what you mean.' Scott looked thoughtful. 'And even if they don't, they can be psychologically beaten into submission by the whole process. Spiritually beaten.'

'What do you mean by spiritually?' Wendy asked.

He thought for a moment. 'I think I mean that when the role you're forced to play in society removes your own sense of who you really are, that's a kind of spiritual impoverishment. Life is hard enough as it is. The one thing we should own is our own self. It's terrible to lose that.'

Wendy was silent. This was a sore point with her. She had always felt she had little control over herself and even less self-knowledge.

Scott shrugged. 'In a way we men are equally hard on ourselves. When we look in the mirror we measure our resemblance to Tom Cruise or Harrison Ford or Donald Trump. Whichever male icon is the best-looking, the toughest, the richest. Sometimes I wonder whether we see ourselves at all.'

Wendy thought of the women's magazines she read. *Cosmo* and the rest. Scott's point was valid for women as well as men. Rare was the woman whose self-image wasn't mediated by a thousand photographs of skinny models and movie stars.

But a combative impulse made her challenge Scott again. 'There's a difference, though,' she said.

'What difference?'

'It's the men who do the choosing,' she said.

'Not always.'

'What do you mean?'

He smiled. 'Look at you, for instance. You can have any man you want.'

'Why?'

'Well, you're beautiful, for one thing. You're bright. You're interesting. You're pretty much everything a man could desire in a woman.'

Wendy sighed. He could not know how far off the mark he really was.

'I'm sorry,' he said quickly. 'That was stupid of me. No one is immune to the pressures of sex roles. I just meant – to me you seem so self-sufficient, so full of originality and character. I can't imagine you being enslaved by anything.'

Wendy had to smile at his characterization of her. It was completely inaccurate, but it indicated so much admiration for her that it was almost worth more than the truth.

Still she felt the need to push him. 'Aren't those qualities yet another description of a man's fantasy? A description of what you want in a woman?'

'You're not a fantasy,' he corrected her. 'You're real. You're not made according to any man's recipe. Besides,' he said smiling, 'wanting isn't getting.'

'What do you mean?' Wendy asked.

'I can't help feeling that you're a bit out of my league,' he said. 'That's one reason I feel relaxed with you.'

*He means I'm rich.* Quick to deprecate herself at any opportunity, Wendy managed to take his compliment in the most unflattering sense possible.

The restaurant's walls were mirrored. As he toyed with his half-empty wine glass, Scott looked at Wendy's reflection. Her body seemed twisted uncomfortably in her chair. She was hunched over her drink, an intent look in her eyes. Her hair flowed over her cheeks, a strand grazing Scott's own hand.

'I've always wondered what it's like to look in the mirror and see someone there who is genuinely good-looking,' he said.

She looked up at him, surprised. 'You're good-looking,' she said.

'No, I'm not.' He shook his head. 'I just look like a person.'

She felt an impulse to argue the point, but gave it up.

'Anyway,' she said. 'I don't see what others see. I see the real me. That's not so pleasant.'

'You're pretty hard on yourself, aren't you?' he observed.

Wendy looked away. She saw Scott in the mirror, his face askance because he was looking directly at her. He had fine hands, she noticed. The hands of someone who could do fine, detailed work. The fingers touching his wine glass looked very relaxed.

'Tell me,' she asked, 'What do you see when *you* look in the mirror?'

He thought for a moment. Then he gave her a sheepish grin. 'Are you sure you want to know?'

'Yes. I want to know.'

'Do you remember *The Little Rascals*?'

'Yes.'

'Do you remember Alfalfa?'

'The boy with the freckles and the cowlick?'

Scott smiled. 'There was once an episode about Alfalfa having a date with a little girl. He was shown primping in front of the mirror. He kept slicking down his cowlick, and it kept popping back up while a sound like *Boing!* was heard on the soundtrack. That's how I see myself. Like a kid with a cowlick and lots of freckles, trying foolishly to look smooth and grown-up.'

Something about this description charmed Wendy.

'You don't have a cowlick, though,' she said.

'Ah,' he corrected her. 'That's because you're looking at me through your eyes. If you looked through mine, you would see it only too clearly.'

*Touché*, she thought. *Maybe he suffers, too, in front of a mirror.*

'You do have freckles, though,' she observed.

'More, in the summer,' he said. 'Especially when I play tennis. Do you play tennis?'

She nodded.

'We'll have to play some time.' Scott gave her a hospitable smile.

She was still looking at his freckles. They were endearing, she decided. The Alfalfa comparison had pleased her.

'Would you like to come back to my place for a brandy?' she asked.

'I'd love it.'

When they came in the door Scott smiled broadly. 'This is great,' he said.

'What is?' she asked.

'I recognize everything here,' he said. 'I've seen it before. I know your place. Two weeks ago I had no idea where in the world you were, what had become of you. Now I know. That's a small miracle to me.'

She served him a brandy and sat down on the couch beside him.

'I'm sorry for what I said in the restaurant,' she said.

'Don't be sorry. You didn't say anything out of line.'

'I said it to test you,' she explained. 'A lot of men don't like hearing that kind of thing.'

'Well, maybe it makes them uncomfortable,' Scott said. 'It makes me uncomfortable, but not because you said it. I can't blame the reporter for the bad news.' He thought for a moment. 'I guess our sex roles don't bring out the best in us sometimes,' he said. 'I'm glad there's more to life than just that.'

Wendy looked at him through narrowed eyes. 'What more?'

'Oh, everything,' he said. 'Music, laughter, movies, books.

Talking, like we're talking now. Having children. You know—living.'

'Oh.' Wendy could not put into words, even to herself, the hopelessness his words had made her feel. Simple things like living seemed light years removed from her.

She sat back against the cushions, letting her thigh graze his own. She felt exposed, nervous. But when he put his arms around her the warmth of his embrace was almost indistinguishable from that of his conversation. The touch of his lips was a thing given rather than an overture to an exploitation of her.

The response of her body shocked her. She felt alarmed, then excited. She returned his kiss, curling her arms around his neck. She liked the taste and feel of him. A flutter of heat went through her, and she guided his hand to her waist.

A cruel little voice inside her mind urged her to get him into bed right away. To use him, to enjoy him. But as he held her closer she felt something else, something new, which threw her off balance.

She stopped him, pressing her hand to his chest.

'I'm sorry.' She sat back. 'I guess I'm not quite ready for . . .' Her voice trailed off. Not quite ready for what? The word on the tip of her tongue would not reveal itself.

'Of course,' he said. 'Let me hold you.'

She got up and closed the curtains. Then she came back to him. She curled her legs under her and put her head on his shoulder.

'Just rest,' he said. And after a moment, 'You're so beautiful.'

*Beautiful.* Wendy closed her eyes, letting the word calm her. She had the oddest feeling that in crossing the path of this man who knew her so little, she was coming back to herself. She was grateful their closeness had gone no further.

Yet she felt closer to him than to any man who had touched her in years.

*Intimacy.* That was the word that had come to her lips, the word she couldn't say.

Across the street Tony Garza stood in the shadows.

It was bitter cold. The lake wind hurled itself across the Outer Drive like a sea monster. But Tony didn't feel it. His body was smoldering under his coat. His hands were clenched.

He knew which window was Wendy's. He had stood here before, watching her, waiting for her silhouette to pass the window, waiting to see what time she turned out the lights.

She had closed the curtains because they were going to fuck. That was obvious.

He had followed them from the moment the fellow picked her up. One of her society faggots, he thought. Just the sort of marshmallow her parents would have picked out for her. They went to a movie together and a late snack, like two nice college kids, and now they were back at her place, where she had invited the fellow in.

Tony knew he was right about Wendy. He had called it from the first night she ever slept with him. She was the creature of her aristocratic parents, a wild young girl who had no mind of her own. Her rebellion had brought her into Tony's bed, where she had known a kind of loving that no man in her society could ever give her. But in the end, an obedient daughter, she would disappear into the life that was prepared for her by her family.

That is, if Tony let her.

And she would perhaps remember Tony in her fantasies. Perhaps she was thinking about him right now, as her boyfriend fucked her.

That's all Tony would ever be to her—a memory.

Tonight, standing alone in the freezing cold while she spread her legs for another man behind that closed curtain, Tony could feel her receding into her separate existence, secure in the knowledge that nothing could touch her, nothing could interfere with her plans.

'Bitch,' he said aloud. 'I'll give you something to remember me by.'

# CHAPTER 29

After the court's decision to grant Calvin Wesley Train a new trial, the Wisconsin prosecutors had seventy-two hours in which to recharge Train with the murder of Harley Ann Saeger.

A bureaucratic snafu occurred, mostly because the State's Attorney was still reeling from the appellate decision. The paperwork for the new charge was given to the new chief assistant, who had been hired only three months ago. The chief assistant's office staff were inexperienced and hampered by the illness of the head legal secretary.

When one of the prosecutors became aware, almost by accident, that the time limit was running out, a frantic rush to complete the paperwork took place, but the new charges weren't ready in time.

The judge, irritated by this show of incompetence in so important a case, did what the law required her to do. She freed Calvin Wesley Train.

Train was spirited out of Wisconsin by Alexander Penn's defense team and put up in a New York hotel while the legal battle over his situation raged.

During this interval Alexander Penn hastily arranged an appearance by Train on the *Larry King Show*. Train did the appearance from a secret studio. In the interview he talked about the unfairness of the first decision in the Saeger case. He also talked about the horrors of child abuse, of longtime incarceration and the existential agonies of the career criminal. He talked at length about being a person of color in a society in which 80 percent of all prison inmates were non-white. He talked about the built-in prejudices of the legal system and the racism of American society.

Penn sat beside Train in the studio. He said he was confident of victory in a new trial.

'Once we get a fair jury whose judgment is not contaminated by the prejudices of the legal system, a jury that can genuinely weigh the facts and hear the truth,' Penn said, 'I have no doubt that Mr Train will be a free man.'

Looking fit and healthy, Calvin Wesley Train seemed already to have put on weight since his release. As Alexander Penn nodded sympathetically, Train expressed concern about his personal safety.

'I intend to fight the charges against me, with Alexander Penn's help,' Train said. 'But I have reason to believe that I would not be safe in a federal prison at this time. My case has embarrassed some important people. I don't intend to surrender until my attorneys have worked out suitable security arrangements for me.'

Neither attorney nor client would amplify on the theme of a conspiracy against Train's life, despite aggressive questioning by Larry King.

*The Larry King Show* was the first step in a media campaign being orchestrated by Alexander Penn to make of his client a martyr and a spokesman for thousands of disadvantaged men and women who had been turned into career criminals by the dual monster of society and the penal system. The campaign was to include an autobiography by Train, currently being ghosted by one of the best and most expensive freelance writers in New York. It was also to include profiles of Train which would appear on A&E, ABC and CNN. A 10,000-word feature article on Train had been sold to *Vanity Fair*.

Finally, Alexander Penn himself had just signed a seven-figure book contract with a major New York publisher. The book was to consist of case histories and reminiscences of Penn's distinguished career, culminating in a long essay on Calvin Wesley Train and his defense.

The name of Susan Shader came up on *The Larry King Show*. Alexander Penn was reminded that Dr Shader's testimony had been cited by jurors as a deciding factor in the Saeger case.

'The psychic, you mean,' Penn said with a smile.

'She is psychic, I understand,' said Larry King.

Penn's handsome face took on a look of intense irony and scorn.

'To say that I am anxious to get Dr Shader back on the stand would be an understatement,' he said. 'I can't wait to get her back on the stand. Without a shred of evidence, she demonized my client before that jury. There are ample verbatim transcripts showing Cal Train's grief and remorse over what happened to Harley Ann Saeger, as well as his complete amnesia concerning the crime. Dr Shader told a naïve and trusting jury that Mr Train felt no remorse at all over what had happened. She is going to pay the price for what she did to my client and to the legal system.'

So confident was Penn of a victory in the new trial that he was already making plans for Calvin Wesley Train after the acquittal. A lecture tour was in the works. Train would speak to church groups, youth groups, and black and Hispanic organizations about the evils of crime, of gangs, and the inequities of the legal system. Negotiations were under way with Court TV for Train to broadcast as a commentator on trials involving racial and civil liberties issues.

The wheels were turning, until the unexpected happened.

Two weeks before Christmas the Penn associate assigned to keep watch on Calvin Wesley Train arrived at Train's hotel room to find the place empty. Train had disappeared without a trace.

No one was more flabbergasted by Train's disappearance, or more personally wounded, than Alexander Penn. He had canceled a lot of commitments in order to devote his valuable time to the pursuit of the Train trial and media campaign. He was gambling everything on his plan to win a Not Guilty verdict in the second trial.

A lengthy meeting of Penn, his associates and the PR consultants resulted in a decision to try to make the most of Train's fugitive status. Penn would make the rounds of the talk shows, building Train up as a new Angela Davis or Patty Hearst, a political prisoner on the run. As soon as Penn's people could contact Train, a new exclusive interview with him would be arranged in which he would explain why he ran away and talk about the legal system that was hounding him.

The plan was sound. Penn and the PR people were in complete agreement. The only thing missing was Calvin Wesley Train.

# PART FOUR

# CHAPTER 30

His bald spot was the only sour note.

The camera was fixed in the ceiling. He had turned it on before starting and let it run throughout.

As he watched it now he could see that he might have done it better. Used two or three cameras, for instance, and cut the video to make a montage. But what he saw was haunting.

She was splayed out on the mattress, her hands and feet tied. Her breasts were firm, only sagging a bit to the sides. Her stomach was flat, her thighs shapely.

He came into the picture as a head and torso moving in from the bottom, obscuring her. A squeal was heard. The wound to her left palm started to bleed, not very much but enough to be picked up clearly by the camera. As he watched he regretted that he couldn't zoom in on the wound. But that would have been impossible without a confederate to operate the camera, and a confederate was out of the question. Not only for security reasons, but because this whole procedure had to be private, like a confession.

In the image he bent to nuzzle her palm. Then he dropped out of the picture. When he returned his shirt was off. He cut her other hand, and she cried out again. She was shaking, pleading through her gag. He made the incisions in her feet, bobbing into the picture like an impersonal technician, spreading wounds and blood and screams.

Her movements were desperate, spasmodic. However, if one stood back and viewed the event as an entire process, with the male coming back into the picture repeatedly and the female reacting to his coming, it was possible to see her as acquiescing in what was happening. Perhaps even enjoying it. This notion sent a hot thrill through his senses, because it most closely approximated the forbidden scene he had witnessed between his mother and the strange man so long ago. The spreading blood, the moans, the acquiescent female flesh not afraid to bleed, a willing participant in its own destruction.

Now the stomach. He was poised over her longer now, his head bent in concentration. Then the knife raised high and plunged into her. Her shriek of agony was so loud it came out distorted on the tape. It was eloquent, tragic.

The wound gaped, a foot long, blood gushing everywhere as the abdominal aorta was hit. For a moment he was out of the picture. The blood told its own story. Then he returned, naked, rubbing his face in the wound. The tremors seemed to pass from her to him, for now she was dying, her struggles ebbing, while his excitement made him frantic. He moved around her as though around a compass, north, east, south, west, his head never more than an inch from the stomach wound.

The holy paroxysm came, difficult to see clearly on the video and yet majestic in its presence. She was dead. He poised himself over her and entered the holy place. The coitus itself was not visible; only his head and back and legs as he squatted atop her and began to thrust. And now, unexpectedly, the bald spot showed its value. It made his entire head look like a penis rising out of her, its mysterious movements spreading blood as a halo. A man made out of cock, ejaculating blood . . .

Watching the screen, he jerked himself hard and fast. High

rasping moans sounded in his throat, drowning his prayers. He was beside himself.

It was over. The figure in the video had collapsed atop her, then rolled to one side, panting. Her eyes were dead. Her body looked like a canvas, painted with bold crimson strokes.

The best part was yet to come. She was alone on the screen. He had gone upstairs to the camera to zoom in on her face. It took a couple of minutes, with nothing happening in the image, but it was worth it. The zoom brought her face closer, closer. The dead eyes bore a rapt expression of communion with the transcendent. She looked at peace.

He lay holding himself, limp now. He repeated the prayers along with the video. *Blessed art thou among women, blessed is the fruit of thy womb* . . .

Still gasping from his orgasm, he froze the frame on her face and hit the Picture-in-Picture button to bring the Virgin up. There she was, fresh and innocent as always, gazing into the camera with her bright trusting eyes. As always, the multiplication of the feminine amazed and uplifted him. The dead girl added exponential depth to the Virgin's innocence. The Virgin's bright clear eyes sanctified and empowered the wounds of the victim. White skin against red blood, life against death . . .

He raised the glass to his lips. Her blood's bouquet sang in his nostrils.

'Oh, true apothecary,' he said. 'Here's to my love.'

He drank. The nectar hit his senses like a bolt of lightning.

'Pray for us sinners . . .' He pressed the fade and watched the divine tandem disappear.

In that last fading image the victim was beautiful as never before. Her innocence restored by red, her specificity created at last by the proximity of the other. He knew now that he had been right all along to plan things around the Virgin. She was crucial to the feminine in all forms and moments. The victim's very soul came from the approach of the Virgin. He would remember this from now on.

From one, to two, and only then One.

Absolution.

# CHAPTER 31

David Gold acted quickly after hearing of Calvin Wesley Train's disappearance.

He had a long conversation with the FBI about Susan's role in the Harley Ann Saeger trial. Gold had a remarkably cordial relationship with the FBI, and had done them a lot of favors in the past. Tom Castaneda, one of the top Chicago agents, was a close friend who owed Gold his life.

The feds put Susan under twenty-four-hour surveillance. They also put men on her ex-husband Nick and his new wife, Elaine, and on Michael. The California FBI was happy to get involved. So was the San Francisco Police, after a little arm-twisting by the feds.

Susan now went nowhere without the company of a CPD tactical officer. Her apartment and office were surveilled by plain-clothes cops working in shifts. Any attack on her would have to be a suicide mission.

David Gold had not been fooled by the hype Alexander Penn had planted in the media about Calvin Wesley Train. He knew Train was a monster, not a victim. He also knew Train had it in for Susan. He had seen the way Train looked at her in the Wisconsin courtroom after her testimony. He considered it more than likely that Train would come after her.

Gold believed in thoroughness. His own attention to detail had lapsed in the Vincent Carl Bruno case, so he was more concerned than ever to give Susan every advantage. With this in mind he made an appointment for Susan with an old friend from Area Six named Jake Gehr.

Jake was a former Homicide detective who had been exiled to Ballistics because of a heart condition, and who was very close to mandatory retirement. Susan made her way to Gehr's basement office at Area Six Headquarters and found the middle-aged officer waiting for her. He breathed heavily and moved with difficulty. The roseate look of his fleshy face, especially around the nose, bespoke chronic heart failure. He looked like a doomed man.

'Doc, how are you?' Gehr asked, holding out a hand.

'I've been better,' Susan said. 'I owe a lot to David for helping me.'

'Have you ever handled a gun before?'

Susan shook her head.

'It's not as hard as it looks. Here, let me show you something.'

He opened a drawer and produced a small automatic pistol.

'This is the Harkness P97 Compact,' he said. 'Nine milli-meter. Ten rounds in the clip. See how it fits in your hand.'

The gun was small, but felt heavy.

'You'll get used to the weight,' Jake Gehr said. 'Dry-fire it a few times. Go ahead.'

He showed her how to work the safety and watched her handle the gun. She pulled the trigger several times. The gun had a cold, dead feel in her hand. It made her uncomfortable.

Gehr was watching her. 'Good deal,' he said. 'I was worried your palm might be too small, but you're all right. The recoil is small, but you've gotta get used to the noise and the smell. We'll go over to the range and practice. Dave told me he'd take care of the registration and everything. After we get you comfy with the piece – ' he actually used the word *comfy*, which struck Susan as oddly funny – 'I've got some special ammo for you.'

He fitted her with a standard belt holster and showed her how to keep the gun behind her back.

'I'm not going to be good at this,' Susan said.

'Don't worry about a thing,' Jake Gehr smiled. 'It's just a question of getting used to it. You'll do fine. You'll probably never have to use it, but we'll get you ready anyway.'

He held the gun in his own hand. 'That's a thousand-dollar piece,' he said. 'You can't shrink it any smaller and still have that much power.'

The Harkness P97 was under Susan's jacket when she arrived for work Thursday morning. She felt rather foolish when she saw Wendy Breckinridge waiting for her.

'You're the early bird,' Susan smiled.

She did not introduce Officer Loftus, an Area Six tac officer who had been assigned to her. She had not been out of sight of a cop except when asleep or in the shower for the last four days.

'I see you have security,' Wendy observed.

'A precaution,' Susan said. 'I'm sorry if it's distracting. It won't be for long.'

'I heard about that Train guy,' Wendy said. 'Are you scared?'

'No. I have faith in the police. I'm willing to take the precautions they advise, though.'

Wendy thought for a moment.

'I'm in a sort of situation,' Wendy said. 'I met this guy. His name is Scott Carpenter. He comes from an old North Shore family, but they lost all their money and moved away a long time ago. He knew me when I was little. He remembers me from that time. It's the strangest thing . . .'

'What is strange about it?' Susan asked.

'Well, it's as though he doesn't know me,' Wendy said. 'But the funny thing is that, in another way, he does know me. He admired me when he was a boy. He had a big crush on me. And now he likes me. He doesn't know about the mess I've turned into. He sees me as this attractive, interesting person.'

'You are attractive, and you are interesting,' Susan said. 'Are you sure he's wrong about that?'

Wendy sighed. 'What I mean is, he sees me as this person who is in control of her life. This very independent person. I tried to tell him how wrong he was, but he . . .' She paused. 'Well, let me tell you what he said. He said I was a fighter as a little girl, I would never let anybody push me around. He thinks I'm still a fighter, and that's one reason I'm so hard on myself.'

Susan thought this characterization showed good understanding. Wendy was stubborn, all right. For years she had allowed no one to interfere with her self-destruction or her self-punishment.

'What do you think of his version?' she asked.

'Well, at first it seemed absurd,' Wendy said. 'He doesn't know what a mess I am, he just doesn't know. But then I began to think there may be some logic on his side.'

'In what sense?'

'Well, he sees me as this beautiful, desirable person. If I run myself down, it's by my own choice. That's how he sees it. I mean, I would be running down someone who is basically good, basically attractive.'

'And you see it differently?'

'Of course.' Wendy's tone was impatient, as though Susan was a bit thick. 'I run myself down because I see what I am.'

'And he sees you as willfully distorting the reality of who you are?'

'Yes. Exactly.' Wendy thought for a moment. 'We had this

conversation about mirror images. He – do you remember
*The Little Rascals*?'

'Yes.'

'I asked him what he saw when he looked at himself in
the mirror. He told me he saw Alfalfa from *The Little Rascals*.
In one episode Alfalfa was primping himself for a date with
a little girl. Trying to comb down his cowlick. Being very
narcissistic, but looking ridiculous.'

'And how did this analogy seem to you?'

'Well, it was charming. Self-denigrating, you know.
Modest. I liked it.'

'Would you say it was accurate?'

Wendy thought for a moment. 'Not physically, no. Scott
is an attractive guy. A good-looking guy. But mentally,
emotionally, I'd say it was accurate. He's self-effacing. He
makes fun of himself. The thing is, though, I think he does
like himself.'

She glanced at the painting of the clown on the wall. Then
she looked down at her hands, which were clasped tightly in
her lap.

'It made me feel . . .'

She broke off. Susan easily sensed the resistance behind
her silence.

'Well,' she offered, 'you think his view of himself is a
generous and honest view. And since he is viewing you with
the same eyes . . .'

Wendy nodded. 'It's as though nothing I could do would
shake his faith in me. Even if he's wrong, you see . . .'

'That would be a new experience for you,' Susan offered.

'Yes. New. Completely new.'

There was a silence. Wendy's knuckles had turned white.
Her hands were clenched tight.

'The night of our first date – the night we met, actually –
I brought him home to my place for a nightcap. We talked . . .

After he left I threw on some clothes to go out cruising. I wanted to get laid. I felt really horny. But then, all of a sudden, I looked at myself in the mirror, and I didn't want to. I put on my nightgown, lay down on the couch, and lit a candle and just sat there, thinking.'

'About Scott?'

'Yes. About the way he treated me, and the way he thought of me.'

'So,' Susan observed, 'mirrors played a role on both the occasions you describe.'

Wendy looked up at her, interested. 'Yes. Yes, they did.'

'Mirrors are highly charged objects,' Susan said. 'They show us what we really are, which no other object can ever do, except a camera. And they show us our own perception of who we are. No one can look in a mirror without correcting or adjusting the image according to one's own needs and fears.'

'I see what you mean.'

'In the end the image that appears in the mirror can be the least reliable of all,' Susan said. 'After so many years of worry and insecurity attached to the image we see . . .'

Susan was thinking of the fear she had felt in Marcie Webb's dressing-room mirror. And of Miranda Becker, who saw the killer's face in a mirror. She had to fight these thoughts off.

'Scott is a mirror that won't allow you to touch up your own image,' Susan said. 'A mirror that insists on showing you in a flattering light. Perhaps an accurate light.'

'Because he doesn't know me . . .' Wendy was struggling with the concept.

'Or because he knows a different you,' Susan said.

There was a silence. Wendy looked past Susan out the window at the lake.

'Do you intend to see him again?' Susan asked.

'I hope so,' Wendy said. 'If he calls. I think he will. I think maybe he will. He likes me.'

'There's no reason he shouldn't,' Susan observed. 'Is there?'

'How can you ask that?' Wendy said. 'You, of all people?'

'You've been my patient for two years,' Susan said. 'I feel very comfortable in asking you. Is there a reason he shouldn't like you?'

Wendy gave her a fearful, troubled look.

'Which answer frightens you more?' Susan asked. 'That there is a reason, or that there is no reason?'

Wendy was silent. She looked away, through the window at the frozen grey lake. Susan could see it would be a long time before Wendy knew the answer to that question.

Wendy turned back, a different expression in her eyes.

'This killer,' she said. 'The Undertaker.'

'Yes.'

'I'm still worried about him. I know it's silly, but I keep thinking about him. Because of Miranda.'

Susan was silent.

'I mean,' Wendy said, 'he's killed two more girls. Girls about my age, more or less. Young girls.'

'That's true.'

Susan was thinking that the three victims all had names that started with the letter M. If Wendy knew this she might be less frightened. On the other hand, Wendy had more than enough cleverness to get around such an obstacle.

Wendy thought for a moment.

'I heard that all the victims had had abortions,' she said.

Susan did not reply.

'Is that true?' Wendy asked.

Susan shook her head. 'You know the rules, Wendy.'

'Sorry. I just thought you might know.' Wendy chewed her lip nervously. 'I know you can't tell me.'

Inwardly Susan cringed at the fact that once again her work with the police was interfering with her therapy. But it could not be helped.

'There is very little you couldn't work into an obsession about this, if you really wanted to,' she told Wendy. 'You know that.'

'Yes, I guess so.' Wendy looked away. 'Meeting men. Going out to bars.' She thought for a moment before adding, 'Meeting Scott. Getting my hopes up . . .'

Susan smiled. 'We all expect to be punished for getting our hopes up. That's the nature of the beast.'

Wendy's eyes took on a challenging look. 'Do you think I should be getting my hopes up?'

'About Scott, you mean?'

Wendy nodded.

'I think you've been very deficient in the hope department,' Susan said. 'I think you could have raised your hopes a long time before this if you had allowed yourself to. If Scott is helping you in that direction, I can only say better late than never.'

'So you think . . . ?'

'I think the image he sees in your mirror is one you should study carefully,' Susan said. 'It's often said that we need to get outside ourselves once in a while, to see with new eyes. Perhaps Scott is offering you this opportunity.'

'Maybe,' Wendy said. 'I might get punished for it, though.'

'By yourself, perhaps,' Susan said. 'Not by a serial killer, though.'

'I guess not.' Wendy's look was sheepish, but still worried. She smiled. 'It's funny. Here I am talking about my fear of a killer on the loose. But you're the one with cops standing guard over you, to protect you from a killer on the loose.'

Susan returned her smile. 'There's another difference. I choose not to be frightened. You choose to be frightened.'

'Yes. I guess I do.' There was infinite fatigue in these words. Wendy was sick and tired of being her own victim.

'The Undertaker is a grandiose symbol for your own guilt,' Susan said. 'As such he can teach you something about your own feelings. What you think you've done wrong, and what the corresponding punishment should be.'

Susan often pointed out to her suffering patients that none of the material they brought forth in therapy was wasted. Even the most ridiculous or painful thoughts had value when one found out what their sources were.

'The Undertaker punishes women for being young, at least symbolically,' Susan said. 'For having sexual organs. For having boyfriends. For wanting love. Perhaps for having hopes. Symbolically, he is an all-purpose weapon. He can punish you for whatever you want.'

Wendy was looking at Susan intently. 'There's something I never told you about myself. I don't know why I kept it a secret. I suppose I shouldn't have. It may help you understand why I worry about the Undertaker.'

'Do you want to tell me now?' Susan asked.

'Yes.' Wendy nodded. 'I had an abortion. About two years ago. Just before I became your patient.'

# CHAPTER 32

Ten days after the finding of Marcie Webb's body, the police still had no clue as to where or when she had had her abortion, or who the father of her aborted foetus might have been.

They also had no clue as to the identity of her murderer, despite the fact that they had samples of his blood, semen and saliva.

The frustration of the authorities was reaching new heights. CPD detectives had visited all the known pro-life groups in the tri-state area. The pro-life people tended to be fanatic in their belief in their cause and sometimes in their willingness to take extreme measures against abortion clinics. But no individual within their ranks fit the profile of the Undertaker. At least not as far as the police could tell.

As for the Satanists, they were a harmless subculture, their activities confined to readings, macabre clothing, a few rituals here and there, and a lot of newsletters and literature. 'Some of them might kill a cat or a rabbit now and then and use the blood in a ritual,' said Rich Sheehan, 'but they're not capable of killing anybody.'

The vampires were another story. The Vice Control detectives had interviewed hundreds of prostitutes, both male and female, throughout the city. Quite a few remembered clients who enjoyed the taste of blood. The female whores knew clients who wanted to perform oral sex on them when they were menstruating. A half-dozen or so could remember men who wanted to inflict minor injuries on them for the purpose of sucking their blood. Not one had ever had a client who wished to draw blood from them with a standard needle and blood bag.

None of the prostitutes could remember a client whose kinks remotely resembled the savagery of the Undertaker. Nor did any of them recognize the composite sketch of the man who had joined Miranda Becker at Pulitzer's Bar.

Marcie Webb's parents, flown to Chicago to identify her body and make funeral arrangements, had spent several hours with Susan and Joe Riccio. They had not known that their daughter had had an abortion. This ignorance made their grief all the more painful, because they had been close to Marcie, who lived with them much of the time in Baltimore.

By now the police knew who Marcie's closest friends were. All were contacted by police in Chicago or Baltimore. None seemed to know that Marcie had ever had an abortion. Joe Riccio interviewed the musicians who worked with her. They were on fairly friendly terms with her, but could not speak of her love life.

'What can I say?' Joe shrugged. 'She was a private person. It seems strange, because her school friends didn't describe her as a loner. She was social, fun-loving, gregarious. But she kept her love life a secret.'

'Not entirely,' Susan corrected him. 'She told the whole world about it in her song lyrics. The words to "Call Me Last Year".'

'How do you mean?'

'The song expresses renunciation and extreme loneliness. I suspect there was something illicit about that particular love affair,' Susan said. 'She concealed it from her friends. When she found out she was pregnant, she aborted the baby without telling anyone. In all probability she didn't tell the father, since she was so secretive about the relationship.'

'Who do you think he was?' Joe asked. 'Somebody married?'

'Probably.' Susan nodded. 'Someone she knew was off limits from the outset. My sense of Marcie is that she was a very upright, self-respecting person. If she got into an illicit relationship, she wouldn't tell anyone about it. Terminating the pregnancy would have been her first thought.'

The pathos inherent in such a relationship seemed to radiate through all the dead girl's music. It helped to explain the world-weary quality that was contradicted by her youth and freshness. A young woman ideally equipped to be a torch singer.

Susan doubted she would ever get to the bottom of this particular mystery. However, she also doubted it was relevant. All three murder victims had had a connection to abortion. Two had had the surgery and one was contemplating it. The fathers of the foetuses seemed completely foreign to the cause of death.

Abortion was the common link.

> O, my love, my wife!
> Death, that hath sucked the honey of thy breath,
> Hath had no power yet upon thy beauty.
> Thou are not conquered. Beauty's ensign yet
> Is crimson in thy lips and in thy cheeks . . .

That night Susan sat reading *Romeo and Juliet* in her bed. The cat was beside her, one paw placed possessively on Susan's leg, enjoying an occasional stroke from Susan's fingers and batting the air languidly with her tail.

She was paying little attention to Shakespeare's eloquence. Her mind was focused on the twin themes of blood and virginity as they applied to Juliet. In the final scene, just before he kills himself on her body, Romeo remarks on

Juliet's rosy cheeks. He does not realize that her cheeks are rosy because she is still alive. The drug she took created the illusion of death, and not death itself. Romeo senses the blood which gives her cheeks color, but does not draw the right conclusion, and dies for his mistake.

Clearly the theme of blood as it connects to virginity was a virtual obsession throughout the play. From the moment Juliet falls in love with Romeo she is eager to sacrifice her virginity for him.

> Come, civil night,
> Thou sober-suited matron, all in black,
> And learn me how to lose a winning match,
> Played for a pair of stainless maidenhoods:
> Hood my unmanned blood, bating in my cheeks,
> With thy black mantle til strange love grow bold,
> Think true love acted simple modesty.

When Romeo is banished for killing Tybalt, Juliet expresses her grief and despair by inviting Death to take her virginity and be her husband, instead of absent Romeo.

> I, a maid, die maiden-widowed.
> Come, cords, come, nurse. I'll to my wedding-bed;
> And death, not Romeo, take my maidenhead!

Juliet never does lose her virginity with Romeo, because she dies before she has the chance to do so. Death is the final and only communion of the two star-crossed lovers.

On her own Susan might not have noticed the repetition of the theme of virginity and deflowering. But her intuition that *Romeo and Juliet* was somehow involved in the killer's delirium about his own murders had sensitized her to the theme, and now she realized how deeply embedded it was in the play.

The phone rang, startling her. She recognized David Gold's ring and picked up.

'Hello?'

'Susan? Gold. I didn't wake you, did I?'

'No. I was reading.'

'Got your gun with you?'

'David, I'm in bed.'

'Get it.'

Sighing, Susan got out of bed, her movement causing the cat to dart away with a small meow of reproach. Susan got the gun off the dresser. It smelled of oil and gunpowder. Unfortunately, her femininity was working against her as a shooter. Her practice sessions at the firing range had left her clothes a smelly mess. The stench of smoke and powder did not predispose her to keep the weapon at the ready.

'All right,' she said. 'It's on the bedside table.'

'Put it in your hand,' Gold said.

'David, really . . .'

'Susan, you have to get used to having it in your hand. That's the only way.'

'All right.' Wrinkling her nose at the smell, Susan held the gun in her hand.

'I've been reading too,' Gold said. *'Romeo and Juliet.'*

'Are you serious?' Susan knew that David Gold was not a reader. She had never even seen him with a book in his hand. For recreation he watched television. At night, before bed, he read magazines or newspapers, but never books. The very idea of Gold poring through Shakespeare was laughable.

'Yeah. I had Josie bring me a copy from the school library. I've got time on my hands, after all. Listen, I see what you mean about the virginity. And the constant references to blood. In a sense, blood is the thing that brings Romeo and

Juliet together at the end. Since they can't consummate their love sexually, they do it by dying together.'

'That's right,' Susan said. 'And in a different sense blood is what separates them, because the Capulets and the Montagues are two different families, two different bloods.'

Gold said ruminatively, 'When Juliet wakes up and finds Romeo dead beside her, she kills herself with his dagger. That reminds me of our killer. The stage directions don't say where she stabs herself, but it seems to me she would use the stomach. And using Romeo's dagger is kind of like using his penis to penetrate herself.'

'Yes, I see what you mean.' Susan smiled again. Gold sounded like an English professor.

'Listen to this,' Gold said. 'This is Romeo talking, after he's been banished:

> *More honorable state, more courtship lives*
> *In carrion flies than Romeo. They may seize*
> *On the white wonder of dear Juliet's hand*
> *And steal immortal blessing from her lips,*
> *Who, even in pure and vestal modesty,*
> *Still blush, as thinking their own kisses sin.'*

'Where is that?' Susan asked.

'Act 3, Scene 3. Lines 35 to 40.'

Susan flipped through the pages to the speech and read it again.

'I see what you mean,' she said. 'It's a strange image. Flies crawling over Juliet's virginal flesh . . .'

'It would strike a chord if you were nuts, and thinking about virgins and death,' Gold said.

'You're right.'

'And the whole part about Juliet looking dead after she

takes the potion is pretty kinky too, if you want to look at it that way,' Gold added. 'A necrophile's delight.'

'Yes.' Susan had been struck by the overtly sexual way Juliet's deathlike state was described in the play.

'You're the one with the second sight,' Gold said. 'But personally I buy the idea that the killer is obsessed with virginity. If you say the play is involved, I'll buy that too.'

'It wouldn't be the first time,' Susan said. 'Killers are always looking for inspiration in literary works or movies or music. Like Jeffrey Dahmer with *Exorcist 3*. Or John Hinckley with *Taxi Driver*, or John Lennon's killer, Mark David Chapman, with *The Catcher in the Rye*. Ironically enough, there is something about murder that inclines to thoughtfulness. Few literary works have had as great an impact as *Romeo and Juliet*. The star-crossed lovers whose deaths are the only thing that can end the feud between the families . . . It is a pretty profound concept.'

'What about the very fact that he reads Shakespeare?' Gold asked. 'Doesn't that tag him as an educated dude? College at least?'

'Not necessarily,' Susan said. 'Killers are often forced into intellectualizing their obsessions, even when they're not educated. Literature provides precisely the climate of alienation, of pain, that killers feel in their megalomania and their paranoia. Also the literary works help them feel legitimate in what they are feeling and doing. So it's possible that our man is not literate in himself, but stumbled onto *Romeo and Juliet* by chance and co-opted it into his delirium. And there's one other thing . . .' She hesitated.

'Go ahead,' Gold said.

'I'm thinking as a psychiatrist,' Susan said. 'Very often in our unconscious mind we go through life with certain misconceptions. Things that we have long since learned to be untrue consciously. Do you see what I mean?'

'Like an inner child?' Gold asked.

Susan smiled. 'What have you been doing? Reading psychology?'

'Just listening to the radio on my way to work.'

'Well, you're right. The way the Undertaker kills the women suggests a terrible fear of copulation. Many small children see copulation as a violent or sadistic act performed on the woman by the man,' Susan said. 'Some children even believe it kills the woman. My guess is that the Undertaker is acting out an unconscious fantasy along these lines. That's why his knife never goes near the vagina.'

'Okay.'

'His obsession with the Virgin Mary expresses his worry about conception, about sexual intercourse,' Susan said. 'The Virgin Mary is the only woman to conceive a child without coitus. Juliet fits right into the obsession, because Juliet is a virgin. And Juliet never does lose her virginity in the play. She dies a virgin.'

'I see what you mean,' Gold said. 'The Undertaker picks out girls who have a virginal quality, a look of innocence. Becker, Mahoney, Webb – they all had that. What I don't understand, though, is why he chooses girls who have had abortions. Isn't that the opposite of being virginal?'

'That's true,' Susan said. 'I'm not clear about it myself.'

There was a silence.

'I wish to hell we knew who the father of Webb's foetus was,' Gold said.

'Me, too,' Susan said.

They said goodbye on that doubtful note. Susan lay in the glow of her bedside lamp, thinking of nothing. A siren sounded outside, moving south to north. Perhaps an ambulance from Northwestern Hospital.

Innocent women, guilty women. Virgins, mothers. Why

Miranda Becker? Why Juliet? Susan's tired mind struggled to undo the tangled threads of the killer's obsession.

The phone rang, interrupting her thoughts. She turned up the volume on the answering machine to monitor the call. Sure enough, it was a hang-up. None of her friends would be calling at this hour. Any professional contact would call her answering service. The machine was for personal calls.

As she lay back against the pillows a thought came to her. She got up, found the Chicago white pages and looked up Marcie Webb's name. It was listed. She went back to the phone and dialed the number.

A recording told her the number was no longer in service. Susan called Directory Assistance and asked for Marcie Webb's number.

'One moment, please.'

The operator disappeared. After a moment a recording gave Susan her answer.

'The number you have dialed has been changed to an unlisted number,' said the impersonal voice.

Susan hung up the phone and pondered. She had had patients who were musicians, actors and theater people. None of them ever had unlisted numbers. Few even truncated their first names in the phone book. They had to be readily available for calls from people who might want to hire them.

Why had Marcie Webb changed to an unlisted number?

It was too late at night to do anything but wonder about this. Susan slept on it and, in the morning, called Marcie's New York agent, Orson Myers. A crisp-sounding secretary asked her to wait, and Myers came on the line after a brief delay.

'Hello, Doctor. To what do I owe the pleasure?'

'Mr Myers, I noticed that Marcie recently had her phone number changed to an unlisted number. Were you aware of that?'

'Yes, I was. She was getting some crank calls and she didn't want the aggravation.'

'What sort of crank calls?'

'She didn't say.'

'Wasn't she concerned about missing professional calls by having an unlisted number?'

'Well, she was. She told me she was going to get an answering service. But I guess she didn't get around to that.'

'I see. Thank you very much, Mr Myers.'

'Do you think this is connected to what happened to Marcie?'

'It could be. We'll find out.'

'Good luck, Doctor.'

# CHAPTER 33

Susan was going over her list of the people closest to Marcie Webb when she got a call from Bob Inkster, the manager of the lounge at the Palmer House. He asked her to stop by as soon as possible.

When she arrived he introduced her to a cleaning woman named Eunice Ardmore, a pleasant African-American woman with worried eyes.

'You're the psychiatrist?' Eunice Ardmore asked, accompanying Susan to the dressing room. 'The psychic lady?'

'Yes. What did you wish to tell me?' Susan asked.

'You want to find out who killed Marcie.'

'Very much.'

'One day last month I came to clean up as usual,' Eunice said, 'and I noticed some lipstick smears on Marcie's vanity mirror. I cleaned them up, but I wondered about them, so I asked her about them. She told me she didn't know nothing, but I thought she looked funny about it.'

'Funny?'

'Worried. You know, upset.'

Susan studied the woman's intelligent eyes. 'What was your conclusion about it?' she asked.

'Didn't have a conclusion,' Eunice said. 'But Marcie looked different to me. As though something had happened. Like maybe somebody wrote something on the mirror in lipstick. You know what I mean.' Her eyebrow raised significantly.

'A message?' Susan asked.

'Like a crank, if you know what I mean.' The cleaning woman shook her head. 'We get crazy people, you know. They come to see performers, they get wild ideas in their heads. Sick ideas. I used to work over at the Shubert Theater. Every once in a while I would find something strange in a female performer's dressing room.'

'I see.' Susan looked at the mirror. 'But you didn't get a clue as to the message itself?'

'No, ma'am.' The cleaning woman shook her head firmly. 'But Marcie looked a little funny when I asked her about it.'

'Thank you very much, Mrs Ardmore,' Susan said. 'I appreciate your letting me know.'

Susan sat down on the chair before the mirror and looked at herself. She had sensed anxiety here the first time she came in, but had written it off as performer's nerves. 'Flop sweat,' as they called it. Now she knew more, both from the phone company and from the cleaning woman. She looked at the mirror and concentrated.

Nothing came. Only a vague uneasiness combined with something like nausea, perhaps.

She had brought a copy of Marcie Webb's head shot, taken from the supply in the singer's apartment. She took it out of her briefcase and looked at it now. The girl was so young, so innocent and full of energy.

'Come on, Marcie,' Susan murmured. 'Give me a clue.'

But Susan saw only her own face in the mirror, the tired brown eyes looking much older and less optimistic than the sparkling eyes of the singer in the photograph.

She tried to see beyond her own face, into the indefinite ether of pure reflection. As though the enigmatic mirror, the most mysterious and troubling of natural objects, could reverse time as well as image.

She heard the singer's haunting voice, at once clear and husky, intoning the words she herself had written.

*If you get lonely*
*Call me last year . . .*

Susan concentrated as hard as she could. The familiar headache was beginning to come on her now, her perennial price for using second sight.

Romeo, Juliet . . . Virgin, intercourse . . . Womb, foetus . . . Blood . . .

She shook her head. Nothing was coming except her own free associations, which were contaminated by her painful concentration on the case.

She got up to leave. A voice sounded behind her as she had her hand on the doorknob.

*Your room is bleeding.*

She stopped in her tracks. She looked at the empty room. It had not been a voice after all. It was an image.

*Your room is bleeding.*

Susan turned back to the mirror. The words were there, scrawled in lipstick in capital letters, enigmatic, frightening.

*Your room is bleeding.*

But the image in the killer's mind was not of a room. It was a woman's womb, pouring out blood like a spring, a source. The lipstick had been used to write out a euphemism for what the killer was seeing. A euphemism all the more terrifying for its refusal to tell all.

*Your womb is bleeding.*

Susan stood poised in the dusty silence, measuring her own insight and the dead girl's fear.

Then she came back to the phone and called David Gold.

# CHAPTER 34

*Your room is bleeding.*

Susan was sitting in a downtown lounge-restaurant patronized by professional people. She was waiting for Meredith Spiers to join her.

The message scrawled on the mirror of Marcie Webb's dressing room in lipstick had haunted Susan's dreams last night. She and David Gold had discussed it at length this morning.

*Your womb is bleeding.* Over the past weeks Susan and Gold had come to know their quarry, as the police often come to a strange intimacy with the perpetrator who eludes them. There was no doubt in Susan's mind that the message on Marcie Webb's mirror had actually referred to her womb, not her room. The killer had euphemized the message, choosing a word that rhymed with the one he didn't want to say. Just as he euphemized the sexual act he wanted to perform on his victims, by respecting their genitals even as he tore at their bodies in a grotesque parody of sexual intercourse.

It was that shrouded quality of the message that made it so scary. *Your room is bleeding.* Marcie Webb must have been very frightened when she saw it. The message, scrawled in lipstick on the mirror in an empty dressing room, had a symbolic appropriateness, as though the dressing room itself were bleeding in lipstick smears.

And who could tell what the killer might have been saying to her over the phone?

'This case is amazing,' Susan told David Gold. 'It's almost as though my entire education in Freud were being retold by this killer.'

'What do you mean?' Gold asked.

'The kinds of symbolism, the displacement, the distortions – it's all so reminiscent of Freud's writings, especially his case histories,' Susan said. 'For instance, when the killer substitutes *room* for *womb* in the message on the mirror, no student of Freud can fail to remember that in German the popular expression for women's genitals was *women's room* or *women's apartments*. And there is an almost universal tendency of dreams to use rooms to represent the inside of the womb.'

'So our killer is a textbook case,' Gold said.

'Yes, a textbook display of anxiety concerning the female genitals, virginity and probably menstruation,' Susan said.

'Why menstruation?'

'I suspect that the image haunting the killer's unconscious mind is that of blood coming out of a girl's or woman's vagina. In prudently avoiding the vagina of his victim he avoids having to see this image. But he inadvertently reproduces it massively in the stab wounds he inflicts. Each stab wound is a symbolic vagina with blood coming out of it.'

Did Marcie Webb make the connection between the crank calls and the message on the mirror? Susan was sure of it. She only regretted that Marcie had not called the police.

'It wouldn't have done any good,' David Gold said. 'I hate to admit it, but the cops wouldn't have given her any protection based on crank calls and a message on her mirror. They would have told her to call them if there were further problems. And told her to get an unlisted number, which she did. The killer would have gotten to her anyway.'

These thoughts were in Susan's mind as she sat with Joe Riccio in the restaurant. Riccio had declined a cup of coffee and was sitting with his hands folded, glancing around him at the patrons and waiters. Christmas decorations were in evidence, as were the customers' shopping bags which bespoke Christmas shopping.

'This gun,' Susan said in irritation. 'I can't lean back. It's giving me a backache at work.'

'You'll get used to it,' Riccio said. 'It won't be for long, anyway.'

Riccio had talked to David Gold about the gun. Riccio had his doubts about Susan's ability to use it in the event of danger.

'Don't worry about it,' Gold had said. 'Jake is working with her on the range, but mostly he's teaching her to keep it in her hand when she's at home. I think she'll be all right.'

'What about the ammo?' Riccio had asked.

'Hollow point expanders,' Gold said. 'Jake got them from a guy on the South Side who deals in special ammo. He told me if she hits the guy anywhere in the trunk, he's dead.'

'Probably a good thing if she's not trigger-happy, then,' Riccio had said.

He saw that Susan was looking at him.

'Do you have much Christmas shopping to do?' Susan asked.

'Enough to keep me busy,' Riccio said. 'My wife does a lot, but I like to do my share.'

'Do you have children?'

'Two girls and a boy.'

'How old?'

'The girls are fourteen and fifteen, the boy is ten.'

Susan was surprised to hear that Riccio had children that old. He was very youthful in appearance.

'Do they share your looks?' she asked.

'You mean the red hair?' He nodded.

Riccio had extraordinary looks. For a northern Italian, he looked precisely, even extravagantly Irish. He had russet hair, pale freckled skin and green eyes. Susan had asked him whether his ancestors looked the same way, and he had told her their looks had astonished fellow villagers back in Italy just as they astonished people today.

'There must have been an Irishman somewhere in the family tree that nobody knows about,' he said.

Interestingly, Riccio's fiery Irish looks did nothing to contradict his taciturn personality. Susan was only now getting used to his wonted silence, and finding it restful. Riccio was a man of integrity who kept his own counsel. When called upon to do a job, he did it without complaint. Gold assured her there was no braver detective on the force.

'He won't smile at you much, but he'll go to the wall for you if you're in trouble,' Gold said.

Susan saw Meredith Spiers coming toward her past the bar. Meredith looked very much the journalist with her dark suit, careful make-up and brisk walk. As always, Susan was struck by the hard professionalism of the young woman, which seemed like a shiny veneer pasted over the face and body of a coed. Meredith had willfully submerged her own innocence and vulnerability under the hard-boiled armor of the savvy journalist. As a psychiatrist Susan thought there had to be a reason for this. She doubted she would ever learn what it was.

'Hello,' Susan said.

'You look all in,' Meredith observed, sympathy in her dark eyes.

'Do I?' Susan smiled wanly. 'It's getting so that I can't even tell when I'm tired.'

'Tell me about it,' the reporter said, lighting a Winston. 'I can't even tell when I'm asleep any more. I do reports in my sleep. Some mornings I wake up thinking it's time to go to bed.'

'Yes, I get that, too. I wake up thinking I've just been with a patient.'

'Is it the case?'

'Yes.' Susan accepted the Diet Coke the barmaid brought. 'This Marcie Webb thing has me going around in circles. There is a sense that we know the killer, we even understand him. But not well enough to catch him or to stop him from killing again.'

She glanced at Riccio, who had slipped away tactfully and now was standing at the bar, his eyes scanning the restaurant through the mirror.

'A lot of the clues are coming from my second sight,' she said. 'David takes them seriously, which is nice of him. But they're not bringing us the concrete insights we need.'

The arrangement Susan and Gold had with Meredith did not require them to keep her abreast of all the clues turned up in the case. Meredith remained in ignorance of many of the less definite ones. But Susan had agreed to give Meredith interviews on the general shape of her work in the case and her feelings about her role.

This was their third informal meeting. At the first two Susan had gone over the history of her work with the police and the basics of her technique as a psychic. She had talked about distortion, resistance and other problems which made second sight a complicated instrument, especially in police work.

Meredith took a long drag of her cigarette, studying Susan's face.

'I'll bet this job gives you some ambivalence about being psychic,' she said.

'Quite a bit, yes,' Susan said. 'There isn't much margin for error in police work. Second sight involves a significant quotient of error. The signals can be confused.' She thought for a moment. 'I hate making errors when so much is at stake. But it's inevitable.'

'And I'll bet you get criticized for it.'

'That's putting it mildly.' It was common knowledge that Abel Weathers hated Susan's participation in major cases. Many members of the police department thought of Susan as a witch doctor. It was only David Gold's fierce loyalty to her that kept her working with the CPD. Gold could point to a dozen cases she had helped solve. Others, of course, could point to psychic insights she had had which led in the wrong direction. The death of Kyle Stewart last year in the Peter Tomerakian case was the most disastrous instance. Stewart had been arrested based on Susan's insight. A tailor-made suspect, he had turned out to be innocent, but had hanged himself in his cell at Cook County Jail before his innocence was realized by the police.

'Does any of this connect with personal issues in your own life?' Meredith asked.

Susan nodded. 'It would probably be correct to say that the tension of the cases revives a pre-existing ambivalence. I've told you that my parents died in a fire when I was ten years old, haven't I?'

'No.' A stricken look passed over Meredith's pretty face at this news.

'I became psychic – or at least I discovered my psychic gift – right after their deaths,' Susan said. 'It's often that way. A shock or trauma, or a loss, will trigger the onset of the gift. Anyway, for me the second sight was contaminated by grief and guilt. I felt guilty as a survivor. I also wished that my second sight had appeared in time for me to warn my parents about the fire. In the years that followed, the second sight was more like a curse than a gift. I couldn't separate it from my guilt.'

'Sounds like a terrible burden for a young girl to bear,' Meredith said.

'It was,' Susan nodded. 'There was a lot of fall-out.'

Susan's teenage years had been the worst time of her life. She and her brother had been sent to live with an aunt. Susan became promiscuous when she was a young teenager, and slept with a lot of boys for whom she felt nothing. She was looking for punishment, and sleeping around seemed to provide it. Then her aunt died of cancer, and Susan's mental health declined further. In the end she went into therapy and pulled herself together. But it was not easy.

'Like a lot of people,' she said to Meredith, 'I eventually healed myself by concentrating on school and achievement. But for five or six years I was in bad shape.' She thought for a moment. 'This has helped me, I think, in relating to my adolescent patients.'

'That's so interesting,' Meredith said. 'I went through something similar, though it came later. My parents got divorced, and my father died soon afterward. I sort of fell apart. It was only when I decided to go into journalism that I pulled myself together.' She looked at Susan. 'There was some man trouble during that period, as you might imagine.'

This remark seemed pregnant with meaning, but Susan only nodded.

'That usually goes with the territory,' she said.

'Being on the hot seat the way you are,' Meredith said, 'does this also connect to your youth?'

'You're very perceptive,' Susan said. 'As a psychic I do work that is going to be debunked and ridiculed by a lot of people. That's a significant choice on my part.'

'There's a parallel there to your psychiatric work, isn't there?' Meredith observed. 'Psychiatry is a controversial science. Psychiatrists are often accused of being frauds. And when they make mistakes, it often gets into the news and causes a lot of embarrassment.'

'Yes,' Susan said, impressed again by the reporter's insight. 'As I've grown older I've realized that something in me wants to challenge other people to reject me, even to ridicule me. Choosing psychiatry as a specialty was one way to accomplish that. Using my second sight in a public arena, instead of just keeping it to myself, was another way. I'm quite sure this all has something to do with the abandonment I felt when my parents died, and with my own need to feel loved and protected.'

Susan did not volunteer the fact that a lot of therapy had been necessary to provide her with these insights. It was not until her training analysis with a legendary Chicago psychoanalyst named Berthe Mueller that she truly understood the dynamics of her professional choices.

'I'm not sure I understand,' Meredith said.

'Well, as a little girl I must have felt my parents' deaths as a rejection,' Susan said. 'I must have been very angry with them for abandoning me. So I chose a controversial profession which dares people to reject me.' She thought for a moment. 'I use my own competence, my experience and preparation, to try to avoid that rejection. But I make the inevitable mistakes that bring on criticism.' She smiled. 'From an emotional perspective, I kill two birds with one stone. I help people, I feel competent, and at the same time I make sure that I'll bring down criticism on myself.'

'I see,' Meredith said, an intent look in her eyes.

'David Gold can relate to this,' Susan added. 'No one attracts criticism more than the police, especially when they make mistakes.'

'I can relate to it, too,' Meredith said. 'Most people hate reporters. They look on us as jackals who feed on people's misfortunes and care only about selling newspapers or getting TV ratings. With every story we write we dig ourselves deeper into that hole.'

'Yes, the analogy is good,' Susan said.

Meredith puffed at her cigarette pensively.

'Personal choices,' she said. 'You know, I entered college as a math major. I thought I was going to become a mathematics professor, maybe a consultant. I never dreamed that six years later I would be a TV reporter.'

'That's interesting,' Susan said. 'I majored in mathematics myself. Long before I had any ambition to become a physician.'

'I was an actress, too,' Meredith said. 'You know – high school drama productions, dreams of Hollywood. I did some college productions, too. As a matter of fact, the acting probably helped prepare me for broadcast journalism.'

'You never know what is going to come in handy,' Susan said.

There was a silence. The evocation of painful subjects and personal feelings had stirred something in Meredith Spiers which she was not saying. Susan could feel it, not only with her second sight but with her years of experience as a psychiatrist.

*Man trouble.* Susan sensed that a love affair had changed the course of Meredith's life. Her admission about her parents' divorce had concealed a truth about another romantic relationship, closer to home. It was not Susan's place to ask about it, but she felt very strongly that Meredith's heart had been broken by a man, and that she was not completely over him even now.

A news report had come on about a bombing at an

abortion clinic in Birmingham. Several patients had been seriously injured, and one of the nurses had died.

Meredith was looking at the TV screen. 'That's a big story,' she said. 'I'll bet they've got reporters from all over the country camped across the street from that clinic.'

Susan nodded. 'Anti-abortion activism is quite a phenomenon. It sometimes reminds me of religious war. The feelings run so high.'

A sidelong look in Meredith Spiers's eyes told Susan that abortion was a sore subject with her. The evasion in that look suggested that Meredith herself had had an abortion. That might be part of the 'man trouble' she had alluded to.

Perhaps to change the subject, Susan said, 'Did you ever hear the story of Joe Louis's paranoia?'

'The fighter?' Meredith shook her head. 'Not that I remember.'

'Well, according to what I've read, near the end of his life Joe Louis became delusional and thought the CIA was following him,' Susan said. 'It turned out that he was in fact delusional and needed treatment. But at the same time, it also turned out the CIA was really following him.'

Meredith laughed. 'No kidding.'

'I mentioned the story in my lecture on distortion in mental life out in California,' Susan said. 'But it hits close to home for me. Sometimes my second sight gives us clues that point in a certain direction. Then we find out the clues were wrong. We abandon that line of inquiry, only to find out too late that it was correct after all, for reasons we didn't understand at the time.'

'Are you worried about that happening with the Undertaker?' Meredith asked.

Susan nodded. 'I have the feeling we're working behind a sort of screen. We have lots of clues to follow, and some of them are pointing directly at the killer. But he remains behind this screen where we can't put our hands on him.'

'That reminds me of journalism, too,' Meredith said. 'Some of our most ridiculous stories turn out to be true. And some of our best ones turn out to be crap. It's the nature of the truth, I guess, to elude us in whatever way it can.'

Susan smiled. Meredith was indeed a bright young woman. She could probably have been a great success as a mathematician. It was odd to see her talent at abstract reasoning fitted into the bag of tricks of a tough City Hall reporter.

'Well,' Meredith said. 'How do you like your salad?'

'It's wonderful,' Susan said. 'I'm glad to know about this place. Do they make things like cheeseburgers and Reubens?'

'Oh, yeah,' Meredith nodded. 'You can fill up on cholesterol in here if you want. The french fries are delicious. And the portions are huge.' She gave Susan a speculative look. 'You don't go in for binge eating, do you?'

Susan laughed. 'No. I'm thinking of Detective Gold. He is an eater, a phenomenal one. Corned beef, pastrami, french fries, ice cream – there's no limit. And he never gains a pound, even though he gets no exercise to speak of. It drives his wife crazy.' She looked around the room. 'He'll want to know about this place.'

'He probably does already,' Meredith said. 'Cops know all the best restaurants.'

A cell phone rang. Both women opened their purses, laughing as they looked at each other.

'Yours,' said Meredith as Susan took out her cell phone.

'Dr Shader,' Susan said.

She smiled at Meredith, listening to the caller.

'How long has he been this agitated?' She said into the phone. 'Did he sleep last night?'

There was a pause as the caller, a psychiatric nurse, responded.

'Is he hallucinating?' Susan asked.

Meredith listened, fascinated by Susan's calm response to the emergency.

'Well,' Susan said, 'let's give him five milligrams Haldol IM stat. No, make that ten. I'll be there in about fifteen minutes.' She smiled apologetically at Meredith. 'I have to run. An emergency.'

'We'll talk again soon,' Meredith said. 'Say hello to Detective Gold.'

'I'll do that. Keep in touch.'

Leaving her salad half eaten, Susan took her coat and left the restaurant. Joe Riccio met her at the door and escorted her through it.

Meredith sat smoking and sipping at her coffee, savoring the brief interval of peace before her own busy day resumed. Then she stubbed out her cigarette, counted her change for the tip and stood up.

She put on her coat and left the restaurant with quick firm strides.

The face of Calvin Wesley Train had appeared on the television screen over the bar. The TV anchor man was saying that the nationwide manhunt had so far failed to determine the whereabouts of the now-famous killer. Meredith did not hear him.

# CHAPTER 35

As Susan was attending to the disturbed male patient at the hospital, she received an urgent message from her answering service. Bob Inkster, the manager of the lounge at the Palmer House, wanted to speak to her right away. After calling him she made the brief trip downtown with Joe Riccio and was met by Inkster at the door of the lounge.

'I should have told you,' he said. 'I've only been here three months. I was brought in from Indianapolis when the old manager got a new job. I've been worrying about your questions about cranks. I didn't see anything significant since I've been here, but apparently there was a guy about six months ago who caused some concern.'

Bob introduced Susan to a cocktail waitress named Pam Benjamin. Pam had been at the Palmer House for nearly twelve years. An enormously tall and well-built woman in her forties, she looked the part of the hard-as-nails cocktail waitress who takes no nonsense from anybody. But she was friendly and well spoken. Her gregarious personality was dampened only by her grief over Marcie's death.

'She was a doll,' Pam said. 'An absolute angel. I've worked with a lot of performers, and some of them are complete jerks. They blame us when the audience gets rowdy. We do our best, but we can't legislate quiet. Bars are bars. Liquor is liquor. It's the nature of the business. This isn't a concert hall. Marcie understood that. She was always sweet to me.'

In answer to Susan's question, Pam said without hesitation, 'Yes, there was a freak in here.' She pointed to a table against the wall. 'He sat at table 22 until we ran him out.'

Joe Riccio was standing by the doorway to the lounge. His eyes followed the direction of Pam's gaze. So did Susan's. The table Pam had indicated was the one that had sent signals to Susan on her first visit here.

'He was a little guy, maybe five feet six or seven,' Pam said. 'On the skinny side, without much hair. Looked like a Casper Milquetoast to me, but he was trouble.'

'How do you mean?' Susan asked.

'Well, he started by requesting songs from Marcie. Her own songs, mostly. He seemed like a big fan. Then he started sending her notes, flowers, things like that. After a while he was overdoing it, and Marcie told Grant about it. Grant was our manager at the time. Grant asked the guy nicely to lay off. The guy didn't take that well and started getting abusive to Marcie in his notes and letters. She was getting spooked, It was bothering her.'

'How did it end?' Susan asked.

'Grant brought a hotel security man down to the lounge one night and had a little chat with the guy. We never saw him again after that.'

'Did Marcie ever hear from him?' Susan asked.

'If she did, she didn't tell me about it.' Pam shrugged. 'Personally I would doubt it. This guy was such a little pipsqueak. I think he ran for cover.'

'Would you be able to recognize him from a photograph?' Susan asked.

'Oh, sure. No problem.' Pam had lit a Virginia Slims and was taking deep drags from it.

'Would your former manager be able to recognize him?'

Pam curled her lip. 'Possibly. Grant wasn't as good with faces as I am, though. You have to be good with faces when you cocktail. People like you to recognize them, greet them. But you could try him.'

'Where would I find him?'

'He's working in some hotel in the Bahamas or somewhere. The personnel guys upstairs could tell you. But if you find a picture, just show it to me. I'll know the bum if I see him.'

'What about your security man?'

'Tommy? Yeah, you could try Tommy. He might remember. But he only saw the guy the one time.'

Susan told Riccio what Pam had told her. Riccio called the personnel office of the hotel from the lounge phone while Susan continued talking to Pam.

'So your own take on the episode, if I understand you correctly, was that this man was not much of a threat,' Susan said. 'More of a nuisance.'

'Yeah, that's how I saw it.' Pam blew smoke out the side of her mouth. She was quite pretty, Susan reflected, in a hardboiled way. 'This guy was too much of a wimp to really hurt anybody. But he was persistent. He had a thing for Marcie and he didn't give up. Not until Grant muscled him a little.' She shrugged. 'That kind of thing is part of the business, you know. Female entertainers have to deal with freaks all the time. It gives you a bad view of human nature – the kind of guys who come into lounges and spend a lot of time. Most normal guys are home with their families.'

Riccio came to murmur in Susan's ear that the former manager, Grant Ellison, was managing a hotel restaurant in St Croix and could be contacted easily.

Susan stood up to leave.

'Pam, you've been very helpful,' she said.

'Any time,' Pam said, crushing out her cigarette and standing up to her full height of at least six feet two. 'I'm sick about Marcie, I really am. I hope you find the fucker who did it. Oops – pardon my language.'

Susan smiled. 'I hope we do, too. I can see that Marcie will be missed. She was a fine artist.'

'Oh, she was going places,' Pam said. 'No doubt about that at all. She had the gift.' She looked around the empty lounge. 'Some nights this place was quiet as a church when she sang. You could have heard a pin drop. It's a terrible loss.'

Pam's metaphor was not lost on Susan. If the Undertaker had been here listening to Marcie Webb sing, he must have conceived the moment in a religious sense. To him Marcie was a Virgin, an exalted figure he came to pay homage to.

Riccio was waiting for Susan. She was about to leave with him, but turned back to Pam.

'By the way,' she asked, 'how did this man pay for his drinks? Cash? Credit card?'

'Cash. Always,' Pam said. 'A reasonably good tipper.'

Susan started to turn away again, but turned back.

'What did he drink?'

'That's the funny thing,' Pam said. 'He didn't touch alcohol. Most of your lounge slobs will be drunk as skunks, but this guy was always cold sober. He ordered Bloody Marys, no booze.'

'I see. Thank you.'

Susan looked at Riccio, but turned back for the third time.

'How did he order them?' she asked.

'Virgin Mary,' Pam said. 'That's what they're called, Doc.'

'He used those words?'

'Sure. Virgin Mary.'

Susan looked at Riccio. He had heard.

*Let's go*, his eyes said.

# CHAPTER 36

*Silent night, holy night,*
*All is calm, all is bright.*
*Round yon virgin, mother and child . . .*

The carol was being sung by a choir on WLS. The radio was in the next room. Meredith Spiers lay in the bathtub, a cigarette in her hand, her eyes half closed.

She wasn't really listening, but her lips did form the words of the carol as she felt the water warm her tired body.

Soon Christmas would be over. Then all the radio stations would drop the carols and return to their usual clamorous mixture of loud music and commercials.

Meredith rarely spent a leisure hour without having the radio on. For one thing, she was afraid of missing some late-breaking story if she didn't keep herself constantly connected to the news. For another thing, silence got on her nerves.

She wasn't always this way. As a teenager and later as a college student, she used to enjoy being alone and reading in an easy chair, especially under a window in the daytime. Natural light on the pages of a book was pretty. Sometimes she would put on some Mozart while she read. But usually her concentration on the book made her forget the music anyway, and she would notice after an hour that the record had stopped playing long ago.

She was more contemplative then. More able to enjoy the

languor of just being alive, feeling moments of time pass over her like small pensive caresses. Sometimes she could even feel the blood flowing through her veins.

Nowadays her friends told her she was like a walking electric current. 'How you keep going at that speed, I don't know,' they said. 'I'd be dead in a week.'

It was true, though she hadn't noticed it so much until others pointed it out to her. She stayed awake at least eighteen hours a day. When she wasn't working she was on the phone, pumping sources, or on the computer surfing through all the online news outlets in search of stories that might be of use to her.

She would long since have become a speed addict had not her natural metabolism kept her so wired. And she would almost certainly have become hooked on sleeping pills had she not discovered that she could function quite well on as little as three hours' sleep.

She was a bit of a coffee addict. Two double shots of espresso in the morning, another two at lunch. And she drank rather heavily when she was with her friends. Jack Daniel's was her brand. It might become a problem if she didn't watch it. Most reporters were drinkers.

Stories, stories . . . She lived for stories, like all reporters. Her antennae were ceaselessly alert for a ripple somewhere in the world that would make a good story. A story the producer would want, if possible. But any really good story would do.

She knew reporters, male and female, who had fucked for stories. Meredith had done it herself. It wasn't hard. You felt nothing and you got value for your time. But over the years she had learned to take advantage of her high public profile. People knew her face, people thought of her as beautiful. She could use a vague promise of a date to get most of what she needed, most of the time. True, the top people at City Hall wanted more; but she was learning how to handle them, too.

She looked at the outline of her naked body under the water. It was a good body. Slim long legs, good hips, firm breasts. Shapely hands which were not seen on the air. She had good coloring, with her fresh white skin and dark hair. Good eyes for broadcasting. 'Burning blue,' they had been called.

A good body – but it had been a long time since it had felt anything. This was an occupational hazard, Meredith told herself a bit smugly. She didn't have time to feel anything.

She lit another Winston from the old one and looked for a moment at the empty walls of her bathroom before closing her eyes again. The smoke felt good in her lungs. She liked the tranquilizing numbness. If she ever tried to quit smoking, it would be hard.

She thought about the Undertaker. Marcie Webb must have been his Christmas victim. He probably wouldn't kill again until the New Year. When would Meredith hear from him again?

She could not deny some feelings of exhilaration at having received e-mails from a murderer. It was exciting, after all. The faceless stranger on the other end of her online service, out there in the anonymity of cyberspace, sitting down to compose words for her, to send her clues. Of course it was horrible – the innocent girls he had slaughtered, and the sick way he had done it.

But at bottom Meredith felt very little about it. She did not allow herself to feel anything – except hunger for a story. If he wrote again, she would sit down with David Gold and scoop the other reporters in town. Gold could get her in to Weathers or Phelan or even the FBI whenever he wanted. She couldn't report the content of the e-mails, but she could get great exposure.

She took a long puff of the Winston, smiling to think of Gold's disapproval of her smoking. Gold was a stand-up guy, very sincere about his work, almost desperate to catch the Undertaker. He wanted to save lives. He was one of the few cops Meredith had met who looked beyond their own cynicism about human nature.

Gold gave lectures to school kids every other week. He traveled to the toughest schools on the West Side, the South Side, the Near North, and spoke to groups of ghetto kids for whom his badge and the color of his skin made him a natural enemy. He urged them to get an education and to resist the temptations of the ghetto, especially drugs and gangs. Susan had told Meredith about these talks, and urged her to go see one.

'He has a good understanding of how young people's minds work,' Susan said. 'He's very sincere, and quite often he is able to overcome their suspicion.'

In Meredith's experience, most cops seemed to have more in common with the criminals they pursued than with society. Like the crooks, the cops were misfits, outsiders, men and women who lived in a violent netherworld ignored by civilized society. The two groups battled each other very much as gangs battled each other in the ghetto. Their goal was not peace, but only territory. They reminded her of little boys playing 'king of the hill' on a dirt pile.

Cops in general were a lot like journalists. Overwork, bad marriages, alcohol, cynicism. They looked to their next collar the same way reporters looked to their next story. They gave little thought to the sufferings of crime victims, because they would lose their objectivity if they did.

Gold was different. He felt the pain of the victims. He called their families long after the crime. Visited them. A good guy.

He was good-looking, too. A bit like Judd Hirsch in

*Ordinary People*, but taller. There was something warm about him that she found attractive. Nothing would come of it, of course. He was obviously devoted to his wife, Carol, a sweet woman. If he had something of a crush on Susan Shader, as Meredith suspected, he sublimated it as a paternal protectiveness which was part of his working relationship with her.

Meredith enjoyed seeing him. She knew he wasn't telling her all he knew about the killer's MO, but she understood. He had to control the flow of information as much as possible. He was dealing fairly with her. He had to catch the Undertaker before she could have her feature story. Meredith was used to quid pro quos. It was how she operated.

She herself wanted the Undertaker caught. She wanted the terror and the pain to end. She also wanted her story. She wanted to put a face and a name to the anonymous presence on the other end of those e-mails.

The cigarette was almost gone. She brought it to her lips, but decided not to take the last acrid puff. She was about to light another one from the ember, but on an impulse crushed it out in the ashtray beside the tub.

She thought about Susan Shader. Lunch with her had been interesting. She hadn't learned anything new about the Undertaker case, but she had learned something about the doctor herself.

She was fascinated by Susan Shader. Her professionalism was impressive, but so was her candor about herself and her past. She had good contact with her own emotions. She must be a whiz at therapy, Meredith mused. She herself had had some therapy in college, but her doctor had been a cloddish Health Service fellow who hated his work and the students he dealt with. Meredith had felt worse after the therapy than before.

But to be Susan Shader's patient must be something quite different, she thought. Something very strong emanated from

Dr Shader's small body and quiet eyes. A strength that wasn't afraid to be feminine. Meredith felt a pang of envy as she compared herself to the other woman. She was a bit intimidated by so much maturity and strength of character.

At age twenty-seven Meredith felt she had accomplished little in the department of maturity or of self-knowledge. She had left her problems behind her by throwing herself into the hurly-burly of broadcast news. It was a convenient escape. Indeed, most of the reporters and editors she knew were every bit as cut off from their real selves as she was. Journalists were not known for introspection.

But Susan Shader had used self-knowledge to make herself better and stronger as a professional as well as a woman. That was a rare achievement.

And Meredith had responded to it, speaking enthusiastically about her own ambivalence about journalism. Talking about her past with real interest, real curiosity. That was rare for her. Usually she didn't think about the past. Not at all.

Meredith lay back under the bubbles, letting her mind stray over those college years which seemed to have led to one disaster after another. Meredith had emerged from her competitive San Francisco high school with a sort of split personality. She threw herself into her mathematics major at Berkeley, but continued cherishing an all-too-typical adolescent dream of an acting career.

The math courses became a dead end, thanks to a failed love relationship which came at the worst possible time, and with the worst possible man. Her participation in college theater productions led, rather predictably, to nothing. When the dust settled she found her two youthful personalities in ruins, and built a new one to take their place – the aggressive, ambitious journalist who knew what she wanted and how to get it. The hard-boiled young woman who could not be hurt, whose armor was ten feet thick.

Superficially it was an effective defense; but underneath, it was not the emotional equipment of a truly mature person. Meredith knew that, and worried about it.

Sometimes she looked back on her mathematics persona, her ambition to become a professor. She had felt very strongly about it at the time. The search for perfect, shining truth through abstract formalisms whose value she could demonstrate in black and white. The dream of sharing those truths with her own students.

That dream was gone now, buried under 10,000 leads and interviews and deadlines. Stories, stories . . .

She also thought back on her college acting career, which had been full of girlish spontaneity and high hopes. The girlish innocence was gone, but acting had helped in its way to prepare her for broadcast reporting. How to steal a scene, how to get noticed. How to get inside the words, to make others feel them. How to use her face, her voice.

She had played Nora in *A Doll's House*, and gotten rave reviews from the Berkeley newspaper. Stella in *Streetcar*. Honey in *Who's Afraid of Virginia Woolf?*. Ophelia in *Hamlet* for the Shakespeare Group. And Juliet, of course. Her last role and perhaps her best performance.

# CHAPTER 37

Michael sat in his second-grade classroom at Glen Grove School, watching with interest as the teacher's special guest held up a large blue bear wearing a flight suit with goggles.

'Magellan lives in Evergreen, Colorado, at the Elk Creek Elementary School,' the lady said. Her name was Mrs Wiedeke, and she visited schools with the bear, who had not only flown around the world on United Airlines, but had flown on the Space Shuttle. 'Now, if I point to the place where Magellan lives on this map of our country, who can tell me what big city is right near Magellan?'

There was a silence. The children were somewhat abashed by the presence of the visitor. Michael squinted at the part of the map she was indicating with her pointer. It was in the western part of the country, but he did not know the name of the city.

'Can I give you a hint?' Mrs Wiedeke asked. 'Magellan, should I give them a hint?'

The bear, sitting on Mrs Kittle's desk, looked enigmatic. Mrs Wiedeke leaned down to whisper something in his ear.

'He's a little shy,' she said to the class. 'But he wants me to give you a hint. There is a football team that plays in this big city, and that football team is going to play in a very special game this January. Can anyone tell me . . .?'

'Broncos,' said a girl in the second row.

'Broncos is exactly right,' Mrs Wiedeke said. 'What is your name?'

'Miriam Braun.'

'Miriam, are you a football fan?'

The little girl blushed. 'No, but my brother is. He got a Super Bowl T-shirt.'

'Can anyone tell me which city the Broncos play in?'

'Denver,' several voices said at once.

'How did you kids get so smart?' the lady asked. 'You're absolutely right. Now, let me show you what happened when Magellan flew all the way around our country. First he got on the plane right here in Denver...' She pointed at the center of the country. 'He flew to a very big city right in the middle of our country, a city where lots and lots of planes have to stop on their way east or west. Who can tell me the name of this city?'

Michael's hand was raised. She turned her infectious smile on him.

'Chicago,' he said.

'Very good. What's your name?'

'Michael.'

'Michael, are you a Cubs fan?'

'Yes.'

'That makes two of us. Of course, I have to be a Colorado Rockies fan because I live just outside Denver, but I'm a secret Cubs fan. You won't tell anyone, will you?'

Michael shook his head.

'Tell me, Michael, who is your favorite Cubs player?'

'Sammy Sosa.' Michael answered without hesitation. He admired Mark Grace, but Sosa, the great power hitter who had broken Babe Ruth's home run record last season, was the closest thing to Michael Jordan on the Cubs' roster.

Mrs Wiedeke gave Michael a conspiratorial smile.

'Well, Michael, I can tell you a secret. Magellan just

happens to be a Sammy Sosa fan himself. But he can't tell just anyone, because . . .'

Michael was enjoying his moment as the center of attention. The lady was very nice. Something about her made you feel like she had known you would be here before she came and had looked forward to meeting you. She was more friendly than Mrs Kittle, who was always somewhat formal in class.

Michael was feeling both shy and important this week. Shy, because he was always a bit shy, even with his friends. Important, because he was accompanied by a female police officer everywhere he went. She was dressed in plain clothes, but she was armed and had a secret radio which she used to talk to other officers.

Her name was Rita, and she had two boys at home, one Michael's age and one younger. She was a San Francisco Police Department tactical officer. She had shown Michael her badge, but she kept it hidden in her purse.

Rita had picked Michael up at home this morning. Daddy had already left for work. Rita spoke briefly with Elaine before taking Michael to the bus.

'Have a nice day, honey,' Elaine had said, kissing him as Rita stood nearby. Michael had blushed at being kissed in front of Rita.

On the bus Rita had sat up front with the driver. When they got to school she melted away into the corridor and didn't come into the classroom. Michael was glad for that.

Mrs Wiedeke was now pointing at New York City.

'Naturally,' she said, 'when Magellan took his flight around the world, he had to make a stop here. Who can tell me . . .'

The fire alarm sounded, making Michael jump.

Mrs Kittle got up from her seat and stood beside Mrs Wiedeke.

'Class, let's show Mrs Wiedeke how well we can go through our fire drill. Everyone line up, now.'

The children lined up, with Michael standing behind Bridget Cadiz as usual. They were led through the hall by Mrs Kittle to the west exit and onto the playground. Mrs Wiedeke, carrying the blue bear, went with them.

When they were on the playground the various classes stood in groups while the teachers talked to each other. The alarm went on ringing for a couple of minutes as everyone waited. Then it stopped. Michael was lost in thought, standing alongside Bridget as the noon breeze rippled his shirt. The sun glided behind a cloud, sending a wave of coolness across his face. His eyes could open wider now, and he looked toward the houses behind which, miles away, was his home.

He happened to meet the eyes of Mrs Wiedeke, who was holding Magellan in her arms. She winked and made Magellan wave at Michael. Michael smiled and waved back.

The janitor was outside, talking to the man who cut the grass. Some other adults who looked unfamiliar were walking to and fro, talking to each other. Michael looked for Rita but didn't see her.

*Are you sorry?*

He stood for a moment listening to the breeze. A dog barked somewhere down the block. A lawn mower started, then stopped. The cloud was bigger now, inching slowly past the sun. It looked like a wolf, Michael thought. A large wolf with long jaws and hollow eyes.

*Is a spider sorry?*

The coolness was spreading. Everything felt grey. Michael's eyes followed the loafing lazy cloud. Slow, slow . . . Then he sensed something on the ground that answered the cloud, or called out to it. Something grey and cold.

*Is a spider sorry for all the flies it caught?*

Michael's skin crawled. He looked over his shoulder into

the trees. He felt something recede from his gaze. A thing that came closer as it shrank away . . .

Calvin Wesley Train held the binoculars without flinching, though the boy was looking right in his direction. The little eyes, magnified by the professional lenses, seemed to see right into him.

Train was beyond the perimeter of the tight security, but not so far away that he couldn't get a panoramic view of everything that was happening.

A young woman who looked like a student teacher held her hand up to her face. The wrist stayed by her mouth an instant too long.

The janitor looked away for a moment, then back at the children.

Alongside the principal a tall woman with dark hair was scanning the playground with eyes that left no doubt as to what she was.

Train made out at least four cops in plain clothes, communicating by wire. The deployment was heavy. The FBI couldn't be far off.

The policewoman had not come out of the school. They must be conducting a search inside. As Train watched, a local squad car pulled up and two uniforms got out. The tall woman left the principal's side and went to speak to them.

The boy was invulnerable, Train realized. The school was staked out. If anything untoward happened, a dozen cops would converge. They were waiting for him.

Train had already checked out the house. No chance there. Cops inside, cops on the street. His only chance to get the boy would be in a shopping center, maybe a movie theater. But it wasn't worth the effort. If he got to the boy, they would nab him within seconds. This was not a suicide mission. He intended to get away. He would come out of this a free man. That was the bottom line.

Train looked at the boy again. The boy's eyes were on his teacher. Odd: a moment ago he had seemed to be looking right at Train, as though he knew.

Shrugging, Train put down the binoculars. He would remain here until the fire drill was over, and slip away later in the day.

He would have to think of something else.

# CHAPTER 38

The police and FBI, desperate for a suspect after two months of terror, pursued the 'Virgin Mary' lead aggressively.

Pam Benjamin worked with a CPD artist to make a sketch of the suspect's face. Simultaneously an FBI sketch artist flew to St Croix to get Grant Ellison, the former lounge manager, to give his own version of the suspect's face. Tommy Ensor, the security man from the Palmer House, could not give a detailed enough description for a sketch, but thought he could pick the suspect out of a line-up.

The police showed Pam's sketch to everyone in the vicinity of the Palmer House, as well as to women who had been victims of sex crimes in the greater metropolitan area in the last several years.

Luck was on the cops' side. An attendant at the parking ramp nearest to the Palmer House recognized the face as that of a regular customer. He clearly remembered the suspect's car, a late-model Taurus with a special antenna probably used to monitor police calls.

The detectives questioning the parking-lot attendant could hardly believe their good fortune when he told them he knew the plate number of the Taurus. In his boredom he made it a hobby to remember the plate numbers of regular customers.

On the basis of the plate number an arrest was made only twenty-four hours after Pam Benjamin had made her fateful mention of the suspect's 'Virgin Mary' drink order.

# BLOOD

To the consternation of Abel Weathers and the Homicide detectives, a reporter from the *Sun-Times* somehow got wind of what was happening and reported the arrest in a hastily assembled story for Thursday morning.

UNDERTAKER ARREST! blared the banner headline. The rest of the media, furious at having been scooped, hyped the story for all it was worth. One reporter, having somehow learned the circumstances of the arrest, published the sensational details.

INNOCENT-SOUNDING DRINK ORDER SINKS UNDERTAKER SUSPECT, announced the headline:

> *An apparently innocent drink order placed regularly with a cocktail waitress at the Palmer House's Palm Lounge has led police to their first prime suspect in the deadly 'Undertaker' slayings*, said the article. *'Dr Susan Shader, psychiatrist and psychic, who has been consulting to the police on the investigation, connected the drink order to certain top-secret elements of the killer's MO. Thanks to the waitress's memory for faces and a parking attendant's memory for license numbers, the suspect was behind bars within twenty-four hours.*
>
> *Now a city and a nation wait with bated breath for confirmation that the as yet unnamed suspect is in fact the dreaded Undertaker, whose grisly string of murders has created a reign of terror over the past two months . . .*

The suspect's name was Timothy Hatch. He was, as Pam the barmaid had described him, a small man, slight of build, with thinning dark hair and a nervous manner. He was a civil service employee who lived alone in a bungalow on the South Side. A bachelor, he had a history of mental health problems and a long string of arrests for minor sex crimes like window peeping, exhibitionism and soliciting prostitutes. He had twice been accused of rape. In both cases the victims withdrew their charges.

He also had a long history of harassing women in the public eye, such as performers, actresses, TV personalities. He would send them fan letters, then flowers or candy, until he became a nuisance. He was the quintessential crazed, obsessive fan.

And he was, in all likelihood, a murderer.

Euphoria reigned within the CPD and the FBI when it was discovered that Hatch's blood type matched that of the semen, saliva and blood believed to be those of the killer, found in the three victims' bodies. The killer was perhaps behind bars at last.

The police were not deterred by learning that most of Hatch's previous crimes had been minor. It was well known that most serial killers had yellow sheets full of minor sex offenses. The progress of a sick personality from fondling or exhibitionism to murder was gradual.

Nor were the profilers disturbed to hear that Hatch was a spindly, ineffectual-looking fellow.

'The vast majority of rapists are little guys,' David Gold explained to Susan. 'Little pimply Casper Milquetoast types. The public doesn't realize it, because of all the hype that paints rapists as big bad dudes. Actually, this guy is the very portrait of the rapist.'

Susan also knew that a great percentage of serial killers were small men who made up for their lack of sexual prowess by assaulting or killing women. Impotence was a virtual signature for serial killers. So was a small penis.

Working under a search warrant granted the day of the suspect's arrest, forensic specialists went over Hatch's unkempt bungalow with a fine-toothed comb. A great deal of pornographic material was present, including magazines, videotapes and some paraphernalia. Pictures of numerous female celebrities – including Marcie Webb – were collected in a scrapbook, and the suspect's desk was full of correspondence addressed to them. News items clipped from newspapers about the murder of the singer were assembled in a file folder. Broadcast reports on the murder, including several by Meredith Spiers, had been saved on videotapes by Timothy Hatch.

The hair, fiber and trace evidence collected from the bungalow was massive. It would take time to assay.

'You did it, kid,' exulted David Gold to Susan. 'You showed them who's got the best nose around here.'

'I'll feel better when we're sure,' Susan said.

A hearing was to be held in a week's time to determine whether the defendant should be bound over for trial. Hatch was represented by a public defender, a fact which surprised Abel Weathers and his lawyers. Could it be that the suspect was throwing in the towel even before the hearing? Or was Hatch simply unaware of the peril of his position?

Susan was besieged with requests for interviews from all the media, with special attention from the cable tabloid shows and the glossy magazine press. Her already high profile as a key witness in the Harley Ann Saeger case, combined with the sensational new trial granted Calvin Wesley Train, gave her more than one claim to celebrity.

Susan refused all the requests. The only journalist she actually talked to before the hearing was Meredith Spiers. Meredith wanted to know, strictly off the record, how Susan had guessed the suspect's guilt. Susan explained the long series of feelings she had been having about the theme of virginity, and how it combined with the obviously religious imagery of the crimes.

'His obsession with the female reproductive organs and especially with virginity is enormous,' Susan said. 'He fits right into the category of disturbed males who view the female genitals with horror, respect and violent hatred all at the same time. His MO can be seen as a symbolic representation of the act of deflowering a virgin. The knife wounds are penetrations that bring blood, just as the penis that ruptures the hymen brings blood.' Susan looked at Meredith, who seemed pensive. 'I'm sorry we didn't tell you all this before,' she said. 'David was worried about the leak. He wanted to keep all the major clues under wraps.'

'No problem. I understand,' Meredith said. 'I don't need that stuff now anyway. I can plug all that into my story later on. Right now I need insight about your working methods and your feelings about your work. You've given me that.'

Meredith knew first-hand that Susan was shunning all interviews and refusing to play the role of a celebrity.

'This is the one part of my profession I can't stand,' Susan said. 'I have a positive allergy to being a public figure. I always feel somewhat violated when people recognize me, when strangers speak to me. It's a shyness built into my nature, I guess.'

'You're not alone,' Meredith said. 'Believe it or not, I can't stand going in front of a video camera. I've never completely gotten used to it.'

Susan was surprised. 'You certainly don't show it.'

'There are techniques you learn,' Meredith shrugged. 'Tricks of the trade. My years as an actress helped, too. I sort of deny the presence of all the people behind the camera. Just as I used to deny all the people beyond the footlights.'

A Chicago PD tac officer was in the room with Susan and Meredith as these words were spoken. Gesturing to him, Susan told Meredith, 'The idea of being guarded, being in danger – being exposed – is something I hate. The day may yet come when I will quit this business just for the sake of having a private life again. I haven't done it before now because David Gold is a persuasive man. He works on my sense of public duty. I can't stand by and do nothing when I might be able to help stop violence from happening. So far that sense of obligation keeps me in the game.'

'I'm glad for that,' Meredith said. 'We need you. The one thing that has struck me since the beginning of this Undertaker thing is that the police had lots of physical evidence, and a lot of leads, including the abortion connection. But it wasn't enough. With all their legwork they couldn't find a suspect.'

Susan nodded. 'Serial killers are hard to catch. They have no motive for a particular victim, and no personal connection to the victim. That's 90 percent of convictions – that personal connection. Without it the police are at a disadvantage. That's where people like me come in. To find a motive.'

'In this case, the idea of virginity,' Meredith said.

'Yes. I guess that was the key.' Susan did not mention her intuition about the killer's concern with *Romeo and Juliet*. The police who searched Timothy Hatch's bungalow had not found a copy of the play or any evidence of an interest in Shakespeare on the suspect's part. Susan was at a loss to account for the massive psychic input she had felt on this score. Perhaps, she mused, she was simply wrong. It would not be the first time.

On Wednesday the hearing was held at the Cook County Courthouse.

The prosecutor assigned by Abel Weathers to handle the hearing was an experienced lawyer named Jack Ousterhoodt. He put Pam Benjamin on the stand to testify to the suspect's obsessive pursuit of Marcie Webb. Grant Ellison, having been flown in from St Croix, corroborated Pam's testimony, as did Tommy Ensor, the Palmer House security man.

Ousterhoodt also produced the documentary evidence of Hatch's obsession with Webb. Hatch's long history of sex crimes was inadmissible, but the eyewitness testimony to his harassment of Marcie Webb was powerful. Timothy Hatch was tailor-made to fit the crime of which he was accused.

Then the People's bubble burst.

Timothy Hatch's public defender responded to the police's testimony by claiming that Hatch was at the movies the night of Marcie Webb's abduction. He produced a parking ticket stub and movie ticket stub to support this defense.

The prosecutors were not very worried about this alibi, for Hatch could easily have ducked out of the movie theater and used a different vehicle to abduct his victim.

But now the public defender produced police records which proved that at the times of Miranda Becker's abduction and the abduction of Mary Ellen Mahoney, Defendant Hatch was behind bars in Joliet Prison, serving a five-month sentence for exhibitionism. It was that incarceration that accounted for the fact that Pam Benjamin and her colleagues had not seen Hatch at the Palmer House in some months.

The public defender concluded that since his client was manifestly not guilty of those offenses, and since the MO in the Webb homicide so clearly matched that of the other murders, the police had not produced sufficient evidence for a court to conclude that Timothy Hatch was probably the killer of Marcie Webb.

The judge agreed.

Abel Weathers's rage nearly knocked the roof off City Hall.

'We arrested an innocent man on the strength of a psychic's interpretation of his *drink order*!' Weathers shouted at his top assistants. 'A *drink order*! Do you have any idea what the media will do to me for this? We're going to be tarred and feathered.'

Weathers knew the media. He was not wrong.

BLOODY MARY DOES NOT EQUATE TO BLOODY MURDER,

read the headline of the *Tribune* the day after the dismissal of the charges against Timothy Hatch.

BLOODY MARY LEADS TO BLOODY MESS, said the *Sun-Times*.

KEY SUSPECT MOCKS KEYSTONE COPS, announced *USA Today*.

It turned out that Timothy Hatch was a career exhibitionist and peeper whose attempted rapes were so ineffectual that the intended victims had hardly taken him seriously. He harassed Marcie Webb as he had harassed a dozen women in public life before her. A harmless psychopath, he had never harmed anyone physically.

Abel Weathers's first official action after his temper quieted down was to have the Chief of Police throw Susan officially off the Undertaker investigation.

Chief Phelan, an old friend of David Gold's who had entertained Susan more than once at his home, explained the reasons to her.

'Abel is pretty excited, but I think he's right. Your profile is too high at the moment, and we're under a cloud of embarrassment. I think your notoriety because of the Train business is also detrimental. In all fairness, I think the CPD overreacted to your lead because they were so hot to catch the Undertaker. But obviously your lead was wrong in itself. I think you should return to your private life, concentrate on maintaining your personal safety, and let the law enforcement people take it from here.'

Susan bowed out with as much dignity as possible. In accordance with Chief Phelan's wishes, she granted no interviews about her role in the investigation or her blunder about Timothy Hatch. The CPD's public relations people handled that. Susan watched in chagrin as Meredith Spiers reported the fiasco on Channel 9's evening news. There was no way for Meredith to sugar-coat the story. The embarrassment of the Chicago Police Department would not be short-lived. The damage was severe.

The city was left to ponder the fact that the Undertaker was still at large. Women, especially those who were pregnant or had had abortions, were warned again to go nowhere alone. Police spokesmen acknowledged that they were 'starting over' in their profile of the killer and that the search could be lengthy.

Christmas intervened to distract the public from the investigation. The Chicago weather, rainy until now, turned frigid. The highest temperature on Christmas Day was two degrees. Wind chills reached record lows for this date. Chicagoans busy buying and then returning Christmas gifts had little leisure to think about the Timothy Hatch fiasco. They were more concerned with how to get their cars started in the deep freeze.

The only sign that people remembered Timothy Hatch was the fact that orders for Virgin Marys were at an all-time high in taverns and restaurants throughout the metropolitan area.

# PART FIVE

# CHAPTER 39

Christmas was on a Thursday. Susan spent the long weekend with Ron Giordano.

They watched football on television, went out to see *Shakespeare in Love* together, had dinner the night after Christmas at an out-of-the-way Moroccan restaurant too dimly lit for Susan to be recognized. Susan need not have worried about being seen, for the place was deserted. Chicagoans were in their homes eating leftovers that night.

They made love. Susan was tense at first, but Ron Giordano's tenderness was an eventual match for her misery. His acceptance of her was a counterweight to her own humiliation and self-doubt.

'I hate to see you go through this,' he said. 'You're only trying to help people, and look what it gets you.'

'You may not be seeing me go through it much longer,' Susan said. 'Even if I wanted to contribute, Abel Weathers and the police may never ask me again.'

'Perhaps that would be best,' Ron said. 'You could live the quiet life of a well-respected shrink. And I would have more of you.'

She nodded against his deep chest. Perhaps it would be best. The idea of a quiet life appealed to her. And no man could be better chosen to share it than Ron Giordano.

Meredith Spiers called to commiserate on Sunday night.

Ron Giordano was sitting on the couch opposite Susan, watching her as she talked to Meredith.

'Did you see my reports on Channel 9?' Meredith asked.

'No,' Susan said. 'I haven't gone near a TV or a newspaper.'

'I don't blame you,' Meredith said. 'They're making it hot for the CPD and for the FBI. It's not a pleasant situation.'

There was a silence. Susan wondered if Meredith would still want to go through with her planned feature article on Susan's police work. Since the story had come to such a sad end, the article might not be worth writing.

'You know, I've been thinking,' Meredith said. 'What happened is precisely what you described to me when we had lunch.'

'What do you mean?'

'The mistake you made is no different in principle from the mistakes the cops themselves make. They follow their leads and sometimes they arrest the wrong suspect. It happens all the time. One guy seems tailor-made for the crime, and it turns out he didn't do it. The difference is your second sight. They won't allow you to make a mistake.'

Susan tried to take comfort from this kind version of events.

'Well, I made a whopper,' she said.

'And I've also been thinking about the other things you said,' Meredith went on. 'About drawing down scorn and derision by your choice of profession. What we're seeing in the media is exactly that.'

'I suppose so,' Susan said. 'It's one thing for the police to be helped by a psychic. The public doesn't mind that so much. It's another for the police to make a mistake, especially a costly one, based on the input of a psychic. That puts egg on their face.'

'To some extent that's true about journalists,' Meredith

said. 'The public likes to read what we write, if it's true. They take our hard work for granted. But woe betide us if we make a mistake. Then we're yellow journalists who couldn't be bothered to check our facts.'

'Yes. I see what you mean.'

Again a silence. Meredith seemed to hesitate.

'You know, there were some things I wanted to say to you the other day,' she said. 'I didn't get a chance, because you had to go to your emergency. I hope we can talk again soon. It would be good for me.'

There was a personal, confiding note in her voice that impressed Susan. Over lunch she had felt that Meredith had more on her mind than she was saying. About her college career, her choice of profession and perhaps her 'man trouble'.

'I'd like that,' Susan said. 'I didn't really think you'd want to talk to me any more.'

'On the contrary,' Meredith said. 'Talking to you when you're down is the most interesting part. Adversity is always the best context for a good profile. Besides, I don't think you'll be down for long.'

'I appreciate the thought,' Susan said.

She said goodbye and returned to Ron's arms.

'I get the impression you like her,' he said, running a finger across Susan's brow.

'She's very nice,' Susan said. 'Bright, too. I think she'll go a long way.'

A few miles north of the sofa on which Ron Giordano cradled Susan in his arms, the Undertaker was preparing to move.

He had watched the news all week, taking in the damage done to the investigation by the Timothy Hatch episode. The police were reeling from their own embarrassment. But they would go back to work with a vengeance. In recent weeks the Undertaker had sensed that they were inching closer to the truth that would lead them to him. He had to keep them off the track, at least for a while longer.

He dressed in dark slacks and a dark windbreaker. He wore black running shoes. He got into his car at ten-thirty at night. The ground lights in the yard were off. The neighbors were all in bed or in front of their television sets.

He turned on the car and set the heater to warm up. Then he looked at the leather case he had put on the passenger's seat in the late afternoon after getting home from work. It was about the size of a salesman's sample case, or perhaps a carrying case for audio tapes or CDs. It was a readily available catalog item for those who needed it. Those who needed it were rare.

He had a pen light and a burglar's tool, procured for this occasion.

Snowflakes swirled over the windshield, too cold to stick, as he pulled out of the garage. He drove through the neighborhood, slowly. Then out onto the suburban streets, past the strip malls and restaurants and gas stations. He kept his speed low, just in case.

When he got to the Edens he headed south, keeping an eye out for cops in the rear-view mirror. He drove south to the junction with the Kennedy, then proceeded to Touhy, where he exited and headed west. The somewhat more urban, seedier neighborhoods were restful to his eye, though there was considerable forest even here.

The neighborhood he sought was easy to find; he had cased it weeks ago in preparation for this night. The houses were respectable ranch affairs. Most had Christmas lights, and a few had the tacky plastic angels and crèches he hated. There were dogs, but they would be inside tonight because of the cold, as would their owners.

He stopped the car in an alley and walked to the house, the bag in his hand. The air was so cold that his cheeks were numb by the time he reached the door. A car came around the corner, but turned left into a driveway.

The Undertaker crept past the poorly kept shrubbery to the back of the house. The kitchen door lock was primitive; he was inside in less than a minute. He stood listening. No alarm. This was as he had predicted it.

He took off his coat and hung it over one of the kitchen chairs. He took off his shoes as well, leaving them on the mat by the door.

He made a brief tour of the living room and dining room. Nothing remarkable; a dull-as-dishwater North Side home. Framed photos of relatives on the walls, a large crucifix in the dining room. Old, old furniture with arm covers that didn't match the original upholstery. No evidence of children.

He darted upstairs for a quick look at the bedrooms, noticing the plank in the ceiling for the pull-down staircase to the attic. Then he went down to the basement.

He used his pen light to scan the room. It was not a finished basement. A washer and dryer, the furnace, a folded-up ping-pong table, a suspiciously large number of folding chairs. On the floor, a large and extremely threadbare carpet, probably imported from upstairs when the owner finally bestirred himself to get a new one.

This was perfect, exactly as he had hoped.

One thing more ... He moved along the walls, looking, looking ... He didn't find it. He had hoped for an old mattress. Oh, well. He would manage without it.

From his pocket he produced a length of old clothesline. He took out a penknife and sliced it in two, then in four, staying on the old carpet as he did so. He dropped one piece under the old couch against the wall, the others in inconspicuous corners of the room.

Then he dropped to one knee and opened the case. Inside

it were vials of blood, each fitting into a little groove, all kept in place by a solid cardboard piece with a Velcro lock.

Using the pen light, he found the three vials he wanted. He took one and stood up. He drizzled a few drops onto the ancient carpet and let them sink in. Then he took a paper towel from the roll upstairs and planted a drop here and there around the basement, rubbing it in so that it looked more like an old stain than a drop.

He returned to the case and switched the first vial for a second. He repeated his procedure, drizzling blood onto the rug and planting traces elsewhere in the basement. Then the third vial.

He stood listening to the silence. The refrigerator shuddered in the kitchen upstairs. A clock ticked. A gust of wind made one of the windows creak.

The most important work was done. But he had to make sure.

He removed more vials from the case, one by one, and planted tiny samples of blood in various parts of the basement, with special emphasis on the rug, the old couch, and – a small inspiration – the stairs. He found the laundry sink and placed samples there, running a bit of water to partially dissolve them.

When he had finished he looked at his watch. Eleven-thirty. It was time to leave.

One more job. From the bottom of the case he took a small vinyl packet tied tightly with rubber bands. He moved to the wide shelves alongside the washer and dryer. They contained assorted paint cans, tools, rags, camping gear. He fitted the vinyl packet between a folded pup tent and an old gray blanket.

He closed the case and tiptoed up the stairs. He put on his coat first, then used one of the kitchen towels to wipe the floor where he had come in. He stood on the mat by the door to put on his shoes. He let himself out and returned to his car. The snow was thicker now in the light of the streetlamps, and starting to stick to the lawns.

He returned to Touhy and drove back toward 94, making sure to slow his speed before the intersections. He took the Edens north and got off at his own neighborhood. The houses were all dark. He used the remote to open the garage door. He let himself in through the kitchen.

He washed his running shoes in the kitchen sink. He had a thorough shower. Then, dressed in his bathrobe, he took the case down to the basement and locked it in the cupboard.

He surveyed the basement. The mattress against the wall, the old furniture, the computer desk. On the ceiling the tell-tale hole in the acoustical tile for the camera.

If they ever came in here they would not have much trouble picking him for the killer he was. There were traces of blood here, too. And fiber, and cord, and hair from his victims, and towels that had been used to clean up the messes he had made.

But they would not come here. They would go to the house he had prepared tonight. He had bought himself the time he needed.

He was ready for his final move. He pondered the way things had gone. He was at peace with himself.

He had never wanted to kill women. He was not a murderer. He himself had saved many lives. He understood the value of life, more than the heedless masses of people who merely lived it.

But this was something that had to be done, this process involving the Virgin. Like the crucifixion, blood had to be spilled in order to create ascension and holiness. Three women had given their lives in this quest. He would give his own. He wanted to finish his own life in a proper manner.

He ate a late snack, put the dishwasher on and went

upstairs to his office. He sat down at the computer and began drafting a note.

*I can help you end it*, he wrote. *I know who the next victim is. I can help you save her. Wait for next message.*

He signed on. This was it, he thought. The last act had begun.

He clicked on the address file.

*MerSpiers@WGN9.com.*

He took a deep breath and sent the message.

# CHAPTER 40

On the Monday after Christmas Wendy broke it off with Tony Garza.

They met in an uptown bar which was also a popular restaurant for steaks and hamburgers. Wendy was dressed in jeans and a cotton top over which she wore a Bears sweater. Her hair was pinned back in a ponytail.

Tony had never seen her looking remotely like this. He understood immediately.

'So,' he said. 'We're saying goodbye.'

She was silent, avoiding his eyes as the waiter came up.

'Beer?' Tony asked Wendy.

She nodded.

'Bushmill's Irish for me. On the rocks. Double,' Tony said.

With a nod, the waiter receded into the cocktail-hour crowd.

Wendy was looking at Tony now. With her hair pinned back, she looked clean and delicate. He felt a throb of pain at the sight of her beauty. To think that he had held that subtle body in his arms so many times, been so intimate with her . . . He should have enjoyed it more, he mused. While it lasted.

'Is it this Carpenter guy?' he asked.

She chewed her lip, concentrating.

'I want to be honest with you,' she said. 'I don't want to

play games. In your own way you've been honest with me, Tony. Right from the start. I owe you that.'

'But you've never been honest with me, have you?' Tony asked.

She shook her head. 'I've never been honest with myself. I couldn't be honest with you. I was too – too screwed up.' She smiled. 'But of course you knew that.'

'And now you're fixed,' he said.

Again she thought before speaking. 'I can't say that. I don't know whether I'll ever be really fixed. Really normal. But I do know I have to try. I can't go on messing myself up any more. I have to make the effort.'

'And Carpenter is part of the effort,' Tony said.

'Yes.' She nodded earnestly. 'Yes, he is. He's not a solution to anything. He's just a human being. It may come to nothing. But he has placed his trust in me. His confidence. And that – that is a starting point for me.'

Tony nodded. He understood her perfectly. He was not the most brilliant man alive, but the pain he had endured in loving this girl had taught him lessons, sharpened his perception. The school of suffering . . .

'And me?' he asked. 'What am I? I should say, what *was* I? Part of the problem?'

Wendy gave him a firm look in which a glimmer of pleading was apparent.

'You invested something in me, too,' she said. 'Something I didn't deserve. Something I couldn't give back. It's too late for me to try. We have to end it.'

'Why?' he asked.

'Because I can't go on treating myself that way,' she said. 'It's not your fault. I can't go on being the person I was with you. It's not fair to me, or to you.'

'So, it's just as I predicted,' Tony said. 'You've picked out one of your society boys to shack up with. And I'm out.'

'Tony . . .' Wendy remonstrated weakly, avoiding his eyes.

Tony's anger was coiled tight inside him. But so was another emotion, one he was less accustomed to. He decided to play the one card he had not dared consider until this moment.

'Suppose I want you in whatever way you want to be with me?' he asked.

'What do you mean?' She seemed not to understand.

'All right. Say you were slumming with me,' he said. 'To cheapen yourself. Whatever. Why can't you be with me on some other basis?' He gritted his teeth. 'Like friends, or whatever. Know what I mean?' He took a deep breath. 'I need you, babe. I won't be the same if you're not around.'

'Tony, you don't need me.' Wendy knew she was not telling the truth. Through all these painful weeks she had learned that Tony did indeed need her. Not only because she was wild, and not only because she was such a contrast from his usual girls. It was because she was who she was.

'I'll forget you said that,' he said. 'Look, babe. I'm asking you to save some room for me in your life. That's all. As a favor to me, if you want to think of it that way.'

Wendy was shaking her head. 'It wouldn't be a favor to you, Tony. Because it wouldn't be real. It wouldn't be right. I just can't . . .'

The waiter arrived with their drinks. Tony downed the pungent Bushmill's Irish in two large gulps. Wendy's beer sat untouched in front of her. Tony caught the waiter's eye across the room but elected not to order another drink.

'Listen,' he said, leaning across the table. 'I slept with you as a rich bitch who was slumming. I slept with you as a confused kid who has never grown up. I slept with you in those ways. I knew how phony it was. I'm a man, I've been around. But I also made love to *you*. The real you. I touched that in you, and you know it.'

Wendy was silent, thinking.

'I suppose I can't deny it,' she said. 'I owe you that much honesty.'

She thought for another moment and decided to challenge him.

'And who was that person?' she asked. 'The real me . . .'

A smile curled his lips. 'A fighter,' he said. 'A girl who won't let the world beat her down.'

Wendy flushed. These were the same words Scott Carpenter had used to describe her. So Tony had known her after all.

'So far you've only been using that stubbornness to fuck yourself up,' Tony observed. 'Poor little rich girl. But there's more to you than that. A guy just has to look beneath the surface.'

Tears had welled in Wendy's eyes at these words, which were also similar to Scott's. She realized that Tony was a human being. In trifling with him she had not only hurt herself, but had hurt him. He had loved her, and his love had made him prescient.

He handed her a linen handkerchief. She took it and wiped her eyes. She had not known he carried cloth handkerchiefs. There was a lot she had not known about him.

'Thanks,' she said, handing it back.

He touched the linen, wet with her tears.

'Baby, don't do this to me,' he said in a low voice.

His eyes were averted. She knew it was costing him a lot to entreat her that way.

'Tony . . .' She touched his hand.

A song had come on the jukebox. The voice of Frank Sinatra sounded in the room. The young Sinatra, singing 'One for My Baby'. The noise of cocktail conversation ebbed.

The words of the song evoked a lover drowning his sorrows in an empty tavern. Sinatra had died last year after a long illness. His death lent a disturbing eloquence to the disembodied voice stating the tragic words. Uncomfortably Wendy glanced at Tony's hand, still curled around his empty glass.

Sinatra had always seemed so young, so cocky. She remembered him in *From Here to Eternity*, in *On the Town* with Gene Kelly. A young sailor thin as a wraith, dancing along the streets of New York. Suddenly it struck her as unbearably tragic that the young man had grown old and died.

'Wendy . . .' Tony's smile was both wistful and cajoling. 'One for the road?'

She was looking at him through wide eyes. She felt as though she was on a high wire between two chasms of her own making. The time had come to choose. There was no breathing space left.

'No,' she said. She stood up.

Eyes turned to her throughout the bar, for her pretty figure stood out to good advantage in her tight jeans. But Tony's eyes remained on the table.

'I'm sorry, Tony. It . . .'

For a long moment she tried to find words. Then she gave up, turned on her heel and walked out.

A patron of the bar, standing by the door, opened it for her, and she slipped through quickly. A breath of cold air hit her face, making her tears feel icy.

Tony had said something as she walked away from him, but in her haste she had not heard it. Now he sat alone, his jaw set, his hand clenched around the empty glass, listening to the words echo in his own ear.

'I love you.'

# CHAPTER 41

The New Year dawned under gray skies, with temperatures near zero and wind chills as low as 25 below, depending on one's proximity to the lake. Those who worked in the Loop, like Meredith Spiers, took the worst of it.

Meredith was at her desk, doodling idly on her blotter at Channel 9, when her phone rang.

'Meredith Spiers.'

'This is your e-mail correspondent.'

It was a woman's voice. It sounded synthesized. Meredith knew there were gadgets that could do that. They could be bought in computer stores and electronics stores. The technology was analogous to that of voice-activated computers.

'Yes,' Meredith said. 'I'm listening.'

'I have to be careful,' the caller said. 'He's suspicious. He's wondering how so much about him has gotten into the media. He's naturally going to look close to home.'

'I understand,' Meredith said. 'Who are you? To him, I mean.'

'I can't tell you that. You'll never know the answer to that. If you did, I would be dead.'

'All right. I want to ask you one question, though.'

'What?'

'How did you know about Baltimore, and about the arts?'

Meredith was testing the caller. There was the possibility that the e-mail she had received was not legitimate.

'I know where he goes. I know what he's thinking. He had his eye on her. The singer.'

'Why didn't you tell me more, so I could have saved her?'

'I couldn't. He would have known it was me.'

There was a silence.

'The next killing will be soon,' the voice said. 'Not later than next week. Do you want to stop him?'

Meredith thought for an instant before saying, 'Of course I want to stop him. I want a story, too, if I can get one.'

'Meet me in the ladies' room at the Northview Theater,' said the voice. 'During the first show of *A Civil Action*, this afternoon. Wait fifteen minutes after the start of the movie. Then go to the ladies' room. If I don't meet you there I'll get you a message within an hour.'

'Northview,' Meredith repeated. 'Fifteen minutes after the show starts.'

'Come alone. If anyone else is with you I won't be there.'

'I understand. I can make it. But you'll have to give me something to make me believe you. I don't go on wild goose chases.'

'I've already given you enough.'

'There are people who could know what you've just told me, because I know it. Tell me something I don't know. Tell me something no one else knows but you.'

There was a pause. Then the voice spoke quickly, urgently. Meredith listened, chewing her lip as she concentrated.

'Really,' she said.

The caller went on talking. Meredith doodled without seeing what she drew. Her mind was racing. What she heard was news to her.

'All right,' she said. 'That's enough for me. I'll be there.'

'Alone,' the voice insisted.

'Alone.'

Meredith touched the mouse to illuminate her monitor.

She looked at her afternoon schedule. The schedule was busy. She had an interview with a city councilman, and a lot of calls to make. Susan Shader had agreed to have a drink with her at five-thirty.

She called the councilman's secretary to reschedule the interview for later in the week. She also called Susan Shader's answering service and left a message for Susan.

Then she got up and left the office.

# CHAPTER 42

Meredith took the Outer Drive to Sheridan Road in her own car, a three-year-old Honda Accord.

She entered the theater in time for the beginning of *A Civil Action*. She mentally counted the minutes and left the theater fifteen minutes after the show began. The lobby was deserted. She found the ladies' room easily. When she entered she saw two teenage girls primping in the large mirror. Hoping to meet boys at the movies, Meredith guessed.

One of the four toilet stalls was closed. Meredith entered the one adjacent to it and waited.

'Jesus,' said one of the girls. 'I look like something the cat dragged in.'

'Never mind,' said her friend. 'It's dark in there.'

'What a scag . . .'

They left, still giggling. Meredith sat waiting. There was not a sound from the next stall. After a couple of minutes she began to wonder if it was empty.

'Is anyone there?' she said in a low voice.

There was no answer. She stood up, left her stall and looked through the crack in the door frame to the closed stall. It was empty.

She looked at her watch. One-twenty-five. It was late. The woman should have shown herself by now.

Meredith went to the mirror. Her face looked tired, but the blue eyes sparkled with expectancy. Those eyes were her best feature. They showed up brilliantly on television, especially when she wore dark outfits. A lot of female reporters used full-iris contacts to make their eyes more noticeable, but Meredith didn't have to.

She brushed a strand of her hair out of her eyes. She applied a touch of color to her cheeks. Then she looked at her watch again.

Sighing, she left the bathroom. She hung around in the corridor for a few minutes, watching the entrance to the ladies' room. A woman went in, left a minute later. Then another.

Meredith now knew she had come here for nothing. The caller had changed her mind, or perhaps not been on the level to begin with.

Meredith used the pay phone in the lobby to tell her editor she was coming back in for the rest of the afternoon.

She left the theater, cursing the time she had lost. This was the middle of the day, always a busy time for her. She usually spent it on the phone doing research if she wasn't actually out on a story.

She went into the parking ramp and up the stairs, not wanting to wait for the elevator. She got into her car with a little grunt of impatience.

'Don't start the engine,' a male voice sounded behind her. 'My gun is pointed at the middle of your spinal cord. You'll never walk again.'

Meredith pursed her lips. She had been taken. It was her own fault. She should have told someone where she was going. Brought someone along, even, as a precaution. This was a murder investigation, after all.

'Who are you?' she asked, realizing only now that the male voice sounded vaguely familiar.

'You'll find that out soon enough. Just don't touch the horn. Don't turn on the ignition.'

Her right hand was already in her purse, looking for the Mace. Cursing, she hit the horn. Nothing happened.

*He must have . . .*

A hand curled around her face before the thought could complete itself. A wet cloth was being pressed to her mouth and nose. The acrid stench of chloroform penetrated her.

She twisted frantically in her seat. But the drug was powerful. Her eyes began to roll up in her head. She coughed, gagged, went limp.

She had time to wonder whether the cold concrete wall in front of the windshield was the last thing she would ever see.

# CHAPTER 43

The morning after her abduction the police found Meredith Spiers's Honda abandoned at a busy rest stop on Route 55 near Midway Airport. A strong smell of chloroform inside the car left little doubt that the reporter had been a victim of foul play.

Meredith's colleagues at Channel 9 had been calling her at home since the previous afternoon. When the police visited the station, Meredith's producer told them that Meredith had signed out yesterday at a little before one, and had called an hour later to say she was coming back in. She never arrived.

Channel 7's mobile unit, monitoring the CPD radios, had arrived at the crime scene in time to learn about the chloroform. The story was spreading like wildfire.

When Abel Weathers learned from David Gold that Meredith had been receiving e-mails about the Undertaker investigation, he exploded.

'What the fuck are you trying to do to me?' he screamed. 'How many more screw-ups can happen to one investigation?'

Gold, sitting in the visitor's chair before Weathers's massive desk, was not cowed by Weather's anger.

'We thought there was a leak in the CPD, or possibly in your office,' he said. 'The best thing seemed to let Meredith run with it for a while. She reported to me personally, and to . . .'

'To who?'

'To Susan.'

'Oh, my God.' Weathers leaned back in his swivel chair. 'With friends like you I don't need enemies. I think you're going soft in the head since you got shot.'

Gold did not particularly regret his secret arrangement with Meredith. He did regret his failure to foresee physical danger to the reporter and to take precautions. When Meredith's last e-mail predicted the abduction of Marcie Webb, Gold knew it came from the killer. He should have put a man on Meredith from that moment.

STAR REPORTER MISSING, ran the headlines. Photos of Meredith's well-known face were all over the papers, and file video of her reports for Channel 9 was being shown at the top of the news on all the local stations.

A meeting was held immediately at City Hall. Present were the lead detectives on the Undertaker case and the FBI point men, including Tom Castaneda.

Like so much of the evidence in the Undertaker case, Meredith's Honda revealed everything and nothing.

'The techs went over the seats and the floor mats,' Rich Sheehan reported. 'They picked up a lot. Her car was messy. We assumed he hid in the back seat, so we segregated the fiber and trace from that area. There are some clothing fibers, but it could be anything.'

Those present shook their heads. Nothing from the car would be of use now. At best the trace evidence might help to convict Meredith's abductor long after he had murdered her.

'Okay,' said Weathers. 'Obviously we have an APB on Spiers. We don't know who has her. If it's the Undertaker, we know she was receiving e-mails from him. He must have used that contact to lure her into a meeting. How about her computer?'

Terrell shook his head. 'We checked her own e-mail files and the online service. She didn't save it.'

Gold raised his hand. 'I don't believe she would have gone to meet this guy without leaving something behind for us in the event she got into trouble. Wasn't there anything in her office, or at home, to give us a clue?'

'We have men in both places right now,' Terrell said. 'Her desk at work is a mess, so is the one at home. We're sifting through. We haven't found anything useful yet.'

'The sixty-four-dollar question is, why did he snatch her?' Weathers said. 'Why Meredith Spiers, and why now? She's well known, her disappearance has to bring an APB and a lot of attention. That means much more danger to the killer. Why is he taking this risk?'

Tom Castaneda raised a hand. 'We might have been getting closer than we thought in the last couple of weeks,' he said. 'He might have been afraid we were about to pick him up. So he abducted Spiers as a bargaining chip.'

'That's possible,' said Rich Sheehan. 'On the other hand, let's not forget we're dealing with a sicko. Maybe he abducted her out of revenge for her cooperation with the authorities. Right, Dave?'

Gold nodded. 'Meredith wasn't using his leaks directly in her reports. I helped her write the stories. It was part of her deal with me. It's possible that he held that against her.'

'The very fact that he was communicating with her indicates a special interest in her,' said Castaneda. 'You know how these guys identify with journalists.'

It was Joe Riccio who offered the explanation the others did not want to hear.

'She could simply be victim number four,' he said. 'It could be as simple as that.'

The others seemed astonished by this suggestion.

'I don't get it,' said Castaneda. 'A famous reporter?'

'Stranger things have happened,' Riccio said.

Gold cleared his throat. 'There's something I should say here, for what it's worth. Susan Shader has had a theory about the Undertaker all along. She thinks the first three victims were substitutes for a woman the Undertaker has in his mind. Clones, tune-ups – whatever. It's possible that Meredith is part of the series.'

Weathers reddened at the mention of Susan's name.

'How does that help us?' he asked.

'It might be a notion to follow up on,' Gold said. 'If the victims have something in common that we haven't identified yet, and if Meredith is connected to them in that way . . .'

'Like virginity?' someone murmured. Suppressed laughter was heard around the table.

Weathers gave Gold a look of reproach. He was embarrassed by the mere mention of Susan's name. Gold realized there was no longer room in the investigation for any of Susan's theories about the killer. Her ideas were too vague to be followed up in any concrete way, and the 'Virgin' notion had already brought about the Timothy Hatch fiasco.

'Whatever the reason is, he's got her,' Castaneda said. 'We need to get her back alive.'

Someone brought a note in to Weathers, who sighed.

'This isn't our day,' he said. 'The media got on to Spiers's connection to the Undertaker somehow. The *Sun-Times* is going to run a banner headline tomorrow that says COULD SHE BE NUMBER FOUR?' He crushed the note into a ball and threw it across the table. 'And this is right after we put the wrong guy behind bars!'

Those present could appreciate Weathers's chagrin. If Meredith Spiers became the Undertaker's fourth victim, the damage to the Chicago PD could last for years. Her death would forever symbolize their incompetence, and the State's Attorney's.

'It will be a fire storm,' said Weathers's assistant. 'Spiers is a star around here. She's a virtual sex symbol in local journalism. This is going to be bad.'

The expressions on the faces around the table left little doubt that they were imagining the pretty face and slim body of Meredith Spiers torn by knife wounds in the pattern of a crucifix.

'What about the Undertaker?' Weathers asked.

'As I say,' Castaneda repeated, 'we might have been getting closer this past week or so. But none of our suspects has panned out.'

Terrell said, 'The pro-life crowd has given us a few good suspects, but they either have alibis or are out of consideration for other reasons.' He shrugged. 'Hatch was the best we had, and he was wrong.'

No one wanted to hear the name of Timothy Hatch mentioned.

'Okay,' Weathers said. 'Let's hit the streets. There's nothing else left for us to do.'

In a spirit of resignation the meeting broke up.

# CHAPTER 44

As soon as he got back to his office David Gold called Susan. He met her at her apartment at six that night. Two tactical officers were in the hall, keeping an eye on the elevator and the stairs, and a uniformed officer from Area Six was inside the apartment. Gold greeted the young man with a handshake before accompanying Susan to the kitchen.

'We had meetings today,' he told her. 'The bottom line is that Weathers is treating Spiers as number four. I tried to float your theory about other ways to view the whole series of victims, but after Hatch he's not gonna pursue anything that has your name on it.'

Susan nodded. 'I understand.'

'I've got to tell you, Susan, I don't think we're going to find Meredith. Not in time, anyway. Our leads are all too thin. Unless the Undertaker offers her for ransom or uses her as a hostage, or something along those lines ...'

Susan opened a bottle of the ale Gold liked and put it in front of him.

'And you don't think he'll do that,' she said.

Gold shook his head. 'She may be dead already. And if she isn't, there's not a damn thing we can do to help her.'

Susan kept her guilt feelings to herself. The Timothy Hatch fiasco was preying on her mind. If the police had not been side-tracked for over a week on that false lead, they might have caught up with the Undertaker in that time. Now

Meredith was gone, and there seemed no way to bring her back.

Susan had thought of nothing but Meredith since the news of her disappearance broke. Meredith's last words to Susan, spoken over the phone, still lingered hauntingly in her mind. 'There were some things I wanted to say to you the other day. I hope we can talk again soon. It would be good for me.'

Meredith Spiers had become a strangely multiple figure to Susan. She was the younger sister Susan had never had. She was also an alter ego for Susan herself. And, in a sense, the patient she had never had.

Susan believed that Meredith's fame and success had not brought her happiness. She even suspected that her career might be bringing her ever closer to some sort of personal collapse, or at least to permanent unhappiness. Susan was not sure she understood the reason for this, but she thought it might have something to do with the shadowy 'man trouble' Meredith had had while a college student.

The sudden change of Meredith's direction bespoke a personal crisis and a defense against that crisis. The defense of achievement, success, fame. Susan's career as a psychiatrist had long since taught her that this defense did not work. Many of her patients were wealthy, successful people. She had come to believe that success was perhaps even more toxic an irritant to mental health than failure.

'I should have had a man on her,' Gold was saying. 'I don't know what I was thinking.'

'It never occurred to me either,' Susan said. 'Maybe because Meredith is so famous.'

*And so hard-boiled*, she thought. Meredith seemed so strong, so savvy and well connected, that it simply never occurred to Susan that she might become a crime victim. Not for the first time in her career, she had been taken in by appearances. A hard fault for a psychiatrist to admit to.

'Well, I guess there's nothing for me to do but sit and wait,' she said. 'Maybe your people will . . .'

'No.' Gold was shaking his head. 'Maybe they will and maybe they won't, but I'm not gonna wait around to find out. I need you, Susan.'

He was sitting at her kitchen table, still a bit pale and flaccid from his surgery, but bearing a determined look.

'What for?' she asked, taken by surprise. She had never felt so helpless. She did not see how she could help him.

'You're the only one who has dared to speculate that the Undertaker had a specific woman in mind when he chose his victims. If that woman is Meredith, that puts you way ahead of the rest of us.'

'Why?'

'Because you know her. Well enough to pick up a reason why he has her in his mind.'

'I don't know her that well, David.' Susan shook her head. 'I know very little about her.'

'Enough to make you prick up your ears,' Gold corrected. 'I'm right, aren't I?'

Susan thought for a moment. 'I did have a couple of interesting feelings about her,' she said. 'I suspected she had had an abortion herself. When we talked about the Undertaker, and once when we saw the TV news about the abortion clinic that was bombed.'

'That's a start,' Gold said. 'I want you to find out more. Find out about her abortion, if there was one. Find out about her past. How she got into journalism. Why she came here.'

'Isn't that rather remote?' Susan asked.

'Not if your theory about the Undertaker is right. Not if Meredith is more than just another victim to him. And I think she is more.'

'What makes you think that?'

'The fact that she's so well known,' Gold said. 'It's much

more dangerous to abduct a famous person. Hard to get up your nerve. Frankly, I don't think he would have been able to pull it off unless he was working his way up to it for a long time. I think he worked his way up by killing other girls. I also think he worked his way up by sending Meredith those e-mails. He was circling her, getting a bead on her.' He looked at Susan through narrowed eyes. 'When you were out in California you told me you thought he had been out there. Right?'

*Methuselah*. Preoccupied, Susan did not quite catch the signal that raced through her consciousness. But she did catch an acute smell of oily smoke, as of engine exhaust.

'Do you smell smoke?' she asked Gold.

Gold shrugged. 'No. I don't smell anything.'

'Do you think he knew Meredith in California?' she asked.

'Why not?'

Susan nodded ruminatively. 'Perhaps . . .'

'He didn't do all this just because he saw her face on the news and took a liking to her. It had to be more complicated than that.' Gold looked at his untouched ale, then back at Susan. 'These feelings of yours, about the Virgin, about *Romeo and Juliet* – they go deeper than seeing a reporter on the news.'

'They're just feelings.' Susan looked unconvinced.

'Strong feelings,' Gold corrected. 'Have you ever felt stronger about anything?'

Susan sighed. 'I suppose not. These things have been keeping me awake nights for weeks. They have to mean something.'

'All I want is for you to operate on the assumption that they do,' he said. 'No one else is going to. Weathers has crossed you off his list. Castaneda won't do anything without Weathers. Not after Hatch. Not one cop is going to look into this angle. Suppose it's the right angle. Suppose it is the only way to save her life.'

Susan nodded wearily. 'What do you want me to do?'

'I want you to find out the things you don't know. What happened at Berkeley to turn her into a reporter? What was the man trouble you mentioned? Why did she come here? Who might have crossed her path along the way?'

Susan was silent.

'Riccio will go with you,' Gold said. 'I fixed it downtown so they won't ream him for it. You need protection, and you need somebody with a badge.'

Susan felt cornered. After the Timothy Hatch débâcle, she had been almost relieved to be just a doctor again, seeing her patients and leading a private life. Now Gold was asking her to throw herself into the fray again.

'What if I come up empty?' she asked.

'What if we all come up empty?'

Susan nodded. 'Where do I start?'

'Our guys went through her apartment today,' Gold said. 'I want you to go over there and have a look around. See what you can pick up.'

'All right.'

There was a silence. Gold contemplated this small, pretty woman whose work he had admired for seven years, and whose gift had helped him put men like Chad Bose and Arnold Haze behind bars. Susan was all too quick to blame herself for every failure as though she was personally at fault. Somehow her education as a doctor, having prepared her for the heavy responsibility of patients' lives, had not prepared her for the consequences of her mistakes in police work. What she could handle in the context of illness, she did not seem able to handle where violence was the issue.

On the other hand, did even the doctors really handle it? Perhaps not. Perhaps this was the reason doctors and cops had in common their high divorce rate, their problems with drugs and alcohol, their high suicide rate. Too much responsibility. Too much potential for failure.

Gold stood up. 'Take your gun.'

'David . . .'

'Have you been practicing?'

She grimaced. 'I've been over a few times. My aim stinks.'

'Make sure you've got it,' Gold said. 'I don't want you getting whacked by Cal Train when you're on a mission for me.'

She nodded. 'All right, David.'

# CHAPTER 45

Joe Riccio drove Susan to Meredith Spiers's Marina Towers apartment. He wore the same poker face Susan had now become familiar with. If he had an opinion about being covertly assigned to babysit her on her private investigation of Meredith Spiers, he gave no sign of it.

Meredith's apartment was something of a disappointment. Despite the spectacular nocturnal view of the Chicago River and the downtown skyline, the place seemed unfinished and a bit seedy, like a student's apartment. The drapes badly needed replacing. The furniture was nondescript. The carpet was stained and in some places fraying.

Meredith was a career girl indifferent to her home surroundings. But Susan saw something else in the disarray of the apartment. Meredith was a girl without a mother. She had told Susan she had not spoken to her mother in years. Most young women Meredith's age lived in apartments whose civilized accoutrements reflected the help and input of their mothers.

This thought sent a pang of loneliness through Susan, for she also was a woman without a mother, and her own apartment in Lincoln Park reflected the fact.

Susan noticed the answering machine by the phone in the kitchen. 'Is this where she took her business calls?' she asked.

Riccio shook his head. 'The answering machine is for

personal calls. She has a voice mail service for the professional stuff.'

The arrangement was similar to Susan's own.

'Everything's dusted,' Riccio told her. 'Touch anything you want.'

The second bedroom had been turned into an office, with a PC and several large cabinets full of computerized files and hard copies. The master bedroom was scarcely more domestic, with crowded bookcases along the walls and piles of folders on the floor against the walls. The bed was queen-sized, with a skirt that matched the comforter, but the large pillows weren't wearing shams. Susan suspected they were in the laundry or perhaps forgotten in the closet.

Susan sighed. It would take days to sift through all the printed matter collected here. She would not even know where to begin.

'Did you check her phone calls?'

Riccio nodded. 'They think the call came on her phone at Channel 9. One of the office boys remembers her talking on her phone in a low voice, just before she left.'

'What about her e-mail?'

'They're going through it. It will take time.'

Susan stood thinking. Why had the Undertaker abducted Meredith? Why now? So soon after the Timothy Hatch fiasco . . . Wouldn't the killer have felt safe now, with plenty of leisure to plan his next murder?

Unless he had a timetable of his own, and was following it without regard for external events. In which case Meredith was, as some of the cops believed, number four.

Susan turned on Meredith's TV and listened to the news as she looked around the apartment. The national media had gotten into the act. Abel Weathers himself was to be interviewed by Larry King tomorrow night. Cable reporters were converging on Chicago. As for the local stations, they were hyping the story as a tragedy that had befallen one of their own, a beautiful award-winning reporter. Channel 9 managed to keep some dignity about the whole thing, offering breaking stories about Meredith's disappearance and, in a hastily assembled special report, an overview of her acclaimed reporting of the past four years.

Instinct told Susan to ignore the massive research files cluttering the apartment. If Meredith had found out anything significant about the Undertaker through her own research, she would have told David Gold about it. Susan doubted that Meredith could have unearthed anything the police didn't already have.

She looked in the logical places for effects of a more personal nature. Dresser drawers, bookshelves, closets. There was not much to find. Like Susan herself, Meredith was a woman cut off from her past, not only by the press of events in her busy professional life but by an emotional barrier that made her loath to look backward.

A banker's box, dumped like detritus in a corner, held journalistic awards and videotapes of awards ceremonies. Searching high and low, Susan could not find a collection of personal letters or a scrapbook. It almost seemed that Meredith was hiding out, trying to make believe her past had never existed.

One thing caught her eye. It was a framed photo of the full professors in the mathematics department at Berkeley. Meredith had spoken wistfully of her mathematics major and the plans she once had for an academic life.

Susan thought it odd, to say the least, that someone as far removed from her erstwhile college major as Meredith Spiers would have kept such a photo. There was no signature, no indication of anything personal about the photo. Just a collection of venerable-looking men in caps and gowns, some of them looking faintly Einstein-esque, with long hair or mous-taches.

Susan was sure the picture concealed something. She looked more closely. A couple of the professors were rather young to be senior faculty. This made sense, she thought. Many mathematicians were prodigies who completed college at an early age and went straight into academia. She had heard of mathematics geniuses who were full professors before the age of twenty.

She ran a finger over the faces. Like a witching rod it stopped almost immediately, pointing to the narrow face and intense eyes of a younger professor. She could tell that Mere-dith's finger had rested on this spot as her own was now doing.

She turned the picture over and followed the key to the names, laboriously turning and returning the picture until she found the correct name.

*Auden, Graham.*

She wrote the name down on her memo pad and put the picture back on the shelf.

On a hunch she checked the filing cabinets, one by one, going through the folders alphabetically in search of the name Auden. In one of the older cabinets in the master bedroom she found a file folder with the professor's name on it. Inside was a small collection of clippings from newspapers about lectures or participation in symposia by Graham Auden. The most recent one was three years old.

Susan stood thinking for a long moment. Then she picked up the phone and called David Gold.

'Gold here.'

'David, this is me. I'm in Meredith's apartment. The only thing I've found is some clippings about a former math-ematics professor Meredith had at Berkeley. His name is Graham Auden.'

Gold seemed irritated. 'You're not telling me the Undertaker teaches math, are you?'

'No. But I have a feeling this professor played an important role in Meredith's life. She changed her major abruptly from mathematics to journalism. When we talked together I had the strong suspicion that she had a failed love relationship in college, and that that had something to do with her change of major. I also . . .'

'What?'

'I also had the feeling she might have had an abortion when she was in college. It wasn't very clear. Just a feeling.'

'Like our victims. Okay . . .'

'David, remember when I was in Berkeley with Michael, I had the strong feeling that the Undertaker had been out there? I know it's a stretch, but suppose the Undertaker was in California when Meredith was. Suppose he's connected to her in some way we don't understand. That alone might explain why he chose her to send those e-mails to.'

'And why he snatched her yesterday?' Gold asked.

'I don't know, David. I feel confused.'

Gold thought for a moment. 'Listen,' he said. 'You're on your own now. Nobody is watching you, nobody can second-guess you. Follow your own instincts. Do you want to go back to California?'

Susan thought for a moment. 'I think so. After I've poked around here some more.'

'Call me when you've decided.'

David Gold hung up the phone in his office and sat with his long legs propped on the desk. The lingering pain and stiffness in his chest and shoulders made him wince.

Police work, he liked to say, involved few surprises. Ninety-five percent of the time the perpetrator turned out to be the first and most obvious suspect. Husband, wife, father, mother. Brother, sister, boyfriend, business partner. Only in rare cases was the solution to a crime not obvious. Police work consisted of pinning down the obvious suspect and getting a conviction. Not in following loose ends into the improbable.

But serial killers were the exception. They didn't kill people they knew. They killed strangers. That was why so few of them were caught.

Gold was willing to give Susan a long leash, and to trust her instincts himself, for the very reason that ordinary police work was not very effective where serial killers were concerned. The manhunt taking place now would probably fail, because it was the nature of a serial killer to slip through the net.

Gold shrugged. He might as well let Susan delve into improbabilities. What was there to lose?

Susan stood in Meredith's silent apartment, listening to the moan of the wind against the windows. She was ready to leave. She was morally certain there was nothing concrete here to help her find out who had abducted Meredith.

On an impulse she went back to Meredith's computer. She opened the online folder and clicked on Meredith's e-mail address book. Perhaps the names of her regular correspondents might yield something.

The list was discouragingly enormous, including e-mail addresses of hundreds of journalistic contacts, friends, public officials, research sources. But there were three addresses kept numbered at the head of the list, rather than alphabetized with the rest. Two of these were producers at Channel 9. The third, Susan discovered by comparison with Meredith's small address book, was a college friend and former roommate named Jill Kaminsky, who lived in Petaluma, California.

Susan looked at her watch. It was only six o'clock in California. She dialed Jill Kaminsky's number. The phone was picked up after several rings and a woman's voice answered, partly obscured by the screams of at least two young children.

Susan identified herself and spoke for a few minutes before hanging up and calling David Gold. He was out of the office, so Susan left a message with the secretary and hung up.

She found Riccio sitting at the counter in Meredith's kitchen, looking through Meredith's phone bills.

'707–555–2174,' she said.

Riccio nodded. 'Couple of times a week,' he said. 'Calls in the three- to four-dollar range. She talks to that number a lot.'

'Good,' Susan said. 'That's where we're going.'

# CHAPTER 46

Meredith woke up with a shattering headache.

Mercifully, the room was in darkness. As she came to herself she realized it was a standard guest bedroom, perhaps in a house. There were windows on two of the walls, with interior shutters. A door to the right of the bed probably led to a small bathroom. The carpet was plush, though she could not make out its color in this light. A couple of oil paintings were on the walls, their forms unclear in the penumbra.

She was naked. The sheets and pillowcase were silk. The bedspread was ornamented with costly brocade. The bed-clothes seemed faintly scented with something expensive.

'Oh,' she said, wincing as she felt the pain crash behind her eyes. She tried to lessen it by not moving. She had had paralyzing hangovers in her time, but this pain was in a class by itself.

She lay limply contemplating her own misery for what might have been five minutes or a half-hour. Then a timid knock came at the door. A man let himself in. Tall, rather thin, with dark hair and a long face. He set a tray down on the bedside table.

'How are you feeling?' he asked.

Meredith pulled the covers up to her neck, her eyes wide. 'Who are you?'

'I hope you're comfortable,' he said. 'I expect you have a whopper of a headache. There's Ibuprofen on the tray. I'd recommend three, but take as many as you like. You're not allergic to it, are you? I can get you Tylenol or aspirin.'

Meredith looked up at him. Her journalist's armor came to eclipse her terror, at least for the moment.

'You'd better turn me loose right now, whoever you are,' she said. 'If you hurt me they'll throw the book at you when they catch up to you.'

He ignored her words.

'The bathroom has a shower,' he said. 'I got a shampoo and conditioner that should work for you. There's a bathrobe in your size hanging on the door. I brought you coffee and rolls. If you can't get anything down now, don't worry about it, that's the drug. When it wears off you'll be famished. Just tell me what you want to eat and I'll try to provide it.'

She was staring at him angrily. 'Who in hell are you?'

He stood at the end of the bed looking down at her. Something in his manner struck a tiny chord in her memory.

'We've met before, haven't we?' she asked. 'I thought I recognized your voice, in the car.'

His hands were at his sides. He bobbed slightly on the balls of his feet. His silhouette in the gloom looked familiar. The tallness, the dark hair and long face . . .

'Is that why you picked me to send the e-mails to?' she asked. 'Because you knew me already?'

He shook his head. 'Because you're you,' he said.

'What is that supposed to mean?' She held the silk sheet more tightly against her chin.

'You don't have to be afraid of me, you know.' He hadn't moved. He stood looking down at her, his hands at his sides. 'I didn't bring you here to hurt you.'

'Then why?' she asked. 'Am I a hostage? Do you want a ransom? Do you want to trade me for your freedom?'

A shudder went through her limbs as it dawned on her that this man was probably the Undertaker.

'None of those,' he said.

'Then why?'

'I told you. Because you're you.'

'What does that mean?'

He smiled. 'I'm so excited. I've been waiting so long for this. You haven't been out of my thoughts for a single minute since it started.'

'Since what started?'

He stood smiling at her. 'You're so beautiful,' he said. 'So much more beautiful than you look on TV. Do people tell you that?'

A pulse of shame went through Meredith when she thought of her nudity under the sheet.

'Who took my clothes off?' she asked.

'They stank of chloroform,' he said. 'They're being cleaned. They'll be here for you when you need them.'

'What am I supposed to do in the meantime?' she asked, her shaking voice belying the irritation she tried to muster. 'Run around naked?'

'You have the bathrobe,' he said. 'If you want clothes, just tell me what to buy. I know your size.'

He moved toward the chair in the corner and touched the switch on a tall halogen lamp. A pallid glow lit the room.

'It's a rheostat,' he said. 'You can have as much or as little light as you want. There's also a good reading lamp beside the bed. What kind of books do you like?'

As he reached to turn off the light she saw his eyes for an instant. Dark, sparkling. They were taking her in during the brief illumination. He was aware of her body. That could work to her advantage, she decided.

'What if I scream?' she asked.

'No one will hear you. Go ahead.'

'What if I break the windows?'

'I'm afraid that won't work. It's been – they're unbreakable glass.'

*It's been tried.* Meredith shuddered again.

'Look,' she said. 'You don't seem like a stupid person to me, but I don't think you realize what you've gotten yourself into. You can't abduct high-profile people like journalists. If anything happens to me they will never, never let you out of jail. Do you really want to spend the rest of your life behind bars?'

'That won't be a problem,' he said. 'You'll understand when the time comes. No one is going to arrest me.'

Meredith was thinking quickly. He seemed at least halfway reasonable. He had been thorough and careful in picking her up. That must mean he was smart. Perhaps she could cajole or manipulate him into letting her go.

'I can help you, you know,' she said. 'I have a lot of contacts. In the police, in government, not to mention the press. I could help you get away. There are things I could trade . . .'

He moved toward the door. On an impulse she squirmed off the bed, pulling the sheet after her, and barred his path.

'Look. I don't know what you think I am,' she said. 'I can get ugly if I have to. I'm not a princess in a tower.'

He grabbed her around her neck and pulled her roughly against his chest. The headache in her temples throbbed wildly.

'No, you're not,' he said in her ear. 'You're a Virgin.'

His arm curled around her waist, holding her to him. She felt tenderness in his touch. 'No one knows that better than me,' he said.

*Susan was right.* Meredith felt a rampart give way inside her. It was all real.

'What are you talking about?' she asked weakly.

He didn't answer. He held her close, swaying slightly in

the darkness. She felt his chin against her forehead. He was much taller than she was, perhaps six feet two or three. His body was hard.

Slowly he guided her back to the bed and pushed her down. She let herself be pushed.

'Now be good and take your pills,' he said firmly. 'Drink the coffee if you can get it down. Take a shower. I'll be back later and we can talk.'

He let himself out. As he opened the door she got another glimpse of the dark eyes. They were deep-set, giving him a melancholy look that was accentuated by his long face.

*No one knows that better than me.*

Meredith pondered his words. As she fumbled for the pain pills, it occurred to her that he had had a beard when she knew him. His cheeks were sunken, giving him a slightly cadaverous air. The beard had masked that.

The pills were in her mouth, the water glass at her lips.

*How are you feeling?* The brisk, helpful manner, the deep voice . . .

Meredith never forgot a face. She prided herself on that.

*Oh, my God.* Meredith choked on the pills, and the water sprayed the silk bedspread. Her hand shook so badly that the glass fell in her lap.

She knew who he was now.

# CHAPTER 47

The old man was a retired civil servant living in a modest town house in Cicero. He was sitting down to his morning paper when two loud knocks came at his door. A tremor of worry shot through his body, but he got up from the table slowly.

'Who is it?' he called.

'Police, Mr Taterik.' Two more knocks, louder, shook the door.

The old man set the chain latch and opened the door an inch. In the next instant, it seemed, eight Chicago policemen were in the small kitchen. Their uniforms made them look outsized and almost unreal. Two of them had guns drawn, the others had their batons out. He caught a glimpse of slush puddles spreading from their heavy boots over his linoleum floor.

'What . . .' The old man could hardly make himself heard over the clamor of the cops as they barked orders to each other. One of the uniforms frisked him while a second pushed him back against the sink. The other cops disappeared into the apartment, their feet pounding on the stairs.

'What are you . . .'

The cop who had frisked the old man was reciting the Miranda in a fast murmur that sounded rather like a Hail Mary. The apartment seemed to be shaking. The old man could only watch in bewilderment as the confusion raged around him.

After a few minutes two of the cops from upstairs came into the kitchen carrying stacks of magazines. They put them on the kitchen table alongside the old man's untouched Entenmann's long john and nodded to the cop who had given the Miranda. The top magazine bore the title *Red Hot Monthly* and displayed a picture of a large-breasted Chinese girl wearing a sanitary napkin and nothing else.

As the uniformed cop in charge checked the other magazines, all of which were devoted to pictures of women menstruating, one of his colleagues came in with a pillowcase full of used tampons. The other cops wrinkled their noses in disgust.

'What about the basement?' the lead cop asked.

'Nothing.'

'Mr Taterik, we'd like you to come downtown with us to answer a few questions. You can call your attorney from there if you like.' One of the uniforms was holding out the old man's down coat, for all the world like a butler.

'Let's go, Mr Taterik.'

A moment later the kitchen was empty, the coffee still untouched on the table. The long john had been picked up by one of the officers, who let the old man eat it in the back of the squad car on the way to the Loop.

Emmet Taterik was one of several hundred summary arrests made that day in the greater metropolitan area. The CPD rounded up every sex criminal in the area, sometimes with little regard for due process. There were no vacations that day and few sick leaves. Cops with head colds and flu muscled rapists and peepers into squad cars. Cops muttering about overtime put the cuffs on exhibitionists, pedophiles and pornographers. The small minority of sex offenders known to go in for vampirism were all in custody by day's end.

Harmless amateur witches and Devil-worshipers, guilty only of conducting rituals involving the blood of mice and rats, were put behind bars.

The FBI's wider search was more ceremonious than the round-up in Chicago itself, but the principle was the same. Every perpetrator with a yellow sheet remotely related to sex crimes was brought in for questioning after a thorough and sometimes legal search of his residence and place of work.

If there was a known sex offender whose private appetites had grown over the years into a thirst for violence that could account for the deaths of three women and the abduction of a fourth, that offender was now in custody. The police left no stone unturned, and were not shy about who they offended. Meredith Spiers was a celebrity crime victim, and if she did not survive her abduction the image of the city of Chicago would never be the same.

By day's end Cook County Jail resembled an airport during a blizzard. Suspects were being interrogated in hallways, in the lunchroom downstairs, even in storage areas. Exhausted cops were sharing convenience food in doorways while suspects, having missed their lunch and dinner, looked on enviously.

It was as cruel a round-up as had been seen in the city in forty years. But it turned up nothing new about Meredith Spiers's whereabouts or the identity of her abductor. The detectives in charge of the Undertaker investigation looked on sadly, for they had suspected in advance that the mass arrests would be futile. From the outset the Undertaker's success in picking up respectable young women had suggested he was no ordinary sex offender. The peculiarities of his MO indicated a sophisticated mind and an obsessionality which would incline him to avoid mistakes rather than to commit them.

The bad news was brought to Abel Weathers at his City

Hall desk, where he was eating pizza with three of his prosecutors. Sighing, Weathers called his wife to tell her he would not be home until late. A meeting with the FBI was scheduled for nine o'clock. He had little hope for good news at that meeting.

Ironically, the only progress made that day came not from the authorities' mass arrests and interrogations, but from Meredith Spiers herself.

While Susan was making her reservations for a flight to California, CPD detectives were crawling over every aspect of Meredith's professional life, searching for a clue to what had happened to her.

Meredith's news producer found herself in a room at Channel 9 with half a dozen cops and FBI men. After lamely offering them coffee, which they refused, she asked how she could be of assistance.

'We need to know something about Meredith's working methods,' said the FBI man who seemed to be in charge. 'Her professional habits, the way she worked.'

'Well, there's not a lot to say,' the woman replied. 'She was – she's very thorough, very professional. She never reveals a source. She never does a story without confirmation from at least two sources. If the story is unflattering to someone in the public eye, she always gives that person an opportunity to respond in the body of the story. Things like that.' She seemed to search for words. 'She's a pro,' she concluded. 'She's got good ethics. That doesn't come along every day in our business.'

'Okay,' said the FBI man. 'Let's say for the sake of argument that she got a call from someone with a hot tip about the Undertaker. What would have been her procedure?'

'Normally she would have called me in to ask whether

she should proceed on it,' the producer said. 'She would at least touch base with me.'

'But she didn't, in this case.'

The woman shook her head sadly. 'No. She didn't.'

'That can only be because the caller told her she had to keep it a secret. There was probably a threat. If she told anyone else, the source would dry up.'

'Yes, I suppose so,' the woman agreed.

A CPD detective now spoke. 'If Meredith is the pro you say she is,' he said, 'she wouldn't just walk away from her desk without some sort of quid pro quo. Something to prove to her that the source was on the level.'

The producer nodded. 'I agree. She wouldn't go off on a wild goose chase.'

'And Meredith was already inside the Undertaker investigation, according to Detective Gold,' said the cop. 'She would know bullshit from truth about the case.'

'Yes, I think so.'

'We can therefore assume that the person on the phone told her something substantive about the case to convince her the call was legit.' The detective was toying with an unlit cigarette.

At that moment a knock sounded at the door and another FBI man came in with one of Meredith's colleagues, a gofer named Trish Calderon.

'This is Trish. She did a lot of errands for Meredith, knew her desk pretty well,' said the FBI man. 'She wants to show us something.'

Trish was an attractive Northwestern journalism student who wore tight jeans which made a visible impression on the men in the room. She was carrying a rolled-up piece of heavy paper.

'This is Meredith's blotter,' she said. 'Meredith was – is – a compulsive doodler. She keeps her keyboard on the blotter, with the monitor slightly to the left. She doodles on her blotter while she looks at the screen or takes phone calls.'

She unfurled the blotter paper to show it to those present. It was a mad jumble of names, phone numbers, isolated words and doodles. The doodles were indeed compulsive. They blossomed from the words like filigrees, embellishments, spreading out in all directions, linking words and numbers.

'I've seen her at work,' Trish said. 'She's very nervous, very intense. She sits on the edge of her chair, chewing her pen when she's not writing. She presses really hard when she doodles. It's like a nervous habit.'

'Does she replace the blotter?' one of the cops asked.

'I replace it for her about once a month,' Trish said.

'Do you ask her first?'

'Oh, yes. Most of the stuff on it is worthless, but some of it she wants to save. It's kind of a joke with us. I tell her it's time to look it over before I chuck it out. She never wants to do it, because she's too busy. I nag her for a couple of days, then she gives it a long look and pulls it up and throws it on my desk.'

One of the cops leaned forward eagerly. 'Do you save them?' he asked.

'No. I just throw them out.'

The producer had taken the blotter from Trish and flattened it out on the conference table, using ashtrays to hold down the corners. The cops gathered around the blotter, looking a bit ridiculous as they peered down at the reporter's messy handwriting and doodles.

'Are you suggesting she doodled or wrote something while she was on the phone?' the FBI man asked.

'I wouldn't be surprised,' the producer said. 'It's an important case. Maybe she thought there was a potential for danger. She might have left something, almost unconsciously, that would be a clue to her whereabouts.'

The detective looked at Trish, trying to keep his eyes from the tight jeans hugging her thighs. 'Would you say you're more familiar with her notes and doodling than anyone else?'

Trish shrugged. 'I'm not that familiar with it myself. I've noticed it when I throw out the blotters.'

'Would you be willing to sit down with a document examiner and share your impressions of what is written or drawn here?' asked the FBI man.

Trish shrugged. 'Sure. No problem.'

'All right,' the head FBI man concluded. 'You guys keep going through her computer. I'll arrange for Trish here to meet with a documents guy right away. We'll go from there.'

# CHAPTER 48

Susan took the same flight to San Francisco that she had taken three weeks ago to see Michael. But this time she was accompanied by Joe Riccio. They drove a rented car up the coast to Petaluma, where Joe followed the directions given Susan by Jill Kaminsky over the phone. It was an easy drive, and within an hour and a half Susan was sitting in the kitchen of Jill's modest tract home, talking about Meredith.

'I've only known her a couple of months,' Susan was saying, 'but I've grown very fond of her. She reminds me of myself, in some ways.'

'You're much softer, of course,' Jill threw in.

'Really?'

'Oh, sure. Definitely . . . Can you hang on a second?'

Jill went to the window and shouted in an astonishingly loud voice, 'Stop doing that to her!' Her two daughters were in the back yard playing. Something in the murmur of their voices must have alerted her maternal ear that trouble was brewing. She came back smiling. 'Motherhood,' she said. 'Do you have children?'

'A little boy,' Susan said.

'Thank your lucky stars you don't have twins,' Jill said. 'The aggravation factor is exponential. It feels like there are eight of them sometimes.'

Susan thought of Carol Gold. 'I think I know what you mean,' she said.

Jill Kaminsky's pretty face was distorted by a slackness and sallowness that indicated permanent exhaustion. The rigors of motherhood were very much part of her, and probably would be for some time.

A remote outpost of Susan's second sight had reacted to Jill's words about the two little girls seeming multiplied. The notion struck a chord. Susan had no idea what it might mean. Now that she was engaged in the desperate search for Meredith her antennae were exquisitely alert, and tiny signals were impacting them like an invisible breeze stirring the petals of a flower.

'But Meredith,' Jill went on, 'she's different now. Since she got into the journalism. When I first met her freshman year, she was very delicate, very vulnerable. I thought of her as a soft girl, a nice girl. She's taken her lumps.'

'Do you mean because of her parents' divorce?' Susan asked.

'For openers, yes. It did something to Meredith. I can't explain it, but it was as though it knocked a wheel out from under her. My own parents got a divorce when I was eleven, but I had long since gotten used to it and never even talked about it. My mom was remarried and everything ... But for Meredith it was a shock she couldn't seem to get over.'

'Were there effects in her private life?' Susan asked.

'She turned in on herself. She studied long hours, like a maniac. She took so many courses – and those math courses were hell, believe me. I had to drop out of Intro to Calculus. I never could understand how she stood it. I hardly ever saw her any more. She lost weight, she was always tired – she was working herself to death.'

'Did she have a social life?'

Jill shook her head. 'Practically nil,' she said. 'I never saw anybody take school more seriously than Meredith. She wanted to be a mathematician, a professor. It was like a crusade with her.'

'But she abandoned it later, didn't she?' Susan asked.

Jill looked troubled. 'Yes, she did. She gave up her acting, too.'

'It's a striking combination, isn't it?' Susan observed. 'A brilliant mathematician who is also an actress.'

'And a singer and dancer, too,' Jill agreed. 'Yeah, she was amazing. I saw her perform. She was really professional. I thought she might even pursue it, go on to Broadway or Hollywood. But she never took it seriously, despite all the time she put into it.'

There was a silence. Susan felt it was time to get to the core of things.

'Jill, I know that Meredith had an unsuccessful relationship with a man at around the time she changed her major. Who was he?'

Jill looked evasive. 'Is his identity that important?'

'It could be. Do you feel uncomfortable talking about it?'

'No, I don't think so. I just feel – it's a painful topic.'

'It could be more important than you know,' Susan said. 'Quite often a seemingly insignificant detail about a person's private life turns out to be crucial to a police investigation.'

Jill thought for a moment. Then she stood up to look out the window at her daughters. She returned to the table and sat down.

'It was a professor,' she said. 'I never knew his name, or which department he taught in. It was sophomore year, the spring semester. I started seeing less of Meredith. She was always busy. But I could tell something was going on. She glowed. She looked so happy all the time. And she looked so pretty. It was as if she were coming into her own.' Jill smiled. 'We talked a lot during that time. It was obvious to me that something had changed in her. She talked about having children, raising a family. About being a woman, about the natural things like childbirth. I was amazed. Here was this girl who could only talk about mathematics three months before . . . She was like a different person.'

'Did you ask her whether she was having an affair?' Susan asked.

'I didn't have to. It was all she talked about. She was like a kid. She brought every conversation back around to this guy, how terrific he was.'

'Did you ask who he was?'

'No. I kind of sensed she would have felt cornered if I did that. She never volunteered it, so I never asked.' Jill's face darkened. 'Then it ended. She told me the guy was married, he had decided to end the affair. He had a child and his wife was pregnant. I think that's what he told Meredith. We talked about it, Meredith and I. She was really devastated. She had thought the guy was going to get a divorce and marry her. I tried to suggest in a nice way that this was an old story – you know what I mean. But I realized Meredith had never thought about that at all. She was completely taken in. Head over heels. She was destroyed when he dumped her. Completely destroyed.'

'And she never told you who he was?' Susan asked.

'Never.'

'Wasn't it about that time that she abandoned her mathematics major?' Susan asked.

'I think so. Around that time. She started journalism the next semester. No, wait. It was that summer. She stayed on campus all summer taking journalism courses, to catch up.' Jill drummed two fingers on the table. 'After that she was a different person. A third Meredith, if you know what I mean. Not the girl from freshman year. Not the lovesick girl having an affair. Different.'

'Different in what way?'

'Hard. Determined.' Jill thought for a moment. 'When I spent time with her, it was as though she wasn't all there. She was channeling so much of herself into her journalism courses and her plans for externships . . .'

Susan threw in an observation. 'But there was at least a homology with her obsessiveness about the mathematics and the man she had the affair with.'

'Homology?' Jill looked puzzled.

'Sorry. I mean a similarity. I take it she was obsessive about whatever she did.'

Jill nodded thoughtfully. 'Yes, I see what you mean. That's true. But still she was different. There was an edge of bitterness about her after she got into journalism. A sort of streetwise quality. Cynical.'

'About journalism itself?' Susan asked.

'About everything. About the world of politics that journalists cover. About using her good looks to become a TV reporter, maybe some day an anchor.' Jill shook her head. 'The old idealism from the mathematics days wasn't there. She was harder.'

Susan nodded. It was clear to her that a great deal of anger had been involved in Meredith's choice of journalism as a career. Anger and resentment. Meredith had wanted with all her heart to be a wife and mother. It was a great leap from that ambition to the plan to become a sexually attractive TV reporter.

'I take it you never drew any conclusions based on the fact that she abandoned mathematics after the failed affair?' she asked.

'What do you mean?' Jill asked.

'Did you wonder whether the professor was in the mathematics department?'

Jill furrowed her brow. 'That's funny. I never did. I guess

I kind of thought the math and science professors were nerds. I just assumed he was from some other department.'

'How has Meredith changed in the years since?' Susan asked.

'She's still driven,' Jill said. 'Personally, I don't think she's happy. I don't think the TV news career was natural to her. I don't think she found herself when she went into journalism. I think she ran away and hid from herself. I talk to her all the time, and she visits me occasionally. I can tell she feels sad by the way she looks at my daughters.'

'Do you mean she's envious of you as a mother?'

'Not exactly envious,' Jill said. 'Just wistful. And a little lost.'

Susan nodded. This was precisely her impression of Meredith. A highly talented, bright young woman, quite capable of using any career she liked to act out her inner conflicts. A young woman who, despite her great intelligence, had made choices that were too narrow for her, too limiting. The divorce of her parents, followed by her painful love affair, had caused damage to her ego organization and led to a distortion of her personality. And, so far at least, she had not found the path that could lead back to her vulnerability and her pain, and rebuild her as a whole person.

She reminded Susan of Wendy Breckinridge, though a superficial observer would have said that Meredith, the successful overachiever, was worlds away from the confused, drifting Wendy. Both had been forced into unhappy choices by the stresses of their growing-up years. Both were plunging down a one-way road, driven by their own stubbornness and perhaps by their need to punish themselves. Turning around would require enormous strength.

'Can I ask you for your personal opinion about something?' Susan asked.

'Fire away,' Jill shrugged.

'What do you think it would take to make Meredith really happy? To undo the damage to her and make her into the person she was meant to be?'

Jill took a deep breath before answering.

'Not journalism,' she said. 'Not success. She's had that, and it hasn't made any difference. I think a man would be the only cure. A good marriage. Children, possibly. But most of all the feeling that someone loves her for herself.'

Susan nodded. She agreed with this formula, though she also thought some long-term therapy would be very good for Meredith.

She had learned what she came here to learn. Meredith's affair with Graham Auden had had a profound, devastating effect on her life. Changed its course, in fact.

It was time for her to leave. But first she had to ask two more questions.

'Did Meredith tell you she had become pregnant through her affair?'

The look on Jill's face told Susan she was surprised by this fact.

'No,' she said. 'I never knew that. Was she really?'

'I'm not sure,' Susan said. 'I need to find out. That's one reason I'm out here. But I have one more question. I hope you won't think I'm trying to embarrass Meredith. When you knew her, had she already lost her virginity?'

Jill looked taken aback.

'Why do you ask?'

'It's something rather tangential, a part of the investigation,' Susan said. 'It could be very important, though. Was Meredith, to your knowledge, a virgin before this affair she had?'

*Methuselah.*

Jill frowned thoughtfully. 'I don't know,' she said. 'She hadn't had a serious boyfriend in high school. She was too busy singing and dancing and acting. She dated some boys at Berkeley, like anyone else. She thought they were boring and immature. We joked about our dates. I dated a lot more than she did, because I wasn't spending half my life on mathematics and the other half on rehearsals.' She thought for a moment. 'The innocence I told you about,' she said. 'The impressionability, the softness . . . Maybe she was a virgin. I don't know. It's not the kind of thing most girls would admit to. It's hard to say. All I can tell you for sure is that no man ever meant anything to her before this affair with the professor. He was her first great love.'

Susan stood up. 'Jill, you've been a great help to me.' She held out a hand.

Jill took it. Her face bore a stricken look. 'I hope you find her,' she said.

'I hope so, too,' Susan said. 'We're doing our best.'

Joe Riccio was waiting in the front yard when Susan emerged.

'How did it go?' he asked.

'Pretty well, I think,' Susan said. 'I'm learning things, but it's slow going. I don't know how much time we have.'

Riccio nodded. The look on his face told her he was thinking it might already be too late. But he kept his thoughts to himself.

*Methuselah.*

This time Susan noted her impulse consciously. It was as though someone was calling out the Biblical name. And the smell of foul smoke in her nostrils . . .

She wondered where such an odd piece of flotsam had come from. She might never find out.

Shrugging, she followed Riccio to the car.

# CHAPTER 49

*My parents got divorced, and my father died soon afterward. I sort of fell apart. It was only when I decided to go into journalism that I pulled myself together.*

Those were the words Meredith Spiers had used during her lunch with Susan, the only time Meredith had spoken about her personal life.

Meredith's mother lived with her second husband, a retired tax attorney, in LaQuinta, California, near Palm Springs.

Her new married name was Scheinmann. She had not come to Chicago to assist in the vigil for Meredith because she suffered from a crippling arthritis that kept her confined to her home. The FBI had sent agents to interrogate her about Meredith, but had come up with nothing worthwhile.

Susan and Riccio turned in the rented car and caught a commuter flight to the Ontario Airport, south of Los Angeles. They rented another car and drove to LaQuinta, a few miles east of Palm Springs. The temperature was eighty degrees. Their winter coats lay useless on the back seat of the sedan. The drive through the desert filled Susan with a slightly surreal tranquility. She found it bizarre that her investigation of Meredith's past should lead to so unlikely a landscape.

Susan had called ahead. She and Riccio found Mrs Scheinmann waiting in a pleasant little ranch house in a desert-landscaped development perhaps ten years old.

Mrs Scheinmann came to the door herself, moving painfully with the help of a walker. Riccio elected to wait outside while Susan questioned the sick woman. Mrs Scheinmann looked prematurely aged by physical suffering and perhaps by something else. But her resemblance to her beautiful daughter was quite palpable. She had the same burning blue eyes and the same quick intelligence.

It did not take Susan long to learn that Mrs Scheinmann's relationship with Meredith was the great chagrin of her life.

'Meredith was our only child, the apple of our eye,' the old lady said. 'We had her late in life, and we doted on her. She was a beautiful baby and an adorable little girl. She excelled at everything – sports, studies, music, acting, you name it. We were thrilled by her. She seemed to take years off our lives just by being so young and beautiful.'

Susan sat on the living-room couch, listening.

'Then our marriage started to go sour,' Mrs Scheinmann said. 'Something about middle age, I guess. Everything seemed to come apart overnight. Meredith was in high school at the time. Abe and I fought a lot. She heard some of it. We were both unfaithful – first Abe, then me. We decided to end it before things got worse. We separated at the beginning of Meredith's senior year, and got our divorce the next fall.'

'Did Meredith continue living with you?' Susan asked.

'Yes. She stayed with me. She was applying to college by that time – she had always had her heart set on Berkeley – and she had a lot of activities. I didn't see very much of her, but I thought we were still friends. I didn't realize how deeply the divorce had affected her. When she went off to college she shut me out. Just closed a door on her past. Abe died that fall, quite unexpectedly, and I realized afterward that Meredith held me responsible for his death. She had been quite close to him, you see.'

It was hard to believe that so much passion had occurred

in the life of this wizened little old lady in her desert retirement community.

'I convinced Roy to buy a house in Oakland,' she said, 'so I could be near Meredith. It didn't really help. In a way it made things worse. She shut me out completely. It was very painful. She would visit me for a day or two at Thanksgiving. She would hardly say a word to me the whole time. She stayed on the phone with her friends and went out in the evening. I was lucky to have so much as an hour with her at lunch. Then she was gone, back into her own life.' She sighed. 'I told myself that I could at least keep an eye on her by being closer. Roy did his best to be friendly to her, but he saw her so seldom that he never really got to know her. I was mystified by her coldness; she had been an affectionate little girl, and charming even as a teenager. I had flattered myself that I could end my marriage and keep my daughter. I thought that daughters and mothers are inseparable. It didn't turn out that way.'

'Did she remain out of touch?' Susan asked.

'She didn't even invite me to her college graduation,' Mrs Scheinmann said. 'I had to go on my own. She won a journalism award at the ceremony. I felt terrible. Then she went to work in San Francisco. She was brilliant as a reporter, aggressive, smart, attractive . . . I had friends calling me all the time to tell me they had seen her reports on television. I had to lie to them and tell them I had seen her recently, which I hadn't.'

'And when she moved to Chicago?' Susan asked.

'She called to tell me she had the job at Channel 9,' Mrs Scheinmann said. 'She didn't even come over to say goodbye. I was terribly hurt. I wrote her a long letter asking what I had done that was so terrible that she had to cut me out of her life. She didn't answer it.'

'So you've been out of touch all these years,' Susan said.

'Yes. That's why this thing, this Undertaker thing, is so awful,' the old lady said. 'I feel so helpless, so cut off.'

'Mrs Scheinmann, were you at all aware of the social life Meredith had at Berkeley? Boyfriends? That kind of thing?'

'Not at all. She was hardly ever in touch. I think I would have been the last person in the world she confided in about such things.'

'Were you acquainted with her roommates or friends at Berkeley?'

'I didn't even know their names.'

Susan frowned. She wondered whether this was a wasted trip. Mrs Scheinmann seemed to know less about Meredith than anyone else.

'Mrs Scheinmann, Meredith indicated to me that her abrupt change from her mathematics major to journalism had something to do with a problem in her romantic life. Would you know anything about that?'

'Not at all. She didn't even tell me she was changing until it was a fait accompli. She just casually mentioned that she had changed her major.'

'Had she been passionate about mathematics?' Susan asked.

The old lady thought for a moment.

'Well, she certainly was serious about it. She took every advanced placement course she could in high school. She went to math camp twice in the summer, over in Berkeley. She had an 800 on her college boards in math. She was a sort of genius at it. But no, I don't think it would be correct to say she was passionate about it. It was a gift she developed because it was so easy for her. However, I do think she was sincere about her plan to become a professor. She liked the idea of helping to develop young minds. She found the university atmosphere exciting.'

'I see,' Susan said. 'Did she ever mention a specific mathematics professor to you at Berkeley?'

The old lady shook her head. 'We were so out of touch by then, she wouldn't have told me a thing like that.'

There was a silence. Susan was not sure what to ask next.

'Was she more passionate about acting than about mathematics?' she hazarded.

'Oh, yes. Much more passionate. The mathematics came easy to her. She had to work for her success as an actress. Her high school was very competitive, with lots of girls trying out for the big roles. Meredith took voice lessons, dancing lessons . . . She used to come home exhausted. But by the time she was a junior she was getting those big roles. Laura in *The Glass Menagerie*, and Kim in *Bye Bye Birdie* . . . She was very good, very talented.' She thought for a moment. 'As I look back, I realize that those years might have been the beginning of the distance between us. She spent such long hours in rehearsal and at her lessons. She never got into any teenage-type trouble – she literally didn't have the time. Abe and I saw so little of her . . . I thought everything was fine, though. I guess I didn't see the handwriting on the wall.'

'And you and your husband were having problems at that time?'

'Oh, yes. I can remember Meredith coming home covered with stage make-up after midnight, and Abe not being at home. Now that I think of it, she must have noticed and been hurt. As I say, I was too blind at the time to see what was happening to us.' She pointed to a bookcase across the room. 'Dear, would you reach me that big blue scrapbook from the top shelf there?'

Susan got up and brought the scrapbook. The old lady had to balance it precariously on her gnarled knuckles.

'Shall I turn the pages for you?' Susan asked.

'That would be nice of you.'

Susan turned the pages. There were programs from several high school productions, the pages turned to the cast list. Meredith had performed in *Camelot, Man of La Mancha, The Fantasticks*, and numerous non-musical productions such as *The Odd Couple* and *Antigone*. A handful of articles from the local papers included rave reviews of her precocious work.

'I kept most of her awards and things like that,' she said. 'They're in a box in the basement.'

Susan turned the pages slowly. The programs from Meredith's high school productions gave way to similar programs from Berkeley. Meredith had played Stella in *A Streetcar Named Desire*. She had also played Honey in *Who's Afraid of Virginia Woolf?*. And Ophelia in *Hamlet* with the Berkeley Shakespeare Society.

'They weren't doing musicals at Berkeley, so Meredith got parts in dramatic plays,' Mrs Scheinmann said. 'I saw her performances, all of them. She was very good, good enough that I half expected her to go on with it and try her luck in Hollywood.'

'Why didn't she?' Susan asked.

'She got interested in journalism and dropped out of acting, just like that,' the mother said. 'I never completely understood why. Young people, you know – they change their minds at the drop of a hat.' Her face darkened. 'Of course, we were no longer close by that time. She wasn't confiding in me any more.'

The pages were turning slowly. There were reviews of Meredith's performances from the college newspaper and the local Berkeley papers. 'Berkeley Co-ed Brilliant in Ibsen Production.' 'Berkeley Drama Group Stages Tennessee Williams with Style.'

'A couple of times,' Mrs Scheinmann said, 'she was in productions without even telling me about it. I had to read about it in the papers. I used to come to them without telling her. I would sit in the audience and the tears would roll down my face, because I was remembering those high school productions, and how proud she used to be when I brought her flowers. But now she wanted no part of me. I knew how terribly hard those kids had to work on those productions. The idea that she was going through all that without so much as a phone call of encouragement from me – it broke my heart to feel so cut off.'

She looked at Susan, whose eyes were still on the scrapbook. Susan had turned pale.

'What's the matter, dear?'

Susan stood up. 'Will you excuse me a moment, Mrs Scheinmann? I need to use your phone.'

Susan swept out of the room. She opened the front door and called out to Riccio. A moment later Mrs Scheinmann heard her voice from the kitchen. She was speaking in low, urgent tones to someone on the phone.

Susan was gone for several minutes. When she came back she seemed in a hurry. 'Mrs Scheinmann, I need to leave you now. You've been a great help. I hope to be back in touch soon.'

'Will you find my girl?' the worried mother asked.

'Yes, we will. I'm sure we will.' Susan left the house without another word.

Mrs Scheinmann sat staring into space for a long moment. Then she picked up the scrapbook and looked at the page it was opened to.

The program was from the Berkeley Shakespeare Society, announcing the production of *Romeo and Juliet* starring Meredith Spiers as Juliet.

# CHAPTER 50

Meredith woke up in a different place. Her headache was gone, but she felt terribly dehydrated. Her skin felt raw. Her joints ached. She wondered if she had been raped while unconscious.

She tried to turn on her side, but the bonds around her wrists stopped her. For some reason this limitation on her freedom brought the headache crashing back. She moaned and closed her eyes.

When she opened them she saw the man sitting beside her.

'You,' she said.

He was dressed exactly as he had been dressed the first time she saw him, in scrub clothes, his mask untied and hanging down on his chest.

'Yes, it's me.' He smiled. 'Have you remembered who I am?'

'Yes.'

Meredith tried to focus on the moment, but it was so skewed by improbability that she was at a loss.

'You don't have your beard any more,' she said.

He was silent, watching her with obvious admiration.

'What are you looking at?' she asked.

'You. You're so beautiful.' He was drinking her in, admiring her. The cold medical face he had worn when he performed her abortion was gone, replaced by an eager, almost adolescent expression which frightened her more than the bonds holding her down or the drug throbbing in her veins.

'I can't believe this is really happening,' he said.

'What do you mean?' she asked. 'What is really happening?'

'You and me. Here. At last.' He let his eyes run over her body. Her skin crawled at the implicit contact. 'I've waited so long for this,' he said. 'It was like an exile, really. I hated being separated from you. Have you ever thought about immigrants? What it must have been like for them to be separated from their loved ones for long years? And the joy of meeting again finally. The warmth . . .'

There was a silence. Meredith struggled for a strategy that would get him on her side, even if only temporarily. A gambit that might keep her alive as long as possible.

'What brought you to me?' she asked.

'Nothing,' he said. 'It was the other way around. You brought me to everything else. Nothing else was real. It was all you. From the beginning.'

'You mean,' she asked, 'the victims?'

'I don't think of them as victims.' A frown furrowed his brow. In that instant he bore the intent expression of a priest pondering a thorny point of theology.

'Was it you all along, sending me those e-mails?' she asked.

'Yes.'

'Why?'

'I needed to feel the contact. I was watching you on the news, every day. Drinking you in. But after a while it became too painful. I had to get in touch.'

Meredith thought for a minute. Pain and anxiety made it hard for her to concentrate. But she could see from the look in his eyes that he was completely obsessed with her. This was a weapon she could use.

She pondered the alternatives of cajolerie and confrontation. An old alternative that every reporter knows. Journalism 301. Gambling, she opted for confrontation.

'Why did you kill them?' she asked.

He thought for a moment. 'They were chosen. Because you were chosen.'

'So you're going to kill me.' She tried for the cynical note, but her voice shook.

He didn't answer. He bent to kiss her stomach. His lips were tender, respectful. But he was kissing the spot where he had torn the victims with his knife. She cried out despite herself.

'Don't do that,' he said and sat up. 'You're looking at it in the wrong way. I'm not going to do anything violent to you.' He paused, as though hesitating whether to let her in on a secret. Then he said, 'I love you.'

Still the rapt, elegiac look in his eyes. Meredith had to fight back her own panic. She knew he was going to kill her. Susan Shader had explained the ambivalence of murderers. Rage mingled dizzyingly with admiration in their attitude toward their victims. Sirhan Sirhan had idolized Robert Kennedy. John Lennon's killer had been a devoted fan. Perry Smith told police he thought Mr Clutter was a fine gentleman. 'I liked him. Right up until the moment I cut his throat.'

Such was the sick creature beside Meredith now. He would love and admire her right up to the moment he killed her.

'How do I know that?' she asked.

'Isn't this enough to prove it?' He gestured to the room, the mattress under her, himself.

'That only proves how sick you are,' Meredith said.

A glare of hatred crept across his features, from right to

left, almost like a wipe dividing one scene of a movie from another. It was the strangest effect she had ever seen on a human face. She knew she was in the presence of pure insanity.

'I'm sorry I said that,' she said. 'I just need to – understand.'

'You don't need to understand,' he said. 'You don't need anything.'

He looked away as though disgusted by her. But he caught a glimpse of her frail body reflected in the mirror, and was touched.

'I'm sorry,' he said. 'I didn't mean it that way. It's important for you to realize that you're safe now, here with me. No one has ever loved you the way I love you.'

He seemed to search for words.

*'Stony limits cannot hold love out,*
*And what love can do that dares love attempt.'*

Meredith was astonished to hear words she remembered very well. She had memorized them when she played Juliet. They were Romeo's words from the balcony scene.

Why Juliet? she wondered. What was in his mind? Could he know she had played the role?

'What do you mean?' she asked cautiously.

'Don't you know?' he asked.

She shook her head, her eyes not leaving his.

'You are the only truly innocent one,' he said. 'I've always known that. I knew it when I operated on you. Innocent through and through. I saw it then.'

Meredith was thinking fast. He was talking about seven years ago. She had been a student. Whatever his obsession consisted in, it had begun then. In this she might find an advantage.

'Did you see me play Juliet?' she asked quietly.

'Yes,' he said, excited. 'You couldn't know how perfect

you were. She was purity itself. And you were so perfect, so unspoiled. You still are. The world can't see it, but I see it. Every day, every night, on my television screen.' He hesitated again, weighing his secrets. 'I've recorded you,' he said. 'From the beginning. I have you on tape. I've watched you thousands of times.' Again that manic glare began to creep over his features, but this time he pushed it back.

'You've watched me?' Meredith asked.

'Juliet was a virgin,' he said. 'No man had ever touched her. And that was you. I knew how pure you were. I sat in that audience and cried like a baby. You were so beautiful.'

*Purity. Innocence. Virginity.* Meredith knew she was afloat in his own delirium. She didn't want to challenge it.

'I was pure?' she asked.

He nodded almost shyly. It was his private treasure that he was sharing with her, though she was its object.

'What about the abortion you performed on me?' she asked. 'Didn't you find me impure then?'

'Not at all.'

Meredith did not know what to make of this. His conception of sex must be too complex and too twisted for her to fathom.

'What about the other girls?' she asked. 'The victims.'

He frowned. 'You're speaking of holy things. You don't really have the right.' He softened. 'I made them pure.'

'Why did you pick girls who had had abortions?'

He ignored her question.

'Why did you pour blood into their wounds?' she asked.

'Blood is communion. Communion means no one dies alone. I think even they understood that, at the end.' He paused. 'I gave them the best of myself. I held nothing back.'

'Is that what you want from me?' Meredith asked. Her nerves were tight as steel. Every response was a gamble. She was walking a high wire, testing each step.

'That's what I have with you already.' He smiled. 'And nothing can take it away from me. You gave it to me when you came to me. You offered it to me. I took it then, and I'll never lose it.'

'Then why am I here?'

He ignored the question. He touched her breast gently. Her skin tingled.

Where to go from here? What to say?

Maddened by his sickness, she blundered.

'You won't get away with it,' Meredith said. 'The police know who you are.'

'Do they?' He seemed curious but not alarmed.

'Yes. They do.'

'Why haven't they been here, then?' he asked.

Meredith thought desperately of Susan Shader.

'You won't get away with it,' she repeated.

His reply took her by surprise.

'I have never intended to get away with it.' The clear, cleansed look of religious ecstasy spread over his face. He was opening his innermost door to her.

'What do you mean?'

'I'm going with you.'

Meredith turned pale. He had check-mated her. The usual way to deal with a desperate criminal is to get him to think about his future, to get him to ponder decisions. The Undertaker was past that. He had made his final decision.

He ran a hand up her thigh to her pelvis. 'So beautiful,' he said. He sighed. 'She died a virgin. Romeo never touched her. But you know that.'

*Ah*, Meredith thought. The twin suicide, brought about by misunderstanding and by the gods. Romeo took poison when he thought Juliet was dead. But Juliet awoke from her drugged sleep, saw Romeo dead alongside her and killed herself with his dagger after trying to take what was left of his poison. The communion of death was better than that of mere sexual consummation. That was the whole point of the play. *And death, not Romeo, take my maiden-head!*

Meredith sought vainly for words to say to the madman beside her. If she could make him feel that she accepted him, even loved him. String him along on the drug of love, to gain time . . .

'You love me, then,' she said.

He nodded, a pious look in his eyes.

'Why didn't you tell me?' she asked.

The glare glinted in his pale irises, lethal, impersonal.

'I did better than that.'

He curled up beside her, his head on her shoulder. She smelled his hair, his perspiration, the normal man smells that belied the sick mind inside his flesh. He spoke:

*'See, how she leans her cheek upon her hand!*
*O', that I were a glove upon that hand,*
*That I might touch that cheek!'*

Meredith lay bound, feeling her lover kiss her breast.

# CHAPTER 51

When the FBI's documents examiner finished going over Meredith Spiers's blotter with Trish Calderon, he called Tom Castaneda, who called Abel Weathers with the news. A meeting took place at the FBI's local office on 219 South Dearborn thirty minutes later. Castaneda was there with his two top agents. David Gold represented the CPD along with Rich Sheehan and an Area Four detective named Rob Gaeth. Abel Weathers came over personally instead of sending one of his assistants.

'What's the deal?' Weathers asked.

It was Tom Castaneda who spoke. 'Have you ever heard of a group called the Stork?'

Weathers shook his head. 'What is it?'

Castaneda deferred to Rob Gaeth.

'It's a splinter group of anti-abortion crazies,' Rob said. 'They've been around on and off for about fifteen years. They harass clients of abortion clinics.'

'That's putting it mildly,' said Castaneda.

'What they do is,' Rob went on, 'they put a dead foetus on the front doorstep of a woman who is considering abortion. Sometimes they'll do the same thing to a woman who has already had an abortion. We've seen them put foetuses in mailboxes too.'

Weathers gave a look of disgust. 'Where do they get the foetuses?'

'They're probably bribing the personnel in clinics some-where, or in hospitals. We've never been able to run that down.'

'It must scare the shit out of the women,' Weathers said.

'It does.' Rob nodded. 'Abortion is traumatic enough in the first place. Some of these women have to go into therapy. But this dead baby stuff is really brutal. I went on a few calls with the detectives. The victims are totally freaked out.' He looked at his notes. 'It's a shadowy organization. They started in Indianapolis, but we picked them up in Gary about ten years ago. We closed them down, but some of them re-formed with a new leader in the early '90s, headquartered out west somewhere. I talked to an undercover cop in Arizona, a woman who had infiltrated them for a while. She was never completely sure, but she thought they were into clinic bomb-ings and attacks on physicians. They had contacts with other groups around the country. You see, there is a kind of under-ground, loosely organized. The national pro-life organizations won't have anything to do with them. They're crazies. They work together on bombs, crank calls, scare tactics, the whole bit.'

Weathers was leaning over Meredith's blotter. Rob Gaeth pointed to a doodle near the bottom of the pad. There was a phone number. Around it Meredith had doodled a cartoon showing a stork with a bundle hanging from its beak. Drops of blood were falling from the bundle.

Castaneda turned to the document examiner, a handsome young FBI man named Roy Cunningham. 'Roy, tell us what you found.'

Cunningham frowned. 'We can't pin down any of the writing on the blotter as to date,' he said. 'Our methods just aren't that precise. The only thing we can really do is to determine which lines were written or drawn first, when two of them overlap.' He reached across the table to point at the drawing of the stork with the baby in its mouth. 'This drawing was done on top of the phone number,' he said. 'She doodled it over the number.'

'What is the phone number?' Weathers asked.

'The number of a movie theater up on Sheridan Road,' said Castaneda. 'It's the number you call for show times.'

'She must have called to check the show time for *A Civil Action*,' said Castaneda. 'I think the caller told her to meet him at the theater. It was only a ruse to get her out in the open.'

'Have you checked out the theater?' Weathers asked.

'Yeah.' It was Rich Sheehan who answered. 'I talked to the teenagers who were working there that day. They saw her come in. The ticket taker thought he recognized her, so he paid enough attention to notice her going back out again about a half-hour after the movie started. The parking lot is unattended, so nobody saw her drive in.'

Castaneda nodded. 'I think he told her to meet him at the theater. He didn't show, so she decided to go back to work. That's when she called in to the station. She must have gotten into her car in the ramp. That's when he snatched her.'

Weathers sighed. 'Okay. What have we got?'

It was Castaneda who summed up. 'I think when she got the call she asked for something concrete to prove to her that the caller was legit. Whoever the caller was, he or she told Meredith about the Stork, and told her the Undertaker was involved with it, or came out of it, or something. Meredith probably hung up, then called the movie theater to check the show time. Then, either while she was on the phone or while she was deciding what to do, she doodled the stork with the bundle in its mouth.'

'And the drops of blood,' Weathers said. 'Okay, so who and where are these Stork people?'

'Well,' said Gaeth, 'that's the thing. They're dissolved. There hasn't been a sign of them in two or three years.'

'What about their membership?'

'Some of them are long gone.' Gaeth looked at his notes. 'Others are still in the area. Their names are on our list. They've either been visited or surveilled. We got nothing.'

'Great,' Weathers said. 'Why are we talking about this, then?'

Castaneda took over. 'It occurred to us that some former member of this group might be out on his own now. He's into blood, he's into death and he hates women who abort babies. He becomes the Undertaker.'

'I see what you mean,' Weathers said. 'The person on the phone spilled something about this to Meredith. Told her about the Stork. Meredith was interested, and made a doodle of a stork with a dead baby in its mouth.'

'Right.'

'But you say we've got nothing.'

'I said nothing on the locals,' Castaneda replied. 'But we ran all the old names through the NCIC computers, just for the heck of it, looking for priors, blood types, MOs, whatever. We turned up a guy who was with them back in the '80s and has been doing time in California on a manslaughter charge, a hit and run. He used to live here. He got out of San Quentin last summer and moved back here. His name is Wayne Hemphill. He's a nutcase with a lot of arrests for harassment, assault, disturbing the peace, stuff like that.'

*San Quentin.* David Gold was thinking about Susan, and about her feeling that the Undertaker had been in California.

'Why haven't we talked to him?' Gold asked.

'We have. Two of our guys paid him a visit last month. He lives in a house up in Park Ridge. He's working as a bartender in his own neighborhood. He's married, but separated. He looked clean to us.'

'Any arrests here in town?' Gaeth asked.

Castaneda shook his head.

The cops were gathered around Meredith Spiers's enigmatic, disturbing drawing of the friendly stork carrying a bloody bundle.

'And there's something about him you'll want to know,' Castaneda added. 'He served in the army as a medic. He had a job as a male nurse down in Indianapolis, but they fired him for pilfering on the job. He later worked as a hospital orderly here at Michael Reese. They fired him too, for stealing drugs from nurses' stations.'

'Dead foetuses,' one of the cops said.

'What about body bags?' Castaneda added. 'This guy would have been perfectly situated.'

Everyone pondered this.

'Let's get a warrant,' Weathers said. 'We need to search this guy's house.'

There was a pause. The final question was on Abel Weathers's lips, but Castaneda answered it before he could ask it.

'His blood type is O,' Castaneda said.

# CHAPTER 52

*A + B = 'ab'*.

Susan was on the commuter airliner between Ontario and San Francisco, sitting next to Joe Riccio. She had put the tray table down and was writing notes in her notebook.

She was excited. Mrs Scheinmann's innocent-looking scrapbook had given her the most powerful confirmation yet of one of the key leitmotifs of the entire Undertaker case. Meredith had played Juliet. Susan had no doubt that the Undertaker had seen Meredith in the role. That proved that the Undertaker had been in California, just as Susan had intuited in the Berkeley hills with Michael.

Juliet was a virgin. She consummated her love for Romeo by death, not by sexual intercourse. Thus she was quintessentially the image of the Undertaker's 'Virgin', his great love and his obsession.

*A + B = 'ab'*.

The equation Susan had written down was from Freud's *The Interpretation of Dreams*. Susan had often quoted it to patients and in her writings and lectures. 'A dream is like a rebus,' Freud said. Its elements were not to be taken at face value, but to be compressed together to create unexpected new ideas. '*A*' and '*B*' together made not '*A + B*' but the syllable '*ab*'.

The rebus metaphor was perhaps the single most powerful view into the heart of Freud's method of reasoning, a method of reasoning that was born with him and may have died with him. It was his unique ability to see disparate things as connected in a secret way that allowed him to perform such spectacular intellectual feats. By looking at '$A + B$' as the syllable '$ab$', he allowed absurdity to play a constructive role in psychoanalysis. Since the unconscious worked often through absurdity, his procedure was successful.

Freud was as much a detective as an abstract thinker – that was his genius. Susan half-wished he was with her now. She needed his ability to make gigantic mental leaps without fear.

$$Juliet = Virgin$$
$$Juliet = Meredith$$
$$Meredith = Virgin$$

Susan looked at the words she had written. She knew they held the secret she was searching for. But she could not make the mental leap that would reveal the hidden pattern.

Someone was speaking to her. She looked up, dazed, to see the flight attendant holding out a pot of coffee.

'No, thanks,' she said.

Riccio accepted a cup. Susan heard the flight attendant pouring it for him. Then she tuned everything out again.

She looked back on the Undertaker case. Three victims, all young, all attractive, all connected in some way to abortion. An unknown way . . .

She tried to put herself inside the killer's mind. A mind obsessed by religious images, by women's sexual organs, by the idea and the substance of blood.

Blood spilled by surgery. Blood spilled by murder.

$A + B$ = ???

Susan closed her eyes. She fought against the roar of the plane for concentration. Ideas tapped at her shoulder and were gone, like goblins. The truth was in her hands, but not as a solid object. It slipped through her fingers like water.

*A + B ...*

Susan shook her head. There was clarity somewhere in this array of facts and obsessions. There was structure. But she couldn't put her finger on it.

She looked at what she had written. Now she wrote: '*Killer + Meredith + California = Undertaker*'.

She smiled, remembering how she played Clue with her brother when they were small children in Pennsylvania. 'Mr Green with the candlestick in the conservatory.'

'*Undertaker with ___ in California*', she wrote.

There had to be more. The crossing of their paths had to have a stronger basis than a chance viewing of Meredith as Juliet at Berkeley. Such a contact would not suffice to unleash an obsession, much less a chain of murders.

The Undertaker used a knife. With this knife he drew blood. Blood which he saved, blood which he used.

A knife with which he killed women. Or transformed them ...

*Blessed is the fruit of thy womb ...*

The Undertaker scrupulously avoided drawing blood from the genitals of the victims. One did not have to be Sigmund Freud to know that the image tormenting the killer was precisely that of blood coming from the genitals of a woman.

Blood comes from between women's legs when they have had abortions. When they have had miscarriages. When they menstruate.

When does blood come from between the legs of a virgin? When she menstruates. When she is deflowered.

'*Victims pregnant*,' Susan wrote. '*Abortion undoes pregnancy.*'

The analytic term 'undoing' – in German *Ungeschehen-machen* – was well known to all psychiatrists. It indicated an attempt to undo a dangerous thought or impulse. But unlike the attempts of healthy people to undo their mistakes – by apology, perhaps, or by doing something to make up for a misdeed – in mentally ill people the attempt was magical, fantastic. It was intended to completely wipe out the distressing misdeed, as though it had never occurred at all. Like Norman Bates in *Psycho*, stuffing his mother and carrying on conversations with her corpse, to undo the fact that he had murdered her. To make her be alive again.

Like killing a woman to make her pregnancy a thing that had never happened at all.

Or killing a woman to make her conception a thing that had never happened at all.

Killing a fertile woman to make her into a Virgin again.

'Doctor?'

Susan came to herself with a start. It was Riccio. He was leaning toward her over his cup of coffee.

'Sorry,' she said. 'Is anything wrong?'

'No. Nothing's wrong. I just thought I heard you say something to me.'

Susan smiled. 'I must be talking to myself. I'm really dead. I'd better take a nap.'

She turned off the light and leaned back against the seat. The roar of the airplane seemed to echo inside her like the heavy breathing of a giant, throbbing, lulling her into sleep.

She woke up long enough to notice her little notebook, still open on the tray table. She wrote one more thing on it before closing it and putting it away.

$A + B = ab$ortion.

In the seat beside her, Joe Riccio sat quietly, looking straight ahead of him at nothing.

# CHAPTER 53

The department of mathematics at Berkeley was located in a venerable ivy-covered building that looked as though it might have been transported from Princeton.

Susan had called ahead to make an appointment with Professor Graham Auden, who said he remembered Meredith and was terribly concerned about her.

She found the professor waiting for her in the departmental office. He was a tall man with long salt-and-pepper hair, and probing dark eyes whose intense expression belied the polite smile on his lips. He appeared to be in his late forties, but something about him was strikingly youthful.

'Would you like some coffee?' he offered. 'I can't promise quality, but I can promise caffeine.'

'Thank you very much.'

He filled two Styrofoam cups, black for Susan and white for himself. They went down the hall to a large office with a beautiful view of the quad. Bright fluorescent lights overcame the rather dim atmosphere of the room, whose walls were covered with pictures of scientists and mathematicians of this and other eras.

Susan decided to get right to the point.

'Professor Auden, Meredith was a student of yours, was she not?'

'Yes, she was. One of my best students, as a matter of fact. She was a loss to our field. She was very creative. She would have become an outstanding mathematician.' He smiled. 'Of course, I understand she has distinguished herself in her chosen field.'

Susan took a deep breath. 'Believe me, Professor Auden, I wouldn't press you this way unless time was absolutely of the essence. We're trying to save Meredith's life.'

'I understand.'

'You had an affair with her, didn't you?'

There was a silence. The professor looked cornered. He glanced out the window as though in search of a refuge.

'How is such a thing relevant?' he asked.

'I'm not entirely sure,' Susan said. 'It could be relevant in a way that would seem absurd to you, especially after all this time. But I need your answer, Professor. Please help me.'

The professor got up and closed the door to the corridor. He returned to his desk and sat down. An odd, sad smile curled his lips, and he looked at Susan.

'Yes, I did,' he said. 'I had an affair with Meredith.' The look in his eyes was very strange. He seemed to be admitting guilt and at the same time taking out a private treasure to share with Susan.

'How did it start?' Susan asked.

'She was in one of my classes. She was brilliant, a born mathematician. Very creative. I gave her an A on her class work that semester and suggested that she try an honors independent study. We allow certain students to do that as a way of skipping intermediate courses and hastening their advancement to graduate work. Meredith obviously had the talent for it. I wanted to know if she had the commitment.' He thought for a moment. 'She came here, to this office. She sat in the chair you're sitting in.'

His eyes clouded at the memory. Susan even thought she saw tears welling in them.

'I gather she was a sophomore,' Susan said. 'The spring semester.'

'Yes.'

'Tell me about her.'

'She was so beautiful,' he said. 'An angel, literally. I remember looking at her and thinking that I had never seen so attractive a creature in my life.' He shrugged. 'I don't know whether that was a weakness of mine, or her own aura. Anyway, I found her irresistible.'

Susan waited for him to continue.

'I'm not a promiscuous man,' he said. 'I had had a couple of one-night stands in the past, but nothing of any importance. It's relatively easy for a man in my position . . .' He thought for a moment. 'An outside observer would probably see what happened as just another case of a horny professor seducing a star-struck student. It's true, I used her admiration for me, I used her youth. Her alienation from her family, her need for affection. But it was more than that, right from the outset. I was in love with her. And, as time passed, she fell in love with me.'

'How long did the affair last?' Susan asked.

'Three months. It started in the spring. She was nineteen.' His eyes were misty. 'What a spring that was! The trees, the blossoms . . . I felt as though I was being born all over again. We had lunch together, picnics on the grass. We took walks in the hills . . . I was like an adolescent. I was simply mad about her. She's a complicated person, you know. Not like her TV image. She's very deep.'

'I know. I've talked to her.'

'You have?' His eyes lit up at the mere recognition that Susan had been in physical proximity to Meredith. In that instant Susan thought he still loved her.

'I spent every minute I could with her,' he said. 'I tried to hide what I was feeling. I didn't – I couldn't . . .'

Susan felt him grappling with his own guilt. He had been afraid of his own passion, but he had also wanted to protect himself from entanglement, embarrassment.

'I felt like I was out of control, every minute of every day,' he said. 'I was as insatiable as an adolescent. And the way Meredith was – not only physically, but the way she accepted me, the way she gave her love – it was bewitching. It was indescribable.'

A beat of silence. He met Susan's eyes. She realized he found her attractive. She herself found him attractive. He did have an adolescent quality despite his graying hair. It shone in his thin body and in the burning intellect behind his eyes.

'How did it end?' she asked.

He breathed a long sigh.

'My wife got pregnant with our third child,' he said. 'I did a lot of thinking. I gave serious consideration to throwing away my family for Meredith. But I'm devoted to my children. In the end, I just couldn't do it. I broke it off with Meredith. I was firm, but I was dying inside. I knew I would never meet another person like her.'

'How did she take it?' Susan asked.

'She was devastated.' He shook his head. 'Like me, she was madly in love. She had thrown caution to the winds. She had assumed I was going to marry her. She simply gave everything. She had no defenses, no fall-back position. I tried to tell her she had her whole life ahead of her . . .'

'Did you use those words?' Susan asked.

'What words?'

'About her whole life . . .'

'I think so, yes. I said, "Meredith, you're very young. You have your whole life ahead of you. I'm a middle-aged man, my best years are behind me." Something like that.' He grimaced. 'Something weak and self-indulgent and hackneyed.' He sighed. 'I think it destroyed her when I ended it. And that destroyed me, that knowledge. I haven't slept a peaceful night since.' He looked at Susan. 'In my own way, I've carried a torch for her all these years. I have a few pictures of her, and a couple of letters. I look at them, I think about her – when I can stand it, that is.'

Susan was looking at him through the eyes of a therapist. She knew his grief was real. She also knew he had changed the course of an innocent young woman's life, probably for the worse.

'Did you know she changed her major that year?' she asked.

He nodded. 'I couldn't avoid learning that,' he said. 'Her name dropped off the course lists. I couldn't contain my curiosity. I looked her up in the student directory. I found out the next fall that she had switched to journalism.'

'Did that make you feel bad?' Susan asked.

'Terrible,' he said. 'The idea that I had had such an effect. As I say, she was such a terrific talent. I had deprived our science of someone who could have made a major contribution. I felt devastated. I felt like a criminal.'

'Did you see her again?' Susan asked.

'Never. It's a big campus. I never crossed her path. Especially since she wasn't coming to our building any more.'

'Did you see her on the stage?'

The professor looked taken aback. 'You know about that?'

Susan nodded.

'Yes, I did,' he admitted. 'I couldn't resist. I went to the production of *A Streetcar Named Desire*. She played Stella. Then, her senior year, I went to see her in the Shakespeare Company, doing *Romeo and Juliet*. She was marvelous. The feeling of youth, of innocence she projected . . . The end of the play was painful for me. When Juliet commits suicide after finding Romeo's body beside her in the tomb, Meredith projected a kind of fatal joy and relief. She got rave reviews for her performance. I couldn't help wondering if . . .'

'If the grief she felt over you was part of her performance?' Susan offered.

He nodded.

There were two more questions Susan had to ask. She could feel the professor's intense pain. She knew she was about to make it worse.

'I have to ask you something difficult,' she said. 'Was Meredith a virgin when you first made love to her?'

He looked shocked. 'Why do you ask?'

'It's something that has come up in our investigation,' Susan said. After a moment's thought she decided not to let him off the hook, but to be direct and even cruel. 'Was she? Did you make her lose her virginity?'

He seemed perplexed. 'No. At least, I don't think so. I've never had sex with a virgin. I think I would have felt something, or she would have said something . . . No, Doctor, I don't think so.'

'Did you know you had made her pregnant?' Susan asked.

He turned pale.

'Are you serious?' he asked.

'Very serious, Professor.'

'Oh, my God . . .' He put his hands over his face. It was easy for Susan to guess his thoughts. The guilt he already felt must have been increased exponentially by the knowledge that he had impregnated Meredith.

'Did she have an abortion?' he asked.

'I believe she did, yes,' Susan said. 'We're investigating that. If you know anything about it, Professor, I would very much appreciate your help.'

'I knew nothing about it,' he said. 'If I had known . . .'

He looked as if she had dealt him a terrible blow. He seemed to grow older before her eyes.

There was a silence. Susan looked at the pictures of his children on the bookshelf.

'Are those your children?' she asked.

He looked wanly at the photos. 'Yes.' The hollow, hopeless tone in his voice told Susan he was thinking how much he would have loved a child borne him by Meredith. He was measuring his own loss as well as the tragedy he had created.

'Can you think of any way you might help me to find out what happened?' she asked.

He sat forward as though fighting to concentrate.

'I didn't know any of her friends,' he said. 'Her parents were divorced. Her father had died. Her mother . . .'

'I've talked to her mother,' Susan said. 'She knows nothing about it.'

'That's right, they weren't close.' Graham Auden nodded. 'Meredith couldn't forgive her mother for the divorce.'

'And you never heard from Meredith again?' Susan asked. 'I'm looking for the slightest hint.'

'Never,' he said. 'Not a word.'

Susan stood up and held out a hand. 'Professor Auden, thank you very much. I'm grateful for your honesty.'

He shook her hand, forcing a weak smile. 'If there's anything more I can do to help, Doctor, please don't hesitate to call on me.'

'I need to find the doctor who performed Meredith's abortion, or the clinic where the procedure was done. Do you have any idea how I might accomplish that?' she asked.

He thought for a moment. 'Maybe she used the Student Health Service. She was a very busy person, a high achiever. I doubt that she could have spared the time to travel far away for a thing like that.'

Again the mask of grief had descended on his features. He was still holding Susan's hand. She disengaged herself as gently as she could. Then he said an odd thing.

'You know,' he said, 'you remind me of her.'

Susan stepped back a pace, a reflexive movement that made her wonder what she was feeling.

'How is that?' she asked. 'We're very different. I'm a lot older, for one thing . . .'

'I don't know really.' He rubbed at his eyes, which were still moist. 'You're psychic, aren't you?'

Susan gave him a controlled smile. 'Yes.'

'Well, never mind,' he said. 'Just find her.'

'I'll do everything I can.' Susan turned on her heel and moved to the door, feeling his eyes on her.

'I'll pray for you.'

She stopped at the door and gave him a last look.

'Thank you,' she said. 'You might pray for Meredith, too.'

# CHAPTER 54

The Undertaker entered the room with a medical bag in his hand. He wore his surgical scrubs, the mask untied so Meredith could see his face.

She felt she knew him now. Knew his smell, the way he moved, the slight Midwest accent in his voice. This was the most terrifying thing of all, this familiarity. For nothing could be so cold or so abstract as the murderous obsession binding him to her. The loneliness of her dying would be terrible, more so than the pain or the loss.

She wondered how crazy he had been the day he aborted her foetus. What twisted thoughts had woven themselves through his brain as he explored her womb?

He knelt by her side and gently pushed a strand of hair from her cheek.

'I've been curious about one thing,' he said.

'What?'

'Who did it to you?'

'Did what?'

'Made you pregnant.'

Meredith tried to focus on the plan she had been thinking out for days. Bind him to her. Use his love.

'A professor at Berkeley,' she said.

'You had an affair?'

'Yes.'

He opened the bag and removed some tubing and other paraphernalia.

'Did you love him?' he asked, his voice as calm as that of any family physician chatting about trivia as he performed his tasks.

Meredith hesitated. Should she admit that she loved another man?

'No,' she said. 'I was young, I . . .'

He smiled, shaking his head. 'Ah-ah. I think you were in love. You don't have to hide it from me. I understand love, after all.'

Meredith was silent.

'I've never been in love,' he said. 'I mean, before you. Oh, an infatuation here and there – you know how it is. But, as they say, when the real thing comes along, you know it.'

He stood up, left the room and returned with an IV stand, which he put next to her. He knelt to pick up a length of tubing from the floor and attached it to a Y connection. He hummed as he worked.

'You know,' he said, 'one thing I've thought about a great deal is the difference between a man's love and a woman's. How can a man possibly conceive a woman's love? All a man does is pursue and spill his seed. A woman shows her love by creating a new human being out of her own body. The two things have little in common.'

He was thinking about all the babies he had brought into the world, and the look in the mothers' eyes when their infant was first presented to them. It was profound, mystical. The foetus being nourished through the mother's bloodstream. Two hearts beating as one . . . How could a man comprehend such a thing?

He connected one end of the tubing to an eighteen-gauge

needle and adjusted the stopcock. A bottle of isotonic saline hung from the stand. He opened the clamp to the saline bottle to clear the tubing of air.

'What are you going to do?' she asked.

'Nothing you need to be afraid of,' he said. 'Just a little transfusion.'

'Why?'

He didn't answer. He fiddled with the stopcock, freeing the tubing of air.

'There. That ought to do nicely.'

He sat down by her side.

'You're so beautiful,' he said. 'You're an angel.'

He kissed her lips, chastely. He stroked her hair. His touch sickened her.

'You're insane,' she said.

The words had slipped out of their own accord. He backed away and looked at her with an expression of the purest hatred.

'I'm sorry,' she said. 'I didn't mean . . .'

He shook his head. He bent to open the medical bag on the floor. He fiddled inside it, breathing hard.

'Don't,' Meredith said. 'I'm sorry. I didn't mean it.'

He produced a small vial of blood with a label. Holding her firmly by her hair, he upended the vial and spilled blood on her face. She began to scream. He bent to lick at the drops. Her face thrashed this way and that, causing his tongue to spread the blood over her in swaths like brushstrokes. Crimson streams ran down her neck. The pungent fleshy smell stank in her nostrils.

He held her jaws apart with strong fingers. His tongue, red with the blood, entered her mouth. She felt his sex hard against her pelvis, moving, pushing.

'This wine . . .'

She felt him shudder. His groan sounded inside her own throat. The tongue pushed deeper, making her gag.

When he finished she saw that his own eyes were full of tears.

'This is my blood,' he said.

# CHAPTER 55

Susan called David Gold.

'I think the killer was out here when Meredith played Juliet at Berkeley,' Susan said. 'Whether he was living and working here, or just visiting, I don't know. I think he became obsessed with her. It was around the same time that she had her affair with the professor, and, I think, her abortion.'

'Okay . . .'

'If she did have an abortion, I need to find the clinic where she had it,' Susan said. 'I don't know what I can learn from it, but I just want to be sure. After all, abortion has been our connection from the beginning. I could be wrong, but . . .'

'You weren't wrong about Juliet,' Gold said. 'Follow your own nose.'

Susan agreed with Professor Auden that Meredith Spiers had probably not left the Bay area to get her abortion.

Meredith was a bright, savvy young woman. Abortion was no longer the secret thing it had been two generations ago. If Meredith needed an abortion she would have been within easy reach of referral to a clinic or specialist. Probably through the Student Health Service. Berkeley was a liberated campus with many women's rights groups.

On their way Susan and Riccio stopped for coffee. Riccio was hungry and ordered a cheeseburger and fries, which he ate without much enthusiasm. Susan watched him for a moment. Then she asked the question that had been in her mind for some time.

'You don't believe in me, do you?'

Riccio gave her a blank look, as though he had not understood. 'What do you mean?'

'My second sight,' Susan said, smiling slightly. 'You don't believe it's real. Do you?'

He took another bite of his cheeseburger and kept his eyes on something over her shoulder as he chewed. Then he took a sip of his coffee.

'I respect Dave Gold,' he said. 'He believes in you. I know you've done some things that have helped in the past. That's good enough for me.'

'But as far as second sight goes, you're a skeptic,' Susan said. 'Isn't that right?'

'Does it show?' he asked.

'No, that's not what I mean. You've been very kind to me. I just mean that, for yourself, you don't believe in second sight.'

'That's right.' He nodded. His expression was neither hostile nor deprecating. He was stating a fact.

'Is there a reason?' she asked.

He thought for a moment. 'No,' he said. 'No reason. I just don't believe in it.'

He wasn't saying what was really in his mind. His Italian roots went deep, and he had grown up steeped in a Catholic tradition which was not without elements of superstition. He had known countless aunts, uncles and grandparents who believed in the Evil Eye and who crossed themselves superstitiously when they feared their thoughts or words might bring retribution from some shadowy source. He remained a Catholic for the sake of his children, but he was secretly an atheist. His wife knew it, but no one else in the family did.

It had taken Joe Riccio thirty years to purge himself of

the religious baggage that had been laid on him in church and in parochial school. He believed in nothing but his power to do the right thing by the woman he loved and by his children. And in the fact that the robbers and gang-bangers and dope dealers and child molesters he had put behind bars over the years belonged there. That the streets were safer with them out of circulation, and that the judges and lawyers who put them back on the streets were criminals themselves.

Riccio realized that in some ways he had had to narrow his perspective in order to be effective as a cop and to remain sane at the same time. But he did not regret this.

If God could not read his thoughts, then Susan Shader certainly could not. That was his opinion.

'Well,' Susan said, 'informed skepticism has always been good enough for me. I don't blame you for not believing what hasn't been proven to you.'

Riccio finished his cheeseburger and wiped his hands with the paper napkin. He seemed content to let the subject drop.

'Let me ask you one more question,' Susan said. 'When I do produce clues that turn out to be valuable, how do you think I'm doing it?'

He thought for a moment.

'The same way any good cop does it,' he said. 'Instinct, experience, brains. You're smart. You pick things up.'

'I see.'

She felt no need to convince him. She enjoyed his skepticism, because it seemed all of a piece with his obvious integrity. She liked Riccio. She suspected, however, that she would never get to know him much better than she did now.

The director of the Student Health Service, a corpulent woman with a friendly smile, welcomed Susan and listened carefully as she told her what she needed.

'This would have been about seven years ago,' Susan said.

'The person I'm thinking of would have been an under-graduate. I doubt that she would have left this area to have the procedure. She was very busy with classes and extracurricular activities.' She grimaced slightly at her own choice of words.

'Well, the clinics here in Berkeley are highly regarded,' said the director. 'No particular one more than the others. Then, of course, there are clinics in Oakland, San Francisco and the surrounding area. A lot to choose from. This could take you some time.'

She got up and took a small glossy folder from a pile on one of her shelves.

'If you start locally, these are the most likely ones,' she said. She put on her reading glasses and read down the list. 'Here's one that's newer than seven years old,' she said. 'I'll cross that out. The rest were in operation during the time you're concerned with.'

'Thank you,' Susan said. 'You've been very helpful.'

The director gave her an intent look. 'I've heard of you,' she said.

'Oh.' Susan was not in a mood to talk about herself.

'Is this about Meredith?' the director asked.

'Yes, it is. Did you know her?'

'No. She was before my time. But I've seen her on tele-vision. A very lovely girl. I hope you find her.'

'I do too.'

Susan used the phone at her motel to call the clinics one by one. The directors were kind about inviting her in to talk, but were chary of promising anything that might violate the confidentiality of one of their clients, past or present. Susan assured them – falsely, she knew – that no such problem would arise.

There were six clinics in the immediate area. On a hunch

Susan had Joe Riccio drive her by them, one by one. She was looking for a feeling, an intuition that might save time.

Her third stop turned out to be the lucky one. Riccio stopped outside the Berkeley Women's Clinic, located at a busy intersection perhaps a mile from the university. She got out of the car under Riccio's watchful eye and walked to the front windows of the clinic, which were closed off by vertical blinds.

She had her hand on the plate glass door, the legend BERKELEY WOMEN'S CLINIC before her eyes, when she heard the complaint of old brakes as a very old and dilapidated flatbed truck came to a stop at the red light. The truck was loaded with what appeared to be second-hand furniture, roped clumsily together and covered by old tarpaulins.

'Hey!' a voice cried from somewhere.

The truck must have stalled, for Susan heard the ignition screeching repeatedly as the driver turned the key. The light turned green, but the truck did not move. A horn was heard from one of the cars behind.

Finally the truck's engine coughed into life, and a great cloud of black smoke rose from the tailpipe, almost obscuring the whole intersection.

'Hey, Methuselah, get a tune-up!' shouted the driver of the car behind the truck.

*Methuselah*.

Susan stood watching as the truck lumbered away in its cloud of smoke, the impatient driver of the car honking his horn again.

Riccio, always on the alert for anything unusual, had heard the commotion and come to Susan's side.

'This is it,' she told him. 'This is the place.'

'How did you know?' Riccio asked.

'A long story,' Susan said.

# CHAPTER 56

A Chicago HBT team supported by a dozen FBI sharp-shooters assaulted the Park Ridge home of Wayne Hemphill in the early morning. They were taking no chances after what had happened to David Gold. They had made sure Hemphill was home alone, and that every house within shooting distance was covered.

Hemphill surrendered without a struggle. A large, heavy man with an ornate goatee and sad eyes, he stood back in silence to let the officers into his home. A court-ordered search warrant was presented to him, and he was Mirandized in front of a dozen witnesses with video rolling, to make sure the arrest stuck.

It took the crime scene specialists less than ten minutes to determine that blood stains from multiple sources were all over Hemphill's basement.

Hemphill was taken to a maximum-security holding cell at Cook County Jail and held under suicide watch while forensic teams from the CPD, the FBI and the Medical Examiner's Office began work on the bloodstains. Three hours after the arrest, at eleven-thirty in the morning, a match was made between a bloodstain on the bottom stair of Hemphill's basement staircase and the blood of Miranda Becker.

One hour later a blood drop on Hemphill's basement rug was matched with the blood of Marcie Webb.

By that time Hemphill was receiving the full treatment

accorded to Ten Most Wanted superstars. His holding cell was under twenty-four-hour video surveillance. His attorney had arrived within an hour of his arrest, and the attorney was in the cell with Hemphill when the arresting officers received word that a bloodstain on the battered couch in Hemphill's basement matched the blood of Mary Ellen Mahoney.

Hemphill had not said a single word since his arrest, with the exception of 'Yes' in answer to the Miranda. The interrogation at Cook County Jail was handled by Abel Weathers himself, with Tom Castaneda and Rich Sheehan in attendance. Video was rolling as Weathers spoke to Hemphill.

'Mr Hemphill, you can do yourself a great deal of good by telling me one simple thing. Where is Meredith Spiers?'

Hemphill listened to a whisper from his attorney before replying, 'On the advice of counsel, I decline to answer any questions at the present time.'

'Mr Hemphill, I want to make very clear to you that your cooperation on this point could make all the difference in the prosecution of this case. By the same token, your refusal to help us locate Meredith could have devastating effects on your future.' Weathers gave the suspect his best piercing gaze.

Hemphill met Weathers's eyes with an almost regretful look as he listened to his attorney.

'On the advice of counsel,' he said, 'I decline to answer any questions at the present time.'

Weathers did not give up. He kept Hemphill in the interrogation room for the rest of the day and through the night. As the evidence against Hemphill mounted, it was made part of the interrogation. Hemphill sat passively in the hard metal chair, not avoiding the interrogators' eyes, accepting a cigarette now and then, but never departing from his stock answer. When his attorney was out of the room for a comfort break, Hemphill remained silent.

In the afternoon a note was brought to Weathers by one

of his prosecutors. A standard hospital body bag, of the same type as those used in the Undertaker killings, had been found on one of the storage shelves in Hemphill's basement.

The cops and the FBI were distressed by Hemphill's stoicism. Surely he realized the extremity he found himself in. Perhaps, on the other hand, it was his awareness of the enormity of the evidence that kept him silent. He had had dealings with the law before. His attorney had probably told him to wait out the initial siege, in the hope that the police would make a mistake that would eventually compromise their case.

Anticipating this, the cops and the FBI worked diligently to make the collection of evidence textbook perfect. Specialists from the State's Attorney's office worked hand in hand with FBI forensics experts to tag and preserve the damning physical evidence in state-of-the-art manner, with video rolling every step of the way to pre-empt a Simpson defense. There would be no 'garbage in, garbage out' DNA arguments this time.

By the end of the day Weathers and the FBI were certain that Hemphill and his lawyer intended to make a deal based on the safe return of Meredith Spiers, but wanted to know for sure what evidence they had on him before negotiating.

'Let's keep the pressure on,' said Weathers. 'Don't let him sleep. We may have our answer by morning.'

By now the interrogators were less annoyed with Wayne Hemphill and his attorney. It was no wonder, after all, that Hemphill was taking refuge in silence. He was the Undertaker.

But where was Meredith Spiers?

The silence of Hemphill made the cops and the FBI fear that Meredith was a card he could no longer play, because she was already dead.

# CHAPTER 57

The arrest of Wayne Hemphill was making headlines on all the cable stations, but Susan did not see them. She was inside the Berkeley Women's Clinic with Joe Riccio.

Susan was greeted at the front desk by an attractive older woman wearing half-glasses and a name tag that said Shielah.

'I'm here to see Mrs Freis,' Susan said. 'I'm Dr Shader.'

'She's expecting you,' said the receptionist with a friendly smile that had probably been refined over the years to reassure frightened clients. 'Come on in.'

She took Susan to the door of the director's office. Mrs Freis was standing in the doorway with her hand held out.

'Dr Shader, glad to meet you.'

'Thank you for seeing me.'

'No problem. Would you like some coffee?'

'Thanks, that would be nice.'

'I'll bring it,' Shielah said. 'How do you take it, dear?'

'Black is fine.'

Mrs Freis led the way into a small, brightly lit office with an executive desk and pictures of grandchildren on the lowboy.

'I used to live in Oakland.' Susan smiled. 'It's good to see this part of the country again. I've missed it.'

'Well, we like it.' Mrs Freis's smile seemed forced. She was obviously girded for a struggle.

Shielah returned with the coffee, handed it to Susan with a smile and left the office, closing the door behind her.

Susan wasted no time.

'I'm working on a murder investigation with the Chicago Police Department and the FBI,' Susan said. 'A person has been abducted . . .'

'I know about the case,' Mrs Freis said. 'I'm very concerned. How can I help?'

'Meredith Spiers had an abortion seven years ago here in Berkeley,' Susan said. 'I have evidence the procedure took place in this clinic. I'd like to know who performed the abortion and what the circumstances were.'

Mrs Freis raised an eyebrow. 'That's a long time ago,' she said. 'Is there a connection?'

'I think there is,' Susan said. 'It's probably better for me not to go into the details, but let me just say that the information could have a major impact on the investigation.'

The older woman frowned.

'The records of all our patients are confidential,' she said. 'I understand your dilemma, but you have to understand mine. There are crazy people out there, violent people who harass patients and sometimes injure them. Physicians have been attacked, even killed. If we gave out information like what you're asking, we might be endangering lives. Not to mention the fact that we would of course lose all our patients.'

'I understand,' Susan said. 'I know it's difficult. I'm a psychiatrist. It would take wild horses to get me to reveal the name of one of my patients. But this is a race against the clock, Mrs Freis. I'm trying to save Meredith's life.'

There was a silence. Susan could feel how torn the other woman was. She wanted to help, but she could not violate a rule upon which the very existence of clinics like this was based.

'Naturally your confidence would be respected,' Susan said. 'No matter what happens, this clinic's involvement in the case would be kept from the public. I can promise you that.'

'Seven years ago ... I'm afraid none of our people have been here that long,' said Mrs Freis, an evasive look in her eyes.

'Not even you?' Susan asked.

'Not even me. I've only been here since '94.'

'What about the physicians?'

The older woman shook her head. 'They've all moved on. Some to private practice or to group practice, some to HMOs, some to other cities. You know how the medical profession is today.'

Susan nodded. She looked at the photos on the wall which showed the smiling faces of the clinic's current doctors, two women and a man.

'I don't suppose they stay in touch,' she said.

'Not with me, at any rate.' Mrs Freis shrugged.

Susan turned back to the older woman.

'Did any of them move to Chicago or the Midwest?'

The director's eyes flicked away from Susan's, then back again.

'I don't know,' she said. 'I'm not sure.'

There was a silence. Susan thought she had struck a nerve.

'I would give a lot to talk to them,' Susan said. 'Their own identity isn't confidential, is it? Their names must have been in the Yellow Pages at the time. No physician can keep his very existence a secret.'

'In this field, such things are becoming necessary,' Mrs Freis said. 'As you know, physicians have been attacked, even murdered.'

'I understand. Please, Mrs Freis. Can you give me their names?'

The older woman drummed two fingers on the desk top, looking at Susan with undisguised irritation.

'Would you excuse me a moment, Doctor?'

Mrs Freis got up and left the room, closing the door behind her. Susan sat looking at the walls, alert to the slightest signal that might help her. The faces of the current doctors in the photographs revealed nothing. When Susan had mentioned Chicago Mrs Freis's eyes had darted to that wall, as though she was remembering a doctor whose face used to be displayed there. But the wall told Susan nothing.

Susan sipped at her coffee, which was surprisingly good, and studied the faces of the grandchildren in the photograph. This was a nice clinic, she reflected. It was clean, reassuring, even homey. Just the place for a worried Berkeley student who needed help with an unwanted pregnancy.

The door opened and Mrs Freis came back in.

'I just spoke to our attorney,' she said. 'The bottom line is, I can't tell you anything about our clients or our doctors, past or present, without their written permission.'

Susan knew what was in the other woman's mind. She might be laying the clinic open to a lawsuit by one or more of the former physicians if she gave out information that violated some sort of implicit contract with them. She was protecting herself.

'I see,' she said. 'So you can't even tell me who has worked here in the past?'

'No, I can't.'

'Even if I could find out the information by looking in the Yellow Pages or the Directory of Physicians from the year in question?'

'All I can suggest is that you do so,' the older woman said. 'It is not my place to tell you. I hope you understand.'

There was a pause.

'All right,' Susan said. 'Thank you for your help.'

Both women stood up.

'I'm sorry I can't do more,' Mrs Freis said. 'I do hope you find Meredith as quickly as possible.'

*It won't be as quickly as it might have been.* Despite the fact that she understood Mrs Freis's position, Susan had taken a dislike to the woman.

'Do you get to Chicago at all in your work?' Susan asked, trying for the collegial note.

'Once in a while. We've had meetings at the Drake Hotel.'

'Really? So have I. I mean, I did when I lived out here. The Drake is a nice hotel. Such a beautiful location, up by the Water Tower.'

A few moments of amicable conversation followed, during which Susan mentioned the names of some of the prominent Chicago specialists in obstetrics and gynecology. Mrs Freis knew them or had heard of them.

'Did I mention that my husband and I used to live in the hills above Oakland?' Susan asked.

'Yes, I believe you did.'

'Our house burned down in the big fire,' Susan said. 'It happened after our divorce, but it still came as a shock.'

'Fires are a danger around here,' Mrs Freis allowed.

Susan paused in the hallway outside the office.

'Would you mind if I took a quick walk through your clinic?'

'Not at all. I'll escort you.' Clearly Mrs Freis didn't want to let Susan out of her sight.

The layout of the clinic was typical, with consultation rooms, examining rooms and a bathroom in the hall. It was nicely decorated, and an effort had been made to avoid the cold, clinical decor of so many medical facilities. The colors and fabrics were warm, there was coffee in a large urn for the patients, and a small TV was on in the waiting room. On the screen Oprah Winfrey was interviewing an actor whose face Susan recognized but whose name she had forgotten.

'Would you mind if I used your bathroom on my way out?' Susan asked.

'Not at all. Help yourself.'

Mrs Freis shook Susan's hand and disappeared into her office.

In the bathroom Susan noticed a striking painting in oils. It depicted a woman standing in a room, seen through an open doorway. The room was bathed in light from a sunset coming through the window, so that the light streamed past the woman's silhouette and out the picture toward the viewer. The oils were lush, the colors very bold. It was an original, the work of an unsung artist of some talent. It had a post-Impressionist quality, with a strong Van Gogh influence in the colors and brushwork.

Susan looked more closely at the picture. It was unsigned. After a moment's hesitation she put her purse on the sink and used both hands to remove the picture from the wall.

A title was written in pencil on the canvas.

*Virgin of the Sunset, 1987.*

No painter's name was given. Susan hung the painting back on the wall and stood looking at it. The color was the centerpiece, with the woman's upright form powerfully silhouetted in the doorway. Susan could almost taste the blood-red pigment. There was a suggestion of gnarled tree branches outside the window, as though the sunset were shining through a wood. The brushstrokes flowed downward from the woman's figure and out through the narrow doorway at the bottom of the picture.

Susan let her fingers stray gently over the crusty layers of paint. She closed her eyes. A slow tremor went through her hands. She put her face to the painting and smelled the oil paint, alert as an animal scenting danger. Then she stood back and took one more long look.

Susan stopped at the reception desk on her way out. Shielah, the friendly middle-aged receptionist, looked up from her computer screen with a smile.

'What is that picture I saw in the bathroom?' Susan asked.

'Oh, that's one of our heirlooms. It's been here for years and years. It gets moved from room to room as we redecorate. It never gets thrown out because everybody seems to like it.'

'It's quite impressive.'

'Yes, it is, isn't it? Very dramatic.'

'Do you know who painted it?' Susan asked.

'One of our doctors painted it. Painting was his hobby.'

'Did he donate it to the clinic?' Susan asked.

'He said it didn't fit the color scheme in his home. When he left us, he didn't take it with him. I guess he didn't care any more.'

'Which doctor was it?'

'It was Dr Tower. He was generous about things like that. Constantly redecorating his house, throwing things out . . . He gave us odds and ends we could use.'

'Roy Tower?' Susan exclaimed. 'Why, I went to medical school with him! He worked here?'

'No, this was Kenneth Tower. Ken Tower. He was a little older than you, dear.'

'Oh. I see.'

'Actually, Ken left to go back to the Midwest somewhere,' Shielah said. 'You might have crossed his path along the way sometime.'

'I wouldn't be surprised. It's a small world.'

Susan glanced behind her at the waiting room.

'The painting,' she said. 'You don't happen to remember where it was hung when you first got it, do you?'

'Hmm . . . Dear, that's a long time ago. I don't – wait. I

do remember! Ken hung it in his own examining room. It stayed there until he left us, I believe. Yes, I'm positive.'

'I can see you've got a good memory.' Susan smiled. 'Thanks for your help.'

'No trouble at all, dear. Nice to meet you.'

Susan found Joe Riccio standing outside the door of the clinic.

'We've got to call David,' she said. 'I know who he is.'

'Who who is?' Riccio asked.

'The Undertaker.'

# CHAPTER 58

It was two p.m. in Chicago.

David Gold was sitting in his office, exhausted from the all-night Wayne Hemphill interrogation, when Susan called.

He had never heard her sound so excited. 'I've found him, David. I know who he is. You've got to arrest him.'

'Slow down,' Gold said. 'What are you talking about?'

'I can't slow down,' Susan said breathlessly. 'His name is Kenneth Tower. He's an ob-gyn specialist. If he isn't in the Chicago area, he's nearby. David, you've got to hurry.'

'Slow down,' Gold told her. 'What makes you so sure?'

'He performed an abortion on Meredith Spiers when she was a student at Berkeley,' Susan said. 'I can't prove it without the clinic's records, but I'm sure of it, David. He's an amateur painter. There's a painting in the clinic called *Virgin of the Sunset*. The secretary told me it was painted by Tower, and he used to have it hanging in his examining room. The painting, David – you'll have to see it to understand. It has everything . . .'

'Susan, we can't arrest a guy for painting a picture.'

'David . . .'

'Susan, listen to me. We pulled in a guy whose basement is full of bloodstains that match the victims. We even found a body bag down there. The guy is a pro-life sicko who used to run a group that dumped dead foetuses on the doorsteps of women who were contemplating abortions. Think about it, Susan. This guy is tailor-made. He's got it all. The motive, the opportunity, the physical evidence . . .'

'You didn't find Meredith, did you?' Susan asked.

'Not yet,' Gold said. 'But we will.'

'David, please. Please listen to me. You've got the wrong man. There is no time. You can save Meredith.'

'Susan . . .'

'David, you sent me on this trip yourself. You can't get cold feet now. You've got to stop him before it's too late.'

Gold sighed. 'I know I sent you . . .'

Gold looked out his window at the frozen sky. In his heart he believed the Undertaker was not on the loose in the city, but being interrogated at Cook County Jail. Susan was tilting at windmills because Gold himself had told her to keep trying. It was over. But how could he make her understand that?

'David,' Susan insisted. 'Please. Help me catch him.'

Gold thought of the consequences if she was wrong again. That would be the end. The pain in his chest was coming back, aggravated by nervous tension.

'All right,' he said. 'Once we find out what Hemphill has to say . . .'

'Now, David. Now. Don't wait another minute. Please.'

Gold stood up. He wished he could slam down the phone and forget this whole ugly case.

'Give me the name again,' he said.

# CHAPTER 59

The Undertaker lay naked in his attic studio.

Canvases in various stages of revision lined the walls.
Three thirty-five-inch TVs were gathered around the bed in
the center of the room, each connected to a VCR. The power
cords were hidden by throw rugs. Photographs of Meredith
Spiers were everywhere. Some were mere eight by ten blow-
ups, in table frames or scattered on the floor. Two had been
blown up into posters at Kinko's. The best one, enlarged at
great expense to the Undertaker by a processing service that
catered to advertisers, occupied most of the interior wall. It
was the glamor shot of Meredith, the one that played up her
sexiness, without of course compromising her essential purity.

The paintings all showed the same subject, the Virgin in a
doorway. Like Monet's cathedrals or Van Gogh's olive trees,
they varied only in the time of day depicted, and conse-
quently the color palette employed. Light from the window
behind the Virgin flowed downward, through her legs and
out of the picture plane toward the viewer's eye. The basic
pattern was unchanging, though in different lights the color
seemed to flow at different speeds.

The Undertaker was reminded of De Kooning with his
'Woman' pictures. The artist's obsession with the one subject
created a power, a focus, which grew stronger with each
successive version, until finally the viewer could hardly fail

to realize that the eye of faith, not of mere esthetics, was creating this Virgin.

The pose was surprisingly neutral when one considered the depth of commitment behind the work. A woman in a doorway, seen from a room away. But this pose had suggested itself to the Undertaker many years ago in a dream, and he had come to see it as a pure icon, like Christ on the Cross or Mary with her infant. The verticality of the female figure, the flowing essence of love emanating from her, the window standing behind like a witness – it all fit together like a prayer. Nothing was unnecessary, nothing was left out.

He looked from the paintings to the three TVs, which were playing the videos of his three rehearsals. He wanted to be surrounded by his best work today, to give himself inspiration. Each of the videos had its good points, of course, but each had important weaknesses as well. Comparison of the three tapes showed the progress in the Undertaker's thinking through the course of the campaign, as well as the deepening of his faith. In retrospect he was sorry that Miranda had come first. She was the most tragic of the subjects and could have benefited from the greater solemnity he brought to the last victim, Marcie. But Miranda had given herself in a good cause. In a way she had purified him and armed him for the challenges ahead.

He was on tenterhooks as his gaze darted from one image to the next. He had to be at his best today. He had to be perfect in his vision, absolute in his devotion. After all, he would not be around to see the results. He was leaving a document that the world would never forget. His own *memento mori* as well as his final paean to the Virgin.

Unaware of any emotion other than homage, the Undertaker was surprised to look down and see the wetness of his sex. He had not looked forward to this day as a day of pleasure. On the contrary, it was a moment of renunciation, of sacrifice.

He took a tissue from the box beside the bed and wiped himself off, ashamed of the betrayal of his flesh. Mortification, he thought. Penance. He lay back and studied the Virgin's many faces, in the photographs and on the screen. Her multiplicity beguiled him. She was so beautiful.

He opened the drawer of the table beside the bed and took out the scalpel. Cautiously he made a small incision in his upper arm, just below the shoulder, and turned his head to lick at his own blood. He felt nothing when the blade parted the flesh, nothing at all. This was proof: today was the day. His spirit was readying itself for higher things.

He sucked pensively at the wound, his mind focused painfully on the Virgin. He did not want her to suffer. Her ascension must be like that of Mary, peaceful and happy. The torments of the Son were not for her. God's arms were open, His heaven saving its place for her.

The blood had stopped flowing. The Undertaker thought about deepening the incision, but gave up the idea. Even this was a sign. His blood was keeping itself for the Ascension. No more rehearsals, no more experiments. He got up and put on his scrub pants and shirt. He washed his hands. He left the studio and made his way to the crawl space. After carefully checking the video camera for power as well as settings, he turned it on and headed downstairs.

The time was now.

# CHAPTER 60

As soon as he got off the phone with Susan, David Gold called Tom Castaneda, who was in his office on South Dearborn.

As Gold had anticipated, Castaneda was unimpressed by his report of what Susan had found in California.

'Dave, you're talking psychic impressions,' he said. 'A painting, the idea of a Virgin, *Romeo and Juliet* . . . What we have in Hemphill is physical evidence, hard and fast.'

'But we don't have Meredith, do we?' Gold challenged.

'We don't now, but we will.' Castaneda held firm. 'Hemphill's attorney is playing it close to the vest, but I think he wants to deal. He's going to give us Meredith in exchange for a plea. The interrogators are putting on the screws. I think we're gonna have a deal by tonight.'

'Tommy . . .'

'Dave, remember what happened with Timothy Hatch. We pulled that guy in based on the fact that he liked Virgin Marys. The egg on our face is still fresh. What if this other thing is no better? The damage . . .'

'What will the damage be if Meredith dies while we're fucking around with an innocent man?' Gold's profanity was in direct proportion to his worry. 'What if Hemphill is another Timothy Hatch?'

'Dave, you've seen this guy's basement.'

'Tommy, I hate to sound like Johnnie Cochran, but it

could have been planted. To throw us off the scent. Think how easy it would be to go in there with a few vials of blood and drizzle some drops here and there.'

'They weren't drops, Dave. They were drops and stains and old caked bits. There could have been five crime scenes down there.'

'That's my point. There's too much.'

'What about the body bag under the folded tent?'

'It could have been planted.'

'Dave, you're reaching . . .'

Gold knew he was losing Castaneda. Though the two men were close friends, the Timothy Hatch episode had soured Castaneda on Susan Shader's input as an investigator. Not even Castaneda's respect for Gold could outweigh the overwhelming evidence against Wayne Hemphill.

'Tommy, just for the sake of argument, say the Undertaker fed us Hemphill to keep us busy. What kind of person would know about Hemphill in advance? A person connected with the abortion business. Now, Susan thinks the Undertaker is an abortion doctor, right here in town.'

'Dave . . .'

'Tommy, think about the MO. The body bag, the blood collected from the victims. Think about the victims' connection to abortion clinics. Who would have access to the clinics' paperwork about past and current clients? A doctor. He could drop in on a clinic, or call them, any time he wanted. Especially a respected doctor.'

Gold was warming to his own arguments. For three months the logic behind Susan's leads had been coiling around his thoughts. Now, at the eleventh hour, it suddenly seemed decisive.

'Tommy, he gave us the upside-down crucifix to throw us off,' he argued. 'He knew we would look to the pro-life crazies because that was the most logical. He saw where we would go. He wanted to keep us from thinking abortion doctor. It worked.'

'Dave, I appreciate your concern,' Tom said. 'But I'm not going in on this with you. All I can suggest is that you call Weathers and tell him your thoughts.'

Gold gave a bitter laugh. 'Are you kidding?'

'I'm not gonna take the responsibility, Dave. Not now.'

The burning in Gold's chest was worse. A wave of weakness flowed over him. He was standing on a tightrope, with no net underneath. Timothy Hatch had removed that net, and so had Wayne Hemphill.

'Okay,' he said. 'Thanks anyway.'

'Dave . . .'

Gold hung up the phone and got to his feet, clutching his chest as the pain stabbed harder.

# CHAPTER 61

Meredith lay naked, watching the Undertaker work.

She was drugged again, woozy and confused. She watched numbly as he set up the IV and swabbed her forearm with alcohol.

'The stopcock is used to clear the tubing of air,' he said. 'Initially I'll use the syringe to pump my own blood into your veins. Then gravity will take over.'

He knelt by her side and stroked her cheek tenderly.

'I hated to have to drug you,' he said. 'But you're not cooperative. It couldn't be helped.' He kissed her lips. 'You'll see, there's nothing to be scared of. Just relax.'

He looked up at the ceiling. Then he stood up. She saw he had a tourniquet on his arm.

He fiddled with the stopcock, then inserted one end of the tubing into his right arm. He knelt and inserted the other end into the needle in Meredith's arm.

'Good.'

He opened the stopcock. She felt the slight pressure as his blood was pumped into her vein.

'Good girl.' He looked up at the ceiling again, then down at Meredith. 'It will all be over soon.'

Meredith mustered the last of her will to fight.

'Listen,' she said. 'We could go away together, you and I.'

He gave her an uncomprehending look.

'We could go away. We could be alone together,' she said.

'You don't have to do this.' Her words were slurred by exhaustion and by the drug he had given her.

He shook his head. 'That won't be necessary. Just relax.'

He stood up and removed his scrub pants. He was naked underneath them. Only now she saw the scalpel in his hand.

'Please,' she said.

'You are so beautiful,' he said. 'They don't understand how beautiful you are.'

'Who? Who doesn't understand?'

She was trying everything. But he didn't respond.

'Now, just relax,' he said, holding up the scalpel. 'You're going to feel a little sting. It will only take a second. The important thing is to relax.'

He took hold of the fingers of her left hand. He kissed her palm.

'I gave you a very slight general anesthetic,' he said. 'You'll feel things, but they won't hurt as much as they would normally.'

Meredith cried out feebly. 'No!'

He made an incision in the middle of her open hand. She felt a brief sting which was numbed by the drug, as he had promised.

He was nuzzling the bleeding hand, kissing it, licking at the blood.

'I love you,' he said. 'I love you.'

At that instant Meredith saw the glint of the lens in the ceiling and understood. He wanted a record of what he was doing to her.

She began to thrash this way and that. Her arms and legs pulled at the cords, her pelvis lifting off the mattress as she struggled.

He kept his face on the bleeding hand, lips pressed hard to the wound. His body settled atop hers. She smelled his sweat, and something else that made her gag. He was getting off on her gasps and her thrashing, she knew, but she couldn't stop.

'You're an angel,' he repeated. 'An angel . . .'

He pulled back abruptly, and sat poised atop her. She felt his thighs squeeze her ribcage. She realized he had been on the point of orgasm and had stopped himself.

He looked at her face. 'Blessed art thou among women . . .'

His eyes darted to her right hand, the unwounded one. He looked at it with undisguised covetousness, the way an aroused man looks at a naked woman's breasts or vagina. She sensed the extent of his perversion. Nausea rose in her throat.

The scalpel was moving toward her hand. She spoke before it got there.

'Kiss me,' she said.

He hesitated, looking down at her.

'Kiss my lips. Let me taste you,' she said.

He pulled back an inch, the scalpel still poised in his hand.

'Kiss my breast,' she said. 'Kiss my nipples. Come on.'

She could see his confusion. He had spent so many years focusing all his libido on innocent parts of women's bodies that he must long since have forgotten how to enjoy the sexual parts, if he ever knew. She wanted to confuse him.

'I want you,' she said. 'Come on. Kiss my nipples.'

His breathing was shallow, his eyes tortured.

'It's all right,' she said. 'Do it. Come on.' She knew her voice was shaking with terror, but she tried to sound inviting. 'Kiss my breast. Suck me. I want to feel you.'

He looked at her breasts. A slow disgust came over his features. He glanced at her unmarked hand.

'Don't you care about me at all?' she asked. 'Don't you want me to feel something too? You've looked at me all this time, you've watched me. You say you love me. Prove it.'

She heard a sound in his throat, a sort of groan. He was

trembling. The unmarked hand was attracting him like a flame. The scalpel came up . . .

'You don't love me,' she said.

He looked down at her in perplexity.

'You don't,' she said. 'If you did you'd want to kiss me. You'd want to make me happy. You don't love me.'

He had gone limp between his legs. He felt confused. She was so beautiful in her nudity. So white, so fresh and clean. And the first flow of blood, like the song of a bird in spring, had made her innocence stand out amazingly. The taste of it was in his mouth. But now her voice was pulling at him, wrecking his focus.

The white palm of her hand drew his eyes like a magnet.

Again her voice, reproaching. 'You don't love me. You don't. Admit it.'

He hated what she was doing. She was asking for filthy things, things that would sully her own purity. He loved her voice, he had coveted it a thousand times in his solitude. But he hated what she was saying. He had to shut her up.

He clamped his left hand over her mouth and fumbled on the floor for the long knife. She was struggling harder, bucking under him and trying to bite his hand. He was losing control of the situation. Where, he wondered, did she get this energy?

He found the knife and raised it over her stomach. He would have to strike now, to subdue her. Then, when she was docile, he would do the rest.

Somehow she got her teeth around the heel of his hand and bit into it, hard.

'Bitch,' he cried.

The knife raised higher, the naked girl bouncing and thrashing, his bleeding hand in her mouth.

'Bitch . . .'

A loud thump from upstairs stopped his hand in mid-air. He looked up at the stairs.

'Police! Open up!'

There were voices, many voices. Shouting. Feet were pounding on the floor above, rushing into all the rooms at once.

He looked at her stomach. It was white and creamy, only inches from his penis. He started to bring the knife down, but the look in her eyes made him hesitate. She was so innocent.

'Police!'

He wanted to explain, to see acknowledgment in her eyes. What was the point of it all, if she didn't understand? His years of devotion . . . But there was no time. The voices were everywhere. A fist banged on the cellar door.

He shrugged himself down onto her thighs and held the knife high.

*O happy dagger! This is thy sheath* . . .

'I love you . . .'

The door crashed open. A voice shouted something that Meredith didn't hear.

There was a loud explosion. The Undertaker shuddered. A flood of blood burst from his chest and inundated Meredith. She screamed.

'You're safe, it's all right.'

David Gold came forward, his .45 still smoking in his hand. The Undertaker lay atop Meredith. The knife was pressed between their bodies. Gold put a hand to the man's neck, feeling for a pulse.

'Still alive,' he said to the others. 'Not for long, though.'

He did not have to tell Meredith. She could feel the Undertaker's blood pumping through her veins in long, slow spasms, a wine she drank without opening her mouth.

Cops were rushing into the room. A medic in a white coat had come to her side and was examining the tubing. He called something to his colleagues. Then she felt him pull out the needle.

Meredith whispered something.

'What?' Gold asked, his face close to hers.

'*Some shall be pardon'd . . .*'

'What?'

Her eyes were open, but she did not seem to recognize him.

'It's Dave, Meredith. You're all right. You're safe.'

'*Some shall be pardon'd, and some punished . . .*' Meredith passed out with the words still on her lips.

Gold held her as he gave the orders for the ambulance and the crime scene personnel. He stayed beside her until the medics took her out. He rode with her in the ambulance to Evanston Hospital. It was only after the emergency room physician had told him she was in no physical danger that he smelled the stench of his own gunpowder and reflected that, after twenty years as a cop, he had finally fired his gun in the line of duty.

# PART SIX

# CHAPTER 62

*Some shall be pardon'd, and some punished;*
*But never was a story of more woe*
*Than this of Juliet and her Romeo.*

Meredith Spiers's murmured words in the basement of the Undertaker's house were also the last words of Shakespeare's *Romeo and Juliet*.

Dr Kenneth Tower, Diplomate of the American Board of Obstetrics and Gynecology and holder of a wall full of honors both as a medical student and as a practitioner, was identified as the killer of the three Undertaker victims the day after his death. Bloodstains and trace evidence in the basement of his Evanston home confirmed that he had killed his victims there. Videotapes of the murders were recovered from his attic studio, along with a collection of about 100 videotapes culled from Meredith Spiers's career in broadcast journalism.

The leather case full of blood samples which had been used to frame Wayne Hemphill for the murders also contained samples from twenty to thirty unknown sources. The authorities set about comparing these to the blood of murder victims in Chicago and elsewhere.

Wayne Hemphill was never charged in the Undertaker murders. He was released with apologies from the CPD and the FBI. However, six months after the termination of the Undertaker case Hemphill was arrested for conspiracy to bomb an abortion clinic, successfully prosecuted and sentenced to twelve years in a federal prison.

Nor was it revealed to the public that Dr Tower had framed Wayne Hemphill for the crimes. As far as the public knew, Hemphill was simply one suspect among others.

The role of Susan Shader in the apprehension of the Undertaker was never revealed. At a joint news conference, Abel Weathers and the FBI's Midwest director described the investigation that led to the death of Kenneth Tower as a 'team effort'.

'The important thing is that Miss Spiers was rescued in time,' said Abel Weathers. 'The tragedy is that three innocent victims had to die before this killer was brought to justice. We send our prayers to their families, and we pray for them.'

Susan acquiesced happily in not being singled out as the woman who had identified the Undertaker and saved Meredith Spiers's life. She had had enough notoriety.

Meredith Spiers would never write the feature article on Susan that would have revealed the key role Susan played in the later stages of the investigation. After recuperating for two weeks, first in a hospital and then at home, she took an extended leave of absence from Channel 9 to consider her future.

She told Susan that the Undertaker investigation had caused her to re-evaluate her motives in deciding to become a journalist.

'I'm only twenty-seven years old,' she said. 'You can start all over again when you're my age. I've never been convinced that I got into this for the right reasons. I don't want my success in news broadcasting to blind me to the choices I still have.'

Meredith asked Susan if she could become her patient. Susan gently refused, being all too aware of the ambivalence her role in the Undertaker case might cause in Meredith. It was hard to be a rescuer at the best of times. It would be easier for Meredith to learn to stand on her own two feet, emotionally speaking, with another therapist. Susan recommended a fine female psychiatrist whose work she knew well.

'If I can't be your patient,' Meredith asked, 'can I at least be your friend?'

'That's an honor I accept gladly,' Susan said. She had come to like and admire Meredith, and looked forward to watching her future development.

A week after the death of Dr Kenneth Tower, the main facts about his life had become known to the authorities.

Tower had been born forty-six years ago to an alcoholic mother who was probably an untreated schizophrenic. The identity of his father was not known. After his mother's death from an apparent overdose of barbiturates, Tower grew up in a series of institutions and foster homes. He worked his way through college and went to medical school at Johns Hopkins, financing his matriculation with student loans. He did his internship and residency in San Diego and completed his Boards shortly before joining a prestigious medical group in San Francisco.

Tower had no criminal record. Since his death the San Diego and San Francisco Police Department had been looking into crimes involving elements of the Undertaker's MO. A prostitute had been found murdered in South San Francisco nine years ago with suspicious cut marks on her hands. A rape victim had been found murdered by a deep knife wound to her stomach. The Tijuana police reported several murders of prostitutes and young girls involving similar features. The crimes had occurred too long ago to be compared with records of Dr Tower's whereabouts at the time.

A closed meeting was held in a conference room at the city office building on North LaSalle to discuss the crimes and their solution. Present were all those who had worked on the case, along with the mayor and the FBI's regional director. As the investigator who had almost single-handedly solved the crime, Susan was asked for her impressions of the clues that led to its solution.

'Dr Tower probably suffered from a narcissistic personality disorder with some schizophrenic features,' Susan said. 'It must have been extremely difficult for him to hide his sickness from others throughout his life, and even more difficult for him to function as a physician. Ironically, his choice of specialty no doubt kept him from a psychotic breakdown. The opportunity to operate on women's sexual organs, to kill foetuses in the womb at the same time that he was bringing other patients' babies into the world, probably gratified his ambivalence about women. We have no evidence that he ever harmed any of his own patients.

'It's hard to speculate about the course things took, in the absence of any sort of records,' she went on, 'but I suspect that Dr Tower saw Meredith Spiers play Juliet at Berkeley. She must have touched him in some profound way. He was impressed by her innocence, her purity. Soon after that time she became his patient at the Berkeley Women's Clinic, and he performed an abortion on her. This event left him obsessed by her. He took an interest in her work as a journalist in San Francisco, and when she moved to Chicago to go to work for WGN he followed her.'

'Why do you think it took him four years to start killing women here?' asked the Mayor.

'I honestly don't know,' Susan said. 'Possibly his proximity to Meredith assuaged his inner cravings for a time. In any case, he finally lost control and killed Miranda Becker. Then Mary Ellen Mahoney, then Marcie Webb. I agree with those of you who have speculated that he used his medical credentials to tap into the records of abortion clinics around the city. However, I also think it possible that he may have haunted some of the clinics and followed the young women who emerged from them until he found suitable victims. We'll probably never know.'

'Do you believe he chose victims from different clinics so that we would follow the pro-life lead?' asked David Gold.

'I do. I think he was being careful. He didn't want us to think the killer might be an abortion doctor. I also think he designed the upside-down crucifix in his victims' abdomens in order to make us think of Satanists. It was an afterthought on his part.'

'You told me early on,' David Gold said, 'that you thought the killer had a specific woman in his mind and was working his way up to her through the other victims. I guess you were right. Tower had a houseful of images of Meredith, and he did abduct her in the end.'

He glanced significantly at Abel Weathers, who had so often debunked Susan's psychic abilities.

'That's right,' Susan said. 'The e-mails he sent were a clever gambit which killed two birds with one stone. He manipulated our understanding of where the case was going. And in the end he used his "Deep Throat" role as a means to entice Meredith to the movie theater, where he abducted her.'

'What about the blood, and the semen in the stomach wound, and all that?' asked Tom Castaneda. 'What was he really about, mentally?'

'I can only speculate,' Susan said. 'But I think the first thing here is his choice of profession. I think that in his mind the act of aborting a foetus had the significance of undoing the mother's fertility, and even of undoing the fact that she had ever had sexual intercourse. He was literally turning her into a virgin by removing her foetus. In the end, though, this was not enough. He had to act out his aggression toward women, so he started killing them. I think the murders were symbolic sexual acts. Though he avoided contact with the vagina, the knife he used was a symbolic penis and the wounds were symbolic vaginas. The proof of this is his depositing of his semen in the abdominal wound.'

'What about the blood from other sources?' Joe Riccio asked.

'He was obsessed with communion,' Susan replied. 'He wanted to use blood as a medium to join himself to all the victims. And, as the transfusion kit at the final crime scene showed, he intended to die with Meredith, as Romeo had died with Juliet. Ironically, I think he wanted to stop himself before he caused too much violence. The reign of terror would have ended with four victims.'

'What about the paintings in his attic, and the one in the Berkeley clinic?' Joe Riccio asked.

'I think he had the painting in his examining room in Berkeley because he needed to remind himself of the secret purpose of his work,' Susan said. 'The painting depicts a woman from whose figure a stream of red paint flows toward the bottom of the canvas and out toward the spectator. Dr Tower was obsessed by the image of blood flowing from between a woman's legs. The cryptic message written on Marcie Webb's dressing-room mirror, *Your room is bleeding*, clearly was meant to signify *Your womb is bleeding*. This was his obsession.' She looked at Joe Riccio, who had been at the clinic with her. 'I wouldn't be surprised if a chemical analysis of the pigment used in those paintings revealed small amounts of blood mixed with the paint.'

The mayor raised his hand. 'What are your impressions as a psychiatrist about his interest in blood?'

'Blood comes from between women's legs in certain important circumstances,' Susan explained. 'A virgin bleeds when her hymen is ruptured. A young girl bleeds when she has her period. A pregnant woman bleeds when she has a miscarriage. Or, when she has an abortion. This is perhaps the core meaning of blood for this killer: a violence occurring in women's sexual organs.' She thought for a moment. 'Again, I can only speculate. We know that as a boy Dr Tower lived alone with his mother. We also know she was promiscuous. The little boy probably saw her having coitus with strange men. I suspect that at some point in his first five or six years, he saw her having sex with a man when she had her period. He saw the man's penis moving in and out of the mother's vagina, spreading blood over her and over the penis itself. This image must have terrified the boy. He saw it as a destruction of his mother's body in which she was somehow acquiescing. Later, when the mother was dead, the son probably worked this traumatic image into his guilt feelings over her death.'

Susan shrugged. 'I think Dr Tower re-enacted this scene in all his killings, while disguising it by keeping the bloody wounds away from his victims' vaginas. I also think that the obsessive image in his paintings, the woman in the blood-red doorway, unwittingly re-enacts the childhood scene. The figure of the woman itself represents a penis, and the doorway represents the vagina.'

Abel Weathers whispered in one of his colleagues' ear, 'What bullshit.' Across the table the mayor was looking at him. Weathers turned red.

'I guess there's no point in asking why the Virgin Mary,' said Rich Sheehan.

Susan smiled. 'She was the perfect woman for him. She conceived Christ without coitus. She was immaculate and fertile at the same time. It was probably inevitable that the woman he chose as his central obsession would be seen as the Virgin.'

Someone laughed. 'But Meredith is Jewish.'

David Gold sat forward with a smile. 'Hey, man, the

Virgin Mary was Jewish. So was Joseph, and so was Jesus. I keep telling you guys, we've got 'em all.'

Everyone laughed.

That night the mayor took Susan and Gold to dinner at Everest, the famed restaurant located forty floors above North LaSalle Street. The mayor, a down-to-earth man who was proud of his police force, congratulated Susan on her hard work on the case, and Gold for firing the shot that saved Meredith Spiers's life.

'You've been good for my city,' he told Susan. 'I know Weathers makes it tough on you sometimes. But I want you to know how grateful I am that you moved here and became one of us. I hope you never leave.'

Gold did a fine job of hiding his distaste for the restaurant's up-scale cuisine. Susan knew how much he would have preferred a pastrami sandwich or a cheeseburger and fries.

Late that night Gold sat on the couch in Susan's apartment, enjoying a glass of Guinness Stout and listening to Susan's explanation of her own failure to see the truth about the Undertaker sooner than she did.

'I think I was misled for the same reasons you were,' Susan said, sitting cross-legged on the floor with a glass of wine beside her. 'Since the victims were clients of different clinics, I assumed the killer had something against women who aborted their foetuses. I just didn't think of an abortion doctor. Probably the wounds themselves also led me astray, because they weren't the scalpel cuts of a trained physician. Also, the final stab wound to the abdomen indicated an uninformed, almost childish idea of where babies grow. This was so crude that it never occurred to me that a physician could be doing the killing.'

'You weren't alone in that,' Gold said.

At that moment the cat appeared in the doorway, looking at Gold through suspicious eyes.

'Hey, Chief.' Gold smiled.

He used this nickname because Carolyn had named Margie after the small-town police chief in the movie *Fargo*, a woman seven months pregnant who overpowered a six-foot hit man on her way to solving a kidnap and multiple-murder case.

For a change the cat came to sit alongside Gold on the couch. He petted her gently as Susan went on talking.

'There was another reason I couldn't see the truth,' Susan said. 'It had to do with my own past. Abortion was a loaded concept in my own mind. When I was a teenager I was consumed with guilt, mostly because of my parents' deaths. I indulged in a lot of self-punishing behavior. Promiscuity was part of it. I slept with a lot of boys when I was fourteen and fifteen. We didn't use birth control, mostly because we were too young and foolish. I missed a period once or twice, and I was terrified that I was pregnant. I knew I would have to get an abortion if I was. My aunt and uncle would have to know. But the emotional significance of a possible abortion was traumatic. If my baby died, that would be the same thing as my parents' deaths. A death I had caused.'

David Gold listened in silence to this confession. He knew these things about Susan from scattered conversations over the years.

'Later on I became over-scrupulous about birth control,' she said. 'When I got married I had irrational fears that I wouldn't be able to conceive a child. Then when I became pregnant with Michael, I had fears of a miscarriage. I had a lot of guilt going.' She smiled at Gold. 'Anyway, in later years I always felt a special bond with my female patients who had had abortions or considered abortion. I understood their terrible ambivalence and their suffering. Child-bearing is one of the most powerful experiences in a woman's life. Abortion turns that experience into a sort of emotional time bomb. I think the clues I got from the Undertaker's victims – the phrase *The important thing is to relax*, and Professor Auden's phrase, *You've got your whole life ahead of you* – should have led me to suspect an abortionist or abortion doctor. But I didn't see it. Perhaps I also didn't want to accept the idea that a medical doctor – a doctor like me – had murdered the three victims.'

'Like us,' Gold said, 'when we find evidence that a cop may be behind a murder.'

Susan nodded.

'In the end, though, my identification with Meredith overcame my own resistances. I got strong signals to the effect that Meredith had had an abortion. I had to pursue them. This led to California, to Professor Auden, and finally to the Berkeley Women's Clinic.'

'Better late than never,' Gold said. 'I shouldn't have doubted you.'

'But you didn't doubt me,' Susan corrected him. 'Not really.'

Gold was silent. He alone knew how close he had come to ignoring Susan's frantic telephone call about Dr Tower. He had doubted her. But in the end he had thought it too dangerous to ignore her intuition.

Susan was looking out the window at the city she had come to love. 'All the females in this case seem connected by invisible threads that are too complex to be disentangled. Young women, ambitious, attractive, troubled . . . Women who got pregnant and couldn't have their babies. I feel so lucky in comparison to them. I have Michael, and they ended up with nothing. Not even life.'

'Maybe they have rest,' Gold said. 'Now that we put the killer under the ground.'

'Rest?' Susan asked.

'Like my Aunt Frances. *Menucha nechona* – remember?'

*Perfect rest.* Susan recalled Gold's theory about punishment and eternal rest.

'Perhaps, David.'

Gold stood up, grunting slightly at the residual pain in his chest and back. 'It's time for you to get some rest, too,' he said. 'Call Giordano. Go to a movie. Take it easy for a while.'

Susan walked him to the door. He turned to pat her on her shoulder, his usual gesture of leave-taking. But he thought better of it and hugged her close, kissing her hair.

'Like I say, kid,' he said, 'you're pretty frightening yourself.'

'I'll take that as a compliment.'

With a wink, Gold closed the door behind him.

# CHAPTER 63

The new year was well under way. Chicagoans were enduring the dawn of the post-Jordan era for the Chicago Bulls and secretly looking forward to spring training. Three more months of frigid gray weather lay ahead. With the Undertaker out of the headlines people could devote their worry to their heating bills and their children's homework.

Susan spent the weekend with Ron Giordano at the Abbey, a quiet resort in Lake Geneva, where they did nothing but relax in their room and sit by the indoor pool, which was located in a lovely solarium. She returned to work Monday morning refreshed and full of energy. She found Wendy Breckinridge waiting for her.

She knew something was different the minute she set eyes on Wendy, who was dressed in a pretty wool skirt and a matching top with a festive appliqué in the shape of a bird. Her hair was pinned back behind her ears. She was wearing comfortable-looking low-heeled shoes and carried a small purse. She had on just enough make-up to add some color to her cheeks. Her smile was as restrained as her outfit.

That was what was different, Susan realized. Wendy looked like herself. Not like a waif, not like a streetwalker, not like a librarian. Like a pretty, vibrant girl of twenty-seven who looked good because she felt good.

'Hi,' she said, sitting down.

'Good morning,' Susan smiled.

'I heard about that guy, the killer,' Wendy said. 'Congratulations.'

'Thank you,' Susan said. 'I'm relieved. So is everyone else.'

There was a silence as Susan thought about Wendy's long obsession with the Undertaker. She expected Wendy to have something to say about it. Instead, Wendy changed the subject.

'I slept with Scott last night,' she said.

Susan nodded. 'Tell me about it.'

Wendy shifted in her chair, nervous and excited.

'We went out to dinner in town, and I invited him over to my apartment,' she said. 'He wanted to see the old family albums, the ones with me as a little girl. We looked at those. Then we were going to watch a movie on TV. We drank a glass of wine. Then it just – happened.'

'Didn't anything lead up to it?'

'Well, yes. We were talking about the old days, about the party where we met when we were little. Scott talked about himself. It was strange . . . The feelings he said he had as a boy were so much like the ones I had as a girl. Shame, inadequacy . . . All these things were in the air between us. He had his arm around me. Then we kissed . . .'

The look in her eyes spoke volumes.

'And it was different – the sex. It started slowly, a kind of soft warmth. All I felt was that he wanted me. I felt protected. He was very tender. Then it became something more, and more and more . . .' She thought for a moment. 'You know,' she said, 'thinking back on all those other guys I've slept with . . . It's kind of hard to describe, but in a way maybe I wasn't really having orgasms with them after all.'

'What do you mean?' Susan asked.

'I'm not sure,' Wendy said. 'I always thought I was feeling something. Sexually. But it didn't really feel *good*. It felt sort of hot and unpleasant. And I would tell myself, *this is it. This is the orgasm.* As though I was –'

'Yes?' Susan said.

'Relieved. Proud of myself,' the girl said. 'It was like, I *showed them.*' She looked at Susan. 'Do you know what I mean?'

'I think so,' Susan said. 'Reassuring yourself that you could feel something, but wanting the feeling as a kind of revenge against others.'

'Yes!' Wendy said. 'That's it. I never realized it until now, but it was a lonely kind of pleasure. It pulled me farther away from other people, instead of bringing me closer.'

Her eyes were sparkling with intellectual triumph. Yet they looked misty.

'God damn it,' she said.

'What's the matter?' Susan asked.

'Why is everything always so hard?' Wendy shook her head in consternation.

'Few things are more complicated than sexual relationships,' Susan said. 'Is that what you're talking about?'

'Yes. No. Yes.' Wendy laughed in consternation. 'Sex, yes. But I think I'm really talking about being wanted.'

Susan looked at her patient. 'What about being wanted?'

'How hard it is. How – great it is.'

Susan smiled. 'I think you've said it all. Being wanted is all we wish for. Yet it can be hard to accept.'

Wendy nodded fervently. 'Yes. Hard to accept.' The intent expression in her eyes showed she was grappling with a truth that did not want to be captured.

Susan hid the excitement she felt. She had spent two years trying to bring Wendy to this moment. Wendy had done the hardest work herself. But one step remained.

'When you haven't been wanted once,' Wendy said. 'I mean – when you weren't wanted once . . .' She sighed in frustration. 'I can't get the words right. When once it has happened . . .'

Susan could feel the resistances behind her patient's difficulty with words.

'When a bad thing has happened once,' she offered.

'When a bad thing has made you feel worthless, yes,' Wendy said. 'When a thing happened that convinced you you could *never* be wanted. When that has happened, you build everything around that belief about yourself. That you could never be wanted.' She looked at Susan. 'Do you see what I mean?'

Susan was silent.

Tears were welling in Wendy's eyes.

'You play that role,' she said. 'The loser.'

Wendy looked at the painting of the clown on the wall. Susan followed the direction of her gaze.

'Happy sad,' Wendy said.

Her tears suddenly overflowed. She held her hands over her face.

There was a long silence between them. Susan, a connoisseur of silences, knew this was an important one. Wendy was on the brink of the most crucial discovery about herself. The heaviest door was open a crack. Pushing it open wider would still be difficult, but not so difficult as five minutes ago. Opportunity was knocking.

'To think I've been carrying this around all this time . . .' Wendy said.

'Carrying what around?'

'This misery . . .'

Susan smiled. 'Everyone carries something around. Even those who seem the happiest. You haven't forgotten Sisyphus, have you?'

Wendy nodded, her small smile expressing gratitude. 'No.'

'We aren't supermen,' Susan said. 'We can't see through

walls. Sometimes the walls were built in great part by ourselves. There's no sin in that. Only human imperfection.'

Wendy was still looking at the painting. She chewed nervously at her lip for a moment. She twisted the tissue into a hard little knot.

'I've always had trouble taking things in,' she said.

'Taking things in?' Susan asked. 'You mean, understanding things?'

'No. Taking things into myself.' Wendy thought for a moment, her eyes on the clown. 'Even into my body. You know – the bulimia,' she added.

'The bulimia?' Susan asked. 'In what way?'

'I needed to undo it,' Wendy said. 'To undo everything. All the things, all the feelings . . . Everything that came into me.' A brittle, artificial smile spread over her face. 'As though I could undo myself.'

There was another silence. The look on Wendy's face was desolate.

She was on thin ice. Susan decided to offer her a hand.

'And the men you slept with?' she said.

Wendy looked at her. 'You mean the bars, the pick-ups?'

Susan nodded.

Wendy was staring at her, hard. 'You mean the condoms. That's it, isn't it? You mean my not letting them use condoms.'

'Why didn't you? Were you hoping an accident would happen?'

'What do you mean, an accident?'

Wendy's eyes opened wide.

'Oh, my God. Like my mother. Is that what you mean? Is that what you're asking?'

'What do you think I should ask?'

'Oh, my God. Was I imitating her all that time?'

'Is that what you think?' Susan asked.

Wendy watched herself twist the ragged Kleenex harder.

'She didn't undo me,' she said.

'No, she didn't.'

Wendy looked at the ruined tissue.

'She could have,' she said. 'But she didn't.'

Susan had leaned forward an inch. She met her patient's eyes.

'Does that mean she wanted you?' she asked.

'No. Yes. No.' Wendy was looking at the clown, who looked exhausted by his painful effort to seem happy.

'She had mixed feelings,' Susan said. 'That's a hard thing to forgive her for, isn't it?'

'She still does,' Wendy said.

'And you?' Susan had sat back.

'Mixed feelings?' Wendy said. 'That's putting it mildly.'

'About your parents, or about yourself?'

'About me because of them.'

'And what about Scott?' Susan asked. 'Are his feelings for you mixed?'

Wendy gave a sad, tired smile. 'No. He likes me.'

'Is he wrong?'

Wendy sighed. 'No. I guess he's not wrong.'

'And can you keep that insight in?' Susan asked. 'Or will you have to undo it as well?'

More tears were flowing down Wendy's cheeks. 'I can keep it in,' she said in an odd, faraway voice.

There was another silence. Wendy looked down into her lap.

'The food,' she said. 'The men . . .'

*Quick*, Susan thought.

'Oh, God,' Wendy moaned. 'It's awful,' she said. 'It's terrible.'

'What is terrible?'

'The things. The food, the substances ... God.' Wendy shook her head. 'It's all so disgusting.'

Susan nodded. 'There's an old saying in psychiatry. The stones we leave unturned aren't left that way because there are hearts and flowers underneath.'

'Yes.' Wendy nodded.

'The substances that entered your body were full of painful meanings derived from a lot of problems,' Susan said. 'Food, pills, semen ...'

'Yes.' Wendy avoided Susan's eyes.

'It's hard to take a thing in when you're not sure you should even be here,' Susan offered.

Wendy nodded. 'They were things that could undo me. Is that what you mean?'

'It was impossible for you to get around that dilemma,' Susan suggested. 'Every feeling, every experience – they all came back to what you call undoing. The fear of it. The fantasy of it.'

'My abortion,' Wendy took a deep breath. 'I did to my baby what they ... I wanted to get revenge.'

Wendy leaned forward, her arms over her stomach.

'Oh, God,' Wendy cried. 'It's so sick.'

A sob shook her. She pulled another tissue from the box, but did not wipe her eyes.

'But you're not sick,' Susan said. 'You knew you weren't ready to be a mother. You made the difficult choice, the painful choice.'

Wendy was silent. She was at the end of her courage. But her next words were a step Susan had not expected her to take this soon.

'The condoms, the men,' she said. 'I wanted it to happen again. For all the wrong reasons. Thank God it didn't happen.'

'Perhaps there was a right reason mixed up in there somewhere,' Susan suggested.

'What right reason?' Wendy asked, her eyes averted.

Susan was silent.

'To make a baby, you mean?' Wendy asked. 'To want it?'

Susan smiled. 'Why not?'

Wendy nodded. She seemed relieved.

'Some day it will happen when you're ready for it,' Susan said. 'The work you're doing now is making that day possible.'

She looked at the clock on her desk. The session was almost over.

'You've opened an important door today,' Susan said. 'Soon, if we work hard, you'll be able to walk through it. Then none of these goblins will seem so terrible.'

Wendy nodded, wiping at her nose. Then she looked at Susan. In her eyes was a hint of the old challenge.

'What about you?' she asked. 'Do you think there is something to like about me, too? Or is it just your bedside manner?'

'After all we've been through together – ' Susan smiled – 'what do you think?'

Wendy nodded, smiling.

'Being liked is a suit that doesn't fit easily,' Susan said. 'Why don't you break it in a little, and we'll talk about it again next time?'

'Yes.' Wendy stood up. 'Okay.'

The two women shook hands. Wendy moved quickly to the door, in her old purposeful way. But she looked back musingly, tenderly, before she let herself out.

'Thanks, Doctor.'

'Don't thank me. You did the hard work.'

Wendy nodded, opened the door and left.

Susan sat in the silence for a long moment. Then, sighing, she smiled and stood up to look out the window. The tired grey lake greeted her like an old friend.

'Good work,' she said.

# CHAPTER 64

Wendy left Susan's building and joined the crowd of pedestrians on Michigan Avenue. For several minutes she simply let herself be pulled along. Then, seeing the sun emerge from behind a bank of clouds, she crossed at a light and went into Grant Park. The Art Institute gleamed under the sudden sun. Though it was the dead of winter, everything looked springlike and new.

Wendy felt cleansed and new herself. She had often felt this way on leaving Dr Shader's office. But today was different. Today, in her own soul, she saw a break in the clouds like the one rising over her head.

In the past her hard-won insights in therapy had made her feel like a soldier in the trenches. The doctor would sometimes tell her, 'It may not look like a great victory, but it is one. You've won a yard or two of the hardest territory in this war.' At these times Wendy would feel exhausted, even discouraged. The uphill battle was so hard, the steps so small.

But today, for the first time, she had in her hand a tiny ray of light which came from another Wendy, another life. For the first time she saw the world through the eyes of another person, a person whose viewpoint was no longer constrained by the rigid self-punishing guilts Wendy had clung to for so long. It was fugitive, hard to grasp; but she had it in her hand. She would not let it go.

She wanted to call Scott. But suddenly she felt hungry,

intensely hungry. She looked at the clock in the Park. Nine-thirty. She had eaten nothing since waking up. She crossed back and hurried her steps, looking for a restaurant where she could get something in a hurry.

She found a sports bar that doubled as a coffee shop in the mornings. As she stood before the window she cast a brief glance at the street reflected in it. She worried that Tony Garza might be following her. But there was nothing in the window other than herself and the downtown traffic.

She went in the door and sat down at one of the high bar tables. The barmaid appeared a couple of minutes later.

'Menu?' she asked with a smile.

'Thanks. And a regular coffee.' Wendy smiled back.

The menu was full of sandwiches and salads, with break-fast foods in a small list on the side. When the waitress returned Wendy ordered french toast with sausage. Her coffee tasted marvelous, pungent and fresh. She saw a small container of cinnamon on the table and shook some over the foamy cup.

Her stomach was grumbling. Her hunger felt different too. The old constraints of her eternal ambivalence about food seemed to have lifted. She remembered the hunger she used to feel as a child, when french fries or popcorn or candy had simple and powerful values to her growing body. She felt that way now.

Wendy turned to watch the pedestrians passing by the window. Their faces were – pedestrian. It was the only word that occurred to Wendy. They were so gray, so routine. Almost all were alone. The Loop was a lonely place. People were on their way somewhere, not living at this moment of passage. Empty, preoccupied faces that looked somehow tragic when compared to the springing happiness inside Wendy.

She ate her breakfast hungrily, savoring the natural scent

and flavor of the food. She had not tasted anything this way in at least ten years. Everything was new, strange, wonderful.

She looked around the bar. Pictures of Michael Jordan, Jim MacMahon, Walter Payton were on the walls, along with team pictures of the Bulls, the Bears, the Cubs from their glory years. Most of the booths were occupied by businessmen in suits, talking earnestly as they ate, or working men with thick hands and preoccupied eyes. In one booth sat two somewhat overdressed middle-aged women wearing careful make-up. They were smoking long cigarettes, Virginia Slims perhaps. Salesladies from Marshall Field or Carsons, Wendy mused.

She smiled. They all looked wonderful to her. They were just people. Imperfect, damaged people, not all that happy perhaps. People on their way through a life whose hurdles were probably a bit too high for them. She felt a budding tenderness for them and, for the first time in her memory, a sort of bond. She was of the same species as they. She belonged to the same world, and wanted to belong to it.

The barmaid brought the check. Wendy sat looking at it, undecided as to her next move. She wanted to call Scott. To see him as soon as possible.

She was about to get up when a hand appeared and covered the check.

Susan's second patient of the day had canceled, so she went into her inner office to make some notes on Wendy's session. She slipped her Zip disk into the Macintosh and clicked through the folder icons to Wendy's file. When the folder opened she started. It was empty.

She closed the folder and opened it again. The contents were gone. She sat chewing her lip in consternation. She knew she could not have inadvertently lost the file. The only way to erase it was to drag it to the trash.

On an impulse Susan opened the trash. Inside it was a single icon, labeled 'Wendy'. She dragged it to the desktop and double-clicked it. A single paragraph greeted her.

Most killers are narrow and circumscribed in their hunt patterns and choice of victims. However, we occasionally see the 'omnivorous' serial murderer who is capable of transposing his aggressive themes into manifold symbolic arenas, and thus of selecting victims of disparate types. Sometimes, to the chagrin of the authorities, such a killer will take the thread of their investigative efforts as a suggestion, choosing for his next victim someone who suits the MO posited by the police. Thus, tragically, the pursuers offer the killer his next prey, like the observer in physics who alters the material at hand by the very act of observing it.

Susan recognized the words. They came from an article she was currently working on.

Her hand had frozen around the mouse. Her own words seemed to mock her. They didn't belong here. Someone had put them here for her to find.

She picked up the phone and dialed a number.

'Gold speaking.' David Gold was in his office at Area Six.

'David, it's Susan.'

'Hey, I didn't expect to hear from you this soon. You're not getting bored already, are you?'

'David, I'm worried about a patient of mine. Her name is Wendy Breckinridge. She left my office about half an hour ago. I think she may be in danger.'

'Do you know where she was going?'

'No. I have no idea.'

'What's her address?'

Susan tried to remember. Her mind was a blank.

'She normally parks in the ramp down the block,' she offered.

'I'll send a man over there. What's her license number?'

'I don't know. You'll have to look up her registration. She drives a Lexus, I think.'

'Can you spell the last name?'

Susan spelled it for him.

'What does she look like?'

'She's twenty-seven. She has long blond hair. She's wearing a skirt and a white top. She's carrying a brown purse over her shoulder.'

'All right. I can have some guys check out the stores and restaurants in your area,' Gold said. 'Take about twenty minutes to get it in gear. What makes you think she's in danger?

'I just opened her file. David, I think someone's been into my files. I – David, it might be Train.'

'Is Loftus out in the hall?'

'I think so. Yes, I saw him on my way in.'

'Go get him. I'll have some more guys over in two minutes. Don't leave your office.'

Gold hung up without saying goodbye.


Wendy looked up to see a man holding her check in his hand. He was handsome. He looked remotely familiar.

'Do I know you?' she asked, wondering if the man was someone she had met in a bar like this one, sometime in the past.

'No.' He was smiling at her.

'To what do I owe . . .' she asked.

'You looked so happy sitting there, I thought you deserved a reward,' he said. 'I figured if I picked up your check, maybe you'd tell me what was making you so happy. Maybe a little bit of it might rub off on me.'

He looked like the working men she had noticed in the café earlier. He wore jeans and a leather jacket. His hands seemed accustomed to manual work, though the fingers were long and rather sensitive. He was a black man, but his features suggested some exotic mixture of races, including perhaps some Hispanic or Native American blood.

'I'll pay myself,' she said, holding out her hand for the check. 'But thanks anyway.'

'Are you sure?' He was gentle, not pushing.

'Yes. I'm sure.'

'Well, then.' He handed her back the check. 'But just tell me – what is there to be happy about on a day like today?'

She smiled at him. He had tawny, soothing eyes. He seemed intelligent.

She glanced at the windows.

'The sun is shining,' she said. 'Isn't that enough of a reason?'

He shook his head. 'It's too cold for it to do any good,' he said.

'Still, sun is better than no sun,' Wendy said.

'I can't argue with that.'

He rested a hand for an instant on the edge of the table. There was a tattoo on his wrist, a tattoo of a snake. It disappeared under the cuff of his shirt.

' "You Are My Sunshine".' He smiled. 'My mother used to sing me that song when I was little.'

Wendy nodded. 'An old song.'

'Your coffee needs a refill,' he said. 'Let me buy you that, at least.'

A trace of Wendy's old bravado came back to her.

'Aren't refills free?' she asked.

He held up his hands in surrender. 'I give up,' he said. 'I can't get you to take anything from me.'

She shrugged.

# BLOOD

'At least let me watch you drink it,' he said.

A siren sounded somewhere outside. A vehicle shot past the window. Wendy didn't see it. She looked up into the caressing eyes of the stranger.

# CHAPTER 65

Wendy Breckinridge's body was found Thursday morning in a forest preserve south of Chicago. The Medical Examiner determined the cause of death as strangulation, which had occurred about sixteen hours after the victim was last seen alive. There was evidence of forcible rape and sodomy.

Ignoring the advice of David Gold, Susan went personally to view the body and consult with the ME. A hurried test of the killer's semen showed that his blood type was consistent with that of Calvin Wesley Train.

There were skin scrapings under Wendy's fingernails, which would provide further physical evidence. Wendy had fought her attacker.

The police had helped Susan search her files. There were clear signs that they had been rifled. Calvin Wesley Train had not picked Wendy at random. He had found her through Susan. Security at Susan's office must have lapsed during her trip to California in search of the identity of the Undertaker. Train must have been watching the office, and seized his chance to get inside.

Susan looked long and hard at the battered corpse of her patient. Wendy had been a troubled girl, but a resilient one. She had what psychiatrists call a 'good neurosis'. She would have developed into a fine, strong person, probably a healthy wife and mother. Calvin Wesley Train had known what he was doing. In rifling Susan's files he had learned of Wendy's obsessive fear of the killer who had murdered Miranda Becker and the others. He had chosen Wendy as a way to hurt Susan herself. He knew Susan would feel responsible for Wendy's death.

Susan went directly from the ME's office to the Lake Forest home of Wendy's parents. She spent a painful hour talking to them about their daughter's courageous fight for mental health. Scott Carpenter was there, looking lost.

'I know – I knew – she was going to be successful in her therapy,' Susan told the shattered parents. 'The very qualities that made her suffer so much from her symptoms – her stubbornness, her imagination – were being turned to her advantage. The same inventiveness and resourcefulness that she had used to punish herself were now being used to free her from her symptoms. I sometimes see this quality in my best patients. They're the ones who give me hope.'

Mrs Breckinridge seemed to take comfort from this admiring portrait of her daughter. But her husband had a hopeless air about him that confirmed Susan's suspicions about his feelings for his daughter. Wendy had stood up to him rebelliously. Even in her self-destructive antics she had shown a spirit that reminded him of himself. He had loved and admired her, but had never told her how he felt. He didn't have to say this for Susan to know it was in his mind.

Scott left with Susan so that he could have a few minutes alone with her. He seemed unbelieving.

'It's all so disjointed, so confusing,' he told her. 'I fell in love with Wendy when we were small children together. I spent my whole life carrying around this image of her as a six-year-old girl in a party dress covered with grass stains.' He shook his head. 'Then, like a miracle, she crossed my path as an adult. I could see she had changed in the interval. So much of her was beyond me, lost in those intervening years. But not all. The girl I remembered was still there somehow.

And then, she was starting to change into something else again, something new. I pinned more of my hopes than I realized on that third person, that new person. Now she's gone. I'm reeling. Falling through space.'

Susan felt the same way. To her also, Wendy had seemed kaleidoscopic, a sort of chameleon who changed her colors so quickly that one could not put one's finger on her. Change, Susan knew, was the great secret to mental health. Rigidity, which Freud called a sort of 'psychic entropy', was the linchpin of mental illness. The secret to recovery was the ability to change. Only the strongest patients had it. Wendy was one of them. Susan felt that this mercurial, changing creature was finally stopped forever. It was a crime against nature. And it had happened not because of Wendy, but because of Susan.

Later that day David Gold came to Susan's apartment. When she opened the door to him she looked physically ill. Her face was pale, her features drawn.

Gold poured himself a beer and went into the living room. Susan was sitting on the couch with her legs tucked under her. Gold sat down in the chair opposite her.

'I hope you understand,' he said.

'Understand what?'

'Train killed Breckinridge because he knew it would make you feel this way.'

'What way?'

'Responsible. Guilty.'

Susan nodded emptily. His insight was correct, but it was unavailing against the flood of painful feelings inside her.

There was a silence. Susan was emptied of mental energy. Gold's attempts to help her were like strong arms reaching from the surface into a pool in which she had already drowned.

'He wanted to hurt someone close to you, in order to

hurt you,' he said. 'He knows what you're thinking now. What you're feeling.'

'Does he?' she asked.

'Sure. You're second-guessing yourself. You're thinking you should have realized he might hit one of your patients. That it might have been Breckinridge. You're thinking you should have seen it coming, you should have warned her. You're second-guessing every move you made with Breckinridge, from the beginning. Am I right?'

She didn't answer. He looked at her through narrowed eyes.

'You're thinking you were too much like her,' he said. 'She reminded you too much of yourself. Maybe you should have referred her. Then she would be alive today.' He looked at her. 'Can you deny it?'

'What makes you so smart?' Susan asked, startled by his insight.

'I'm not smart. I just know you well.' Gold picked up his beer, then put it down without taking a sip.

'Thank you, David.' Susan sighed. 'I think you're right about me. I'm just sorry Train was so smart in figuring it all out.'

'Murder is easy,' Gold said. 'It's being alive that is messy and hard. Being alive, and . . .'

There was a silence. Outside the window a chilly rain was falling. Gold's eyes rested on Susan. He said nothing. He was giving her room for her hopelessness, she realized. He knew she needed to feel it completely before mustering her forces to fight it.

'What now?' she asked at length.

'We try to catch him before he kills again.'

'Do you think you will catch him?' she asked.

'We'll try. He's smart, but he's not invisible. It's only a matter of time.'

*Time*, Susan thought. The word had never sounded so hopeless.

Gold left a few minutes later. Susan took a shower, put on a pair of cut-off jeans and a T-shirt, and made herself a sandwich. She took it into the living room and curled up on the couch to eat it. The meal was tasteless. She watched a CNN report about the President's sex life, shaking her head. She surfed a few stations, watching the faces of struggling actors in TV movies and sitcoms. The face of an evangelist shot by, eclipsed by a professional wrestler holding up both arms and shouting at the camera. The human struggle to survive, to endure . . .

She felt something wet fall on her hand. She looked up at the ceiling, fearing a leak. Then she realized her eyes were full of tears. She put down the sandwich impatiently and walked into the bathroom. Surprisingly, a sob came from deep inside and shook her hard as her face came into view.

Poor Wendy, she thought. Like Joe Louis with the CIA, she thought she was in danger because her neurosis wanted to torture her with that notion. And it turned out that she was in danger after all. Her story was a comedy of errors whose last act was death. A death Susan could have prevented if she had been more clever.

*First do no harm.* The physician's oath came back to haunt Susan. If Wendy had never been her patient, she would be alive today.

Susan went into the bedroom and picked up the phone. She started to push the 'Auto 1' button for Nick's California house, but then thought better of calling. Her tears were coming steadily. She did not want Nick or Michael to know she had been crying.

She turned on her computer and found an e-mail from Michael.

*Dear Mom,*
*Today we went to the mall and I saw The Prince of*
*Egypt with Elaine. It was kind of loud, but I liked*
*it. Elaine bought me popcorn and made the man put*
*extra butter on it. My fingers were a mess.*

   *I miss you Mom. Call me up sometime soon. I*
*drew a cartoon today, two mice and a rabbit. I'll*
*send it to you real soon.*

   *I miss you. Call me up real soon. I'll tell you*
*about the movie.*

   *I hope you're not sad.*
*Love,*

                  *Michael*


Susan smiled. Her son was trying to cheer her up. She wrote him a brief e-mail and turned off the computer. Then she went to bed.

The room seemed more empty than usual. Despite the penumbra she saw how thick the dust on her bedroom bookshelves was. A pile of unread magazines and medical journals was on the windowsill. It had been growing taller for months. In the closet were cardboard boxes that were dumped there right after she moved in, and not opened since.

The apartment was like her life, she mused. Unfinished, in flux, up in the air. For years, it seemed, she had not really sat down to think about herself. About where she was going, who she was. Her divorce had obviously left her more wounded than she liked to think. Though she had made a good life for herself here in Chicago, with good friends, patients and colleagues, she was still running away from the past.

But life was real here, every bit as real and as profound as anything that had happened in the past. In this city Wendy Breckinridge became her patient. Now Wendy was dead. As dead as the parents Susan had lost as a little girl. As dead as her marriage.

Proust was right, she thought. We are made up of countless tiny selves. And when a loved person dies, it takes a long time for all those selves to be informed of the event. A moment ago Susan's tears had come from the lonely, desperate teenager she had been back in Pennsylvania, a girl who felt exiled from the world and wanted to hurt herself as Wendy had done, for being different, being tainted.

A girl ground under the heel of time, covered over by thick layers of forgetfulness, eclipsed by long years of hoping and building and coping. And it had taken Wendy's death to bring her to life, to bring her tears to Susan's grown-up eyes.

But Wendy would never have those years. Wendy's battle was over.

*It isn't fair*, Susan thought.

The words had a long, deep currency in her office. They had been spoken by countless patients who looked back over their lives and wondered whether they had been hurt more by what the world gave or by what they themselves took. That was the great enigma, the endless quest and question.

Susan turned off the light. She felt more tears quicken in her eyes. She fought them back, staring at the ceiling. She thought about Michael, about the news he would tell her when she called. Gradually the image of Wendy began to recede, eclipsed by the patient murmur of the living world, which insulates us from all things past.

Sleep now, she thought. Time for death tomorrow.

# CHAPTER 66

Time passed. The promised January thaw did not come. Winter temperatures set records. The air was so cold that even the lake snow could not stick. The flakes wandered the downtown streets like refugees in search of a home.

People stayed inside. The city was hibernating, as it did every year at this time. The faces behind car windows were empty. Sounds rang hollow in the cold. Spring seemed a long time away.

The railroad yard was vast, covering dozens of acres. Freight cars and flatbeds still in use were kept on the tracks nearest the dispatch building. Damaged and older cars were shunted to outlying areas. The skyline of Gary was so dimmed by the pollution that it looked as though it was behind a scrim.

The sun had set half an hour ago and the sky was darkening quickly. The distant sounds of traffic and machinery mingled with the city's neutral hum. A dog barked hoarsely. A faraway siren sounded.

A man wearing work pants and a parka made his way along the deserted track in the oldest and saddest corner of the yard. His hair was grey. He wore a stocking cap with a faded Bears insignia. He shuffled slowly, a battered tool case in his hand. He had the gait of an alcoholic. He hummed tunelessly as he walked.

He had gained fifty pounds. His moustache was shaved

off. There were tattoos on both his hands. The old one, on his wrist and arm, had been removed.

He was not recognizable as Calvin Wesley Train. Not unless you knew him very well.

He had used the place as a hideout before. Over the past ten or twelve years the yard had changed little. Some of the older cars were in the same places they occupied when Train was last here. They were never touched by the railroad, and were visited only by occasional tramps. A few cranes and other pieces of heavy construction equipment were here, and two shacks used by maintenance workers.

Train made his way silently to a little shack tucked among the tracks and took a long look in the filthy little window. Then he stood like a deer in a forest, watching, listening.

This was to be his base of operations. He had chosen it with care. Since the death of Wendy Breckinridge the nation-wide manhunt had grown more intense, and in Chicago it was particularly hot. Nevertheless he had calculated that it would be smarter to dart right under the net than to try to lay low somewhere.

He had planned a way to get to the Shader woman before they realized he was in the neighborhood. It required some subtlety, and especially disguise. He had worked it out to the smallest detail. If necessary, he would finish her in the hospital where she did her supervisions. He would be disguised as a patient. The escape route was the difficult part, but he had called in some chips from two old friends in the neighbor-hood. One of them would put him up for a night, the other would drive him north to Canada afterward.

When Shader arrived at the hospital for her rounds Monday morning, he would be waiting.

He used his key in the lock. There was some hesitation, for the lock was old and rusty. But the door creaked open.

Train stood in the silence, lighting a match. The old oil

lamp was where he remembered it from last year. He shook it; there was oil in it. He lit it, and a pale glow illuminated the shack.

There was one central room with a kitchen counter at the end, big enough for a hotplate and some foodstuffs. A tiny bathroom containing only a toilet, no sink. An old wooden office chair. A card table.

Train stood measuring the silence. This would do. He only needed two nights.

On the table was a folded issue of *Sports Illustrated* from years ago. The face of Michael Jordan looked out from its cover.

Train moved to the kitchen, where the ancient hotplate, used by him last year, had not moved. He opened the cupboard. A can of beef stew had an appetizing look, but when he touched it he saw it was empty. The beaming face of an old woman shone on the label. AUNT MOLLY, read the label. OLD FASHIONED HOME BEEF.

At that moment a voice came through the old window, borne aloft by a quirk of the wind. Train stood still, listening.

'*The idea of a censure resolution is obviously dead now,*' said the voice. '*With the resignations of Gingrich and Livingston, the incredible notion of a Democratic victory arising out of the Monica Lewinsky scandal seems to have become a reality.*'

The voice trailed off, drowned out by a siren somewhere beyond the yard.

Train stood waiting. Silence returned.

He set down the tool bag carefully. It was heavy. It contained a hand-held semi-automatic weapon and several clips of ammunition. There were also knives, some smoke bombs and two grenades in case of emergency. He intended to get her alive and take her with him. If that failed he would finish her in one of the hospital storage rooms. If there was time he would rape her. He might have to do it after she was dead. He could smell her sex right now. He had smelled it in his prison cell in Wisconsin, and again in the courtroom. He had not gone a day since without thinking of this.

When it was over the security on her family would die down. He would wait a while, then go back and do her little boy. He owed her that.

He stood for a moment, thinking. He had a knack for clearing his mind when action was the priority. There was nothing in his head but the means and the opportunity. Death was near, he could feel it. That strengthened him.

He moved to the bathroom. The little door was ajar. It pulled outward. The toilet was old, but it worked. Better than having to go outside in this weather, he thought.

He pulled the door toward him. He stepped back a pace when he saw what was inside it.

He was at a loss for words. Susan Shader sat on the toilet, looking as cool as if she had come here to have tea with him.

He stepped back. She stood up. He saw the boots she was wearing under her skirt. She wore a leather coat over a sweater. The gun in her hand was an automatic, probably nine millimeter. The details came to him with remarkable clarity, though only a few seconds had elapsed.

She didn't move toward him. She stood framed in the little doorway. She had him trapped. There was nowhere for him to retreat.

'I should have known,' he said. 'I didn't take you seriously enough. Your gift, I mean.'

She was looking at him, noting the changes in him.

'You've changed,' she said.

'We've both changed,' Train replied. 'No one gets through the world without changes.'

There was a silence. They seemed like statues, planted

here a long time ago, still facing each other. They had a long past between them, he reflected. She knew a lot about him.

'Are you sorry?' she asked.

'For what? For Wendy?'

'For all the things you've done.' The tone of her voice told him she had come here to end it for him. He decided to keep her talking.

'Sorry?' he asked, stepping back a pace, his thoughts on the table. He could hook a foot around it, slide it toward her. 'That's a question. Is a snake sorry for all the mice it's killed? Is a spider sorry for all the flies it caught? It needs their blood.' He looked at Susan. 'What about you, Doctor? Are you sorry for all the lambs and calves you've eaten? How about the snails?' He shrugged. 'We do what is in our nature.'

'I only wanted to hear you answer,' she said.

She moved forward a pace, the gun pointing at him.

'So, this is the end,' he said, edging to his right, toward the table.

She gestured with the gun. 'Back to the center of the room,' she said.

*Keep her talking. One more sentence.*

'What are you going to do?' he asked.

'That's up to you.'

He nodded at the gun in her hand. 'Go ahead,' he said. 'You won't be doing anything I don't want you to do.'

He felt confident. He knew this wasn't something she really knew how to do or was trained for. She wasn't a fighter. He had a huge advantage over her, even though she had the gun.

'Go on,' he insisted. 'I tried to get to your little boy when I escaped. They had him too well covered. I was going to do him first. I decided to take Wendy instead.'

Still she stood immobile, staring at him. He was struck by her lack of emotion. She seemed attentive, focused.

'I am sorry,' he said. 'Try to understand that, after.'

'I know you're sorry,' she said. The gun trembled faintly in her hand.

'Remember what I told you in the jug?' he asked, poising his weight on the balls of his feet. 'I said I would like you to be the one who dropped the pill on me. Remember? I said you had a nice face.'

She was listening to his words. This was the moment.

'Let me just ask you one favor,' he said.

He seemed to stumble sideways. He touched the wall with his right hand, gave it a hard push for leverage. The knife had appeared in his left. He came at her, quick as a running back dodging into a hole in the line.

She never moved. The gun flashed. The bullet entered Train's chest before he heard the blast. He gave her a last empty look which seemed to acknowledge something already lost and forgotten.

Then he fell at her feet, blood spreading over the floor under him.

Susan stood looking down at him. She watched the pool grow. It was thick, sticky, and very red even in this light, for there was oxygenated arterial blood. The heart was not pumping, but the trunk vessels were hit. The body's six liters were being voided by the force of gravity. An army of paramedics with transfusion gear could not have saved him.

The roar of the gun still echoed in the room. She had known there would be no time to aim. She had used her gift to poise herself inside Train's chest, and let his heart attract the bullet.

She knelt beside him and felt his neck for a pulse. Nothing.

She remained where she was until she realized the blood was spreading around her boots. She stood up, moved to the chair and sat down. She noticed the gun in her hand and put it on the table.

There were sounds outside the window. A siren, then another. A dog barking. On the wall was an old Playmate of the Month centerfold. The naked girl sat at a dining room table, a cup of cocoa or coffee in her hand.

A voice sounded somewhere outside. *'I don't know if the President feels he has gotten away with something, John, but I'm sure he and his supporters are thinking, All's well that ends well . . .'*

A gust of wind drowned out the voice.

A half-hour passed, then an hour. Susan sat looking at the dead man on the floor. She wanted to leave, but something held her here. A waiting for something. A halting of the breath of time. She thought of Wendy. Of Harley Ann Saeger. Of Miranda Becker. Of dead people who should not be dead, and living people who should never have been alive.

Time moved slower, the seconds crawling by like tired animals. She wished David Gold were here. Then she was glad he wasn't.

Slower, faster . . . Time moved at various speeds, each one tailored to a hope or a memory. Only death was still, the final measure.

She stood up. A word came to her lips.

She looked down at Calvin Wesley Train.

*'Menucha nechona,'* she said.

# JOSEPH GLASS

## Eyes

Pan Books £5.99

'Everything suggested that the killer's last move was to take a long look at himself in the mirror. *But not with his own eyes.*'

As the freezing rain of a Chicago winter turns to snow, homicide detectives attempt a news clampdown on the death of Patsy Morgenstern. For Patsy, it seems, has become the third victim of a pattern serial killer who ceremonially removes his victims' eyes.

Facing mounting criticism, Homicide Detective David Gold turns for help to Dr Susan Shader, a criminal psychiatrist – and a woman who holds the fragile, debilitating gift of second sight. Susan can feel the chill of the killer's presence at the horrifying murder scene. But she is facing an opponent more ruthless and dangerous than she's ever encountered before.

An opponent who won't stop until he has closed her eyes ...

'If you want a potent cocktail of chills and sleepless nights, EYES will satisfy.'
*Time Out*